# COLLINS
# COBUILD

英語語法系列

# 連詞
# Linking Words

## Sylvia Chalker

BANK *of* ENGLISH

商務印書館

## Collins Cobuild English Guides: Linking Words

### Editorial Team

| | |
|---|---|
| Author: | Sylvia Chalker |
| Founding Editor-in-chief: | John Sinclair |
| Editorial Director: | Gwyneth Fox |
| Editors: | Jane Bradbury |
| | John Williams |
| Editorial Assistance: | Alice Grandison |
| | Sean Lynch |
| | David Morrow |
| Computer Staff: | Jeremy Clear |
| | Tim Lane |
| Secretarial Staff: | Sue Crawley |
| | Michelle Devereux |

## Collins Cobuild 英語語法系列：連詞

| | |
|---|---|
| 主　　編： | 任紹曾 |
| 譯　　者： | 劉萬存 |
| 責任編輯： | 黃家麗 |
| 出　　版： | 商務印書館 (香港) 有限公司 |
| | 香港筲箕灣耀興道 3 號東滙廣場 8 樓 |
| | http://www.commercialpress.com.hk |
| 發　　行： | 香港聯合書刊物流有限公司 |
| | 香港新界大埔汀麗路 36 號中華商務印刷大廈 3 字樓 |
| 印　　刷： | 美雅印刷製本有限公司 |
| | 九龍官塘榮業街 6 號海濱工業大廈 4 樓 A |
| 版　　次： | 2017 年 1 月第 7 次印刷 |
| | © 2000 商務印書館 (香港) 有限公司 |
| | ISBN 978 962 07 1392 7 |
| | Printed in Hong Kong |
| | 版權所有　不得翻印 |

# 目錄

# 前言

《連詞》是《Collins Cobuild 英語語法系列》中的一本。這套系列針對學英語的人特有的難點提供指導。

作者西爾維雅·雀卡 (Sylvia Chalker) 是英國一位編寫英語語法書的名家。我們為她能接受邀請編寫這本書倍感高興。

大家都必須記住，語言的構成不只限於孤立的前後不相干的話；所以，學習語言的人不管在書面語言還是口頭語言裏，都要能夠識別和運用各種連接手段，將不同的句子、分句連成話語，並把話語與更大範圍的語境聯繫起來。我們希望這本書會使學習者信心十足地處理好英語中這一關鍵而又一直為傳統語法書相對忽視了的問題。

同其他 Cobuild 出版物一樣，本書是研究 Cobuild 語料庫 (The Bank of English) 收集的例證的成果，該語料庫是一個現已擁有 3 億多詞的巨型語料總匯。本書的例證直接取自語料總匯；詞頻高低決定詞彙在本書的突出程度。強調用真正的語言能確保學英語的人能看到操英語的人所使用的語言連接手段，然後以自然而令人信服的方式在自己的寫作、會話中加以應用。

我們希望這本書既能有助於讀者又能使用方便。如果讀者對改進 Cobuild 出版物有甚麼看法、建議，請來信告知。我們的電子郵件地址（e-mail address）是 editors@cobuild.collins.co.uk，它能保證使用本書的人與我們保持便捷的聯繫。讀者亦可以用下列地址給我們寫信：

Cobuild
University of Birmingham Research Park
Vincent Drive
Birmingham B15 2SQ

# 引言

有時一個人能用單句來表達自己的意思，但是，人們用的許多話語，不管是書面的還是口頭的，都是由比單句更長的語段組成。

本書討論的是用來連接句子與句子、分句與分句並表示它們之間關係的詞和短語。"連接詞語"（或"連接副詞"）這一術語有時只是在狹義上表示我們在此處稱作連接語的詞語，但本書從廣義上還探討其他的"指稱詞"和"連接"手段。

第 1 章對兩類重要的連接詞語，即連接詞和連接語的區別進行說明。

第 2 章集中討論連接詞，特別是並列連詞和副詞連詞，同時也討論意義相似的連接語。

第 3 章亦討論連接語，但僅限於沒有相應的連接詞的連接語。

第 4 章討論關係從句、名詞從句與主句相連接的手段。同時也兼顧非限定小句、無動詞小句與主句的連接、常常是無任何連詞的連接。

第 5 章探討代詞、限定詞以及其他一些詞在指稱和替代書面語和口頭語中成份所起的作用。

第 6 章探討用名詞指稱其他名詞（或名詞詞組）或語篇段落的方式。

第 7 章集中討論只在會話時使用的某些非正式連接詞語。

第 8 章討論句子附加狀語。它們屬於副詞的一個重要類別，但從語法角度來看，又不屬於連詞。把它們列入本書有兩個理由，第一，有的語法書把它們作為句子，副詞同連接詞混在一起，因為像連接語那樣，它們可用以對整個句子進行評註，而不作句子的一個部份。但是它們的功能和用法不同於連接語，所以需要對這兩種副詞加以區分。第二，像在前兩章敍述過的真正意義的連接詞語那樣，它們的作用是幫助聽話者或讀者更容易地理解話語。

隨後是一整套練習。練習的一部份是短語和句子，另一部份是較長的語篇段落。所有的練習以各章討論過的連接詞語及其功能為依據，可以在課堂使用，以強化和檢測學生對連接詞語的了解。練習還配有答案，使之成為自學的理想練習。

大家有必要明白，許多英語詞和短語都不止一種意義，不止一種語法功能。本書的重點放在這些詞語的連接功能上，但它們之中的許多詞語還可另作他用。


　　　　　　　　　　　　　　西爾維雅・雀卡 (Sylvia Chalker)

# 英漢語法術語對照表

以下的英漢語法術語對照表提供本書使用的部份最重要的語法術語的簡短定義。正文對許多術語都給予詳盡的定義和充分的討論。書後的索引中可以找到準確的術語作為參考。

**absolute clause 獨立從句**：有自己主語的非限定小句或無動詞小句，如：weather permitting。

**adverb clause 副詞從句**：在句子裏的作用相當於單個副詞的從句，如：I'll come **as soon as I can**.

**adverbial 狀語**：作用與副詞一樣的一個詞或一組詞（包括單個副詞）。

**apposition 同位語**：一名詞後的名詞短語或名詞從句，前後兩個部份指同樣的人或物，如：There was **a danger / that they would decide to leave**.

**complement 補足語**：使動詞（特別像 seem 或 be 這種動詞）意義完整的詞、詞組或分句，如：You seem **upset**… The fact is **I can't afford it**.

**complex sentence 複合句**：由一個主句和至少一個從句組成的句子，如：I didn't buy it, although I liked it.

**compound-complex sentence 並列複合句**：有兩個或更多的主句和至少一個從句組成的句子，如：I put my arm around him and steered him to the sofa, where he collapsed.

**compound sentence 並列句**：兩個或更多的主句由並列連詞連接而組成的句子，如：They picked her up and took her into the house.

**concession 讓步**：特定從屬連詞、連接語和某些從句連接後表示的對比概念。

**conjunct 連接性狀語**：連接語的別稱。

**conjunction 連接詞**：連接兩個分句、短語或單詞的詞。有兩種連接詞，即並列連詞和從屬連詞。

**connector 連接語**：連接兩個單獨句子的副詞或狀語，如：I can't

do anything just now. It won't matter a lot, **though**.

**content disjunct 內容評註性狀語**：表示對自己的敍述所持的態度的句子附加狀語，如：**Fortunately**, the weather that winter was reasonably mild, 或對自己的敍述的可能性所持的態度的句子附加狀語，如：**Perhaps** they might help him.

**co-ordinated clauses 並列分句**：由並列連詞連接的兩個分句，如：This is really confidential and I've not told it to anyone.

**co-ordinating conjunction 並列連詞**：連接語法類型相同的分句、短語或詞的詞，如：and、but 或 or。

**co-ordinating pair 成對並列連詞**：由句中分隔開的兩個詞或短語構成的並列連詞。常用的成對並列連詞有 both…and、either…or、not only … but also 和 neither …nor。

**co-ordinator 並列連接詞**："並列連詞"的別稱。

**correlative 關聯詞**："成對並列連詞"的別稱。

**defining relative clause 限制性關係從句**：指明被説及的人和物的關係從句，如：The office **that had been cleared for them** was austere but functional.

**demonstrative 指示詞**：指 this、that、these 和 those 中的一個詞，用在名詞前，如：**this** woman，或用作代詞，如：**That** looks nice.

**determiner 限定詞**：指包括 the、a、some 和 my 在內的一組詞，用在名詞前。

**discourse marker 話語標記**：口語中一個詞或短語，其作用是向受話者發出如何理解正在説的話的信號，如：**Now look here**, you're wrong.

**disjunct 評註性狀語**："句子狀語"的別稱。

**ellipsis 省略**：略去不用但又能從上下文別處加以"補充"的詞，如：Come if you can.省略了第二個 come。

**fluency filler 補白語**：英語口語中無特定意義的詞語或語音，其作用是使人感到講話者説話流利，如：**Well I mean you see** the Scots are very proud of their country.

**'-ing'-clause** -ing -小句：結構像從句，但其動詞都是不帶限定助動詞的現在分詞，如：It was certainly the best meal I had had **since leaving home**.

**nominal clause** 名詞性從句："名詞從句"的別稱。

**nominal relative clause** 名詞性關係從句：屬wh-詞從句的一種，通常不表示疑問，其 wh- 詞有雙重功能，在主句裏代表某物；在關係從句中作關係代詞，如：**What you need** is a change of scene，此句的 what 大致上等於 that which。

**non-defining relative clause** 非限制性關係從句：提供有關某人、某物的附加信息，但又無需起確指作用的關係從句，如：Paul's father, **with whom he had had a close relationship**, died suddenly.

**non-finite clause** 非限定小句：不含限定動詞，但又像從句的結構，如：Water is liquid, but **when heated** it becomes vapor.

**noun clause** 名詞從句：在句子裏的功能與名詞或名詞短語相同的 that- 從句或 wh-詞從句。

**pro-form** 替代形式：意義籠統的詞或短語，如here、there、now 和 then；像代詞替代名詞那樣，用來替代更為具體的詞或短語。

**quantity pronoun** 數量代詞：可用來表示量而又無需確指具體的量或數的代詞，如 both 或 many。

**reduced clause** 縮略從句：其限定動詞被省略卻又能被推斷出來的從屬結構，如：She wanted to sleep **if possible**.

**reduced relative clause** 縮略關係從句：與關係從句功能相同，但缺少主語和限定動詞的結構，如：He took out a folder **containing my proposal**，該句的 containing 等於 that contained。

**sentence adjunct** 句子附加狀語：表示說話者對自己說的話（說的內容）的態度，如：**Personally**, I think you'd be better off here in the States，或者解釋說話者說話的方式（說話風格）時用的副詞或狀語，如：We're getting a little tired of it, **frankly**.

**sentence adverb** 句子副詞：見 8.2 節。

**stative verb** 狀態動詞：be、seem 或 know 這樣的動詞，用來描述狀態而不是描述動作，通常不用於進行時態。

**style disjunct 語體評註性狀語** ：一種句子附加狀語，用來解釋說話者是怎樣說話的，如： **Quite honestly**, I don't know if it was worth it.

**subject-auxiliary inversion 主語助動詞倒裝**：助動詞加句子主語的詞序排列，譬如，出於某些前置否定詞語的需要，如： Not only **did they** win, but they also changed the nature of their team.

**subordinate clause 從屬分句**：不能單獨存在、依附於另一分句的分句。從屬分句包括副詞從句、名詞從句、關係從句及非限定小句和無動詞小句。

**subordinating conjunction 從屬連詞**：引導從句的連接詞。

**subordinator 從屬連接詞**："從屬連詞" 的別稱。

**substitution 替代**：指不用原詞而用其他的詞，特別是指不用原詞而用代詞，不用謂語而用do、so和not，以避免重複，如：I asked him to telephone me, but he failed to **do so**.（請注意替代與省略的區別，後者指把詞略去不用，如：…but he failed to.）

**'that'-clause that- 從句**： 用連詞that引導或不用任何連詞引導的從句，例如，用來轉述他人的話的 that- 從句，如： She said **that she'd wash up for me**… She said **she'd wash up for me**.

**'to'-infinitive clause to-動詞不定式小句**：用 to 引導、動詞為原形的非限定小句，如： **To do this**, you need to be firm and assertive… **For the attack to succeed**, surprise was essential.

**verbless clause 無動詞小句**：不帶動詞但又能推斷出動詞，類似從句的結構，例如： She wanted to sleep **if possible**.

**'wh'-clause wh-詞從句**：wh-詞引導的從句，通常用來轉述問句，如： She asked **what I'd brought with me**.

## 本書正文排印說明

本書正文第一次提及和作為要點提及的詞項（詞和短語）及語法術語用**粗體字**排印；正文前的《英漢語法術語對照表》已對許多術語下了定義。

斜線號或括號用來表示可供挑選的短語形式，例如：generally/ broadly/ roughly speaking 代表 generally speaking、 broadly speaking 和 roughly speaking ，而 without (any) doubt 既指 without doubt 又指

without any doubt。

　　作為例證的句子短語用普通斜體字母排印，並將被解釋的詞或短語用粗體表示。說明語法結構錯誤的例句，用 ✗ 符號標出，說明與之相對應的正確例句，用 ✔ 符號標出。

# 譯者的話

## 內容簡介

本書是論述英語連接詞、連接語的專著。

第一部份是本書使用的語法術語、各術語的簡短定義及說明相關術語的例證。

第二部份是本書的主體,用 8 章的篇幅討論句內和句際的連接所使用的並列連詞、連接語;引出狀語從句的從屬連詞、連接語;由wh-詞或 that 引導的關係從句、名詞從句與主句的連接;用來避免重複、表示返指、預指但同時又起到連接作用的代詞、限定詞和名詞;會話中特有的連接詞、連接語和句子附加狀語。

其次是相當數量的練習,共 16 套,並附練習答案。

最後是按字母順序排列的索引。

## 實用價值

連接詞和連接語是詞與詞、短語與短語、分句與分句、句子與句子的連接及連句成篇的重要手段。人們表達自己的思想時,在個別場合,可以用一個詞、一個短語、一個句子,但在絕大多數場合,卻需要用比詞、短語、單句更複雜、更長的話語,才能傳遞更多的信息,才能變換增加交際的方式。因此,連接的重要性不言而喻。但傳統語法在很長時間裏未突破句子界限,忽略了對連接詞和連接語這一重要語言現象的深入研究。

西維爾雅·雀卡 (Sylvia Chalker) 是英國一位編寫英語語法書的名家,她以現代語言學研究的新成果為指導,視世界各地中級和中級以上英語學習者為對象,利用電腦技術和龐大的語料庫,結合自己成功而豐富的寫作經驗,突破傳統語法的句子界限,口語和書面語研究並重,編出了這本既精彩又起到示範和補缺作用的書。

作者研究連詞問題的方法和處理這一問題的方式極具啟發性和創新性,為學習英語和對英語連接手段有興趣的人展示了研究和處理語言問題的方向。它在內容上是英語教師在教學和進修過程中用得上的最新參考書,是英語學生難得的好教材;書中的有些章節是研究話語分析、篇章語言學學者參考借鑒的好材料。

## 本書特點

### （一）例證豐富、權威性強

本書用了大量的例證，都選自 Cobuild 語料庫（The Bank of English），是操英語的人在實際生活中使用的語言，生動、自然、可靠，可供學英語的人在口頭、書面交際時不斷地反復模仿學習。

### （二）依據詞頻編排、重點突出

本書論述的詞項、短語不以傳統的字母順序而是以使用頻率的高低分類、編排，重點突出、層次清楚，能保證本書讀者在學習時分清主次，有所側重，收到事半功倍的效果。

### （三）突破句子、展示篇章結構

本書引用了許多突破句子界限、展示句際關係和語篇結構的例證，讓讀者學到的不只是單個的句子而是有章法的話語。

### （四）強調指代的連接作用、新穎獨到

本書第 5、6 章論述起指代和連接作用的代詞、限定詞、名詞，新穎獨到，行文清楚，通俗易懂，又輔以大量例證，令人耳目一新，實為本書的精華所在，值得讀者認真學習，並主動地在自己的閱讀和寫作時加以運用。

### （五）突出會話連接、有利於避免口語的書面語氣息

第 7 章專門介紹會話中用的多種連接手段，為學習英語的人弄清了會話中許多起連接作用的詞語的確切意義，為提高口頭表達的能力和效果創造了有利條件。

單獨敍述句子附加狀語，劃清三大類狀語的界限

本書第 8 章用單章敍述在句子結構中有相當獨立性、但卻表示作者或說話者對話語的態度、從而能將信息傳遞人和接受人聯繫起來用的副詞、短語，統稱句子附加狀語或評註性狀語，將其與連接性狀語和作為句子一個成份的狀語區別開來，把這一向來不受重視而又繁雜的語言問題理出了頭緒，為學習者提供了方便，為研究狀語的人做出了示範。

提供語體信息，強調語言使用得體

本書多處為讀者提供有關口語、書面語的語體信息，強調語言使用，使我們這些把英語作為外語來學習和使用的中國人，在學會用英語交流時，還能有意識地做到語言表達的得體性。

### （六）配備練習、注重實際運用

本書配備大量的練習，讀者可以通過做練習來鞏固、復習和檢查自己學習正文部份的效果。

### （七）英漢索引，方便查閱

本書的索引像一本以字母順序排列的小詞典，便於讀者查閱有關的詞項、短語和進行相互參照。同時，索引又能在一定程度上起到補償本書不以字母順序編寫的不足之處。

## 使用建議

這是一本不可多得的論述連接詞、連接語（又叫Conjunct — 連接性狀語）、指稱、替代和句子附加狀語（又叫 disjunct —評註性狀語）的語法專著，雖篇幅不長但內容卻十分豐富，它對起指稱、連接作用的名詞和起連接、評註作用的狀語的論述處理多有創新獨到之處，實屬英語學生、英語教師和從事語言研究的人必備的優秀導讀書籍和工具書。書中數以千計的例證是地道的語言範例，值得任何一個想學好英語的人在口頭和書面表達時作為樣板來模仿學習。

正文後的練習是本書的一個重要部份。為了提高學習成效，本書的讀者應該耐心地做完練習。為使學習富於挑戰性和趣味性，做練習時需要不時參閱有關章節的敍述，並在完成練習之後才參閱練習答案。

劉萬存
浙江大學

# 鳴謝

我們感謝 Gill Francis、Martin Hewings、Susan Hunston、Elizabeth Manning 以及 Debbie Seymour 在本書製作過程中所提供的協助。

# 連接詞和連接語：提要
# Conjunctions and connectors: outline

## 連接句子的語法方式
## Grammatical ways of joining clauses

**1.1**　當一個人要在書面或口頭上敍述複雜得難以用一個單句（只有一個限定動詞的句子）表達時，自然可用若干單獨的句子。有兩種簡單可行的連接句子方式：

- 可用 and 這樣的**並列連詞**將單句連接起來。原來的單句成了同等重要的分句（**並列分句**），從而構成**並列句**。

*This is really confidential **and** I've not told it to anyone.*
這事確屬機密，而且我也未曾告訴過任何人。

- 也可以使原來的單句成為新句的主句，用 when 這樣的**從屬連詞**，使從屬（即次要的）**分句**依附於主句。新構成句子就是**複合句**。

*We also tend to trust people more **when** they look at us directly.*（main clause followed by subordinate clause 主句後隨從屬分句）
當別人敢於正視我們的眼睛時，我們往往也會更加相信他們。

**1.2**　用並列連詞或從屬連詞或者同時用並列和從屬連詞，可將兩個或更多的分句連成一個句子。並列分句和從屬分句並存所構成的新句子就是**並列複合句**。

*I put my arm across his shoulders **and** steered him to the sofa, **where** he collapsed.*
（main+main+subordinate 主要分句＋主要分句＋從屬分句）
我用手臂抱住他雙肩並把他架到沙發旁，他就倒在沙發上了。

*He had always loved Clara **and** he had always hoped **that** he could make her love him.*（main+main+subordinate 主要分句＋主要分句＋從屬分句）
他一直都愛着克拉拉而且一直期望他能使她愛上他。

*It was still early, **and although** she was fatigued her mind was restless.*
（main+subordinate+main 主要分句＋從屬分句＋主要分句）
時間還早，而且，雖然她感到很累，她的腦子卻一刻不停。

*He had always written like that, **although when** he was small Sofia had taught him to write 'D' the proper way.*（main+subordinate+subordinate 主要分句＋從屬分句＋從屬分句）
他一直都那樣寫字，雖然，在他年幼時，索菲亞已經教過他字母 D 的正確寫法。

**1.3**　表示兩個分句，特別是單獨句子間的另一種較為鬆散的連接方式是用一個較為特殊的詞，稱為**連接語**（有時又稱**連接狀語**或**連接性附加狀語**）。例詞有 moreover、nevertheless、otherwise。

## 連接詞和連接語：語法上的差異
# Conjunctions and connectors: grammatical differences

**1.4**　連接詞和連接語的意義有許多相同之處，而且有的詞，如 before、though 和 nowhere 既有連接詞又有連接語的功能。不過，這兩類詞語在語法上卻有諸多不同之處（見 1.5－1.10 節）。

**1.5**　**連接詞**通常把兩個（或更多）分句連成一句，往往在分句間用逗號，但是有時也可以不用標點符號分開。

> ***Before*** *you decide to be a soldier, you have got to read these books.*
> 你決定當兵前，必須閱讀這些書。

> *Ms Johnson was looking very embarrassed,* ***though*** *she was smiling.*
> 約翰遜女士看上去很尷尬，儘管她在笑着。

> *This was a selling job,* ***however*** *you look at it.*
> 不管你怎麼看待這個工作，它還是個銷售的工作。

與連接詞不同，**連接語**通常連接的是兩個獨立句子，所以在第一個句子的句末有句號。

> *Now he's more focused on his work.* ***Before***, *he was distracted, always making plans to go out.*
> 現在他對自己的工作更為關注。在以前，他卻精力不集中，總是打算外出。

> *'I can't do anything for several days,' he said. 'It won't matter a lot,* ***though***'.
> "數日來我甚麼事也幹不成，"他說，"不過，關係倒不是很大。"

> *There was no longer any abdominal pain.* ***However***, *the patient experienced low back pain and cramps in the legs.*
> 腹部不再感到疼痛。然而，病人卻感到腰部痛、雙腿抽筋。

當然，標點符號的使用有選擇的餘地，但是在有連接語的兩個分句間用逗號總是顯得連接不夠緊密。

**1.6**　**連接語**在分句裏起着比較獨立的作用，因此，總是用逗號將其與所在句的其餘部份分開。

> ***Before***, *I had oysters for breakfast and now I've changed them for porridge.*
> 過去，我早餐吃牡蠣而現在我改吃麥片粥了。

> ***However****, the patient experienced low back pain.*
> 然而，病人感到腰部痛。

**連接詞**是分句的一個部份，一般不用標點符號將其與所屬句分開。

> ***Before*** *you decide to be a soldier…*
> 在你決定當兵前……

**1.7**　由**從屬連詞**引導的分句缺少句子其餘部份時，在語法上是不完整的。

- ✘ ***Before*** *you decide to be a soldier.*
  在你決定當兵之前。
- ✘ ***Though*** *she was smiling.*
  雖然她仍然笑着。

有**連接語**的分句（或句子）無疑是返指先行句子，但在語法上卻是完整的。

- ✔ ***Before****, it would have been impossible.*
  在過去，那是不可能的。
- ✔ *It won't matter a lot,* ***though****.*
  不過，關係倒不是很大。

**1.8**　絕大多數**連接詞**位於所屬分句的句首。**連接語**通常也位於句首，但是其中有不少隨後出現（而且有的連接語如 though，肯定隨後出現）。

> *I have read and enjoyed the article you sent me. I do feel that several paragraphs are somewhat distorted,* ***however****.*
> 我讀過並欣賞你送來的文章。不過，我的確感到有幾個段落多少有些不符事實。

**1.9**　絕大多數由**連接詞**引導的分句都能位於主句之前。只有個別例外，如由 so that 引導的結果從句和並列分句的第二個分句。而有**連接語**的句子由於能返指先行句子，因此不能出現在被連接的兩個句子的第一句裏。理由是連接語不能表示預指。

- ✘ *I do feel that several paragraphs are somewhat distorted,* ***however****, I have read and enjoyed the article you sent me .*
  我的確感到有幾個段落多多少少有些不符事實，然而，我讀過並欣賞你送來的文章。

**1.10**　儘管有的連接詞能引導**縮略從句**，但**連接詞**通常引導的是有主語和限定動詞的限定分句。不過值得注意的是，並列連詞 and、 but 和 or 還能用來並連單個的詞。

> *Hodge is disappointed,* ***but philosophical*** *about the decision.（…but philosophical…*
> 等於 *…but he is philosophical…*……但他是泰然自若的……）
> 賀治對這決定感到失望但又泰然。

***Although certain** I had not actually broken a rib or two, I knew that something had gone wrong.*（*Although certain...* 等於 *Although I was certain...* 雖然我肯定……）
雖然我肯定自己沒有弄斷一、兩根肋骨，但我知道肯定出了問題。

***If possible**, choose a restaurant in advance.*（*If possible...* 等於 *If it is possible ...* 如果這樣做可能的話……）
如果可能，事先選定一家飯店。

與連接詞不同，**連接語**與分句在語法上的關係並不那麼緊密。它只是用來表示說話者或寫話者對後接的話語如何與先行的分句或句子聯繫作出判斷。因此後接話語是不能 "縮略" 成 "連接語加短語或單詞" 這樣的縮略從句的。

✘ *Hodge is disappointed, **nevertheless philosophical** about today's decision.*
賀治對今天的決定感到失望但又泰然。

這個句子在語法上是錯誤的，因為 nevertheless philosophical 這一後接分句是不能縮略的。

## 並列連詞：它們的語法及意義
## Co-ordinating conjunctions: grammar and meaning

**1.11** 主要並列連詞有 **and**、**but** 和 **or**。

**And** 是意義最籠統的連詞。有時用來將一句話附加到另一句話上，產生一定的意義連接。

*The vehicle was muddy **and** the carpet inside needed sweeping.*
車身上有泥而且車內的地毯需要清掃。

先後時間的事件或有因果關係的事件也可用 **and** 連接。

*She caught Mark's arm **and** pulled him to his feet.*
她抓住馬克的手臂並把他拉着站起來。

*Russia spans 11 time zones **and** desperately needs satellites for a communications network good enough to attract Western investors.*
俄羅斯跨越 11 個時區，因而極需人造衞星提供良好的通訊網絡來吸引西方投資者。

*I think you're a great family **and** I'm glad I'm going to join you.*
我認為你們是一個了不起的家庭，因而我很高興將和你們在一起。

連接詞 **or** 通常表示一種選擇，此外還有其強調形式 **or else**。

*The new rules may not always be properly tested **or** they may simply be ignored.*
這些新規定可能並非總是經過嚴格檢查，或者可能乾脆無人過問。

*The smell wasn't so bad in here, **or else** he was getting used to it.*
這裏的氣味不是很糟，不然就是他在習慣這種氣味。

**But** 表示對比，引導的是意外的事。

*He went to his study, **but** he couldn't work.*
他去了書房，但卻無法工作。

*Dean faced a similar charge **but** it was withdrawn.*
迪恩面臨類似的指控，但該指控卻撤回了。

# 成對並列連詞
# Co-ordinating pairs

**1.12** 另外還有幾個由成對的詞構成的並列連詞，被稱作**成對並列連詞**（又稱作**關聯詞**）。它們中的第一個詞對第二個詞起到強調作用。

主要的成對並列連詞有：

| | |
|---|---|
| **both…and** | **not only…but (also)** |
| **either…or** | **neither…nor** |

用 **both…and** 連接兩個分句時，強調兩個都是真實的或可能的事實。用 **either…or** 連接的是兩種選擇。用 **not only…but (also)** 強調兩個相關的事實，尤其是強調第二個事實；有時這些是令人吃驚的事實，其中第二個事實更為令人吃驚。用 **neither…nor** 連接的是兩個被否定的部份。

**1.13** 成對並列連詞與主要並列連詞一樣，通常連接語法上同等的詞或短語。可用 either…or、not only…but (also) 連接完整的有主語和限定動詞的分句。若 not only 位於句首，要求主語助動詞倒裝（必要時，得用助動詞 do ）。然而，not only 也可以位於主動詞前，無須倒裝。

***Either** you're lying **or** he must be an absolute wimp.*
要麼你在說謊，要麼他一定是個十足的窩囊廢。

***Not only** did they win, **but** they **also** changed the nature of their team.*
他們不僅贏得了比賽，而且還改變了球隊的性質。

*They **not only** printed my letter **but** they paid me £5.*
他們不僅把我的信印出來，而且還付給我 5 英鎊。

▶ **注意** ◀ 有人會認為第 3 例有錯，因為由 not only…but 連接的兩個成分在語法上是同一類型：printed my letter 是動詞＋賓語結構，而 they paid me £5 是完整的分句。如果省略句中的第二個 they，才算語法正確的句子。在句子 They not only printed my letter but paid me. £5 裏， printed my letter 和 paid me £5 都由動詞＋賓語構成。

**1.14**　以下再列出一些成對並列連詞的例句。

*Most of our flights have **either** taken off **or** landed by 11:30 pm.*
絕大多數航班在晚上 11 點 30 分以前已經起飛，或者已經到達。

*They **either** ignored the situation **or** treated it lightheartedly.*
他們對局勢不是根本不聞不問，就是漫不經心。

*The National Bank was a place where women were **either** secretaries **or** oddities.*
在國家銀行裏，女性不是秘書就是怪人。

*The claims were **not only** quite false **but also** very nearly dishonest.*
這要求不僅是相當無根據的，而且幾乎是不誠實的。

*This will benefit **not only** the employers **but also** the workers.*
這不僅給僱主，也給工人帶來了好處。

*He **both** loved it **and** hated it.*
他既喜歡它又討厭它。

*Most unconfident people will have experienced their fair share of punishment **both** from others **and** from themselves.*
絕大多數得且過的人都將既從別人又從自己身上得到應有的懲罰。

*Coeducation suits **both** boys **and** girls.*
男女合校的教育既適合男孩也適合女孩。

*My client wants **neither** to buy **nor** to rent this flat.*
我的客戶既不想買也不想租這套房子。

*I told them that **neither** the kidnappers **nor** my wife had turned up at the appointed time.*
我告訴他們綁匪以及我妻子都沒有在約定時間露面。

*He dared show **neither** pleasure **nor** pain.*
他不敢表示快樂也不敢表示痛苦。

## 作連接語用的 nor、neither 和 either
## Nor, neither and either as connectors

**1.15**　可以只把 **nor**、**neither** 用在一個否定分句之後引導另一否定分句。在第一個分句可用 not、never 這種完全否定詞，或者 hardly 這種廣義否定詞。在 nor、neither 後需要主語助動詞倒裝，動詞詞組一般是省略形式。在 nor、neither 前也可以有連接詞。

*She didn't want anyone to know, and **neither** did I.*
她不想有人知道；我也不想有人知道。

*He wouldn't want the trouble. And **nor** would I.*
他不願遇到麻煩，我也不願遇到麻煩。

*She appeared not to recognize me. And **nor** did I desire it.*
她擺出不認識我的樣子。我也不想她認識我。

*He could hardly look at it, **nor** examine it in my presence.*（...nor examine... 是 ...nor could he examine... 的省略）
有我在場，他對它幾乎不能看一眼，也不能仔細打量。

另外，否定句可以含否定詞，句末加 **either** 。

*He never had any failures, but he **never** had any great successes **either**.*
他從未經歷過失敗，但也從未取得過大的成就。

*'I haven't really got anything planned. Are you doing anything?' — 'No, I **haven't** got anything planned **either**.'*
"我還真的沒有計劃做甚麼。你在計劃做甚麼嗎？" —— "沒有，我也沒有計劃做甚麼。"

## 並列連詞與從屬連詞的比較
# Co-ordinating and subordinating conjunctions compared

**1.16** 不少的連詞有一部份像並列連詞同時又有一部份像從屬連詞。它們是 **yet**（意義為 but）；**for**（意義為 because）；**so**（意義為 as a result）和 **then**（意義為 next 或 therefore）。

在語法上，**並列連詞**與**從屬連詞**有若干不同之處。從1.17－1.21的各節說明它們之間的區別。

**1.17** 並列連詞 and 、 or 都能連接兩個以上的分句，除最後一個 and 或 or 不能省略外，其餘的都可省略。

*He grabbed my purse, opened it **and** stuffed it full.*
他抓住我的錢包，把它打開並把它塞得滿滿的。

*You can pay cash, send a cheque, **or** use your credit.*
你可以付現金、寄支票或用信用卡付賬。

然而也有例外情況。別的連接詞包括 but ，在語義上是不能連接兩個以上的分句的，在下面的句子裏的第一、二兩個分句間，我們知道連詞是 and ，而不是 but：

*He failed, got into debt, **but** then found a job in Brussels.*
他失敗了，並且欠了債，但後來卻在布魯塞爾找到一份工作。

用 and 、 but 、 or 也能將兩個從屬分句連接起來。

*His wife had insulted him constantly at restaurants, because he ate too much bread **and** always finished off the meal with a rich pastry.*（and always finished off... 是 and because he always finished off... 的省略）
他妻子在飯店用餐時經常羞辱他，因為他麵包吃得太多並且總是在用餐結束前吃油酥餅。

*In the letter Annie said she was sorry to have run off without a word, **but** that she was happy with her marriage and work.* （...but that she was happy... 是 ...but said that she was happy... 的省略）

在信裏安妮為自己不辭而別表示抱歉，但她說她的婚姻生活愉快，工作也順利。

*Tennison could recognize an emergency when he saw, **or** as in this case heard one.* （...heard one. 是 ...when he heard one. 的省略）

坦尼森能辨別出他所見的，或像這種情況下所聽到的，是緊急事件。

**1.18** 用 and、or 或 but 連接的是主語相同的分句時，可將這幾個連詞後的分句的主語省略。

*He went up **and** found the bed hadn't been slept in.*
他爬了上去並發現床鋪未有人睡過。

*I'd have been happy to attend the game, **but** have been advised by others not to.*
我本來是樂意去參加比賽的，但人家卻建議我不要去。

*As time went on he lapsed into long silences **or** became offensively off-hand.*
隨着時間的推移，他陷入長時間的沉默或令人討厭地簡慢。

如果助動詞相同，連詞後分句的助動詞也可省略。

*You should write to them **or** give them a ring some time.* （or give them... 是 or you should give them... 的省略）

你應該給他們寫信，或者在甚麼時候給他們打個電話。

兩個屬於並列（and）關係的否定分句主語相同時，第二個否定分句的主語（以及與第一分句相同的助動詞）可以省略。這時用 **or** 連接兩個分句。

*He didn't keep them **or** have them printed.* （即：He didn't keep them and he didn't have them printed. ）

他沒有把它們留下來也沒有把它們打印出來。

Yet、so 用於 1.16 節提及的意義時以及 then（意義為 next）引導的分句的主語與另一分句相同時，可將其主語省略。

*There was a connection that I did not understand, **yet** felt.*
有一種我無法理解但又能感覺到的聯繫。

*Iron absorption has been extensively studied **yet** is still poorly understood.*
對鐵的吸收作用已經作了廣泛研究，但對它的理解仍然少得可憐。

*I tried for the prison service and was turned down and **so** went to the job centre.*
我試圖去監獄服務，但被拒絕了，所以就去了職業中心。

*For a little while she waited, **then** went out herself.*
她等了一會兒，後來就自己離開了。

*He sighed, **then** continued.*
他嘆了口氣，然後再繼續做下去。

在 for 引導的分句和**從屬分句**裏用的主語和別的詞與其他分句裏的主語或詞相同時，該主語或詞是不能省略的。

✗ I bought it , **for** liked it . （不能省略 for 分句的主語 I）

✗ I didn't buy it, **although** liked it . （不能省略 although 分句的主語 I）

**1.19** 並列連接詞 and、or、but、yet 和成對並列連詞能連接短語或單個詞，這一點同引導從屬分句的大多數**從屬連詞**不同。

*You should be able to divide the housework, shopping **and** cooking between you.*
你們之間應該就家務、購物和燒飯進行分工。

*It's difficult **but** worthwhile.*
這不容易但值得。

*Then add raisins, nuts, **or** little pieces of chocolate.*
然後添加葡萄乾、果仁或小塊巧克力。

*We're expecting to go back to London later today, **or** maybe on the first shuttle tomorrow.*
我們期望今天晚些時候，或者明天乘坐第一班區間車回到倫敦。

*Quiet, utterly genial, **yet** dignified, this gentleman struck me as a perfect example of 'a good citizen'.*
這位紳士文靜、很和藹，而又端莊體面，給我的印象是個十全十美的"好公民"的榜樣。

*Most of them are **either** dead **or** out of the country.*
他們當中絕大多數人不是已經亡故就是在國外。

**1.20** 正如 1.19 節列出的例句所示，**並列連接詞**引導的分句通常要位於與其有關的分句之後。譬如，不能把：

*He didn't want to be seen, **so** he carefully sauntered off in the opposite direction.*
他不想被人看見，所以他小心翼翼地往相反方向走開。

改成：

✗ **So** he carefully sauntered off in the opposite direction, he didn't want to be seen.

由 then （意義為 therefore ）引導的主要分句可以位於 if-從句之後。

*If he says he's got evidence, **then** he's got it.*
如果他說有證據，那麼他就掌握了證據。

但是，這兩個分句的次序是不能顛倒的。不能說：

✗ **Then** he's got it, if he says he's got evidence.

與此不同，許多**從屬分句**可以位於主要分句之前。

***Because** it is electric, there are no polluting exhaust gases.*
因為這是電動的，所以就不會排放污染環境的廢氣。

*Before the boys could answer, an angry voice was heard outside.*
男孩們還來不及作出解答，就從外面傳來一把憤怒的聲音。

*After they had played two sets, they went into the clubhouse and had lunch.*
他們在打完兩盤後，就進入俱樂部會所吃午飯。

由並列連接詞引導的分句只能是"第二個分句"的規則看起來如此合情合理，以至有人認為任何用 and、but 或 or 開頭的句子都是不符合語法的。不過，只要這些句子，像第二個分句那樣，返指的是前面出現的句子，還是可以接受的。

*You don't do a lot of checking in this particular job, unless you've been specially asked to. **And** in this case nobody was.*
除非對你們提出過特別的要求，否則這項特定的工作中你們不用進行大量核對。而且在這次，對誰也沒提出過特別的要求。

*This wine will develop in a few more years. **But** it's excellent stuff right now.*
這種葡萄酒的開發將需要幾年的時間，不過它現在的質量已是很好的。

*Nobody took any notice of his opinions. **Yet** he remained proud and confident.*
沒有人理會他的意見。然而他卻仍舊自傲自信。

**1.21**　在**並列連接詞** and、but、or、for 之前不能有另外的連接詞，但是在 yet、as 和其他**從屬連詞**之前卻可以用 and、but 或 or。

*I was sure he was telling the truth **and yet** I did find it hard to believe.*
我肯定他在說實話，不過我的確感到難以相信。

*They could not see the river **and so** they did not know which way to run.*
他們看不見那條河，所以他們不知道往哪條路跑。

*I do go out at night **but** only **if** I can use the car **or if** I'm not on my own.*
我在晚上的確外出，但只是在我可以使用汽車，或沒有人和我在一起的情況下才這樣做。

# 從屬分句：提要
# Subordinating clauses: outline

**1.22**　從屬分句根據其在句子裏的作用可劃分成三大類型。

- **副詞從句**：副詞從句的作用和單個副詞一樣，它們與句子的其餘部份的連接通常是用從屬連詞。

- **關係從句**：關係從句一般用關係代詞引導，它們的作用往往是形容詞性的（所以偶然又被稱作形容詞從句）。

- **名詞從句**：名詞從句又分為 that-從句和 wh-詞從句，它們與句子其餘部份的連接通常用 that 或 wh-詞。這兩種類型的名詞從句在本書中統稱名詞從句，是因為其作用與名詞相似。譬如，它們可作動詞的主語或賓語。

絕大多數連接詞和其他從屬連接詞是單個的詞（如 although, because, if, who, that），但有的由兩個或兩個以上的詞組成（如in case, as long as, on condition that）。

# 2 狀語從句的連接詞及與之相關的連接語
# Adverbial conjunctions plus related connectors

## 副詞從句
## Adverb clauses

**2.1** 在句子裏，**副詞從句**起着與單個副詞幾乎相同的作用。請比較下列例句：

*I'll come **tomorrow**.(time adverb)*
我將於明天來。（時間副詞）

*I'll come **as soon as I can**.(time clause)*
我將盡早來。（時間從句）

引導狀語從句的連接詞很多，從句涉及到時間、條件、讓步、對比、目的、理由、結果、地點、方式等意義。

上述各種意義一部份也可以用連接語表示，因此本章把狀語從句的連接詞和連接語並在一起，在適當之處，説明它們相同的意義或語法上的區別。

**2.2** 有的從屬連詞可以引導縮略從句。這種分句可以是非限定小句：

*While waiting for the water to boil he made another trip to the bedroom.*
等水燒開的時候，他又去了一次寢室。

*'I had to copy the patterns by hand,' she says, 'and had no idea how they would look **when finished**.'*
"我不得不用手工仿畫圖案，"她説，"而且對畫好後會是甚麼樣子心中無數。"

也可以是無動詞小句：

*She wanted to sleep **if possible**.*
可能的話她要睡覺。

與此相反，所有的連接語之後一般要求完整的分句或句子。

# 時間：連接詞
# Time: conjunctions

**2.3**　時間從句把主句的時間同另一事件或另一時段聯繫起來。　這種聯繫一般由連詞交待清楚，句子的時態遵循通常的規則。注意要是主句表示將來，時間從句則用現在時態，因為從句提供的是"背景"而不是對將來的預告。時間從句中用現在時表示將來這個規則，也適用於條件從句。

主句的事件或狀態可以先於時間從句的時間：

*Everything is carefully cleaned **before** it is passed on to you.*
把它交給你之前，一切都已仔細清洗過了。

也可以後於時間從句的時間：

*Zoe's confidence was shattered for a few months **after** her bag was snatched.*
提包被人搶了以後，柔依在幾個月的時間裏完全喪失了信心。

也可以與時間從句表示的時間共時：

*He could have come **while** I was getting a coffee.*
他可能是在我等咖啡時來的。

## when

**2.4**　使用意義很籠統的 **when** 時，時態格外重要。從句、主句是簡單過去時的動作時， when-從句的動作先於主句。

***When** Tweed **arrived**, he **was shown** into Fairweather's office.*
推德到後，就被領進費爾韋塔的辦公室。

***When** they **took** the baby from me to clean her up, she **let out** a couple of good screams.*
他們把女嬰從我這裏抱開去清洗時，女嬰用力地大叫了兩聲。

▶注意◀ 並列連接詞 and 有時用來聯繫兩個有先後順序的事件，所以，想把兩個事件置於同等重要的地位，就可以用 and 連接，譬如可以説 Tweed arrived and was shown into Fairweather's office.（推德到了並被領進費爾韋塔的辦公室。）

When-從句裏的**狀態動詞**表示已經存在狀態，為主句提供一定的"背景"。

*She died **when** we **were** quite young.*
在我們還很小的時候，她就去世了。

*He only drank **when** he **was** sure of being alone.*
在他確信只有自己一人時，才喝酒。

When- 從句的過去完成時態強調第一個動作先於第二個動作。

> ***When*** he ***had finished***, he turned out the light.
> 當事情做完後，他把燈關掉。

> ***When*** he ***had read*** this and ***risen*** to his feet he saw all the bystanders around him smiling.
> 當他讀完站起來之後，看見所有的旁觀者圍着他在笑。

When-從句指將來，用簡單現在時或現在完成時（不用 will）。

> I'll try to explain ***when*** I ***see*** you.
> 我見到你時，將設法向你解釋。

> What will you do ***when*** you ***go*** back?
> 你回去後準備做甚麼？

> ***When*** you ***have finished***, you will be shown to your bedroom.
> 你事情辦完後，將領你去寢室。

> ***When*** you ***have solved*** this mystery will you return to England?
> 你破了這個謎之後，將返回英格蘭嗎？

**2.5** When-從句用其他時態時，可以表示第二個或晚些時候的事件，常常打斷了早些時候的事件。

> ***When*** the phone rang, he was making himself a cheese sandwich.
> 當電話鈴響時，他正在為自己做乾酪三明治。

> We were driving around outside ***when*** unfortunately three old ladies emerged from the hotel and came straight across in front of us.
> 我們正在外面開車兜風時，倒霉的是有三位老年婦女突然從飯店出來，直接從我們面前穿過。

> We had just gone to bed ***when*** we were startled by a forceful knocking at the door.
> 我們剛剛就寢，就給重重的敲門聲嚇了一跳。

**2.6** 有時可以用 on the way、at the moment 或 the first time 之類的短語加上 that-關係從句代替連接詞 when 引導的時間狀語從句。

> So do you ever go to the college of an evening ***on the days that*** you're working?
> 那麼你有沒有在工作日的晚上去上大學呢？

> This came ***on the day*** I got my last bank statement.
> 這是在我收到銀行結算單的那天到的。

> He arrived ***at the very moment that*** the Civil Service was preparing radical administrative changes.
> 他正是在行政機構準備進行重大改革時來到的。

> ***At the very moment*** my husband proposed to me, I said, 'Yes, I'll marry you'.
> 我丈夫向我求婚時，我對他說：「好的，我嫁給你。」

> ***The first time*** I came here, I had the best night's sleep for months.
> 我第一次來到這裏就睡了數月來頭一個晚上的好覺。

同樣，用 day 或 moment 之類的名詞後加上 when-關係從句也可以代替 when-狀語從句（參閱 4.10 節）。

> *Matty enjoyed talking to Mr Halloran, whom he met **on the days when** the greengrocer brought his van around.*
> 馬梯喜歡同哈洛蘭先生談話，他們在蔬菜水果商開着貨車在附近售貨的日子裏碰面。

> *There was a wave of dissatisfaction with President Bush's economic policy **at the very moment when** that policy was starting to come right.*
> 就在布什總統的經濟政策開始理順的時候，出現了對該政策不滿的浪潮。

當然，如果不需要把時間表示得很明確，可以只用 when-狀語從句。

> *Do you ever go to the college of evening **when** you're working?*
> 你上班時是否晚上也上大學？

> *…whom he met **when** the greengrocer brought his van around.*
> ……在蔬菜水果商開着運貨車在附近售貨時他碰到的人。

## after

**2.7**　**After** 表示主句的事件或狀態後於從屬時間從句的事件或狀態，時態的使用與 when-從句相似。

> ***After** Don told me this, he spoke of his mother.*
> 多恩向我講述這事後，又說起他的母親。

> *He reached here right **after** we did.*
> 他剛好在我們到了以後來到這裏。

> ***After** Dena had gone to bed he studied the picture again as he drank a brandy.*
> 鄧納去睡後，他一邊喝白蘭地一邊又把圖片研究了一番。

> *Laura went for a ride on her moped **after** Ian had left for work.*
> 洛拉在依恩去上班之後，騎了一回自己的摩托自行車。

> *They were doing it long **before** we got here. And they'll be doing it long **after** we leave.*
> 早在我們到達之前，他們就在做那事。我們離去以後很久他們將仍舊做那事。

> *A letter will be sent to your family doctor as soon as possible **after** you have left hospital.*
> 你出院後，我們將盡快寄一封信給你的家庭醫生。

## since

**2.8**　**Since** 指的是過去時間的某個起點，說明從這一時間點開始直到現在仍然在繼續、或者從這一時間點開始一直繼續到過去晚些時候的某種狀態或一系列事件。Since-從句通常要求用過去時，主句用完成時。**Ever since** 是 since 的強調形式。

*These drugs **have been** the mainstay of medical treatment **since** they first **became** available in 1950.*
這些藥品自從 1950 年第一次使用以來，一直是醫療上的主要藥物。

*Things **have improved since** the inspector **wrote** his report.*
自從檢查官寫過報告後，情況已經有了好轉。

*He**'s been** there **ever since** you **left**.*
自從你離開後，他一直在那裏。

*A lot **had happened since** they last **met**.*
自從他們上次見面後，已經發生了許多事情。

*The family **had lived** in the Manor House **since** it **had been built** in 1573.*
這座莊園主的住宅 1573 年建成後，這個家族一直住在那兒。

▶注意◀ 在有 since 的句子裏，主句用現在時或簡單過去時通常是錯誤的。

✗ *He **is** there since you left .*

✗ *The family **lived** in the Manor House since it had been built in 1573.*

然而，在下列句子裏，動詞 be 的簡單現在時或簡單過去時形式卻是正常的用法，因為這種句子強調的是已經流逝的時間的長短。

*It **is** over ten years **since** we left college.*
我們離開大學已經 10 年了。

*It**'s** ten days **since** the accident happened.*
事故發生已有 10 天了。

*It **was** forty years **since** Ingrid had first arrived in California.*
自英格銳德最初到加利福尼亞以來，已有 40 年了。

## before, until, till

**2.9** **Before**、**until** 都表示主句的事件或狀態先於時間從句的事件或狀態。但是 until 強調的是主句事件或狀態的終結點。

*Mr Major spoke to Mr Kohl shortly **before** the Chancellor flew to India.*
在德國總理科爾飛往印度前不久，梅傑先生和他進行過一次談話。

*I was already an old person **before** I stopped acting in that way.*
在我停止那樣的表演之前，我已經是一個上了年紀的人。

*They had known each other for only three months **before** he left Brisbane.*
他離開布利斯本前，他們倆才結識了 3 個月。

*Read the document carefully **before** you sign it.*
在簽字前，你要仔細閱讀文件。

*They talked about Stephen **until** they reached Canterbury.*
到了坎特伯雷，他們才停止談論史蒂芬。

*We waited **until** Bruno's brother came and told us the news.*
我們一直等到布魯諾的兄弟把消息告訴我們為止。

*Until* it happens, you tend to be complacent.
在這種事件發生之前，你常常會自鳴得意。

*You will sleep and stay asleep **until** you are told to awake.*
你會一直睡，睡到有人叫醒你為止。

*Would you mind not questioning Pauline **until** you have studied the journal?*
請你審查完每日大事記錄後再向潑林提問行嗎？

**Till** 的意義與 until 相同，更常用於口語和非正式書面語。

*He took a pencil out of his jacket and fumbled around **till** he found an old envelope.*
他從夾克衫裏拿出一支鉛筆，笨拙地找來找去，直到發現一個舊信封為止。

*He'll have to wait **till** we've finished here.*
他只好等待，直到我們在這裏辦完事情為止。

**2.10**　注意，用 before、until 引導的時間從句裏也許是一些不能確定的事件，從而使人產生疑慮：這樣的事會發生嗎？這樣的事發生過嗎？

*At this rate we'll capsize **before** we get to Rocky Isle.*
照這樣的速度，在我們到洛磯島之前，我們的船就會傾覆。

***Before** she had time to say a word, Andrew appeared.*
她還來不及說話，安德魯就出現在她面前。

*She had put the phone down **before** he could press her for an answer.*
在他逼着她作出答覆之前，她已經擱下了電話。

*People always interrupted him **before** he had finished what he was trying to say.*
別人總是在他未能說完他打算要說的話之前就打斷了他的話。

*She doesn't believe anything **until** she has seen it in print.*
不親眼看到白紙黑字，她甚麼都不相信。

*He could authorize nothing **until** he had spoken to the new minister.*
不和新部長談過，他甚麼事都不能批准。

## while, whilst, as, as long as

**2.11**　**While** 及其不常用的變體詞 **whilst** 用以連接兩個同時發生的事件。**As** 也可起到 while 的作用，但是後者表示有一定連續性的動作或狀態，而前者表示較短暫的動作，通常含義為 at the very moment。

*Dad was home **while** his wife was working.*
父親留在家裏而他太太卻在上班。

*She had just crept out **while** he slept.*
在他睡覺時她溜了出去。

*Someone else fetches the horse **whilst** the owner is at work.*
另外一個人在馬的主人幹活時把馬給牽來了。

*She grinned to herself **as** she lay awake in the dormitory.*
她醒着躺在宿舍裏時自個兒咧着嘴笑。

*As* he looked at the coin, his whole expression changed.
在審視硬幣時，他表情全變了。

The telephone began to ring *as* he unlocked the door.
他開門時，電話響了起來。

'Did you get my letters?' — 'I received one just *as* I was setting out.'
"你收到我的那些信嗎？"——"我正準備動身時收到一封。"

有時 as long as 的意義與 while 相似，是 while 的強調形式。

I'll never forget those soldiers *as long as* I live.
我生命尚存，就不會忘記那些戰士。

然而，as long as 更為常見的是條件意義（參閱 2.34 節）。

## whenever, every time, each time

**2.12** **Whenever** 、 **every time** 和 **each time** 表示某些一再引起相同動作發生的事件。

I seem to catch the most appalling colds *whenever* I attend funerals.
每次去參加葬禮，我似乎都要患上可怕的感冒。

*Whenever* this was discussed Miss Lewis became very agitated.
每次對這事進行討論，路易絲小姐都會變得很激動。

We go to Disneyland *every time* we're in Los Angeles.
我們每次到洛杉磯時，都去參觀迪斯尼樂園。

*Each time* she went out she would buy a plant.
每次外出她都會買一樣植物。

## as soon as, immediately, the minute/second/moment...

**2.13** **As soon as** 、 **immediately** 表示引起一個動作或事件接踵而至的動作或事件。

*As soon as* he gets the money, he'll pay you.
他一收到那筆錢，就付給你。

Let me know *as soon as* any of them turn up.
他們當中一有人露面就通知我。

I'll be marrying again *as soon as* circumstances allow.
一旦環境許可，我就再婚。

A microphone was put under my nose *immediately* I got off the horse.
我一下馬就有人把傳聲器遞到我嘴邊。

在較為非正式的場合，也能用 the minute 、 the second 和 the moment 之類的慣用語表示 as soon as 、 immediately 的意義。

*I'll telephone **the minute** there's any change.*
一有變更我立即用電話通知。

***The moment** I closed my eyes, I fell asleep.*
我一合上眼，就睡着了。

*She put down the receiver **the instant** she recognized my voice.*
她一聽出是我的聲音，馬上就放下電話聽筒。

☞ 與 2.6 節比較。

## once

**2.14** **Once** 用作連接詞時，也可以表示 as soon as 或 when 的意義。Once 從句所述事件的發生導致（並常常決定）主句中的事件。

*The smell will disappear **once** the hair is dry.*
頭髮一乾，那種氣味就會消失。

***Once** I decided what to do. I stopped worrying.*
我一決定了要幹甚麼，就不再發愁。

## no sooner…than, hardly…when, hardly…before

**2.15** 成對從屬連詞 **no sooner…than**、**hardly…when**、**hardly…before** 強調第二個事件如何緊接着第一個事件。No sooner 和 hardly 位於句首的分句的主語和助動詞倒裝。這類連接詞主要用於書面語。

*He was **no sooner** inside his cabin **than** the door opened again.*
他剛進小屋門又開了。

***No sooner** had she taken the knife from its hiding place **than** she dropped it.*
她剛從藏刀處拿到刀卻又給丟了。

*The ambassador had **hardly** begun speaking **when** he was again interrupted by the president.*
大使剛開口説話，又給總統的插話打斷了。

***Hardly** had the meeting begun **when** a share holder leapt to his feet.*
會談剛剛開始，就有一位股東猛地從座位上站了起來。

*I'd **hardly** closed my eyes **before** I was called out again.*
我剛要閉上眼又有人叫我出去。

# 時間：非限定小句和無動詞小句
# Time: non-finite and verbless clauses

**2.16** 部份而不是全部時間連接詞可引導非限定小句或無動詞小句。

When、after、since、before、until 和 while 可引導 -ing -小句。

**When making** records in the 1920, sound engineers often made two recordings for safety's sake.
音響工程師在上世紀 20 年代錄音時，為了保險起見通常做兩個錄音。

**When lifting** weights off the floor, bend your knees and keep you back straight and long.
把重物從地上舉起時，要雙膝彎曲背部挺直。

**After being** colonized by Spain, Haiti was ceded to France in 1697.
海地成為西班牙殖民地後，在 1697 年被割讓給法國。

It was certainly the best meal I had had **since leaving** home.
這應該是我離家後吃得最豐盛的一頓飯。

The people will report to you **before making** any major decisions.
這些人在作出任何重大決定前都會向你報告。

The 65-year-old accepted his judgement **until hearing** a radio broadcast in 1988 about a similar case.
直到在 1988 年聽到一次類似案件的無線電廣播後，那位 65 歲的老人才接受了對他的判決。

We decided to maximize our return on each product **while hoping** our superior quality would win out.
在希望我們的優良品質能取勝的同時，我們還決定最大限度地增加每種產品的利潤。

**2.17** When 和 until 後可隨過去分詞。

Water is liquid, but **when heated** it becomes vapour and **when frozen** it is solid.
水是液體，但加熱後，變成氣體；凍結後，變成固體。

A man is guilty **until proved** innocent.
一個人只有被證明是清白後才稱得上是無罪。

Grill for 15 to 20 minutes, turning occasionally **until cooked**.
燒烤 15 分鐘至 20 分鐘，不時翻轉直到燒熱為止。

Once 可後跟 having 加過去分詞。

On the other hand, **once having seen** this apartment, who'd have the courage to complain?
另一方面，一旦看過這套公寓房，誰還會有勇氣發牢騷呢？

**2.18** When、whenever、while、once，偶然還有until，可引導無動詞小句。

The full figures, **when available**, will show imports remaining at a high level.
詳盡的數據，在可以獲得時，將表明進口仍維持在高水平上。

We avoided one another, **whenever possible**.
無論何時只要可能，我們都互相迴避。

Greenwood continued to talk daily with Fennymore **while in Florida**.
在佛羅里達期間，格林伍德繼續每天與芬尼摩爾交談。

**Once inside her apartment** she felt an urge to brush her teeth.
一走進自己的公寓套房，她就馬上想刷牙。

*Cover and put in a cool place **until ready** to serve.*
將其加蓋並放置於陰涼處，直至可以使用。

**2.19** ▶注意◀ 時間從句在一定的語言環境中能具有條件、原因或理由的意義。

*He became very lonely. He's always like that **when** he's away from home.*
他感到非常孤寂，離家在外，他總有那種感覺。

*There is a gift shop selling a variety of attractive items including our own honey **when** available.*
禮品店銷售形形色色的誘人的商品，有貨源時，包括我們的那種呱呱叫的玩意。

*He was a silent man who stammered **whenever** he tried to talk rapidly like his friends.*
他是一個沉默寡言的人，每當他試圖把話說得像他朋友們那樣快時，就要口吃。

*She is to receive £3 million damages **after** a car crash left her brain-damaged.*
由於一次汽車碰撞，她的大腦受損，故此，她將得到 300 萬英鎊的賠償金。

# 時間：連接語
# Time: connectors

## after, afterward(s), later, subsequently

**2.20** 這些詞語表示一事件在先提及的事件或先提及的時間之後晚些時候發生。**After** 和 **afterward(s)** 通常意味着兩個動作之間只有短暫的間隔。After 作為副詞連接語，主要用於口語，有的人認為，這是不規範的用法。

*It's the first time I've ever heard him talk in such a blatant fashion. **After**, he said 'I bet you quote that in some interview!'*
這是我第一次聽到他吵吵嚷嚷地談話。後來，他說："我敢肯定你在某一次訪談中引用了我那次的話。"

*Write down those ideas. We can discuss them **afterwards**.*
把這些想法記錄下來，我們以後可以展開討論。

*We shared a cigarette. **Afterward**, she rested her head on my shoulder.*
我們倆合抽了一支香煙。後來她把頭枕在我的肩上。

**Later** 和 **subsequently** 意味着先後兩個事件間有較長的間隔。Subsequently 在語體上比較正式。

*At Cambridge University, he gained a first in English and **later** completed his PhD thesis in early 19th century poetry.*
在劍橋大學，他的英語得了第一名。後來他做完了關於 19 世紀早期詩歌的博士論文。

*Several players needed police protection and then the remainder left the field. The referee **subsequently** brought them back and made them all shake hands before resuming.*
幾位球員需要警察保護，隨後其餘的球員就離開了球場。後來裁判把他們帶了回來，並在繼續比賽以前讓他們相互握手。

## before, earlier, previously, hitherto

**2.21** 帶這幾個詞語的分句表示在時間上先於前面的句子或分句（或者先於由上下文確定了的時間）的事情或情況。用這些詞語使過去和現在形成對比，而用 **previously**、**hitherto** 使這種對比格外鮮明。Hitherto 屬於相當正式的詞語。

> *Now he's more focused on his work.* **Before***, he was distracted, always making plans to go out.*
> 現在，他比較專注自己的工作。在過去，他注意力不集中，總是打算外出。

> *She was a trifle unbalanced, perhaps even suicidal at the time.* **Not long before** *she had attacked and beaten a complete stranger.*
> 她曾有點不正常，當時也許還有自殺傾向。此前不久，她攻擊並毆打過一個素不相識的人。

> *Several government officials were injured.* **Earlier***, two bridges and several buildings were damaged by fires.*
> 幾位政府官員受了傷，在早些時候，兩座橋樑和幾幢建築物為火災所損壞。

> *What about the dead man on the runway? You* **previously** *said that if any of the hostages were harmed you would move in immediately.*
> 飛機跑道上的死者該怎麼處理？你先前說過的，要是有人質受到傷害，你就會立即出擊。

> *These expeditions marked a significant change in British policy.* **Hitherto** *they had been fighting a defensive war in Europe and America.*
> 這些遠征標誌着英國政策上一個重要的變化。到目前為止，他們在歐洲、美洲進行的一直是防禦戰。

## meanwhile, in the meantime, simultaneously

**2.22** **Meanwhile**、**in the meantime** 表示兩個時點間的一段時間，但兩者之間有細微的區別。In the meantime 強調直到第二時間點才發生或進行的事。如果沒有 until then（直到那時）的特定含義，只是表示發生在另一事件發生過程中的事，meanwhile 更為可取。

> *'I will be back with them as soon as I can,' he promised. '***In the meantime***, try to get some rest.'*
> "我將盡快和他們一起回來，"他承諾說，"在此期間還要設法休息休息。"

> *The government will manage the company until it can be dismantled or sold.* **In the meantime***, its 28 offices will remain open.*
> 政府對公司的管理將維持到公司可以被解散或出賣為止。在此期間公司的 28 個辦事處仍將辦公。

> *Elizabeth dried her hair and changed her clothes.* **Meanwhile** *I fiddled with my mobile phone.*
> 伊麗莎白在吹乾頭髮，更換衣服。而我這時正擺弄着手機。

> *Sauté the onion and celery in a small frying pan.* **Meanwhile** *melt the margarine in a saucepan.*
> 在長柄平鍋裏嫩煎洋葱芹菜。同時，在煎鍋裏化開人造牛油。

**Simultaneously** 是語體正式的詞語，表示兩個動作同時進行或兩個事件同時發生。與 meanwhile、in the meantime 的不同之處在於 simultaneously 可表示兩個短暫的事件。

> At that moment a vivid bolt of lightning flashed across the cove. **Simultaneously** a deafening crack split the air.
> 在那一刻，耀眼的閃電劃過小海灣的上空。同時，震耳欲聾的一聲霹靂撕裂了天空。

當然，有時也可用書面用語 at the same time。

> The program uses so little of the computer's processing power that it is possible to do other things **at the same time**.
> 作這個程序所用上的電腦的處理能力簡直微乎其微，所以完全有可能同時做別的事情。

**2.23**　除了以上討論過的詞和短語外，還有許多可以使用的副詞表達式，指出某個事件發生的時間，將這個時間同語境時間聯繫起來。

> He was in the Congo in 1968. **After that**, he made an appearance in Nicaragua in the mid 1970s.
> 1968 年他在剛果。此後，70 年代中期他又在尼加拉瓜出現。

> Pioneer 10 left our solar system in June 1983. **At that time** it was nearly 3 billion miles from the earth.
> 先驅者 10 號探測器於 1983 年 6 月飛離我們的太陽系，那時，它離地球的距離已近 30 億英里。

> 'Why would anyone take any notice of us?' Terry said at last. **At that very moment** three girls cycled past.
> "為甚麼沒有人注意我們呢？"特里最後說道。這時，有 3 個女孩騎車而過。

許多像上述例句中類型的短語的意義隨that這樣的指示詞而定。有關指示詞的詳盡論述，參見 5.4 節。

## 條件：連接詞
## Condition: conjunctions

**2.24**　條件分句說明某事發生的條件。

時態的使用部份取決於說及的是過去、現在還是將來，部份取決於條件和結果的可能性和不可能性的程度。說及想像的情況時，主句要用情態動詞。

### if, unless

**2.25**　條件分句最常用的連接詞是**if**。如果if-從句先行，有時，特別是在主句似乎是必然產生的結果時，用then加強主句。**Unless**的通常意義為if...not。If和unless都能用來引導非限定小句和無動詞小句。

**2.26** 有時，條件句裏表示的是現在或過去發生的有規律的、有代表性的或常規的事。這時，if 含有 when 或 whenever 的意義。

*If you tell a man of ordinary build and average strength what needs doing, he does it.*
如果你告訴一個體格平常、力氣一般的人需要做甚麼，他會去做。

*These glands all react if challenged by infection or trauma.*
如果受到感染或損傷，這些腺體都會有反應。

*Unless the case is settled out of court, it can often take years before it comes to trial.*
如果此案不在庭外和解，通常要等數年才會審理。

*Unless otherwise stated the price of the holiday applies to each of two people sharing a room.*
如果未加別的說明，假日的優惠價只適用於雙人間的客人。

*You had to be nice to him if you wanted to get on.*
如果你想出人頭地就得對他好。

*Nobody could use the computer **unless** they knew the password.*
不知道密碼，誰都用不成電腦。

**2.27** 有 if- 從句的句子的主句有時為祈使句。

***Work** together, **if** possible.*
可能的話，就一起做。

*If you want to attract schoolchildren to science and technology, **make** the lessons more practical.*
如果想讓學童對科學技術感興趣，就要使功課更具應用性。

*If you are threatened with court action **do not** panic.*
如果有人用法庭訴訟威脅你，不要驚慌。

*If serving the soup cold, **blend** the ingredients thoroughly.*
如果這種湯冷吃，要把各種湯料攪勻。

**2.28** 有時條件可能是真實的，或者過去是真實的，不過我們並不肯定或者並不知道。

*If you believe that, then you've got a very low opinion of yourself.*
如果你相信那樣的事，那麼你就太低估了自己。

*If you were involved in that attack, if you've been lying to me, you ought to leave straightaway.*
如果你參與了那次攻擊，如果你一直在對我說謊，那麼你就應該馬上給我離開。

*If they are right, the universe has so little mass that its expansion is hardly slowing at all.*
如果他們的看法是正確的，那麼宇宙的質量是那樣的小，以至宇宙的擴展幾乎不會緩慢下來。

*Unless it's in the form of insurance, the guarantee could well be worthless.*
如果保證書不採取保險的形式，它就很可能毫無用處。

條件句也可以對未來的事件進行猜測。

> **If** I accept it will be for that reason.
> 如果我接受的話，那是出於那種理由。

> You don't have to let us into the property but we can get a warrant **if** you refuse.
> 你沒有必要讓我們走進那座房屋，但是如果你拒絕的話，我們可以弄一張許可證。

> The population will grow without limit **unless** kept in check by starvation. (unless kept in check... 是 unless it is kept in check... 的省略)
> 人口如果不受到飢餓的抑制，將會無節制地增長。

認為將來事件不可能時，在條件從句裏用過去時形式，有時用虛擬形式 were 取代 was。

> **If** I **won** £1 million tomorrow I'd go to my mother's house, pack her bags, and send her away.
> 假如我明天贏到100萬英鎊的話，我就要到我母親家去，收拾好她的行李並把她送走。

> I wouldn't have enough to live on **if** the operation **wasn't** success.
> 假如這項交易辦不成功的話，我將難以維持生活。

> Six out of 10 said they'd be disappointed **if** the President **weren't** deposed.
> 百分之六十的人說，假如不免除總統的職務，他們就會感到失望。

> My son is the only one whom I would worry a lot about **if** my husband and I **were** to separate.
> 萬一我丈夫和我分手的話，我的兒子將是我唯一十分擔心的人。

**2.29** 人們有時想像一個已經知道與事實相反的現在事件或過去事件。這時，在條件從句裏用過去時態（或虛擬式的 were）。

> **If** I **knew** that, I shouldn't feel so helpless.
> 假如我知道那事的話，我就不會感到這麼無助。

> **If** I **were** in that position and **thought** I **could** win, I should certainly sue. (If I were in that position... 即：I am not in that position. 我不處在那種地位。)
> 假如我處在那種地位並認為自己會獲勝的話，我一定會提出訴訟。

> **If** he **had lived**, some day Michael would have done something important. (If he had lived... 即：Michael died. 他當時去世了。)
> 假定麥克爾當時在世的話，他本可做出了不起的事。

**2.30** ▶注意◀ Unless 與 if...not 的意義並不完全相同。Unless 強調例外的事件，所以準確地說，它的意義為 "除非"（except if）。當條件與已知事實相反時，必須用 if...not，不用 unless。

> It would have been comic **if** it had **not** been so frustrating. (...if it had not been so frustrating. 即：It was frustrating. 這事令人感到灰心受挫。)
> 即使這事不是那麼令人感到灰心受挫，也是使人感到好笑的。

*If the body had **not** been on the path it would have been ignored.* （*If the body had not been on the path...* 即：*The body was on the path. 屍體在路上。*）
如果屍體當時不在路上，就會無人過問。

✗ *It would have been comic **unless** it had been so frustrating.*

✗ ***Unless** the body had been on the path it would have been ignored.*

在下面這樣的句子裏，用 unless 也是不可接受的：

*I'll be glad / sorry if they do **not** come tomorrow.*
如果他們明天不來，我將感到非常高興 / 遺憾。

該句裏主句的真實性取決於從句裏的否定行為或事件，而這一行為或事件被看作是一種可能，而不是例外。

# 間接條件
# Indirect condition

**2.31** 有時，特別在説話時，用 if-從句把話説得緩和一些，而不是表示主句成立所依賴的條件。

*He looks a bit weird **if you ask me**.*
要是你問我，他看上去有些不自然。

該句的 if-從句大體上等於 "要是你徵求我對他的看法，我以為他看上去有點不自然。" 事實上，即使沒有人徵求説話者的看法，他的想法還是這樣的。

以下例句也包含這類間接條件句。

認為自己將要説的話可能會冒犯他人時，用類似 if I may say so 或 if you don't mind me / my saying so 的間接條件句來緩和説話語氣。

*Utter nonsense, **if I may say so**.*
如果我可以這樣説的話，我就説：一派胡言。

*This is an irrelevant and, **if I may say so**, a rather naughty remark.*
這話毫不相干，而且要是可以這樣説的話，還相當低級。

*You're acting a little strange, **if you don't mind my saying so**.*
要是你不介意我直言，你的行為有點古怪。

一個人對某事進行解釋，而又感到不是解釋得很清楚時，用 if you see what I mean。

*It isn't my fault, not really. **If you see what I mean**.*
那不是我的過錯，真的不是。你明白我的意思嗎？

*They seemed almost like mother and daughter, but a mother and daughter who had switched roles, **if you see what I mean**.*
彷彿她們倆像母女，不過母親成了女兒，女兒成了母親，你明白我的意思嗎？

一個人知道他的看法是對的，而又不想給人造成不禮貌或傲慢的印象時，用 if I'm not mistaken。

*And you're Mr Allan Kelling, the owner of this property, **if I'm not mistaken**.*
你是艾倫·克林，這塊房地產的主人，我沒有弄錯吧？

***If I'm not mistaken**, one of the twins was named after me.*
如果我沒弄錯，雙胞胎中的一個取了我的名字。

# 其他條件連接詞語
# Other conditional words

另外還有各種不常見的條件連接詞語，它們中的絕大多數只引導限定分句(2.33－2.38節)。其中有幾個是分詞形式的連接詞語 (2.36－2.38節)。

## on condition that

**2.33  On condition that** 強調某人採取行動前必須事先認可的條件。

*He only took her to the hospital **on condition that** she did not say who had done this.*
只有她不說出是誰做的，他才帶她去醫院。

*I reluctantly agreed to a postponement **on condition that** the sale should be completed and the boat handed over by 31st August.*
只有銷售事宜得以辦妥，並在 8 月 31 日前交付那艘船，我才勉強同意延期。

## only…if, only if, as long as, so long as

**2.34  Only…if**、**only if**、**as long as** 及其使用頻率較低的變體 **so long as** 除能表示要認可的先決條件外，更多地是表示某事發生前，必須具備一定的條件。

*A pilot will **only** be hired **if** he signs a statement to say that he will accept no orders from the passenger.*
只有簽署了保證不接受乘客命令的聲明，機師才會得到聘用。

*She's **only** be happy **if** she got a thousand miles away.*
只有她到了千里之外，才會感到幸福。

*My kind of magic works **only if** you keep on believing.*
只有你深信不疑，我這種魔法才靈驗。

*They can go into journalism for all I care **as long as** they're happy.*
只要他們高興，他們去從事新聞工作我也不在乎。

*I could cook you some dinner **so long as** it's scrambled eggs.* （即：Scrambled eggs is the only dish I am able or willing to cook for you.炒蛋是唯一我會或願意替你做的一道菜。）
只要是炒蛋，我就能替你準備這餐飯。

## in the event of, in the event that

這兩個短語的意義是：“如果某個事件發生 —— 常常是令人不愉快的事件發生。”不過，這種事件未必會發生的。**In the event of** 當然是介詞短語，而不是連詞，所以後接名詞或 -ing 形式。它遠比語體相當正式的 **in the event that** 常見。

***In the event of** a foreign war or domestic agitation, what would be the resisting power of our institutions?*
如果爆發一場對外戰爭或出現國內動亂，我們各種機構的抵抗力會有多大呢？

*A life assurance scheme is one where, in return for a monthly payment over a specified period, you are guaranteed a sizeable payout **in the event of** your death.*
人壽保險方案指在規定期限內，每月交納款項，如果死亡可取得一筆可觀的死亡保險金。

*Being on patrol was the only excuse I could think of **in the event of** my being caught at the farmhouse.*
正在值勤巡邏是我在農舍被逮住時能想出的唯一藉口。

*We shall give you assistance **in the event that** you suffer illness, personal injury or death during the period of your holiday overseas.*
你去海外度假期間如果生了病、受到個人傷害或死亡，我們將向你提供幫助。

## provided(that), providing(that)

**2.36** 這是兩個具有分詞形式的連接詞，意義與 if 、 as long as 相似。

***Provided that** both birds are healthy I cannot see why a mating should not produce healthy chicks.*
只要兩隻鳥都健康，就沒有理由說他們的結合生不出健康的雛鳥。

*You will probably find this the most pleasant week of the diet **provided** you don't experience a reaction to it.*
只要沒有產生生理上的反應，你也許會感到這是最舒服的節食週。

*I believe in freedom to do what I wish, **providing that** it does no harm to my neighbour.*
只要不給鄰居帶來危害，我喜歡自由自在地做我喜歡的事。

*Mother will believe me **providing** I tell her what she wants to hear.*
只要我說母親要聽的話，她就會相信我。

## assuming(that), given that, considering (that)

**2.37** **Assuming that** 或 **assuming** 的含義是，假定第一件事是真實的，那麼第二件事也勢必是真實的。

*These two basic factors must continue to apply in the future, **assuming that** the country remains peaceful and politically stable.*
假定這個國家仍舊太平並保持政治上的穩定,那麼這兩個基本因素必會在將來繼續起作用。

***Assuming** I convince you, you can convince Waddington in turn.*
假定我使你信服,你接下去就會使瓦丁頓信服。

## Given that 除了表示第一件事的真實性是肯定的以外,與 assuming(that) 的意義相似。

***Given that** no decision is ever 100 per cent right, it's how we feel about our decisions that counts.*
鑑於沒有十全十美的決定,我們對自己的重要決定也持有同樣的看法。

*I don't see what I can do for you, **given that** you have no evidence.*
鑑於你拿不出證據來,我就不知道我能替你做點甚麼。

## Considering that 或 considering 也用來引出真實或肯定的事,但主句表示的往往是令人吃驚或對照鮮明的結論。

***Considering that** they are such an important part of undergraduate courses, lectures are often presented in a remarkably poor manner.*
鑑於演講課在大學本科課程中佔了很重要的地位,這些課就顯得上得非常差。

***Considering that** the event had happened such a short time before, a surprising amount of information had already been collected.*
鑑於該事件不久以前才剛發生,已經獲得的信息算是驚人地多了。

*These devices were very sophisticated **considering** they were homemade.*
考慮到這些裝置都是自製的,它們已經算是很複雜的了。

## suppose(that), supposing(that)

**2.38**　作連接詞用的 suppose(that)、 supposing(that) 含有 let us suppose (讓我們假定) 或 let us imagine (讓我們設想) 的意義,因此整個句子表示的是設想的和假定的情景所帶來的影響。

***Suppose** you buy a lottery ticket and then win a big prize. The moment you hear that you have won, you feel ecstatic.*
假定你買進一張彩票,然後得到了大獎。在你聽到你得獎的那一刻,你定會感到欣喜若狂。

*Just **suppose that** Daniel and I were ever to get married. Would you come to the wedding?*
假定丹尼爾和我要結婚了,你會參加我們的婚禮嗎?

*Now **supposing** there were only one of those stamps, and **supposing** it was worth a million dollars. And **supposing** the man who owned it suddenly came into possession of a second stamp, its duplicate. What do you think would be the valve of each of those two stamps?*
假定只有一張這種郵票,假定這張郵票值100萬美元。然後又假定這張郵票的主人一下子有了第二張郵票,即第一張郵票的複製品。你認為這兩張郵票各值多少錢?

*Even **supposing that** people can agree on such choices, the result will be a rigid set of rules.*
假定人們同意採用這些可供選擇的辦法，其結果會帶來一整套嚴格的規則。

**2.39** ▶注意◀ 除了用從屬連詞，也可用其他辦法表示條件意義。

- 條件意義有時寓於屬於主句的分句裏。因此，後接 and 的命令句可以帶條件意義。

  *Do that again **and** I'll kill you.* (即：*If you do that again, I'll kill you.* 如果你再犯，我就宰了你。)
  如果再犯，我就宰了你。

Or 及其強調式 or else 也可以隱含起威脅作用的條件意義。

*You will apologize **or** you will leave my house.* (即：*If you do not apologize, you will have to leave my house.* 如果你不道歉，你就得走出我的家門。)
你得表示道歉，否則，你就得走出我的家門。

*Do as I say **or else** you'll be flying this plane alone.*
照我說的辦，否則，你就得獨自駕駛這架飛機。

- 條件分句有時不用連接詞表示，而是用主語和助動詞倒裝表示。

  *Well, I'll be in my room **should you** want me.* (倒裝部份 ...should you want me. 等於 if you want me.)
  那麼，如果你需要我的話，我就在我的房間裏。

  *You'd be surprised **were I** to tell you how often that question arises.* (倒裝部份...were I to tell you... 等於 ...if I were to tell you...,...if I told you...)
  假如我告訴你那問題發生得多麼頻繁，你會感到吃驚的。

  *He would not have advanced the funds **had he** known that the balance sheet falsely indicated the firm was solvent.* (倒裝部份 ...had he known that... 等於 ...if he had known that...)
  要是他知道資產負債表虛假地表明了那家公司有支付能力，他就不會預付資金了。

  *Who is the mysterious CIA major whose identity would surprise so many people **did they** but know it?* (倒裝部份 ...did they but know... 等於 ...if only they knew...)
  那位身份使許多人吃驚的神秘的中央情報局少校是誰？要是他們知道就好了。

▶注意◀ 上例帶 but 的結構一般不多見，而且語體相當正式。

## 條件：連接語
## Condition: connectors

otherwise, if not, if so

**2.40** **Otherwise** 和 **if not** 返指先行陳述句或疑問句，並關注在陳述句或疑問句提及的情況不真實或不曾發生時會產生的影響。

*Your secretary told me that you would be coming over. **Otherwise** I should have felt compelled to call you at home.* （即：*If I had not known you were coming over, I should have felt compelled...* ，如果我不是知道你要來，我就覺得有必要……）

你的秘書告訴我你要過來，否則，我就覺得有必要往府上給你打電話。

*You may as well go ahead with the wedding. Think of all the telephoning you'd have to do **otherwise**.*（即：*...if you cancelled the wedding.* 如果你取消婚禮的話。）

你還是做好婚禮的各種準備為好。要取消婚禮的話，得打多少電話通知別人啊。

*Are you pressed for time, Mr Bayliss? **If not**, I suggest we have lunch before going to the house.*

貝利斯先生，你時間很緊嗎？如果不緊的話，我建議去那個地方之前我們先用午餐。

**If so** 也用於返指，但卻表示某事是真實的或發生了的。

*Does what I do scare you? **If so**, I will stop.*

我做的事嚇着你了嗎？如果這樣，我就停下不幹了。

*They must decide if such a plan can be implemented and **if so**, when.*

他必須決定這樣的計劃是否能實施，而且要是能實施的話，又得決定何時實施。

# 讓步：連接詞
# Concession: conjunctions

**2.41**　說話者有時想把非常令人意外的兩個陳述句合併起來，實現這種合併可用**讓步從句**。說話者"承認"那種似乎與主句的陳述相矛盾的令人意外的事實。

## although, though, even though

**2.42**　最常見的從屬讓步連接詞有 **although**、**though**、**even though**。這三個連接詞都能引導非限定小句或無動詞小句。

*Animal tests are often used, **although** there is no guarantee that the results will be the same as the effects on humans.*

我們常常用動物進行試驗，儘管我們無法保證試驗結果與在人身上做試驗取得的效果一樣。

*The inquiry refused to blame the American pilots, **although** implying strongly they were at fault.*

調查結果拒絕指責美國飛行員，儘管有強烈的暗示是他們出了差錯。

*He produced a bottle of sherry from a cupboard and, **though** it was three in the afternoon, poured out glasses for all.*

他從櫃子中拿出一瓶雪利酒，儘管此時是下午 3 點了，他還是給大家斟了幾杯。

***Though** certain of ultimate victory, Haig expected the coming four months to be 'the critical period'.*

雖然對最後勝利毫無疑慮，海格料定未來的 4 個月將是關鍵時期。

*I've always loved this part of London, **even though** it been spoiled like everything else.*
雖然倫敦的這個地區已像別的地方一樣被糟蹋了，我卻還一直喜歡着它。

帶 though 的讓步從句有時可以把形容詞或副詞置於句首進行強調。在這種從句裏 as 與 though 相同。

**Important though** *it is, this is not the beginning of the process.*
這雖然重要，但不是該過程的開端。

**Quietly though** *I had spoken, the medical superintendent heard.*
雖然我說話聲音很輕，醫療負責人卻聽到了。

**Nice as** *this would be, reality is unfortunately different.*
雖然這很美好，但現實卻不幸並非如此。

## while, whilst, whereas

**2.43** 有時 **while**、**whilst** 和語體更為正式的 **whereas** 可隱含對比的意義。While 和 whilst（但不包括 whereas）有時可後接非限定小句或無動詞小句。

*She was tall with reddish hair, **while** I was short with dark hair.*
她個子高、頭髮泛紅，而我卻是矮個子、黑頭髮。

*Many Russians, **whilst** approving the new warmth in superpower relations, found it strange that President Gorbachev should have been mobbed as a hero.*
許多俄國人，在贊成超級大國之間親近的同時，卻對成羣集隊圍住戈爾巴喬夫總統把他視為英雄又感到不可思議。

*They seem to think that brute force solves every problem, **whereas** you and I know it achieves little or nothing.*
他們好像認為無情的暴力可以解決一切問題，而你我卻認為暴力不起多大作用或者根本不起作用。

## not that

**2.44** 人們常常把這個短語像連接詞那樣使用，其意義大致上等於"儘管情況不是如此……"（although it is not the case that...）。它可以用來提供附加信息，經常用於糾正說話人認為某人可能持有的不大準確的印象。如果 not that 先出現，第二個分句前要用 but。

*They won't get any fingerprints from these rubber gloves, **not that** any of them would know what to do with a fingerprint if they had one.*
他們從這些橡皮手套上將取不到任何指紋，不過，並不是說要是他們有了指紋就知道該怎麼辦。

*That would of course have been the end of my career. **Not that** it's much of a career.*
當然那本會是我事業的終結。不過，並不是甚麼了不起的事業。

*'Why?' — 'Well, **not that** you'd understand, **but** I can't miss this opportunity.'*
"為甚麼？" ——"唉，並不是說你會諒解，而是我不能失去這個機會。"

*'Did you smoke on the plane?' he asked slowly. 'I always do. **Not that** I'm nervous exactly **but** it helps me not to be.'*
"你在飛機上吸煙嗎？"他慢吞吞地問道。"我經常吸，但並不是説我乘飛機時感到緊張，而是吸煙使我不緊張。"

## much as

**2.45**　**Much as** 把 although 和 very much 這兩種意義結合在一起。

**Much as** *he longs for our marriage, he's completely absorbed in the making of maps.* （Much as he longs for our marriage... 等於 Although he longs very much for our marriage...）
雖然他非常渴望我們結婚，不過，現在卻一心埋頭於地圖的製作。

☞ 比較 2.79 節：**方式**。

## granted that

**2.46**　**Granted that**（又一分詞形式的連接詞）的意義與 admittedly（公認地）或 it is true that...（誠然的）相似。主句的敍述或提出的問題要根據從句提供的背景來考慮。

**Granted that** *killing a dog was not the sort of thing to be encouraged, it was easy to imagine that the punishment might possibly go too far.*
的確，殺狗是不應該予以鼓勵的行為，但不難想像，對殺狗的懲罰也許會因此做得過份。

**Granted that** *the firm has not broken the law, is the law what it should be?*
的確，那家公司沒有違反法律，但法律應該是那樣的嗎？

# 條件加讓步：連接詞
# Condition plus concession: conjunctions

**2.47**　有的從屬連接詞既有條件意義又有讓步意義。

## even if

**2.48**　**Even if** 不同於 if。主句的事件或狀況總會出現，並不為從句的條件所左右。

**Even if** *you know that these worries are ridiculous, at lower levels your mind remains restless and anxious.* （Even if you know... 等於 Although you may know...）
即使你明白這些憂慮是荒唐可笑的，不過在情緒低落時，你心中仍然會感到焦慮不安心神不定。

*He used to be very anxious if he had to make a speech, **even if** it was only a speech to his old school.* （即：He was always anxious before making a speech; where he made the speech did not affect the situation. 演講前他總是焦急不安；演講的地點並不能影響他的心態。）
如果他要演講，他總是焦急不安，哪怕演講是在以前呆過的學校進行。

# if not

**2.49**　這個短語引導縮略從句，既有 even if 又有 although perhaps 的意義，表示 "即使" 或 "雖然也許" 某事不是如此。

*I lived among people who probably thought me fortunate **if not** rich.*
我生活在可能認為我雖然不算富有但卻幸運的人們中間。

*She took great care to listen to the child's answers, which were emphatic **if not** always absolutely clear.*
她仔細聽著那個孩子的回答，回答雖不總是非常清晰但卻斷然有力。

*I breathed a little easier, **if not** more deeply.*
我呼吸得鬆快了一些，雖然還不太深。

*The states would have the power to tax, **if not** the power to issue their own currencies.*
那些州即使不能得到發行自己貨幣的權力，但它們將得到徵稅的權力。

# whether...or

**2.50**　Whether...or 引導的是兩個互相對照的條件，但這兩個條件都承認主句的陳述不對其產生任何影響。

*They say we're to stay on here **whether** we like it **or not**.*
他們說不管我們高興與否，我們都得在這裏呆下去。

*So these people were promoted **whether or not** they had any professional skills.*
因此，不管這些人有無專業技能，都得到了提升。

*But who would describe herself in those terms, **whether** she's in her forties **or** seventies?*
不管她是 40 幾歲還是 70 幾歲，誰會用像她那樣用這樣的詞語來形容自己呢？

# whatever, whichever, whoever, wherever, however, no matter what/who/which/how

**2.51**　人們可以認可這些連接詞引導的任何條件，但是主句的事件總會發生，不為任何事所左右。

***Whatever** happened in the future, my suggestions would count for nothing.*
不管將來發生甚麼樣的事，我的建議都無甚價值。

***Whatever** they offer, my people will pay more.*
不管他們提供甚麼東西，我們的人都肯多付些錢。

***Whichever** way they fall to the ground, one sharp end has to stick up.*
不管它們以甚麼方式落地，尖利的一端必須向上豎起。

*How she loves your new friends, darling, **whoever** they are!*
親愛的，不管你的新朋友們是誰，她都喜歡！

*__Wherever__ I looked, enemies lurked.*
我所看之處，都潛伏着敵人。

*His body began a traumatic shivering, __however__ tightly he wrapped his arms across his chest.*
他的身體開始痛苦地顫抖，不管他把雙臂在胸前抱得多緊都不能自制。

*No sea wall, __however__ high and well built, is inviolable.*
海堤不管造得多高多牢，都會被衝垮的。

*__No matter what__ my friend replied, the salesman would say 'Great. Great. Glad to hear it.'*
不管我朋友回答甚麼，那個售貨員都説：〝好極了！好極了！很高興聽到你的回答。〞

*Inflation might take off again, __no matter who__ is elected.*
不管誰當選，通貨膨脹都可能開始。

*He always woke up early __no matter how__ late he had gone to bed.*
不管他睡得多晚，總是一早就醒了。

## albeit

**2.52**　這是一個罕見又正式的詞，用來削弱主句的陳述，其意義大致等同於 although 、 admittedly 或 even if ，一般後接縮略從句。

*The road was packed but traffic was moving, __albeit__ slowly.*
道路擁擠但車輛仍在運行，雖然速度緩慢。

*In the United States he was a hero, __albeit__ a somewhat tarnished one.*
他在美國仍是英雄，雖然已稍微失去昔日光彩。

# 讓步：連接語
# Concession: connectors

**2.53**　含讓步和對比意義的連接語包括：

| | | | |
|---|---|---|---|
| *however* | *though* | *even so* | *still* |
| *nevertheless* | *nonetheless* | *all the same* | |

這裏列出的連接語的意義大致等於 despite this （儘管這樣）。

▶注意◀ Though 和 although 都是連接詞（見 2.42 節），但是，如同下列帶 though 的例句所示，只有 though 可用作連接語。與別的連接語相比， all the same 和 still 用得更為隨便。

*This was not an easy decision. It is, __however__, a decision that we feel is dictated by our duty.*
這是一項艱難的決定。不過，我們感到這是受到我們責任感驅使而作出的決定。

*There's no direct evidence that such sweeteners cause cancer. **However**, research into additives is going on all the time.*

沒有證據直接證明這些甜化劑致癌。不過，對各類添加劑的調查研究卻一直在進行。

*They even had food for a day or two. **Nevertheless**, he was not relaxed.*

他們甚至還有一、兩天的食物。然而他並不感到輕鬆。

*Though not generally thought of as a serious handicap in physical terms, eczema has **nevertheless** crippled some people's lives because of its effects.*

雖然從生理上講，一般認為濕疹不會帶來嚴重的後果，不過因其作用，濕疹已經使許多人的生活受到了破壞。

*She was hounded by a man who eventually broke into her home with a gun. Usually, **though**, the stalker is threatening but non-violent.*

她受到了一個最後破門而入的持槍者的追逐。不過，通常，這種追蹤者只是威脅人而不對人施以暴力。

*These exercises will make you more aware of how you stand, sit, lie, breathe and move. Do follow the instruction carefully, **though**.*

這些鍛煉將使你更加注意自己的站相、坐相、睡相、呼吸和走動。不過，一定要注意按規程鍛煉。

*You can't go on negotiating ceasefires which are quite clearly signed in bad faith. **Nonetheless** he will go on negotiating them.*

對顯然是不抱誠意簽署的停火協定你不能再繼續談判下去。儘管如此，他還將繼續就停火進行談判。

*His chances look somewhat better than his predecessor's, but **even so** the prolonged period of political bargaining and intrigue is not necessarily over.*

與前任相比，他的機會看起來略勝一籌，儘管這樣，長時間在政治上的討價還價和陰謀詭計不一定就已經結束。

*Impossible, you say. **All the same** it has been done.*

你說那不可能。但是那已是木已成舟。

*I shouldn't think you'll need me at all. But I'll be there **all the same**.*

我想也許你根本就不需要我。儘管這樣，我還是會到場的。

*Without those items, the company would have come in with a $250 million loss. **Still**, that's a big improvement over the same quarter of one year ago.*

沒有那些貨品，公司就要損失2.5億美元。儘管這樣，同一年前同季度相比，還是有了很大的好轉。

*It was a joke of course, but where exactly was the humour in saying you didn't dance very well. **Still**, because I couldn't see the joke didn't mean that there wasn't a joke.*

這當然是笑話，但是說你舞跳得不好的幽默之處到底在哪裏呢？儘管這樣，這還是個笑話，雖然我不懂這個笑話的意義所在。

## anyway, anyhow, in any case, at any rate, in any event, at all events

**2.54** 所有這些詞語的含義都是 whatever happens（不管發生甚麼事）或 whatever is (or was) the case（不管情況如何）。因此，有時對先行的陳述就有一定的懷疑成份。Anyhow 不如 anyway 常見，而 at all events 則比較罕見。

*She did fall. She said herself she tripped. **Anyway**, what does it matter now?*
她的確摔倒了。她自己説是絆了一跤。但即使這樣，現在又有甚麼關係呢？

*'She could at least say she isn't guilty, if she isn't.' — 'I don't see why she should, since she knows very well that you're not going to believe her **anyway**.'*（粗體部份等於 whatever she says）
"假如她無罪，她至少可以説自己無罪。"——"我不明白為甚麼她要那樣説，因為她很清楚不管她説甚麼，你都是不會相信的。"

*Whether it was his main subject or not I really can't remember. But **anyhow** he got on extremely well with the professor.*
我的確不記得這到底是不是他的主科。但是，不管情況如何，他與那教授相處得很好。

*There was nothing in our agreement to keep me from showing my pictures, and the arrangement was only for a limited time, **anyhow**.*（即：whatever you think was in our agreement. 不管你認為這個協議內容怎樣。）
我們的協議裏沒有任何規定不讓我展出我的照片，但是不管怎樣，這種展出安排的時間很有限。

*It is impossible to foretell what they may attempt. **In any case**, we must be prepared to meet a very strong attack.*
無法預知他們的意圖。不管怎樣，我們必須作好迎接猛烈進攻的準備。

*The woman made a strange noise in her throat. It might have been speech; **at any rate**, the old man seemed to have understood it.*
那婦人的喉嚨裏發出一種奇怪的聲音。也許她在説話；不管怎樣，那個老頭好像懂了她的意思。

*Did the General know of the plot? But **in any event** the General wasn't worried.*
將軍對那個陰謀了解嗎？但不管怎樣，將軍是不擔心的。

*'Congratulations!', they said, 'it's an honour you deserve.' — 'That's as maybe. **At all events** it's an honour I declined.'*
他們説，"祝賀你！這是你受之無愧的榮譽。"——"也許是這樣的，但不管怎樣，我謝絕了那榮譽。"

☞ 另見 3.5 和 3.17 節。

## at least

**2.55**  **At least** 引出使某一情況不致變得很糟糕的情況，因而含有 so things could have been worse（所以情況本來可能會更糟的）。

*My wallet and credit cards were stolen. **At least** they didn't take my passport.*
我的錢包和信用卡被盜了。不過，他們沒有偷走我的護照。

*Most of the crew were drowned. But **at least** their death was instant.*
大多數船員都淹死了。但至少，他們死得很快。

*He hadn't met a single friendly face since he'd arrived. Except Katherine. She **at least** had a sense of humour.*
自他到達以來，他還沒有見過一張友好的面孔。凱瑟林除外，無論如何，她有幽默感。

☞ 另見 3.17 節。

## for that matter

**2.56** 可用這個短語表示説話者對陳述之後補充的信息的認同，強調陳述和補充信息兩者的真實性。

*He was only nineteen and clearly in a state of shock. **For that matter**, so was everyone.*
他當時只有 19 歲，顯然是愕得不知所措。而且，每個人都是如此。

*I had no love for the lady. But **for that matter**, nobody else did either.*
我不愛那位女士。而且，另外也沒有一個人愛她。

## having said that, that said

**2.57** **Having said that** 和語體更正式的 **that said** 起着讓步從句的作用。其含義大致等於 although I agree or admit what I have said（雖然我同意或承認自己説過的話）。Having said that主要用於口語，不過，在事實上這兩個短語都可以用於書面語。

就語法而言，像其他分詞一樣，having said that 從理論上應該依着於後接分句的主語，但它已經成了固定的短語，與主語無依着關係。不過，仍有人覺得這種用法不當。

*Success doesn't happen overnight. **Having said that**, we've confident we can get the club back into the Premier League.*
獲得成功不是一朝一夕的事。雖然這話不錯，不過我們有信心使球隊重返甲級聯賽。

*They do use organic ingredients whenever possible and the menu changes daily. **Having said that** the food is rather ordinary.*
他們一有可能就用有機配料並每天都更改菜單。雖然這話不假，食物卻毫無特別之處。

*I couldn't rest my heel on the floor and work the brake at the same time. **That said**, taxis are very easy to drive.*
我不能讓腳後跟着地同時又踩刹車，雖然這話不錯，開出租車卻很容易。

*Clearly, you do relate to your young man and he to you. **That said**, have no illusions. It might end tomorrow.*
顯然，你與你的情人相處甚好，他與你也不錯。雖然這話不錯，但不要有幻想。也許你們這種關係明天就會結束。

## alternatively, instead, by/in contrast, conversely

**2.58** 這些連接語主要用來強調對比。

**Alternatively** 和 **instead** 常常含有選擇的意義。

*Sieve the soup through a colander. **Alternatively**, liquidize it in a food processor.*
用濾鍋對這種湯進行過濾。但也可以在食品處理機裏將其液化。

*There were several taxi-cabs waiting, but he decided to walk down to the main road **instead**.*
有幾輛出租汽車在等候，但他卻決定步行到主幹道上去。

*Amy didn't look round. **Instead**, she was looking straight ahead of her.*
艾米沒有環顧四周，而是一直往前看。

**By contrast** 和 **in contrast** 引導有明顯差異的陳述。

*Each territorial acquisition needed a garrison and so the army increased in size. **By contrast**, the size of the fleet declined.*
每佔領一處新的領土都需要派駐軍，因此陸軍擴大了。相比之下，艦隊的規模卻縮小了。

*He has virtually no experience of running anything. The other candidate, **by contrast**, is a sincere, caring man who made a fortune in business before going into public life.*
他幾乎沒有管理的經驗。相比之下，另一位應聘人在步入公眾事務之前就是一名誠實、關心人的人，已經發財。

*In the larger neighbourhood I felt very unsafe. **In contrast**, others grow up in places where they never confronted serious danger.*
在這較大的社區我就會感到很不安全。相比之下，別人都是在從未遇到過嚴重危險的地方長大的。

**Conversely** 是語體正式的詞。用來說明前後兩個事件或兩種情況相互有關聯。但這相互對立的情況，都發生或屬實。

*Some people can eat more than others and still not gain weight. **Conversely**, some people can eat less than others and still gain weight.*
有的人能比別人吃得多卻不增加體重。與此相反，有的人比別人吃得少卻要增加體重。

*Eclipses of the Moon can only occur at Full Moon: **conversely**, eclipses of the Sun can only occur at the time of the New Moon.*
月蝕只能在全月時發生；與此相反，日蝕卻只能在新月時發生。

## on the other hand, on the contrary

**2.59** 不要混淆這兩個短語。**On the other hand** 引導的是與剛說過的話形成對比的另一論點。有時候用 **on the one hand** 引導第一個論點。要是說話者試圖做到公正而溫和，可用這兩個短語來"平衡"兩個論點。

***On the one hand**, I felt sorry for them, but **on the other hand**, I felt they knew something I didn't know.*
一方面我替他們感到惋惜，但另一方面我感到他們知道一些我不了解的事。

*She is not afraid of, or ashamed of, being successful, but **on the other hand** is prepared to sacrifice ambition for other rewards if she so chooses.*
她對出人頭地既不怕，也不難為情，但另一方面，要是她願意，她就準備為了別的報償而捨棄抱負。

*Southern parts of Cornwall had a monthly total rainfall of less than 2 mm. **On the other hand**, many parts of the country suffered from thunderstorms.*
康沃爾郡南部各地月降雨量不足 2 毫米。另一方面，英國的許多地方卻遭暴雨侵襲。

On the contrary 是語氣很強的短語，強調與先行陳述的主要意義形成對比。如果對已經説過的話不同意或認為不對，也可以用這個短語。

*In the end I still felt there was no way I could lose. **On the contrary**, I thought I would win too easily.*
我最後仍然感到我絕不可能失敗。恰恰相反，我認為我會輕而易舉地獲勝。

*'You've an educated fellow. Don't you know that nothing is connected?' — '**On the contrary**, Mr Kennerly, everything is connected.'*
"你是有學識的人。難道你不知道事事都沒有聯繫嗎？"——"恰恰相反，肯那利先生，事事都有聯繫。"

☞ 比較 **then again**、**there again**：見 7.22 節。

## at the same time

**2.60**　**At the same time** 涉及到兩個或多個同時發生的事件（見 2.22 節），但它引導的卻是與説過的話略有矛盾的陳述或者相反的論點。

*I was glad to be away from my difficult mother, though I missed her **at the same time**.*
我很高興離開我那不易相處的母親，雖然我同時又想念她。

*The results have been disappointing. **At the same time** the research is in its infancy.*
研究的結果一直令人失望。不過，研究是處在起步階段。

## despite, in spite of

**2.61**　▶注意◀　這是兩個帶讓步意義的常用語，但既不是連接詞也不是連接語，而是介詞，所以後接名詞（或名詞詞組）或者 -ing 形式（見 4.33 節）。其後從來不直接跟限定分句，但常常跟 the fact that 引出的從句。

*They wore gloves **despite the fact that** it was warm.*
雖然天氣暖和，他們卻帶着手套。

*Why did you go ahead with that office party **in spite of the fact that** one of your employees had recently died?*
你為何不顧你們的一名僱員新近去世的事實，還仍然要舉行辦公室工作人員的聚會？

# 除外
# Exception

## except (that), only

**2.62**　**Except that**、**except**、**only** 引導的從句表示對主句的例外。

*I can't think of anything else. **Except that** I should have your signature as well as Roger's on these two copies.*
我想不起要做甚麼事，只記得要羅傑和你在這一式兩份的文件上署名。

*Miss woods said that she touched nothing in the room, **except that** she turned on the light.*
伍茲女士説，除了開燈之外，她沒有碰過房間裏的任何東西。

*That was when Frances started to sing: she didn't know why exactly, **except** it seemed the right thing to do.*
那是弗郎西斯在開始唱歌的時候：她不確切知道為甚麼要唱，只覺得好像應該唱一唱。

*I think she was as confused about him as we are, **only** she didn't give a damn.*
我認為她同我們一樣對他這個人感到困惑，只不過她全不在乎。

## otherwise

**2.63**　**Otherwise** 有時表示 except for this（除此之外）或 apart from this（除了這點之外）。

*Of its recommendations, only one, that CBC operate an all-news channel, has been realized. **Otherwise**, little has happened.*
在所有的建議中，只有一條，即要加拿大廣播公司開通全新聞頻道的建議，成了現實。除此之外，就沒有辦成甚麼事。

☞ 另見 2.40 節。

# 目的
# Purpose

## to, in order to, so as to, in order for...to

**2.64**　通常用帶 **to** 的簡單不定式小句表示目的。

*A man in gold suit and a top hat hurried forward **to** open the front door.*
一位身着金黃色服裝、頭戴大禮帽的男人急匆匆地走過來打開前門。

*You need to put your point of view and perhaps alter your approach. **To** do this, you need to be firm and assertive but not aggressive.*
你需要擺出自己觀點，也許還要改變自己的方法。為此，你要堅決、自信，而不是咄咄逼人。

相比之下，**in order to**、**so as to** 是更為明確的目的的標記。

*They need travelling papers **in order to** exist in the bureaucratic world.*
他們需要種種旅行證明，以便能在官僚體制的國家裏生存。

*I never drank **in order to** get drunk.*
我喝酒從來不是為了要買醉。

*If we were in a decent hotel we started eating in our bedrooms **so as to** be alone.*
如果我們呆在體面的飯店裏，就可以在臥室裏開始用餐，以便無人干擾。

*She shielded her eyes **so as to** see him better.*
她用手遮住眼前的陽光以便把他看得更清楚。

當動詞不定式小句的主語不同於主句主語時，可用 **in order for...to**。

***In order for** her **to** quit there had to be some alternative occupation she could take up.*
為了她離職方便，需要安排另一個工作給她做。

*You do not have to eat hot foods **in order for** your body **to** create warmth.*
你不必吃辣味食品使身體產生熱量。

## so that, in order that, so

**2.65** 目的限定從句由 **so that**、**in order that** 或 **so** 引導。In order that 在語體上相當正式，而省略了that的so卻主要用於口語。這類從句中通常要用情態動詞。

*He arranged for the taxi to come at six **so that** she would not have to wait long at the station.*
他安排出租車在 6 點鐘來，以免她在車站久等。

*Eat small portions **so that** your digestive system is not overloaded.*
吃小份食物，以免你的消化系統負擔過重。

*We only married **in order that** the child should be legitimate.*
我們是為了孩子能成為合法婚生的才結婚。

*I went between twelve and one o'clock **in order that** I might find the men at home.*
我在 12 點到下午 1 點之間這段時間去，目的是為了在家裏找到他。

*He may have taken up smoking early in life **in order that** he has something to do with his hands.*
他大概在年輕時就吸上了煙，為了手上有事做。

*Take notes **so** you will remember it all.*
請做筆記以便記住全部內容。

*Come to my room **so** I can tell you all about this wonderful play I saw in Boston.*
到我房間來，以便我向你敘述我在波士頓看到的好戲的方方面面。

## so as not to, in order not to, so that...not, in order that...not

**2.66** 表示否定目的的不定式小句由 **so as not to** 或 **in order not to** 引導。偶爾也由 **so that ...not** 或 **in order that ...not** 引導否定限定從句。

*I left quietly **so as not to** disturb any of the hotel guests.*
我悄悄地離去，以免打擾飯店旅客。

*He talked to the bird softly **so as not to** frighten it.*
他輕輕地對鳥說話，為了不至驚嚇了它。

*She slept in a separate room **in order not to** disturb him.*
她在另一房間睡覺，為了不至打擾他。

*He must consume 2250 calories daily **in order not to** lose or gain weight.*
他必須每日消耗2250卡路里熱量，以使體重不致減輕或增加。

*Miss May took the little girls out of the house **so that** they might **not** hear their mother screaming.*
梅依小姐把小姑娘們從家裏帶到戶外，以免她們聽到自己母親的尖叫聲。

*She put down her glass **in order that** it should **not** reveal how her hand was shaking.*
她放下手裏的玻璃杯，以免人家看出她那只手在發抖。

# 理由：連接詞
# Reason: conjunctions

## because, 'cos, since, as, for

**2.67** 原因從句主要由 **because**、**since**、**as**、**for** 引導。其中以 because 最為常見，而且常在非正式口語中縮略成 'cos。

*Another advert has been banned from children's TV **because** it frightens youngsters.*
另一種廣告被禁止在兒童電視裏播放，因為這種廣告使兒童害怕。

***Because** she was my mother, I expected her to know the right choice.*
由於她是我的母親，所以我期望她能作出正確的選擇。

*What I've got in the bowl is four ounces of wholemeal self-raising flour, **'cos** obviously wholemeal's better for us.*
我在那個碗裏有四盎司自發的全麥麵粉，因為很明顯，全麥麵粉更有益我們的健康。

***Since** this is a special occasion, I've already decided to treat myself to a taxi.*
由於這是個不尋常的時刻，所以我已經決定享受一回坐出租車去。

*The subject was mentioned, but only in passing, and **since** I wasn't asked to elaborate, I didn't.*
那個題目被提到了，但只是附帶地被提及；由於沒有要求我詳加說明，我就作罷。

*'You surely know them,' I wanted to add, '**since** you seem to know everyone.'*
我想補充說，"你肯定認識他們，因為你好像人人都認識。"

*It was not a wise decision in the long run, **as** we had not reckoned on the dramatic rise in house prices.*
從長遠觀點來看，這不是一個明智的決定，因為我們不曾期待房價大漲。

表示理由的 for 語體正式，不常見，而且由 for 引導的從句只能在主句之後。

*Clients are in for a shock, **for** they too will be subjected to new scrutiny.*
顧客會感到震驚，因為他們也將被置於新的監視之下。

## in that, insofar as, to the extent that, seeing that, now that

**2.68** 以上是引導理由從句的另一些連接詞。

**In that** 的語體相當正式，引出解釋。

*I am an optimist **in that** I believe that human beings do not always perversely try to make life worse for themselves.*
我是樂天派的人，因為我認為人類並非總是違反常情地力圖使自己的生活變差。

*Most of them are not in reality engineers, **in that** the work they do is mostly clerical.*
他們中的大多數人實際上都不是工程師，因為他們做的主要是辦公室工作。

**Insofar as**（也寫成 **in so far as**）和 **to the extent that** 也屬語體正式的詞語，用來限定已經說過的話，提出其真實的確切理由或唯一理由。

*He didn't want power, particularly, or even money; he valued them not for themselves but only **insofar as** they brought him independence.*
他不是特別要權，甚至也不要錢；他不是看重權錢本身，而只是因為這兩樣東西給他帶來了獨立性。

*I think his offer will be received well, **in so far as** they will see that he wants to make some kind of a compromise.*
我認為他的出價將得到積極的回應，因為他們會注意到他希望做出某種妥協。

*The tenets of this sacred art exclude women **to the extent that** only men are allowed on the stage during a recital.*
這種神聖藝術的原則把婦女排除在外，竟然在演奏會上只有男人才允許登台。

**Seeing that** 通常含有幾分原有的字面意義，等於 because someone saw or realized that（因為某人了解或意識到）情況確是如此。

*****Seeing that** I was covered with dust, she brought a bowl of hot water.*
見我滿身灰塵，她端來一盆熱水。

*****Seeing that** losses on their existing loans were inevitable, the banks therefore cast around for other means of making big profits.*
認識到現有貸款的損失已不可避免，那些銀行試圖尋求別的方式來獲取巨額利潤。

然而，在大多數非正式英語裏，seeing that有時卻沒有原有的字面意義，純粹用來引出原因或提供解釋說明。

> *Seeing that you had a police escort, the only time you could have switched cars was en route to the airport.*
> 由於你們有警察護送，唯一你們本可更換汽車的時間是在去機場的途中。

> *I'm just ringing to check everything's OK, **seeing that** it's Crime Prevention Week.*
> 我按了一會兒鈴來核實是否平安無事，因為這是預防犯罪週。

**Now that** 也含有幾分原有的字面意義，等於because at this time（因為在此時）。

> *Now that she was retired she lived with her sister in the village of Lindleham in Berkshire.*
> 因為當時已經退休，她與妹妹住在英國伯克郡的林達漢姆村。

> *Now that you have kept your part of the bargain, I will keep mine.*
> 既然你已經履行了協議中有關你的條款，我也將履行我的條款。

## in case, lest, for fear that

**2.69** 用in case、lest、for fear that 藉助對可能會發生的事情的預測或擔心，對主句表示的行為進行解釋。Lest 和 for fear that 的語體正式，而 lest 後有時接虛擬語氣謂語動詞的從句。

> *He wasn't going to use his car **in case** somebody recognized it.* （...in case... 即：...because somebody might recognize it, and he did not want to be recognized.因為有人可能會認出他的車，他不願被人家認出來。）
> 他不打算用自己的汽車，因為怕有人認出他的車。

> *I think I ought to stay **in case** Ian suddenly comes back.*
> 我認為我應該留下不走，因為伊安可能會突然回來。

> *I was afraid to open the door **lest** he should follow me.* （...lest... 即：I wanted to prevent him following me.我想阻止他跟蹤我。）
> 我怕把門打開，因為他可能會跟蹤我。

> *British officers were forbidden to keep diaries **lest** they were captured and their secrets betrayed.*
> 英國軍官被禁止記日記，因為怕他們被俘而洩密。

> *He refused to say anything **lest** he **say** something foolish.*
> 他拒絕開口說話，因為他怕說出蠢話來。

> *They did not want to admit to any shortages of food **for fear that** it might reveal a weakness to be exploited by their enemies.*
> 他們不想承認食物短缺，因為怕暴露弱點後被敵人利用。

> *I said that I was ten years younger **for fear that** I would be turned down for the job.*
> 我把年齡少報了10歲，因為怕人家不肯給我這份工作。

# 理由：連接語
# Reason: connectors

**2.70** 列舉理由，可用 **for one thing**（原因之一）或 **in the first place**（首先）。

*The Manor was a house full of interest.* **For one thing** *it was said to be haunted.*
莊園是一座引人關注的建築物。原因之一是據說這個地方鬧鬼。

*Very little was known about Lassa fever.* **In the first place** *it was difficult to recognize.*
對拉沙熱病的了解不多。原因之一是該流行傳染病難於認別。

**For one thing** 之後，還可以用 **for another**。

*He did not immediately recognize her.* **For one thing***, she had the sun behind her;*
***for another***, *she was without her glasses.*
他沒有立即認出她。一則是她背着陽光，二則是她沒有戴眼鏡。

☞ 另見 3.18 – 3.21 節：**列舉**。

# 結果：連接詞
# Result: conjunctions

**2.71** 結果從句位於主句之後。表示結果的從句由 so that、such that、in such a way that 引導。

*The alley was curved* **so that** *now he could not see the taxi.*
小巷彎曲，結果他無法看見那輛出租車。

*Drink can suppress your appetite* **so that** *you are not eating sensibly in the first place.*
飲酒會抑止胃口，所以你首先明顯地不能吃東西。

*She swung her shoulder bag* **so that** *it caught him full in the chest and pushed him backwards.*
她揮動自己的背包，結果包直砸在他的胸上，使他踉蹌後退。

*He actually suffered a great intolerance for alcohol,* **such that** *a single drink could produce violent, disruptive behavior.*
他真的對酒精很過敏，以至於喝一杯酒就能使他產生激烈的破壞性的行為。

*The length and complexity of the case were* **such that** *a fair trial was not possible.*
時間拖得長、案子又複雜，結果使公平的審判不可能進行。

*The mind reflects on itself* **in such a way that** *we become conscious of consciousness.*
腦子可以作用於自身，所以我們能意識到自己的意識。

So 或 such 可以同 that 分開，用在主句裏。在比較隨便的英語裏，從句裏的 that 經常被省略。

*I knew him **so** well **that** I was not surprised by this news.*
我對他很了解，所以並不為這個消息感到吃驚。

*Was it possible to have **so** much pain **that** it could no longer hurt?*
痛得很厲害以至不再感到疼痛，這種情況可能嗎？

*Sometimes he was **so** busy thinking **that** he forgot to eat.*
有時他忙於思考結果連吃飯都忘了。

*They were **so** surprised, **(that 被省略)** they didn't try to stop him.*
他們非常吃驚，以至他們沒有設法去阻止他。

*The champagne was of **such** superior quality and **such** a good year **that** she had already drunk more than she should have.*
這香檳酒質量高，年份好，結果她已經喝過了量。

**2.72** 表示結果的動詞不定式小句由 **so...as to**、**such as to** 引導。

*We are not **so** young or stupid **as** not **to** know our own feelings.*
我們並非年輕或愚蠢得不知道自己的心情。

*If a modern society is prosper, its political, social and economic arrangements must be **such as to** stimulate and satisfy those with most to contribute to the common good.*
如果要使現代社會繁榮昌盛，其政治、社會及經濟方面的計劃一定要激勵和滿足那些為共同的利益作出最大貢獻的人。

*Will you please act in **such** a way **as to** put their minds at rest?*
你行為可不可以注意一些好使他們放心？

# 是目的還是結果
# Purpose or result？

**2.73** 目的和結果肯定是密切相關的 ——人們確定目的是為獲得結果。帶so that 的目的從句通常以情態動詞為標記，而帶 so that 的結果從句一般以普通動詞為標記。然而，事情並不那麼簡單，有時，特別在脫離具體的語境時，就不清楚這種從句表示的是目的還是結果，或者既是目的又是結果。

*She also organized her eating, **so that** she was taking more fruit and vegetables and less starch.*
她還對自己的飲食做了安排，結果她多吃水果和蔬菜，少吃澱粉類的食物。

**2.74** 為了起到特別的強調作用，可用 so 置於句首，然後加上形容詞或副詞的句型來表示結果意義。這時需要倒裝主語、助動詞的次序。

***So successful have they*** *been that they are moving to Bond Street.*
他們是那麼成功，結果他們將搬到邦迪街。

# 結果：連接語
# Result: connectors

**2.75** 引導結果或後果的連接語包括：

| | | |
|---|---|---|
| *therefore* | *so* | *as a consequence* |
| *thus* | *because of this* | *in consequence* |
| *as a result* | *consequently* | *accordingly* |

*He previously worked in the Ministry of Finance. He comes, **therefore**, with a great deal of experience and expertise.*

他以前在財政部工作過。因此他來的時候已有豐富經驗和專門知識。

*These birds truly enjoy flying and should **therefore** be housed in lengthy aviaries.*

這些鳥確實喜好飛行，所以應該用很長的大鳥舍關養。

*The second millennium did not commence until January 1, 1001. **Thus** the second thousand years does not finish until December 31, 2000.*

公元的第二個千年到了1001年1月1日才開始計算。所以第二個千年要到2000年12月31日才算結束。

*Most study groups are held during the day, **thus** avoiding evening or rush–hour travel.*

大多數學習小組在白天進行學習，從而避免了傍晚或交通高峰時的乘車。

*Firms can contract out work to one another, and **thus** acquire specialized services, equipment and skills none of them could possess alone.*

公司之間能夠互相承包工程，結果，這些公司就有了獨家公司不能擁有的專項服務、設備和技術。

*Only part of the restaurant was being used, and **as a result** the tables were closer together than usual.*

餐館在那段時間只有一部份被用了起來，所以，餐桌比平常擺放得擁擠。

*On their travels they indulged their hobby of collecting antique furniture. **As a result** their home had become something of a museum.*

他們在每次旅行時，盡興地滿足自己收集古董傢具的嗜好。結果他們家成了類似博物館的地方。

*Our son is at school near here, **so** that's another reason for not moving.*

我的兒子在附近學校上學，因此那是我們不搬家的另一理由。

*I was still unsure about the need for a book. **So** I consulted several academic experts on Foucault.*

我仍然不能確定是否需要一本書。所以，我請教了幾位研究法國物理學家傅科的專家。

*I travel the globe six months of every year. **Because of this** I honestly believe that I know more about the airline business than any of my competitor.*

我每年有六個月時間在作全球旅行。因此，我堅信我對航空公司事務的了解比任何一名競爭者都多。

*Both were adopted Korean girls, and **because of this**, felt almost like sisters.*

她們倆都是被領養的韓國姑娘，因此感到自己幾乎像是親姐妹。

*He has attained superstar status, he has achieved a massive following and, **consequently**, he now has power, success and unlimited money.*

他已經有了超級明星的地位，有了一大批追隨者，因此，他現在有權力、有成就，還有用不完的金錢。

*The love affair itself never comes alive. **Consequently**, the novel's moral dilemmas fail to grip.*
那個戀愛事件本身從來就不吸引人。因此，小說中描寫的是是非非也沒有感染力。

*500,000 tourists visit the region annually. **As a consequence**, tourist traffic must be regulated and subjected to very tight restrictions.*
每年有 50 萬旅遊者訪問那個地方。所以，對旅遊用車必須加以管理和嚴格限制。

*Alice had to take four sleeping pills before she could get back to sleep and **as a consequence** failed, for the first time in her life, to turn up for a 7.00 am call.*
阿麗斯在重新入睡前不得不服用四片安眠藥，結果生平第一次未能根據通知早晨 7 點到場。

*Once Alastair got so carried away that he attempted to speak through his snorkel, and nearly drowned **in consequence**.*
有一次，阿拉斯特興奮得有點忘乎所以，試圖借助潛水通氣管説話，結果差點被淹死。

*The Party identified itself with the welfare and happiness of people. It was **in consequence** trusted by the people.*
那個黨全力謀求人民的福利和幸福，因而受到人民的信任。

*Peace is not secured by alienating people, but rather by uniting them. **Accordingly**, the goal is to learn to live together in tolerance and mutual understanding.*
和平不是通過使人民疏遠而是通過使人民團結得到的。因此，目標是學會在相互寬容和相互理解中共同生活。

*The financing of social services affects everybody. They are, **accordingly**, the object of much heated discussion by economist and politicians.*
為社會服務提供資金對大家都有影響，因此，成了經濟學家和政治家熱烈討論的話題。

## hence

**2.76　Hence**（因此）可以引導另一句子或分句，但通常卻是引導一個單詞或短語，所表示的事物被認為是先行句子或分句的結果。

*Linguistics, then, is the field which classifies the pronunciation, grammar, meaning and use of language and **hence** provides terminology to talk about these matters.*
那麼，語言學是對語言的發音、語法、意義和使用進行歸類的學問，因而為討論這些語言問題提供了術語。

*My guess is somebody on our side arranged it, some dirty tricks operation; **hence** the deathly silence.*
我猜想是我方的某個人進行了佈置，耍了卑鄙下流的花招；因而出現了死一般的寂靜。

## thereby

**2.77　Thereby**（因而）也具有 as a result（結果）或 in this way（這樣）的意義，但是卻不能用在新句的句首。

*She hit the soldier's outstretched arm, and **thereby** saved the life of a demonstrator whom he was about to shoot at point-blank range.*
她擊中了那個士兵伸開的臂部，這樣保住了這個士兵打算近距離槍殺的示威者的性命。

*Smokers stay longer in hospital, **thereby** depriving non-smoking patients of treatment.*
吸煙者住院的時間要長些，因而使非吸煙病人喪失了治療機會。

## then, in that case, in which case

**2.78    Then**（那麼）引導符合邏輯的推斷或顯而易見的結論。

*'I have not stolen any money.' — '**Then** you must know who did.'*
"我沒有偷過錢。"——"那麼你肯定知道是誰偷的。"

*If this argument is right, **then** there are many new things to worry about.*
如果這個論據成立，那麼就會出現許多令人擔憂的新情況。

**In that case**（那麼、在那種情況下）引導的是假定先行的陳述屬實時，勢必會產生的結果。如果先行的陳述是不可靠的或是假設，就用 **in which case**（此時、在這種情況下）。

*'I'm sure all the obvious methods have been checked.' — '**In that case** there's not much I can do.'*
"我肯定那些顯而易見的方法已經全部檢查過了。"——"那麼我就沒有多少事可以做了。"

*Either I know my job, **in which case** I shall know the answer to your questions. Or else I don't know my job, **in which case** I probably shouldn't be here.*
要麼是：我了解自己的工作，在這種情況下，我將知道你問題的答案；要麼就是：我不了解自己的工作，在這種情況下，我也許就不應該來。

# 方式：連接詞
# Manner: conjunctions

**2.79**    方式從句解釋怎樣做事，即做事的方式。

**As**、**like** 大體的含義是 in the same way as（以同樣的方式）或 in a similar way to（以相似的方式）。可以在 as、like 前用其含義為 exactly（正、完全）的 just。Like 有引導方式從句的功能，主要用在口語裏，並被一部份人認為是錯誤的用法。

*In the end I could always do **as** Harry had suggested. I could go to the press and tell the story.*
最後，我總能按哈瑞的建議辦事。我會去向新聞界講述真相。

*The round clock at the rear of the room ticked loudly, **just as** I remembered.*
正如我記住的那樣，在屋子裏後方的圓鐘發出響亮的嘀嗒聲。

*I mean, **like** you said last night, the fact that you're a soldier doesn't mean to say that you want to kill.*
我的意思是就如你昨晚説過的那樣，你是當兵的並不等於説你嗜好殺人。

**Much as** 的含義是 in roughly the same way as（以大致上相同的方式）。

> *She grasped the pen in her fist with the point down, **much as** a young child would do.*
> 她把鋼筆一把抓在手裏，筆尖朝下，跟幼童握筆時的樣子差不多。

> *I serve my country **much as** you serve yours.*
> 就像你為自己的國家服務那樣，我為我自己的國家服務。

> *The jury will decide pretty **much as** you tell them to, won't they?*
> 陪審團將像你要求他們的那樣判決，對不對？

## as if, as though, like

**2.80**　**As if**、**as though**（彷彿、好像）表示某種比較，這種意義可以是虛擬的，也可以是對某事的印象或信念。用 as if、as though 可引導非限定小句。**Like** 用於這一意義時在語體上很不正式，常常被認為是不正確的用法。

> *You talk **as if** she was someone you once knew.*
> 你把話說得好像她是你過去一度認識的人似的。

> *She said the word **as if** the meaning escaped her.*
> 她講出了那個單詞，卻好像忘了詞義。

> *They looked at me **as though** I hadn't a clue to the meaning of activism.*
> 他們看着我，彷彿我對激進主義的意義一點兒也不知道一樣。

> *She lifts his hand **as if** to lead him somewhere.*
> 她牽起他的手，像要把他帶到某個地方去。

> *He paused and looked round the room **as if** saying goodbye to it.*
> 他停了下來，將屋子環顧一番，彷彿是在向屋子告別。

> *Lucas stepped toward the burnt house **as though** hypnotized.*
> 盧卡斯向燒毀的房子走去，好像被人施過催眠術似的。

> *You sound **like** you remember them.*
> 你的話使人覺得你還記得他們似的。

**2.81**　方式從句也可用 **the way**（方式）、**in a way**（以某種方式）或 **in the way**（以這/那樣的方式）引導。Way 的後面有時可接 that。

> *People like you **the way that** you are.*
> 人們都喜歡你處世的作風。

> *You end up making a happier life for yourself by understanding yourself **in a way** you never have before.*
> 用從未有過的方式來看待自己，你最終就能替自己營造一種更加幸福的生活。

> *He treated Haig's suggestions as if they were commands, probably **in the way** they were intended.*
> 他把黑格的建議當作命令，可能正合乎黑格提出建議的用意。

*Then you can paint your nails **in the way** you apply nail varnish.*
然後，你可以像用指甲油那樣來染自己的指甲。

*These cats and dogs caught birds **in the way** they might, in Europe, have caught mice.*
這些貓和狗像過去在歐洲捕捉老鼠時可能用過的方式來捕捉鳥類。

# 地點：連接詞
# Place: conjunctions

**2.82**　如果需要從句而不是單個副詞來說及某事發生的地方或位置，可用 **where**、**wherever** 或 **everywhere** 引導的從句。

*I'm so glad to see you back **where** you belong.*
我很高興看到你回到了你自己的住處。

***Where** the lane ends, continue on a narrow woodland footpath which rises briefly before running downhill.*
在巷子的盡頭，就是一條狹窄的林間小道，先是一小段上坡路，然後就是下坡路。

*Ramesh can take this document **wherever** he likes to have it checked.*
拉麥西可以把這份文件帶到任何一個地方去加以核對。

*Collect Mrs Selby and take her **wherever** she wants to go.*
接走塞爾比太太，並帶她去她要去的地方。

***Everywhere** I went in Tibet, Tibetans kept remarking on the strange weather.*
在西藏，無論我走到哪裏，都有藏民在不停地議論那兒的奇異天氣。

**2.83**　許多用 where 或 wherever 引導的無動詞小句的含義與其說是表示地點，還不如說是表示時間和條件。

*Even after the military takeover a week ago, the people **wherever possible** continued to encourage us.*（…wherever possible… 等於 …when and if it was possible… 當一有可能時……）
甚至在一週前的軍事接管之後，人們還在一有可能的時候就繼續對我們進行鼓勵。

*The local committees draw up lists of qualified practitioners who can test sight and make up glasses **where necessary**.*
各地方委員會列出能在必要時驗光配鏡的合格的醫務人員名單。

# 比較：連接詞
# Comparison: conjunctions

**2.84**　比較從句將一人與另一人、一物與另一物進行比較。有兩種比較從句。

• 第一種用來表示比較的人或物從具有的某種屬性來看是相同的（或不同的）。

- 第二種用來強調差別，説明一個人或物與另一個人或物相比，具有更多或更少的某種屬性。

在比較從句裏，常常出現省略，即略去與主句相同的成分，或者出現替代，即用帶動詞 do 的短語來避免重複主句的動詞短語。

## as...as, not as...as, not so...as

**2.85**　表示同等比較用 **as...as** 。

*She was just **as** rude to the boys **as** the girls.* （…as rude to the boys as the girls. 等於 …as rude to the boys as she was to the girls.）
她對男孩同對女孩一樣粗魯。

*One fetched for oneself and ate **as** much **as** one could.* （…as much as one could. 等於 …as much as one could eat.）
食物自取，能吃多少就吃多少。

*John Kempton was now **as** strong **as** could be expected.* （…as strong as could be expected. 等於 …as strong as it could be expected that he would be.）
約翰‧坎普頓現在的身體要多結實就有多結實。

*He's **as** angry **as** anybody at the news.*
對那條消息他同大家一樣生氣。

用 **not as...as** 或 **not so...as** 表示不同等比較。

*She would**n't** have known her **as** well **as** you did.*
她本不可能像你那麼了解她。

*The job was **not as** difficult **as** the look of the place implied.*
這個工作沒有像那個場地給人的印象那樣難。

*She was **not so** innocent **as** he'd first thought.*
她沒有他起初想像的那麼單純。

## -er...than, more...than, less...than

**2.86**　強調差別的比較從句用 -er 比較級形式加 **than** 引導。

*Well there can be some girls that are **better than** boys but mostly the boys are **cleverer than** girls.*
不錯，有的女孩是比男孩更優秀，但是大體上，男孩比女孩更聰明。

*It is **easier** to arouse a tiger **than** to ride it.*
激怒老虎比騎老虎更容易。

*He was back **sooner than** she expected.*
他回來得比她預期的要早。

表示比較通常都有 **more** 或 **less** 這樣的詞。

*He felt **more** tired **than** he had ever felt.*
他感到過去從未有過的累。

*I've already said **more than** I intended to say.*
我講的話比我原先打算要講的多。

*I've been wrong much **more** often **than** I've been right.*
我出錯比我正確要經常得多。

*Tony looked **more** tanned and handsome **than** ever.* （…than ever. 等於 …than he ever looked.）
托尼看上去比以前曬得更黑、長得更英俊。

*The new men, not wanting to appear **less** tough **than** the veterans, kept silent.*
新兵一聲不吭，因為他不想表現得不如老兵那樣吃得苦。

*The prospect is ultimately **less** attractive **than** it seems.*
前景最終不如表面上那麼有吸引力。

**2.87** 當比較從句第二分句在 as 或 than 後只有主語，而且這個主語又是代詞時，有的人堅持要用主格代詞。

*She is just as foolish, as stupid, as impulsive **as I**.* （…as I. 等於 …as I am.）
她跟我一樣地愚蠢、頭腦遲鈍、容易感情衝動。

然而，這種用法很正式。遇到這種情況時，可將 as、than 看作介詞，用含主語意義的賓格代詞，這種用法既普遍又無錯。

*They're fighting the same war **as us**.* （…as us. 等於 …as we are.）
他們同我們打的是同一場戰爭。

*She arrived earlier **than him**.* （…than him. 等於 …than he did.）
她比他先到。

# 比例
# Proportion

**2.88** 英語有兩種相當獨特的句子，由兩個分句組成，用來表示比較，但又包含結果意義。

- 第一種由兩個平行分句組成，都由 **the** 引導，然後再加比較級形式。

***The more** I thought about it, **the more** confused I became.*
我對此考慮得愈多，就愈感到迷惑不解。

*He is the most versatile actor on TV. **The more** shows he does **the better**.* （The more… the better. 即：He should do more shows. 他該多做些表演。）
他是電視上最為多才多藝的演員。他演得愈多，就演得愈好。

***The more** stress one experiences, **the higher** the cholesterol levels tend to be.*
人的壓力越大，其膽固醇水平就可能越高。

*He believed that **the less** you said, **the more** likely you were to be heard.*
他認為,話説得愈少,就愈有可能讓人聽取。

- 第二種比較少見。第一分句用 **as**,第二分句用 **so** 引導。發生在第二個分句的情況在一定程度上取決於發生在第一個分句的情況,而且兩種情況同時發生。

*__As__ the genetic secrets of muscle growth unfold, **so** the prospects for genetically manipulating muscle fibres improve.*
隨着肌肉生長的遺傳奧秘的揭開,在遺傳上控制肌肉纖維的前景也就更好。

*__As__ the cost of keeping money in the bank increases, **so** it's spent faster.*
隨着在銀行存錢的費用增加,人們的錢花得也更快了。

# 優選
# Preference

**2.89** 另一獨特的以 **rather than** 或偶爾以 **sooner than** 引導的分句可用來表示優選。這樣的分句後接不帶 to 的動詞不定式而不是限定動詞。

*__Rather than engage__ in a long report over the telephone, I had invited him to lunch with me at home on this quiet Sunday.*
我寧肯邀請他在這個安靜的星期日來我家共進午餐,而不是在電話裏同他長談。

*Rosemary had thought it important enough to come herself, __rather than send__ one of the maids.*
羅斯瑪麗認識到此事很重要,得親自來,而不是派一名女傭來。

*They will sink us __sooner than permit__ our safe arrival in any British port.*
他們寧可將我們沉入水中而不願讓我們安全抵達英國的任何一個港口。

# 3 連接語：解釋說明
## Connectors: explaining

**3.1** 有些連接語的意義與連接詞引導的副詞從句表示的意義沒有關係。有時說話者把這些連接語作為標誌，表明自己通過增加信息、舉例、重新措辭、列舉或總結的方式來對已說的話作進一步解釋。

## 增加
## Adding

**3.2** And 之類的並列連詞和 not only...but also 之類的成對並列連詞當然具有增加的意義。在某種意義上，所有的連接語都有增加的意義，因為它們都能增加一定的信息。但是有些連接語是增加信息或提供更多論據的特定標誌（3.3–3.12節）。

### moreover, furthermore, further

**3.3** 這是三個比較常見、語體比較正式的用語，表明說話者在為自己的論點增加信息或者提供更多的支持。

*Most streets in Tokyo are safe at night.* ***Moreover****, the juvenile crime rate actually has fallen in recent years.*
東京的絕大多數街道晚間都安全。再說，近年來少年犯罪率實際上已經下降。

*They seem to know exactly what they're doing and,* ***moreover****, make you want to admire them for it.*
他們似乎都明確自己在做的事情，此外，他們還使你為此對他們表示欽佩。

*The organization has both limited powers and limited funds.* ***Furthermore****, it has no right of access to countries outside the treaty.*
那個組織的權力和資金都有限。而且，該組織也無權進入條約之外的國家。

*His enormous reputation is almost entirely posthumous. It is based,* ***furthermore****, on very little actual production.*
他那如雷貫耳的名聲幾乎是死後才有的。而且，其名聲是建立在寥寥無幾的作品基礎之上的。

*No single British field sport has been subjected to abolition by law.* ***Further****, hunting with hounds continues to thrive throughout the British Isles.*
沒有哪項野外運動為法律所取締。再說，帶獵犬出獵還繼續在不列顛羣島盛行。

## in addition, additionally, what is more, on top of that

**3.4**　這是另外幾個可以用來表示增加信息的連接語。其中，以 **in addition** 最為常用。

*He is incapable of using rhythm and pace for dramatic effect. **In addition**, he stumbles over words.*
他不會用節奏和速度使講話產生戲劇性的效果。此外，他說話時結結巴巴。

*Even on the simplest voyage there is a feeling of adventure and excitement. When, **in addition**, you are in your own boat you realize just how lucky you are.*
甚至最普通的航行也會給人歷險和刺激的感覺。此外，一坐在自己的船裏，你就意識到自己多幸運啊。

*Banks are run by people, and people make mistakes. **Additionally**, like all industries, banks will have their share of dishonest workers.*
銀行由人經營，是人就要出差錯。此外，像所有行業一樣，銀行也會有不誠實的工作人員。

*Barely three months later they are engaged in an unholy row. **What is more**, it is a row over basic principles.*
不到三個月，他們就大吵了一場，而且是一場關於基本原則的爭吵。

**On top of that** 是語體比較正式的用語。

*That day the heat was unbearable, **and on top of that**, tsetse flies bit me every time I slowed down.*
那天酷熱難忍，此外，我一放慢速度，採採蠅就咬我。

*I won't tell a lie on your behalf. And **on top of that**, it's the stupidest lie I've ever heard.*
我不會為你而說謊。此外，那將是我所聽到的最愚蠢的謊言。

*You'll be interviewed, of course. **On top of that**, we'd like you to describe what happened in your own words.*
當然，你會受到採訪。再者，我們將樂於請你用自己的話敍述發生的事。

## besides, anyway, anyhow

**3.5**　**Besides** 用來增加信息，有時用以強調附加的或重要的觀點，有時對已經說過的話進行解釋。

*The doctors couldn't talk English and **besides** they were never around.*
醫生們不會講英語，此外他們也從未露過面。

*I want to share my paintings with my clients. **Besides**, my apartment is too small for them all.*
我要把我的畫作與客戶分享。再者，我的公寓房太小，無法陳列全部畫作。

*Martin sat on the bank at one side of the lay-by, watching the parked lorries and waiting. **Besides** he was tired.*
馬丁坐在路旁停車處的邊上，注視着停泊的貨車，等在那裏。此外，他也累了。

**Anyway** 、 **anyhow** 也有增加信息的意義。

*It's not joyriding, **anyway**. It's stealing, isn't it?*
而且，這不是用借來的車兜風。這是偷車，不是嗎？

*We cut all scenes of sex and violence because it is against our religion. **Anyway**, it's bad for the children.*
因為與我們的宗教信仰不符，我們剪掉了所有色情暴力的場面。而且色情暴力對兒童產生不好的影響。

*I thought it was best to warn him. **Anyhow**, Cheryl wanted him to know.*
我認為最好是告誡他。此外，切瑞爾也想讓他知道。

## after all

**3.6    After all** 引出對先行的陳述的進一步說明或補充理由，因為先行的陳述試圖解釋說明的是略有非同尋常或令人不解的事物。

*Her speaking in German was hardly peculiar. **After all**, it was her native tongue.*
她用德語講話並不奇怪。德語畢竟是她的母語。

*Her contradictions were not so unusual, not if you stopped to think about it. Most people, **after all**, were a mix of good and evil.*
她身上反映出的矛盾不足為奇，要是你仔細想想，就不感到奇怪。絕大多數人畢竟都是善與惡的混合體。

*I'm not advising you to throw away your makeup or forget about your appearance. **After all**, we do live in a world where beauty counts.*
我不是勸你丟棄你的化粧品，也不是勸你忘卻自己的容貌。畢竟我們是生活在人們重視美的世界上。

▶ 注意 ◀ 不要把有這一特別含義的 after all 與 finally 或 lastly（3.23 節）相混淆。

## above all

**3.7    Above all** 的作用是補充比已經講過的話更為重要的論點。

*And it's far from silent there. **Above all**, of course, there's the singing of the birds and the squeaks and rustling movements of small animals.*
那裏遠非寂靜。當然，尤其是那裏有鳥兒啾鳴的歌聲，有各種小動物吱吱的叫聲或沙沙移動的響聲。

*Rather than a 70 mph limit she said a better idea might be a device the automatically restricted cars to the speed limit. **Above all**, the association wants a change in car advertising.*
她說更好的辦法是用能將汽車車速自動控制在速限內的裝置來替代每小時70英里速限的規定。最重要的是，聯合會還想對汽車廣告作出改進。

# indeed

**3.8** **Indeed** 的作用是補充進一步的評論，以強調已經説過的話的真實性。

*The Great Bear rotates about the sky and is always visible at night in the Northern Hemisphere.* **Indeed***, during a total eclipse, it is visible in the daytime as well.*
大熊星座在天空轉動並在北半球的夜晚總是可以見到。事實上，日全蝕期間，在白天它也可以看得見。

*Those with chapped hands should try treating them with my special herb lotion.* **Indeed***, the lotion is so safe that it can even be recommended for treating swollen eyes.*
那些雙手皮膚皸裂的人應該嘗試我所特製的草藥護膚劑來進行治療。事實上，該護膚劑非常安全，甚至可以推薦它來治療眼睛發腫。

## to cap it all, to top it all

**3.9** **To cap it all** 和 **to top it all** 偶爾用來引導具有總結性的並且有些令人意外的話。

*We had frosts in April and May.* **To cap it all** *we even had nights of frost in June.*
我們那裏在 4 月和 5 月都有霜。更有甚者，在 6 月夜間也有霜。

*They have little or nothing of value left to sell. And* **to top it all***, some have also been beaten up by the airport security guards.*
他們沒有多少或者根本沒有剩下值錢的東西可以變賣。更有甚者，他們中的一些人曾被機場保安人員毒打。

## also, too, as well

**3.10** 偶然用 **also** 引導句子以增補另一條理由。

*I can't remember ever being bored.* **Also***, Anastasia, I can't remember you ever complaining of boredom before.*
我不記得自己曾感到過厭倦。另外，安娜斯塔西婭，我也不記得你以前抱怨過厭倦。

*Please be as generous as you can with extra donations. It is* **also** *helpful if you subscribe by Banker's Order.*
請你們盡量慷慨作額外捐贈。另外，要是你們委託銀行定期匯款認捐也能起到幫助作用。

而 **too** 、 **as well** 不能用在句首引出句子，事實上，是把它們用在句末。

*Oh I do feel ill. My arm hurts,* **too***.*
啊，我確實感到生病了。此外，我的手臂也痛。

*He was just another child from the shelters. There were other children* **as well***.*
他只是來自收容所的另一個孩子。另外還有別的一些孩子。

*Write down what is said or done and when. Ask a friend or colleague to take a note* **as well***.*
記錄下説過的話或者做過的事以及説話、做事的時間。另外，讓一個朋友或同事也作記錄。

## similarly, likewise

**3.11** 如果要補充與講過的話相似的事實或者細節，可用 **similarly** 或 **likewise**，其含義與 in the same way 差不多。

*The only reason he used a rental car company more than once was that there weren't enough to avoid repetition. **Similarly**, he never used the same passport twice, nor the same credit cards.*
他不止一次地租借一家汽車租賃公司的車只是因為這種租賃公司不多，無法避免重複。同樣地，護照、信用卡他從不用上兩次。

*The job has given me great pleasure and has taken me to places I would not otherwise have visited. **Likewise** I have made marvellous friends and acquaintances.*
這個工作給我帶來許多樂趣，使我到過許多我本來不會去的地方。同樣，我也結交了些很好的朋友和熟人。

*Working women, especially if they have children, may not have time for community activities. **Likewise** working men.*
上班的女性，特別是有孩子的女性，就可能沒時間參加社區活動。上班的男性也是如此。

## equally

**3.12** 要補充說明另一類似的情況同樣是真實的或相關的，可用 **equally**。

*In that situation, he would lie. **Equally** in my situation I would want to believe he was lying.*
他在那樣的情況下會說謊。同樣地，處在我的情況下，我也會相信他在撒謊。

*What will the 19,000 Syrian troops do? And **equally**, what will the 10,000 French troops do?*
那1萬9千敍利亞軍隊會幹甚麼呢？同樣地，那1萬法國軍隊又會幹甚麼呢？

# 舉例
# Giving examples

**3.13** 如果想要舉例說明自己在談論的事，可用 **for example**、 **for instance** 或 **e.g.**。這裏的e.g.是拉丁用語exempli gratia（含義為 for example）的縮寫形式。它原先是書面用語，但現在常常用在口語裏。

*Most of us can take simple precautions to minimize the risk. **For example**, we avoid walking in parks or deserted city areas after dark.*
我們大多數人都可以採取簡便的提防措施把危險降到最低限度。譬如說，天黑以後，我們就不在公園裏、也不在無人的街區步行。

*He seemed unaware of some rather basic details about you. **For example**, what you look like.*
看來他對你的某些基本情況一無所知。例如，對你的模樣。

*The new test has some similarities to a conventional IQ test, but also some significant differences, it does not, **for instance**, have a test of vocabulary.*

新型考試與傳統的智商測試有些相似之處，但也有些很不一樣的地方。譬如説，新型考試不考詞彙。

*Recognizing priorities is another vital ingredient to the effective use of time. **For instance**, at home you may be faced with several jobs which need attention, **e.g.** cooking the evening meal, ironing clothes for tomorrow, housework, washing the car.*

認識到辦事有輕重緩急是有效利用時間的另一要素。譬如説，在家裏你可能有幾樣要料理的事，如做晚飯、燙好明天要穿的衣服、家務、洗車等。

# 重新措辭
# Rewording

**3.14** 有時説話者換一種方式重述説過的話，竭力把自己的意思表達得更清楚。英語有好幾個連接語可以起到這個作用。當然用這樣的連接語時，説話者也許只是對自己説過的話換一個説法，或者糾正自己説過的話，或者説出與原話很不一樣的話。

## in other words, that is to say, that is, i.e., namely

**3.15** 這些是表示一個人對自己口頭或書面剛作出的陳述重新措詞時用的幾個主要連接語。這裏的 **i.e.** 是拉丁語 id est（含義為 that is）的縮寫，像 e.g.一樣，i.e.的使用已經從書面語擴展到口語。而 **namely** 的使用更常見於口語。

*For the past century or so, geologists have worked on the basis that the present is the key to the past. **In other words**, they use processes familiar today to explain how ancient rocks formed.*

在過去的一個世紀左右的時間裏，地質學家一直把以今推古作為自己工作的基礎。換句話説，他們用現代人熟悉的過程去解釋古代岩石的成因。

*The onus is on the shopkeeper to provide goods which live up to the quality of their description; **in other words**, they must not be bad or off.*

店家的職責是供應質量符合產品説明的貨物；換句話説，貨物絕不可低劣也不可低於標準。

*A film is made at twenty-four frames a second. **That is to say** that the camera takes twenty-four photographs each second.*

電影以每秒 24 幀的速度進行製作。就是説，攝影機一秒鐘要拍攝 24 張像。

*A portrait painter or a landscape artist fakes, **that is to say** he rearranges nature to a better angle for his purpose.*

肖像畫畫家或者風景畫畫家都不是刻板地寫實，就是説，為了作畫的目的，將自然重新安排在一個較理想的角度。

*Then I didn't hear a thing from them until yesterday, **that is**, the last day of February.*

然後，直到昨天，也就是 2 月的最後一天，我才聽到有關他們的一點消息。

*Some teachers may be more effective than others because they explain better.*
***That is***, *they employ qualitatively different kinds of verbal interaction with student.*
有些教師比另一些教師也許更有成效，因為他們的解釋更清楚易懂。換句話說，他們採用的是完全不同的與學生進行口頭互相溝通的方法。

*And please don't say anything until we're there;* ***that is***, *if we ever get there.*
在我們到那裏之前，請甚麼都不要講；就是說如果我們到得了那裏再說。

*Anyone could learn this way. Any man,* ***that is***.
任何人都能學會這個招數，說得確切些，任何男人都學得會。

*The advertisement was taken as it was intended,* ***i.e.*** *straight-talking and fair.*
這個廣告的意圖為人們理解。具體地說，說話直截了當，合情合理。

*Many ponies are kept at grass livery,* ***i.e.*** *they live outside all year round.*
許多小種馬都在牧場由人代養，也就是說它們一年到頭都生活在戶外。

*He held the receiver to his ear long enough to establish what he already knew,*
***namely*** *that the line was cut.*
他把受話器貼近耳朵聽了很久來確認自己已經知道的情況，即線路斷了。

*…the shortage of housing in the area to which he decided to move,* ***namely*** *Tower Hamlets.*
……他決定遷入的那個地方，即哈姆萊特，房屋短缺。

# 糾正
# Correcting

## or rather, or better still

**3.16**　如果要對自己說過的話進行更仔細的重新措詞並要表明自己事實上是在糾正自己說過的話，可用 **or rather**、**or better still** 或另一意義相似的短語。

*I explained to him how far things had got,* ***or rather*** *had not got.*
我向他說明形勢發展到何種程度，或者更確切地說向他說明形勢沒有發展到何種程度。

*They were astonished at men marching up with such courage,* ***or rather*** *madness,*
*to certain death.*
他們對人們走向必然死亡所表現的勇氣，或者更確切地說是所表現的瘋狂，表示驚訝。

*Beneath the conscious mind are all the manifold levels of what is called the*
*unconscious,* ***or better***, *the subconscious mind.*
在有意識的思維之下，是多層次的被稱作無意識的，或者不如說是下意識的思維。

*You should think of your customers as partners,* ***or better still***, *family.*
你們應該把自己的顧客視為夥伴，或者更確切地說視為家人。

*Maria was standing in the doorway of the apartment,* ***or more correctly***, *leaning*
*against on side of it.*
瑪麗亞當時站在公寓門口，或者說得準確些，是靠在公寓門口的一邊。

## at least, anyway

**3.17**　**At least**、**anyway** 有時用來修正原話。因此，在有的場合起到糾正原話的作用。

*Mums and Dads do help their children. As far as I can see. I help mine or **at least** I think I used to.*
爸爸、媽媽確實幫助自己的子女。就我所知是如此。我也幫助我的孩子，至少我認為我過去常常是這麼做的。

*I couldn't promise to marry him. Not yet, **anyway**.*
我不能答應嫁給他。不管怎樣說，還不到時候。

# 列舉
# Listing

**3.18**　如果要對自己正在提出的一些要點進行強調，可用表示列舉的連接語。主要的**列舉連接語**在 3.19 － 3.24 節進行論述。

## first, second, third…
## firstly, secondly, thirdly…

**3.19**　很明顯，這是一些與時間有關的詞（但 first 除外，另見 3.20 節），幾乎全都用來列舉論點或理由。

*There were always two certainties about 1993. **First**, that devaluation and interest rate cuts would bring an economic upturn. **Second**, that it would bring the Government some political relief.*
關於 1993 年，有兩件事總是可以肯定的。首先，貶值和利率降低會帶來經濟上的好轉。其次，經濟的好轉又會給政府帶來幾分政治上的輕鬆。

*He was disappointed in the lack of action after his speech. '**First**, I wanted the government to acknowledge what I had said, and they didn't. **Second**, I expected the local authority to try to do something about it.'*
他演講之後當局並沒有所行動，對此他感到失望。"首先，我曾要求政府接受我的意見，但他們沒有。其次，我期望地方當局對此設法採取一些措施。"

*They are angry with me **firstly** because I went to the United States, **secondly** because I didn't come back after the war and **thirdly** because I came back.*
他們生我的氣，第一是因為我去了美國，第二是因為戰後沒有回國，最後是因為我後來又回來了。

*…**Secondly**, a lot of junk mail emanates from abroad. **Thirdly**, we would be unable to impose realistic sanctions on transgressors. **Fourthly**, I feared that the deluge of extra work would swamp our decidedly finite resources.* （即：寫話者是在解釋為甚麼使垃圾郵件不合法是不切實際的。）
……第二，有大量的垃圾郵件從海外湧入。第三，我們將不可能對違規者實施可行的制裁。第四，我擔心處理這些大量湧入郵件的額外工作將會耗盡我們那實在是有限的資源。

## first, then, next

**3.20** 因為用 **first** 、 **then** 、 **next** 及另一些偶爾用的詞（如 second）來表明數個事件發生的先後順序，所以在列舉一系列的指令時，有時也使用它們。

First 把最先發生的事件與後來發生的事件聯繫起來。Then 、 next 像 after 、 afterwards（另見 2.20 節）那樣，可能暗指事件之間僅有短暫的間隔，或者幾乎不存在間隔。

> **First**, the organization sought and found young people with talent. **Then** they assessed them for other capacities.
> 首先，該機構尋求並找出有才幹的年輕人。然後，再對他們的其他能力進行評估。

> **First** he loosened the pin on the grenade. **Next** he wired the body of the grenade to the door handle.
> 他先把手榴彈的保險栓鬆開。然後，用金屬絲把手榴彈繫在門把上。

> **First**, the buyer/seller approaches a stockbroker or commercial bank and instructs them to buy or sell a specific number of shares in a particular company. **Second**, the stockbroker or bank approaches a market maker to buy or sell the shares as instructed.
> 首先，買方/賣方與證券經紀人或商業銀行進行接觸並指定買進或賣出某公司的一定數量的股份。然後，經紀人或商業銀行與證交所接觸，根據買方/賣方要求買進或賣出他們的股份。

> Let your arms slowly drift down to your sides again. **Then**, slowly screw them up into fists. Hold tight like that, and **then** relax again. **Next**, your back.
> 再將雙臂緩緩地旋下到身體兩側。然後，慢慢曲臂握拳。嚴格保持這一姿勢，然後再放鬆。接下去是你的背部。

> Gallagher secured the paddles inside the canoe. **Next** he hung Onyschuk's backpack from the branch of a tree.
> 加拉赫把槳固定在獨木舟裏。然後將奧尼蘇克的野營背包掛在一棵樹的樹枝上。

## first of all, in the first place

**3.21** **First of all** 是起強調作用的短語，其含義是 before anything else（首先、第一），可以指時間，也可以指理由。

> **First of all**, I'm going to explain what I believe is going on.
> 首先，我打算説明我認為是正在發生的情況。

> It was a marvellous place to begin one's management career. **First of all**, there were so many different aspects of transport on which to try my hand.
> 這是開始一個人的經營管理生涯的好地方。首先，那裏有涉及運輸許多方面的工作讓我初試身手。

不過，**in the first place** 引出的幾乎總是理由。

*No, sir, that wouldn't work, and you know it.* **In the first place** *your interests and Miss Radcliffe's may not totally coincide.* **Second***, in the course of my investigation I may uncover information detrimental to her reputation.*

不，先生，那不成，而且你也知道那不成。第一點，你和拉德克里弗小姐的興趣並不完全一樣。第二點，在調查過程中，我也許會發現有損她名聲的情況。

**In the first place** *she didn't want to leave him.* **Secondly***, she had no intention of abandoning any part in the film he was producing.*

首先，她不想離他而去。其次，她沒有打算放棄扮演他在製作的電影中的任何角色。

*A tight authoritarian system isn't going to work* **in the first place** *and,* **in the second place***, if they try to adopt it, there's nobody to support them.*

嚴厲的權力主義制度將行不通，這是一；其二，要是他們採用這種制度，也沒有人支持他們。

## to start with, to begin with, for a start

**3.22**　這幾個短語，同以上幾節論述過的絕大多數短語一樣，也可以表示時間或理由。

*Aim at a short walk* **to start with***, say for 20 minutes on flat ground. Then begin to increase your speed and distance. Eventually you should be able to take a brisk walk at least three times a week.*

首先，爭取進行短距離步行，比方說，在平地上步行 20 分鐘。然後，逐漸增加行走的速度和距離。最後你就能每週至少進行三次輕快的步行。

**To begin with** *I thought of Terry as a really nice, fun person. Then one day he said he was seriously in love with me.*

起初，我認為特里是一個很友善、有趣的人。後來，有一天他說他認真地愛上了我。

*'What should I write down?'* — *'The precise name of the wine,* **for a start***.'*

"我應該把甚麼記下來呢？"——"首先是記下那種酒的準確名稱。"

*You've been listening to too much propaganda, young man. So now you're going to hear the truth.* **To start with***, our civilization is older than yours.*

年輕人，你一直以來聽到的宣傳太多了。因此，現在你要聽聽真實的東西了。首先要說的是，我們的文明比你們的文明更古老。

*This really was a romance, but the obstacles were insurmountable.* **To begin with***, they were both married.*

這確實是個戀愛故事，但有着不可逾越的障礙。首先是他們倆都已結婚。

*After the engine was in full production it was discovered that it was a major disaster.* **For a start***, it weighed not 600 but 656 pounds.*

那種發動機完全投產後，才發現是件重大的失誤。首先發動機的重量不是 600 磅而是 656 磅。

## finally, lastly, last but not least

**3.23**　進行列舉時，不管是按時間先後，還是按邏輯順序，還是別的甚麼，都可用 **finally** 或 **lastly** 來表明列舉的最後一項。（注意，下面第 1 個例證用的 then 完全是一個列舉詞。）

*Then* there are the needs of the individuals. We all like to be praised and to fulfil our ambitions. *Finally*, there are the needs of the team which must work as a cohesive unit.

其次是個人的各種需要。我們都喜歡受人稱讚、實現我們的抱負。最後是緊密團結共事的集體的各種需要。

*Working for too long a time, without adequate rests or change, is likely to cause errors to increase and lead you to become otherwise inefficient generating yet more work. **Lastly**, overwork can be a way of masking other problems.*

工作時間過長，沒有足夠的休息或調節，可能使差錯增多，並且在其他方面效率低下，結果反而增加了工作。最後，過度工作可能將其他問題掩蓋起來。

*Cream the butter and sugar to a smooth consistency and gradually add the egg whites. **Lastly** blend in the flour and vanilla essence.*

將黃油和糖攪拌成均勻的糊狀並緩緩加入蛋清。最後再摻入麵粉和香精。

**Last but not least** 的含義是指，雖然最後提及某事物，但實際上卻仍然重要，並不是事後的補充。

*We thank the Mental Health Foundation, British Heart Foundation, and the Chest, Heart and Stroke Association for supporting our research. **Last but not least**, we thank the patients themselves without whose enthusiasm and personal experience this book would not have been written.*

我們感謝精神康復基金會、英國心臟病基金會和胸、心臟和中風協會對我們研究的支持。最後同樣重要的是，我們要對病人表示感謝，沒有他們的熱心和親身經歷，這本書是無法寫成的。

*Problems can come from photocopier fluids, solvents, aerosols, cleaning agents, air purifiers and, **last but not least**, the fabric of the building and its furnishings.*

問題可能出自複印機液、溶劑、噴霧劑、除垢劑、空氣淨化器，最後也同樣可能出自建築的結構或它的傢具陳設。

## one final point, a final point

**3.24** 表示論據的結束部份或一系列理由的最後一條，也可用**one final point** 或 **a final point** ，當然，這兩個短語並不是連接語。

*Thirdly, I always find that live interviews with interesting people add zest and sparkle to any piece of research. **One final point** is that I actually knew a good deal about some of these subject myself before writing this book.*

第三，我總是發現現場採訪有趣味的人能增加調查的熱情和生氣。最後一點是在寫這本書前，我實際上對有的採訪對象已經很了解。

***A final point** I'd like to make about the grip is the position of my right index finger.*

關於這種握法我想說的最後一點是我右手食指的位置。

# 總結
# **Summing up**

## to conclude

**3.25** 舉出最後一點前，可用 **to conclude** ，但因為説話者經常樂於對自己説過的話進行總結，所以也可以用 to conclude 引出總結。這是比較正式的用語，適用於對一本書或一個講座進行總結。

> ***To conclude**, I would like to make some points about Christian mysticism as a whole.*
> 最後，我想就整個基督教神秘主義談幾點。

> ***To conclude**, seapower was once more a vital component of the British and American conduct of the war.*
> 總之，海軍實力又一次成為英美戰爭行動的關鍵力量。

## all in all, to sum up, in conclusion, altogether

**3.26** 這些是用作總結的詞和短語，可表示説話者要對自己剛説過的話進行總結或者提出自己的論據或陳述可證明的結論。

> *Ten years now she'd been alone, but she'd spent them usefully. She enjoyed her life and had some good friends in the village. **All in all**, she'd been very lucky.*
> 十年來她一直獨居，但日子卻過得充實。在那個村子裏她生活愉快，交了些好朋友。總的來説，她一直都很幸運。

> *…In difficult and chronic cases changes were brought about only through this type of treatment. **To sum up**, many people were helped through this treatment and most of them were people with chronic conditions.*
> ……疑難病症和慢性病症只有通過這種治療才能好轉。概括地説，許多人通過這種治療得到了幫助而且其中的絕大多數都是慢性病患者。

> *…Pedometers are not too expensive and are available from most sports shops. **In conclusion**, walking is a cheap, safe, enjoyable and readily available form of exercise.*
> ……計步器價格不是很昂貴，而且在大多數體育用品商店都有售。最後，步行運動花錢少、安全、使人愉快而且是不受任何條件限制的體育鍛煉形式。

> *I like Peter very much. He's amusing, clever, and enlightened. **Altogether** a charming fellow.*
> 我很喜歡彼得。他有趣、聰明、開明。總之，是一個討人喜歡的人。

## in short

**3.27** 需要進行簡短的總結時，可用 **in short** 。

*I want to believe you are wholly innocent of those boys' deaths. I want to believe you never played about with drugs or silly games. **In short**, I want to believe you are a victim.*

我願意相信你對那些男孩的死是完全無辜的。我願意相信你與毒品和荒唐事毫無關係。一句話，我願意相信你是位受害者。

*By the time of President Tito's death, **in short**, federal institutions were fatally weak.*

一句話，在鐵托去世時，聯邦機構已經是致命地軟弱無力。

*We had a record player and a few records, and we used to make a lot of noise going out into the hall to fetch water for tea. **In short**, girls having fun.*

我們曾有一台唱機、幾張唱片，而且我們到大廳取水泡茶時常常發出陣陣的喧譁聲。一句話，我們是一羣玩得很開心的姑娘。

# 説明話題
# Stating your topic

## as for

**3.28**　有時説話者可能需要對談論的話題稍作改變，他們借助另一個不同但又與原話題相關的話題來實現這樣的轉移。辦法之一是用 **as for** 加名詞詞組或-ing形式構成的介詞短語。

*His other major victories came in 1988 and 1989. **As for** the future, Fignon would say little.*

他另外取得的重大勝利是在 1988 年和 1989 年。至於未來會怎樣，費格農不願多説。

*Dr Maturin could speak fluently in Latin and Greek, and **as for** modern languages, to Jack's certain knowledge he spoke half a dozen.*

馬圖林博士能流利地用拉丁語和希臘語説話。至於現代語言，據傑克的可靠消息，他會講六種。

*She was finished with 'good works'. **As for** going back to the United States, that was impossible.*

她以"優秀作品"結束學業。至於回到美國去，那是不可能的事。

## as regards, as to

**3.29**　**As regards**、**as to** 與 as for 相似，用來對話題稍作改變，或者談論同一話題的另一方面。

*There was a lab at the college and I did a little experimental work in botany there. **As regards** research, there were just no grants at all.*

學院裏有一個實驗室，我在那個實驗室做了些植物實驗。至於研究，壓根兒就沒有經費。

*This makes it difficult to ascertain the exact time of death. However, it is thought that a more detailed post mortem will give the answer. **As to** motive, police are still baffled.*

這使得確定死亡的準確時間非常困難。不過，據信一次更詳細的屍體剖檢將提供答案。至於動機，警方仍感迷惑不解。

## with reference to

**3.30    With reference to** 是交代話題時使用的正式用語。在正式的信函時，有時用於信的開頭，本節選用的例證是一封給一家科學雜志社的信。雖然 with reference to 的位置可以在話篇開頭（這不同於 as for、as to），它所指的當然是收信人或讀者已經知道的某封信或某篇文章。

***With reference to*** *J.C.A.Craik's third rainbow, I have been intrigued by a related phenomenon, that of seeing a rainbow apparently reflected in water surface.*

關於 J·C·A·克雷克描述的第三類彩虹，我已經對一個相關的現象產生了興趣，即看見一道被清楚地映在水面上的彩虹。

# 4 關係從句、that-從句、wh-詞從句及其他
## Relative clauses, 'that'-clauses, 'wh'-clauses, and others

**4.1** 如1.22節所述,從屬分句不僅包括副詞從句而且還包括關係從句、that-從句及wh-詞從句。有時又把that-從句和wh-詞從句統稱為名詞從句。此外,還有與各種限定從屬分句功能相似的非限定結構和無動詞結構。

## 關係從句
## Relative clauses

**4.2** 人們常常用形容詞補充關於某人或某物的信息。但是,有時只用形容詞還嫌不夠,那就要用**關係從句**(或稱形容詞從句)。關係從句直接位於它所修飾的名詞(或代詞)之後。

關係從句句首,一般以關係代詞 who、whom、whose、which 或 that 開頭。

關係從句有兩大類:**限制性和非限制性關係從句**。

## 限制性關係從句
## Defining relative clauses

**4.3** 限制性關係從句提供限定或確定說話者談論的人或物所不可缺的信息。
關係代詞在關係從句裏作主語時,用 who 或 that 代表人。

*I'm looking for someone **who might be able to help me**.*
我在找一個可以幫我忙的人。

*Women **who have this condition** are often overweight.*
處於這種情況的女性往往體重偏重。

*Do we want the people **that use the beaches** to pay for it?*
我們希望使用沙灘的人付費嗎?

關係代詞作從句主語時,用 which 或 that 代表物。

*The office **which had been cleared for them** was austere but functional.*
為他們清理過的辦公室雖然簡樸但卻實用。

*It can be seen now as an unnecessary and grave mistake **which led to a political disaster**.*
現在可以把它看成是引起政治災難的一個多此一舉而又嚴重的錯誤。

*Jealousy is an energy **that takes us over**.*
妒忌心成了一種左右我們的力量。

*Think of a word **that sums up how you feel**.*
想出一個概括你的感受的詞。

**4.4** 關係代詞是從句賓語時，用 whom、who 或 that 代表人。嚴格地説，用 who 作賓語是不正確的，但其使用頻率卻在不斷增加，而且用 whom 給人拘泥之感。

*And then there was Clara, that woman **whom Clarence had married**.*
此外還有克拉拉，那位與克拉倫斯結婚的那位女士。

*Also with them was a woman friend **who I last saw thirty years ago**.*
同他們在一起的還有一位我 30 年前見到過的女性朋友。

*Many of the youngsters **who we have helped** are now married.*
我們幫助過的年輕人很多現在已結婚。

*After all that killing, it's enough to be alive and well with someone **that you love and trust**.*
在那場屠殺之後，能和自己所愛所信的人同活在世、身體健康已經心滿意足了。

當該賓語指物時，用 which 或 that。

*Grace sat down in the leather chair **which her brother had originally offered her**.*
格瑞絲坐在她兄弟一開頭就要她坐的皮椅上。

*The kind of music **that David Bowie and Brian Eno were doing** was very much in the direction of experimental music.*
大衛‧布益和布萊‧伊諾在創作的那種音樂非常接近於實驗音樂。

此外，作賓語的關係代詞常常省略。

*It is a portrait of a person **we don't know**.*
這是一幅我們不認識的人的肖像畫。

*That bestseller book **I wrote** made me a lot of money.*
我寫的那本暢銷書使我掙了一大筆錢。

*He never listened to a thing **I said**.*
他從來不聽我的話。

**4.5** 關係代詞作介詞賓語時，如果介詞位於從句末尾，可用 that 代表人和物。

*A lot of people must have looked carefully at the person **that** they were living **with**.*
許多人一定仔細觀察過與他們生活在一起的那個人。

*We're very much interested in the background of the people **that** we're talking **to**.*
我們對我們正與之交談的那些人的經歷很感興趣。

*Take the statistics of science **that** we looked **at** earlier.*
把我們早些時候查閱過的科學統計數據帶走。

此外，這種情況下使用的 that 也可以省略。

*No matter how hard they work, the person **(that**被省略**)** they are responsible **for** is working twice as hard.*
無論他們花多大力氣，他們負責照管的那個人都要付出雙倍的力氣來工作。

*There was no one else **(that** 被省略**)** he could talk **to**.*
此外再沒有一個他可以交談的人。

*The only thing **(that** 被省略**)** I'm concerned **about** is reusable products.*
我唯一關心的東西就是可回收再利用的產品。

但是，介詞位於關係代詞之前時，必須用 whom 代表人，用 which 代表物。

*The only people **with whom** he could discuss the plan were those who knew of it already.*
可以同他一起討論計劃的最合適人選是那些對計劃已經了解的人。

*She would be safe in Jehol now, with her dying Emperor and the little son **through whom** she hoped to rule China.*
她在熱河就安全了，那裏有她那行將去世的皇帝陛下，和可以利用來實現她統治中國願望的年幼的皇兒。

*The book stands as a monumental testimony to the historical circumstances **in which** it was written.*
該書是寫作此書時所處的歷史環境的不朽見證。

*This is something **for which** you must constantly be on the lookout.*
這是你必須一直密切注意的事。

# 非限制性關係從句
# Non-defining relative clauses

**4.6** 非限制性關係從句提供關於某人或某物的附加信息，但是何人或何物在原句已經交待清楚。這種從句在書面語裏比在口語裏更為常見，而且用逗號把從句與句子的其餘部份分開。

**4.7** 用 who（主語）、whom（賓語）代表人，which 代表物。非限制性關係從句是比限制性關係從句正式的結構，所以作賓語時，寧可用 whom 而不用 who。

*My brother, **who** is a gourmet, took him on tours of France.*
我的兄弟，一名美食家，帶他去法國周遊。

*Unfortunately Frank Wolf, **who** would never have agreed, was away at the time.*
真可惜，弗蘭克·烏爾夫當時不在，此人是絕對不會同意的。

*He spent much of the evening with Walter Cronkite, **whom** he had hardly seen in the thirty years since they had worked together at CBS.*

他與沃爾塔‧克讓凱特一起度過了大半個晚上。自從不在美國哥倫比亞廣播公司共事以來，他倆已經有 30 年幾乎沒有見過面了。

*Paul's father, with **whom** he had had a close relationship, died suddenly.*

與他關係親密的保爾的父親突然死了。

*Flex your knees so that your feet, **which** should be together, are flat on the floor.*

彎曲你們的雙膝，但雙腳並攏，平展地站在地上。

*Well I remember, for example, our meetings in London in 1954, **which** you certainly remember.*

我記得很牢，比如説，我們 1954 年在倫敦一次次的會面，這些你肯定記得。

*Today the menu consisted of smoked salmon mousse, with **which** they were drinking a delightful white wine.*

今天的菜餚中有燻鮭魚奶油凍，品嚐着這道菜，他們開心地喝着白葡萄酒。

## whose

**4.8** **Whose** 的含義是 of whom 或 of which，用來敍述所有關係或其他某種密切的關係。可用在限制性、非限制性關係從句裏，既指代人又指代物。

*He was an officer **whose** career meant everything to him.*

他是一名軍旅生涯對他來説就是一切的軍官。

*He married a woman **whose** name I forget.*

他娶了一個我忘了其名字的女性為妻。

*There is a wonderful story about Lord Uxbridge, **whose** leg was shot off at the Battle of Waterloo.*

有一個描寫阿克斯布里奇勳爵的精彩故事。這位勳爵的一隻腿在滑鐵盧之戰被擊中而失去。

*Even a state like Austria-Hungary, **whose** very existence depended on balance and law, was affected by the dominance of military strategic thinking.*

甚至像奧匈帝國這樣的國家，它的存在取決於力量的均衡和法律，也受到了軍事戰略思想佔支配地位的影響。

*For repairing a modern, hardback book **whose** cover has fallen off, they charge about £15.*

修復一本封面已脱落的現代版本精裝書，他們收取 15 英鎊左右的費用。

*The butcher shot pigeons and sold them to the people on **whose** land he had shot them.*

那個殘殺者射殺鴿子並將鴿子賣給射殺地的人。

**4.9** 書面語可用 some、each 或 many 等代詞加 of whom、of which 或 of whose 引導關係從句。

*The room was packed with people, **many of whom** Amy had never seen before.*

屋子裏擠滿了人，其中的多數人艾米以前從未見過。

*He devotes most of his words to two topics: money and health, **each of which** he seemed to lack in equal measure.*
他用大部份篇幅論述兩個論題,即金錢和健康,而這兩樣他都同樣缺乏。

*He remains a great admirer of Warhol, **several of whose pictures** he now owns.*
他仍然非常愛慕沃霍,還藏有幾張沃霍的照片。

同樣也可用數詞以及比較級、最高級短語加 of whom、of which、of whose 來引導關係從句。

*They heard voices ahead, two voices, **one of which** suddenly rose above the other in anger.*
他們聽到前面傳來聲音,是兩個聲音,其中的一個突然因氣憤提高嗓門壓住了另一個。

*There are 50 families here. Between them they only have 11 family names, **five of which** go back to the names of the original settlers.*
這裏有 50 家人。他們中只有 11 個姓,其中 5 個可追溯到最早的移民的姓。

*They have two sizes of mixing bowl, **the larger of which** inverts over the scales for easy storage.*
他們有兩個大小不同的和麵缸,大的那個為了便於存放倒放在廚房磅秤上。

*She gave birth to eight children, **the youngest of whom** died in 1954.*
她生過 8 個孩子,最小的一個死於 1954 年。

此外,of 可以置於關係從句句首,從而要略微改動從句詞序。

*Her haunting landscapes, **of which many** were painted in the Dordogne, seem to express a profound sense of fear and foreboding.*
她的狩獵風景畫,其中多數創作於法國多冬尼河畔,似乎表現出一種深沈的懼怕和不祥的預感。

*He had fifteen children **of whom three** went into the Army.*
他那 15 個孩子中有 3 個去當了兵。

☞ 有關縮略關係從句,見 4.27 節。

## when, where, why

**4.10  When、where** 有時起關係副詞的作用,既引導限制性關係從句又引導非限制性關係從句。另見 2.6 節。

*Magnus is there waiting for the day **when** we shall be together.*
馬格納斯在那裏期待着我們團聚的日子。

*He showed me maps of his country and the place **where** his family had a country house.*
他給我看他國家的地圖和他家的鄉間別墅所在地的地圖。

*We live in the mountains, **where** life is hard.*
我們住在山裏,那裏的生活艱難。

有時 **why** 作為關係副詞在 reason 一詞後引導關係從句。在 reason 後用 that (或者省略 that）也可以引導這樣的關係從句。

*There must be **some reason why** he looked pleased.*
他看上去那樣開心肯定有某種理由。

***The reason that** they liked the restaurant was its anonymity.*
他們喜歡那家餐館的理由是它的默默無聞。

*That is **the reason** (**that** 被省略) I asked you.*
那是我詢問你的理由。

## whereby

**4.11** **Whereby** 是語體正式的連接詞，其含義大體上等於 by which 或 in which way，用來説明一種制度、過程或計劃是如何發生的。

*A routine was established **whereby** the men worked in the mornings and played football in the afternoons.*
人們確定了男人們上午幹活、下午踢球的慣例。

*Poirot and Hastings had devised a plan **whereby** one or the other would leave the hotel first; then, after an interval, the other would follow.*
卜依拉特和哈斯廷斯已經制訂了一項計劃：兩個人中的一人先離開飯店，等過了一定時間後另外一個再跟着出去。

*This is the system **whereby** the European Union automatically gets the cash from some British taxes.*
這是歐盟借以從英國部份税款中自動獲取現金的體制。

# 其他關係從句
# Other relative clauses

**4.12** 可以用關係從句説明一事發生在另一事之後。

*There was laughter again, **which** the corporal silenced.*
又傳來了笑聲，後來給下士制止了。

*The left hand still held a pair of pliers, **which** Kelly took and used to tighten the wire yet more.*
那只左手還拿着鉗子，後來凱里把它接了過來用它把金屬絲收得更緊。

*The new aircraft design was submitted to the Ministry, **who** promptly rejected it on the grounds that there was no immediate requirement for it.*
新型的飛機設計方案呈送到了部裏，不過部長立即予以拒絕，理由是目前還不馬上需要這樣的方案。

**4.13** 可以用 which 引導的從句對先行的分句進行評論。

***He was probably talking to himself**, **which** he often did now.*
他也許在自言自語，他現在常常如此。

*Her only commitment tomorrow is a rehearsal at the Conservatoire during the afternoon*. *Which* *means the morning is the time to make contact.*
她明天的唯一安排是下午在藝院排練。這就是説明天上午是同她聯繫的時機。

*She looked like a ghost*, by *which* I mean that she seemed not entirely alive.
她看起來像個鬼，我這樣説的意思是她好像完全沒有活力。

# 名詞從句
# Noun clauses

**4.14**　Wh-詞和that不僅用來引導關係從句，也用來引導功能很像名詞或名詞詞組的從句，譬如説，作動詞的主語、賓語或補足語。這時，常常把這兩種從句稱作**名詞從句**（或**名詞性從句**）。下列的幾個例證説明這兩種從句與名詞詞組的關係。

*We didn't like **the hotel**.* （the hotel 是一般的名詞詞組）
我們不喜歡那個飯店。

*We didn't like **the hotel we stayed in**.* （…the hotel we stayed in 是帶關係從句的名詞詞組）
我們不喜歡我們住的那個飯店。

*We didn't like **where we stayed**.* （wh-詞從句 …where we stayed 是名詞從句）
我們不喜歡我們住的地方。

在以下幾節裏，上述的説明同樣適用於 that-從句和 wh-詞從句，我們為了敍述方便起見，在所有合適的場合，將用**名詞從句**這一術語包括以上兩類從句。

術語 wh- 詞從句也包括 how 引導的從句。

**4.15**　名詞從句最常見的用法之一是在轉述結構裏作賓語，用在表示説法和想法的動詞之後。

*He explained **that** he couldn't be more specific.*
他解釋説他不可能説得更具體。

*She said **that** she'd had a card from him.*
她説她已經收到他寄來的明信片。

*He explained **how** the climate was just right for growing sugar.*
他説明那種氣候如何宜於種植糖料作物。

在這種結構裏，從句的 that 常常被省略。

*She said (**that** 被省略) she knew nothing of the plans.*
她説她對那些計劃一無所知。

*When he took the job people agreed (**that** 被省略) he was a good choice.*
當他接受那份工作時，大家都同意他是最佳人選。

被轉述問句用 wh-詞從句或 if-從句。

*Finally she asked **what** I'd brought with me.*
最後她問我身邊帶着甚麼。

*I wonder **who** he's with.*
我不知道他同誰在一起。

*A stewardess enquired **whether** he really was Mr H. Hughes.*
一個空姐詢問他是否真的是 H ‧ 休斯先生。‧

*I asked **if** we could stay for a while.*
我詢問了我們是否可以呆一會兒。

(有關轉述結構的詳盡論述，見《Collins Cobuild 英語語法系列：5. 轉述法》)。

**4.16** **名詞性關係從句**有時不指問句而是指另一特殊類型的 wh-詞從句。這種從句不同於其他名詞性從句(含抽象意義)，可以指具體的人或物。名詞性關係從句的功能像名詞或名詞詞組，但又有點像關係從句。它的 wh-詞有雙重功能，其含義是 that which 、 the thing(s) which 或 the person(s) who 。

***What** you need is a change of scene.*
你需要的是改變場景。

*The driver will take you to your address to let you get your passport and to pack **what** you need.*
駕駛員將送你到你的住處去取護照和收拾你需要的行李。

*That's **who** I'm paying the rent to .*
那位就是我向其交付租金的人。

***Whatever** I did there was motivated by fear.*
我在那裏所做的一切都是恐懼所致。

***Whoever** did this must be caught.*
任何一個幹出這種事的人都必須抓起來。

*You know **where** I'll be.* (…where… 等於…the place where…)
你知道我將會在甚麼地方。

然而，純粹的名詞(或名詞性)從句和名詞性關係從句之間的界限並不總是一清二楚。它們在句子裏的功能相同。因此，4.17－4.23節用的名詞從句和 wh-詞從句這兩個術語適用於名詞(性)從句和名詞性關係從句。

**4.17** 除了在轉述結構裏作賓語外，名詞從句還可以作其他動詞(非轉述動詞)的賓語。從句的 that 有時省略。 Wh- 詞從句還可以是非限定小句。

*He saw **that a police car was parked outside**.*
他看見有一輛警車停在外面。

*He doesn't mind **who uses it**.*
他不在乎誰用那件東西。

*Anxiously, Gill looked up at the clouds to see **which way the wind was blowing**.*
吉爾焦慮不安，遙望天空的雲層以便確定風向。

*I suggest you call **whichever girlfriend you had your eye on for the weekend** and warn her you'll be working.*
我建議你打電話給你已經看中的隨便哪個共度週末的女友，提醒她你在週末要上班。

*That shows **how desperate she is**.*
這表明她是多麼絕望。

*Over the years I've learnt to remember **how to survive**, and **how to forget pain**.*
數年來我已經學會了記住怎樣掙扎求生和怎樣忘卻痛苦。

**4.18** 名詞從句也可以作補語，譬如說作動詞 be 的補語。

*The fact is **that I'm going to get married**.*
事實上我打算結婚。

*The fact is **we couldn't think of anything else to do**.*
事實是我們想不出另外還有甚麼事可做。

*My problem, put baldly, is **that I've doubts about Carmela's suicide**.*
我的問題，直言不諱地說，是我對卡梅拉的自殺有懷疑。

*I hope that wasn't **why he was so angry**.*
我希望那不是他如此生氣的原因。

*Yes, Andy Holden was **who I meant**.*
是的，安第‧霍頓就是我所指的那個人。

**4.19** 名詞從句也可以作句子主語。這時，整個句子通常用形式的非人稱代詞 it 引出，名詞從句置於句後。在有非人稱代詞 it 的句子中，其 that-從句的 that 可以省略。

***It** emerged **that they shared a mutual passion for sailing**.*
情況清楚了，是他們都非常喜歡帆船運動。

***It** was odd **(that 被省略) he had no means of identification at all**.*
奇怪的是他根本沒有證明身份的東西。

***It** was a mystery to me **why he never appeared to be especially popular with his colleagues**.*
為甚麼他從未格外受到同事們的歡迎對我來說是一個謎。

此外，名詞從句可以出現在句首（不用非人稱代詞 it）。比較常見的是 wh-詞從句，而 that-從句卻相對地罕見。位置在句首的 that-從句的 that 不能省略。

***What he did at home** was perhaps even more remarkable.*
他在主場的表現也許更加引人注目。

***That he was rescued at all** was a matter of coincidences.*
他的獲救實屬巧合。

**4.20** Wh-詞從句有時用在介詞之後。

*She crossed **to where he stood**.*
她走到對面他站的地方。

*Their father often reminisced **about when he had worked as a New York City police detective**.*
他們的父親常常回憶他在紐約市當警察偵探的往事。

*Afterwards you can talk **to whoever you like**.*
然後，你就可以同你樂意交談的人説話。

*It was no longer a case **of who would win**, but when.* （…but when.是…but of when. 的省略）
那已經不再是誰取勝的問題，而是何時取勝的問題。

*There was no record **of whom she had phoned**.*
沒有她給誰打過電話的記錄。

**4.21** That-從句、wh-詞從句可用在某些形容詞之後。

*Fowler was **angry that** the contract had not been placed with his firm.*
福勒對還沒有與他的公司訂立合同感到生氣。

*I really am **glad (that** 被省略**)** I decided to come.*
我對自己決定來實在感到高興。

*I can't even be **sure how** old those bones are.*
我甚至無法確定這些骨骼的年代。

**4.22** 名詞從句，尤其是 that-從句也能用來作名詞詞組的**同位語**，對名詞詞組進行解釋説明。被解釋説明的名詞常常是與轉述和想法有關的名詞（如 fact、belief）或其他一些名詞（如 danger、possibility）。

***The fact that many of us eat too much junk food** can hardly have escaped anyone's notice.*
我們中的許多人過食不利於健康的小吃，這個事實是不大可能無人注意到的。

*He had condoned it at first in **the belief that he was genuinely helping further the cause of science**.*
基於他是在真誠地促進科學事業的信念，他最初已經對此表示寬容。

*The producer may then use the logo in the wine label as **evidence that the wine is 'verified' as organic**.*
屆時，廠家可以利用果酒標簽上的那個標識，作為這種果酒已經"證實"是有機物的證據。

*There was **a danger that many of the country's important foreign workers would decide to leave**.*
存在着一種危險：那個國家中很多重要的外籍工作人員將決定離去。

*They called their child Indiana, prompting **the question, what's wrong with a good old English name**?*
他們管自己的孩子叫印第安納，結果引發了這樣的問題：用地道的歷史悠久的英語名字有甚麼不對呢？

**4.23** ▶注意◀ That-名詞從句有時看上去像關係從句，但它們的功能是不同的。

*He had heard **rumours that** old Fritz's heart wasn't as good as it used to be.*
( 名詞與 that- 從句是名詞與同位語的關係)

他已經聽到了謠傳，說老弗瑞茲的心臟不如以前。

*I am aware of **the rumours that** have recently been circulating about me.* (名詞與 that-從句是先行詞與定語從句的關係)

我已經了解到了最近一直在擴散的關於我的謠言。

# 非限定小句和無動詞小句
# Non-finite and verbless clauses

## 有連接詞小句
## With conjunctions

**4.24**　與非限定小句、無動詞小句一起用的、引導狀語從句的連接詞已經在第 2 章進行過論述。這種小句被看作省略了主語和動詞 be 的縮略從句。

*Each firm, **when deciding** upon its pricing and other market strategies, must explicitly take into account the likely reactions of its competitors.* (...when deciding... 等於 ...when it is deciding...)

每家公司，在確定自己的價格和市場策略時，必須明確地將競爭對手可能作出的反應考慮進去。

*My patients, **if given** the opportunity, would freely converse about their problems **whilst sitting** in my waiting room.* (...if given... 等於 ...if they were given... ; ...whilst sitting... 等於 ...whilst they were sitting...)

如果給他們機會，我的病人坐在我的候診室時，會毫無保留地訴說自己的問題。

*She wanted to sleep, **if possible**.* (...if possible. 等於 ...if that was possible.)

如果可能的話，她想睡覺。

*His working life, **although not unstructured**, allowed him a kind of freedom.* (...although not unstructured... 等於 ...although it was not unstructured...)

他的工作生涯，雖經過仔細安排計劃，仍然給他某種自由。

**4.25**　非限定小句裏的 -ing 分詞有時應該作為一般時態而不作為進行時態理解。

*He described that prospect as 'unlikely', **although accepting** that any signs of recovery were weak.* (...although accepting... 等於 ...although he accepted...)

雖然承認復甦跡象渺茫，他還是把復甦的前景說成 "不可能"。

*Peterson, **after having looked** the plan over, said, 'Fine, why don't we let Kim try it in his region?'* (...after having looked... 等於 ...after he had looked...)

彼得森對整個計劃很快地審查後，說："好的，我們幹嗎不讓基姆在他的地方試試這個計劃呢？"

***Before leaving**, he asked Sam for an account of his movements during the previous afternoon.* (Before leaving... 等於 Before he left...)

離開前，他要求山姆對前一天下午的活動進行滙報。

## 無連接詞小句
## Without conjunctions

**4.26** 有的非限定小句和無動詞小句不帶連接詞。鑑於這種小句不帶連接詞，所以，嚴格地說，不宜在本書詳細討論。不過有幾點還是值得注意。

**4.27** 名詞或名詞詞組之後的非限定小句可以具備類似關係從句的功能。

*A person **standing very close to the fire** receives more heat than someone **standing further away**.* （兩處的粗體部份等於 ...who is standing...）
站在靠近爐火的人比站在離爐火更遠的人接受到更多的熱。

*He took out a folder **containing my proposal** and slammed it on his desk.*
（...containing my proposal... 等於 ...which contained my proposal...）
他取出一個放着我建議書的文件夾並往他的桌子上一摔。

*We wish you every success in maintaining the high standard of journalism **set by your magazine**.* （...set by your magazine. 等於 ...which has been set by your magazine.）
我們祝願你們在堅持貴雜志社提出的新聞工作高標準方面取得完全的成功。

這種小句有時被稱作**縮略關係從句**。

**4.28** 某些非限定小句和無動詞小句有時含有時間、理由或條件意義。然而，由於沒有用連接詞，到底是哪一種並不清楚。事實上，有時候也不清楚表示的是上述三種意義中的一種還是應該將其解釋成縮略關係從句。

***Looking out of the window**, Holly said, 'You're usually in the shower by this time.'* （Looking out of the window... 等於 While she was looking out of the window...）
往窗外看時，何莉說："你在這種時候，總是給陣雨淋着。"

*Cassandra sat down, **not wanting to get in his way**.* （...not wanting to get in his way. 等於 ...because she did not want to get in his way.）
卡珊扎坐了下來，不想妨礙他的出入。

***Not having encountered an atlas before**, she could not make head or tail of maps.* （Not having encountered an atlas before... 等於 Because she had not encountered an atlas before...）
因為過去從來都沒有接觸過地圖冊，她對那些地圖摸不着頭腦。

***Overcome with emotion**, Irena burst into Polish.* （Overcome with emotion... 等於 Because she was overcome with emotion...）
由於過分激動，愛瑞娜突然說起波蘭語來。

***Unhappy**, **not wanting to see more**, she went back to Seymour House.* （Unhappy, not wanting to see more... 等於 Because she was unhappy and didn't want to see more...）
因為不高興、不想再看下去，她回到了希姆爾大廈。

*It had been easy for me to avoid the issue, but now, **faced with the man himself**, it was impossible to dissemble.* （...faced with the man himself... 等於 ...when I because I was faced with the man himself...）
以前我很容易避開這個問題，但此時當着他本人的面我就不能掩飾了。

*Given time*, *these questions will answer themselves.* （*Given time...* 等於 *Provided that we/you/they are given enough time...*）
只要有時間，這些問題就會自行解決。

*The will of the people*, ***inspired by God's holy truth***, *must prevail.*（*...inspired by God's holy truth...* 等於 *...because/when/if it* 或 *which is inspired by God's holy truth...*）
人民的意志，一旦為上帝神聖的真理喚起，一定能獲勝。

**4.29** 在某些語言環境中，-ing 小句可以表示結果，即表示隨接發生的事。

*Both machines crashed near Hatfield*, ***killing their crews***.
兩架飛機在哈特菲爾德相撞，結果機組人員全部喪生。

*These developments will lead to local monopolies*, ***leaving customers with less real choice***.
這些事態將產生地方壟斷，結果使消費者沒有真正選擇的餘地。

# To- 動詞不定式小句
# 'To'-infinitive clauses

**4.30** To-動詞不定式小句有多種功能。常常被用來表示目的（見2.64節）。有的用來作連接語，如 to start with 、 to sum up （見 3.22 和 3.26 節）。

To- 動詞不定式小句可以有自身的主語，其位置在小句開頭，由介詞 for 引出。

***For me to question you about your homeland*** *goes contrary to all the laws of honour.*
我就你們國家的情況盤問你們與一切道義準則背道而馳。

***For the attack to succeed***, *surprise was essential.*
要使進攻取得成功，突然襲擊是至關重要的。

To- 動詞不定式小句有時表示結果，即某種行為之後出現的情況。

*I arrived* ***to find*** *the hotel officially closed.*
我到達之後才發現飯店已經被正式關閉。

*He took his washing machine in for repair, only* ***to be told*** *it needed replacing.*
他把自己的洗衣機送去修理，結果被告知需要更換新的。

# 帶介詞的小句
# Clauses beginning with prepositions

**4.31** 有的非限定小句和無動詞小句由介詞引導。這樣的小句，以及引導小句的各種介詞在 4.32 – 4.37 節論述。

## by, in, on

**4.32** 這三個介詞之後可用 -ing 小句。

**By** 表示方法或方式。

> *Appointments may be made **by calling** 414 6203 on weekdays.*
> 在工作日，可撥打電話 414 6203 進行預約。

> ***By learning** how the mind works, scientists hope to construct better computers and software.*
> 通過對人腦思維的了解，科學家期望製造更好的計算機和軟件。

> ***By staying** in this room you have become a carrier of the illness.*
> 你在這個房間呆過，就成了這種疾病的病原攜帶者。

**In** 可以表示時間和原因雙重意義。

> *I believe I am right **in saying** that I have rather a large influence over a good many people my own age.* （…in saying… 等於 …when I say…）
> 我認為我說我對許多同齡人有相當大的影響時，我的判斷是正確的。

> *Even the foul weather and my illness couldn't totally account for my disappointment **in returning** to a holiday destination I remembered fondly.* （…in returning… 等於…when I returned…）
> 甚至惡劣的天氣和我的疾病也無法完全解釋自己回到給我留下良好印象的度假地時感到的失望。

> *All agree however that the company has been irresponsible **in refusing** to discuss the issue.* （…in refusing… 等於…because they are refusing…）
> 然而大家都一致認為，拒絕討論那個問題，公司是不負責任的。

**On** 加 -ing 小句的意義是 when 。

> *She had a mild attack of hysteria **on reaching** Jamaica, when she realized her mother had actually died.* （…on reaching… 等於…when she reached…）
> 一到牙買加，當她了解到自己母親確已去世時，她表現出輕度的歇斯底里。

> *Their faces lit up **on hearing** their own language.*
> 一聽到有人用他們自己的語言講話，他們臉上露出欣喜的神色。

> *He arrived, but, **on hearing** what the crime was, he turned round instantly and left.*
> 他來了，但當聽到這項犯罪是怎麼回事時，他立即掉頭就離開了。

## despite, in spite of

**4.33** **Despite** 、 **in spite of** 表示讓步，含義大致等於從屬連詞 although 。

> *Being the first child meant that she was given the conventional male education **despite** being a girl.*
> 儘管她是女孩，作為家庭的第一個孩子意味着給她的教育卻是對男孩的傳統教育。

*None of our players is taking anything for granted, **despite** starting hot favourites.*
儘管比賽一開始我們的選手就成了最有希望的獲勝者，但他們沒有一個把取勝看作理所當然的事。

*Corbett helped himself liberally, **despite** having already eaten.*
柯貝特自己動手大吃大喝起來，儘管自己早已吃過東西。

***In spite of** getting better for a while, when April came along, her appetite disappeared and by the end of April she was dead.*
雖然身體好了些時候，但隨着四月的到來，她失去了胃口，到了四月底就逝世了。

*The Duchess is very active **in spite of** not having been in particularly good health of late.*
儘管近來身體不是特別健康，公爵夫人卻很活躍。

☞ 另見 2.61 節。

## without, with

**4.34** **Without** 加 -ing 小句表示不屬實的事或沒有發生的事。

***Without looking up** at me, he said, 'Why did your friend go to the museum?'*
沒有抬頭看我一眼，他卻說：" 你的朋友為甚麼去博物館？ "

*I would never go to bed **without locking** my door.*（即：*I always lock the door before I go to bed.* 我睡覺前總是鎖上房門。）
我從來不會不鎖房門就去睡覺。

*Julius, I can't keep using your phone **without paying** for it.*
朱麗葉斯，不付電話費我就不能老是用你的電話。

***Without wishing** to be unkind, she's not the most interesting company.*（即：*I don't wish to be unkind, but I think she is not...* 我不想刻薄，但我認為她不是……）
我不想刻薄，但我認為她不是最有趣的夥伴。

**4.35** **With** 、 **without** 常常引出有自身主語的非限定小句和無動詞小句。這樣的小句說明主句裏的事件發生 (或不發生) 時所處的情況。

*Expenses should be cut by at least 10 per cent, **with most savings coming from reduced fees to brokers**.*
有了主要來自降低經紀人手續費省出的錢，開支應該至少降低百分之十。

***With the door shut and the air-conditioning on**, it was almost as though we were locked into some mysterious space capsule.*
在門被關上、空調開着的情況下，我們彷彿被關進了神秘的太空艙一般。

***With Habib away**, Hassan's attitude seemed to have changed.*
哈比卜不在，哈桑的態度好像有了變化。

*One man was taken away **with blood pouring down his face**.*
一個男子給帶走了，鮮血從他臉上直往下流。

*She is slumped in her chair **with her hands folded between her knees**.*
她重重地往椅子上一坐，十指交叉放在雙膝中間。

*I'm going to eat it and enjoy it **without you staring down on me like an old sheep**.*
我準備在你沒有像饞貓那樣盯着看我的時候享受吃它的樂趣。

*She wants to do that **without them knowing she helped**.*
在他們不知道是她幫過忙的情況下,她願意辦那件事。

*I'd be lost **without you here**.*
沒有你在這兒,我會一籌莫展。

▶**注意**◀ 有時 -ing 小句的主語用所有格形式的名詞、代詞來代替賓格形式的名詞、代詞。現在認為這種用法比較過時或者屬正式語體。

***With my getting back** so late, we haven't had time to go over the timetables.*
我回來得很晚,我們沒有時間看時刻表。

*Travis had joined them, **without Larry's spotting** his approach.*
拉瑞沒有看到他走近,查維斯已走過去同他們聚在一起。

*She did not understand why she could not say anything **without its being** interpreted as a sign of madness.*
她不能理解為甚麼她説甚麼都被理解為愚蠢的表現。

## with all

**4.36** 用 **with all** 加名詞或名詞詞組構成的小句可表示理由或讓步。

***With all the rush**, I'd failed to fasten the top strap correctly.* (With all the rush... 等於 Because of all the rush...)
由於忙亂,我沒有把上面的帶子紮牢。

***With all her advantages**, she was nowhere near an equal match for him.* (With all her advantages... 等於 Despite all her advantages...)
儘管她有許多有利條件,但仍然遠不是他的對手。

*Japan, **with all its uniqueness**, still has to find its place in the international order which we are trying to build.*
儘管有其獨特之處,日本仍然需要找到它在我們試圖建立的國際秩序中的位置。

## for all

**4.37** **For all** 加名詞詞組可以表示讓步意義(等於 despite),或者説明某事是不重要的或不成功的。

***For all his ultra-Irish name**, he looked Australian.* (For all his ultra-Irish name... 等於 Despite all his ultra-Irish name...)
雖然他姓地道的愛爾蘭姓,但樣子卻是澳大利亞人。

***For all his jokes and laughter** he was a dangerous and ambitious man.* (For all his jokes and laughter... 等於 Despite all his jokes and laughter...)
儘管他會説笑話,笑聲又不斷,卻是一個危險而又野心勃勃的人。

*I ran back for a gun and searched the woods, **for all the good it did me**.*（…for all the good it did me. 等於 …it did me no good.）
我跑回去取槍並對樹林進行搜查，儘管這對我並沒有好處。

**For all** 加 I care、I know 這樣的小句表示的意義與字面意義相反，分別等於 I don't care、I don't know。

*You can go right now, **for all I care**.*
你即使馬上就走，我也不在乎。

*Everybody's nervous the first day on a job, she assured herself. **For all she knew**, that was true.*（即：She didn't know; it might have been true. 她不知道情況是否真的是這樣。）
她確信頭一天上班大家都會緊張。雖然她並不清楚，但情況卻可能是如此。

***For all we know** he may have been in the drug business for years.*
我們全然不知道，他幾年來大概一直在做藥品生意。

# 獨立小句
# Absolute clauses

**4.38** 沒有從屬連詞但具有主語的非限定小句稱為獨立小句。有時用這種小句來說明主句裏發生或存在的事所處的環境（比較 4.35 節）。實際上，在下列例證的獨立小句之前，都可以插入 with，而意義並不因此有所改變。

*I could see her standing on the sidewalk, **blood running down her neck**.*
我看見她站在人行道上，鮮血順着頭頸往下流。

*He ordered Gough to carry out rigorous inspections of cavalry divisions, **the aim being to prepare them for the role set forth in the memorandum**.*
他命令戈弗對騎兵師進行嚴格的檢查，其目的是讓他們在擔當起備忘錄規定的角色上做好準備。

*The Captain was bent over the radar, **his eyes glued to the scanner**.*
船長埋頭看着雷達，雙眼緊盯着雷達上的掃描器。

**4.39** 有時獨立小句表示條件意義（if、provided that）。如下列例證所示，含條件意義的獨立小句通常都是習慣用語或固定表達式。

*You and your circumstances may well change. **That being so**, what was right of one time may no longer be right for you now.*（That being so… 等於 If that is so… 或 If you and your circumstances change…）
你及你所處的環境很可能會發生變化。如果這樣的話，過去對你合適的事也許現在就不再合適了。

***Other things being equal**, most hostel tenants would prefer single to shared rooms.*（Other things being equal… 等於 Provided that there are not other circumstances that could affect their decisions…）
如果其他條件一樣，住在寄宿宿舍的多數房客將願意住單人間而不願與別人合用一間。

*A helicopter would pick up the two yachtsmen, **weather permitting**.* (...weather permitting. 等於 ...provided that the weather was good enough.)
天氣許可的話，直升飛機將把兩名帆船運動員救起。

*From now until November, when, **God willing**, the rains will come, I shall be in the Luangwa valley in Zambia.*
從現在起到十一月，如果一切順利，雨季即將到來，我將在贊比亞的盧旺瓦谷地。

# 5 指稱：代詞和其他替代形式
# Reference: pronouns and other pro-forms

**5.1** 人們説話、寫文章時，往往要返指自己已經提及的事項（偶爾還要預指自己將要提及的事項）。英語有多種不同的指稱方式可使人們避免重複。實現指稱用的詞，嚴格地説，不是連接詞，儘管把連接語也算作連接詞，但它們起到的作用是連結和避免重複，有時是避免單詞的重複，有時是避免分句的重複。

實現指稱用得最多的是代詞，通常是代替名詞或名詞詞組，但有時也代替一個完整的分句。此外，有的限定詞、形容詞、副詞、名詞、動詞也用來實現各種不同類型的指稱和替代。實現返指最常見的方式之一是用 the 加名詞或名詞詞組，返指已經提及的人或物（誠然，the 還有許多別的用法）。

*He had an advance from HarperCollins to do a book. If he wasn't going to do **the** book right away, he'd have to pay **the** advance back.*
他從哈卜柯林斯公司拿到了一筆為編寫一本書的預付款。如果他不打算立即把這本書編寫出來，就得退還這筆款子。

## 人稱代詞和限定詞
## Personal pronouns and determiners

**5.2** 返指（或預指）人或物，不管被指稱對象是出現在同一個句子裏還是在先行句子裏，常用方式之一是用人稱代詞和屬格形式（如she、her、hers、it、they、them、their 等）。

*At the beginning of **his** working life Taggart had joined a training scheme run by the BBC, and there **he** had met Jane.* （注意粗體的 his 表示預指，he 表示返指。）
在參加工作的初期，塔加特參加過英國廣播公司舉辦的培訓班，他在那裏認識了簡。

*In **her** fright Rosetta seized Gabriel's hand, **he** felt **her** plump, soft palm, and entwined **his** fingers with **hers**. Gabriel's hand was cold and rough and **it** pressed hard, harder all the time.*
羅塞達在恐懼中抓住了加布雷爾的手，他接觸到她那豐滿柔軟的手心，把他的手指與她的捏在一起。加布雷爾的手冰涼而粗糙，越捏越緊。

*Brand, surprised and none too warm, reluctantly indicated **he** had no objection. After all **he** was a guest. Normally **it** was a haven of peace tucked away in the hills above Salzburg. But not today. When they returned **they** would find **it** in the same immaculate order in which **they** had left **it**.* （顯然，he 指代 Brand。但是不清楚 it 和 they 指代甚麼：也許 it 指代 a house。此處例證中的代詞返指先行句子裏所明確的物和一些人。）

布蘭德，感到驚訝又毫無熱情，勉強表示他不反對。畢竟他是客人。通常情況下，它是薩爾茨堡之上為小山隱蔽的安寧去處。但今天不是這樣。當他們回來時，他們會發現它與他們離開時一樣的乾淨整潔。

# 數量代詞和限定詞
# Quantity pronouns and determiners

**5.3**　**數量代詞、限定詞**（如 another、both、neither、many 以及數詞）可以代替表示人或物的名詞詞組。即可以不再使用名詞而只用數量代詞、限定詞指稱已在文中其他地方被提及的名詞（或名詞詞組）。這種用法其實就是一種省略。請看下列例證。

*Had he found the gold or the dead man, or **both**?*
他找到了黃金還是死人，還是兩者都找到了？

*She began to consult doctors, and **each** had a different diagnosis.*
她開始去找醫生們看病，但是各個醫生都有自己不同的診斷。

*Thousands of new diets are dreamed up yearly; **many** are soon forgotten, **a few** are sufficiently effective to become popular.*
每年都有數千種的食品、飲品開發出來：其中多數很快被人忘卻，但有幾種能產生滿意的效果，得以盛行。

*The most startling thing about Goa are the four great Catholic churches built in old Goa and now surrounded by jungle; **two** had been abandoned to nature but **two** were still in use.*
印度果阿最使人驚奇之處是有四座宏偉的建於古代果阿、現在為叢林所包圍的天主教堂：其中兩座已經棄而不用但任隨風吹雨打，但其餘兩座仍在使用之中。

*She was seventy years old but everyone thought she'd last another **ten**.*
她有 70 歲了，但大家都認為她會再活 10 年。

# 指示詞
# Demonstratives

**5.4**　**指示詞**（this、that、these、those）也能起到與數量代詞、限定詞類似的作用，指稱已在文中其他地方出現過的名詞。

*In **this** and the final chapter we look more closely at the way home ownership has changed.* （this 等於 this chapter。）
在這一章和最後一章我們對家庭所有權改變的方式進行更加詳盡的探討。

*For **that** and other reasons, the conviction was unsatisfactory.* （that等於that reason。）
因為那個理由以及別的理由，定罪令人不滿意。

*People are beginning to realise the true scale of the problems facing them. Some of **these** are Germany's alone, though with powerful European side-effects.* （these 等於 these problems。）
人們開始意識到他們所面臨各種問題的真實情況。其中的一些問題雖說能在歐洲產生巨大的副作用，卻只能算德國自己的問題。

*She told me she loved me more than all my brothers and sisters combined. She was afraid to show it because they would be jealous. **Those** were her exact words.* （those 等於 those words。）
她告訴我她對我的愛超過我兄弟姐妹加在一起對我的愛。她不敢把這種愛表示出來因為他們會妒忌的。這些是她的原話。

**5.5**　指示詞也能起到籠統的替代作用，但通常指代的是物而不是人。

*The cost of the operation in 1990 and 1991 will be nearly 10 million dollars. Over half of **this** relates to personnel costs such as salaries, fees and travel expenses.*
在1990和1991年的營運支出將接近1000萬美元。其中有一半多是薪金、專業服務費和差旅費等與員工相關的支出。

*A century earlier, Messina had had a famous architectural seafront, lined with elegant palaces. Only remnants of **that** remained now.*
一個世紀前，意大利的墨西拿市有過著名的、以建築風格著稱的濱海區，沿海濱馬路有一排典雅的宮殿。但現在只有斷壁殘垣。

*An alternative to cash is investment in Government bonds, also known as gilts. **These** represent money borrowed by the government to finance its Public Sector Borrowing Requirement.*
可以替代現金的就是投資政府債券，又叫金邊證券。這種證券作為政府借款，向政府的公共借款補需基金會提供資金。

*I'm quite happy if you ignore the format of the essay and just produce a sheet in which you say '**These** are my thoughts'.*
要是你不去理會文章的格式，只要交出一紙，上面寫着"這些就是我的想法"，我會感到十分高興。

*Rights? You ceased to have **those** from the moment you were brought here.*
權利？從你被帶到這裏那一刻開始你就不再享有權利。

*Clements put three packets of ammunition on the arm of Malone's chair. 'We found **those** in a steel box in the garage.'*
克萊門茨把三盒彈藥放在馬龍椅子的扶手上。"我在車庫的一個鐵盒裏發現了這些東西。"

**5.6**　然而，those 有時可以指代人們，不過，後面必須有附加的詞語。即使 those 返指名詞或名詞詞組，這一條件也不能缺少。

*Yes, you can trust a botanist; at least, **those from the Royal Botanic Gardens**.*
是的，你可以信賴植物學家；至少信賴那些來自皇家植物園的植物學家。

*The public is only interested in generals who win battles, not in **those who lose them***.

公眾只對打勝仗的將軍有興趣，而不是那些打敗仗的。

# 替代：one 、ones
# Substitution: 'one', 'ones'

**5.7** 作代詞用的 **one** 能代替單數具數名詞，**ones** 能代替複數具數名詞。One 可以不帶任何修飾詞語單獨使用，而 ones 需要有修飾詞語才能起到替代作用。

*I have an aspirin, if you want **one***.
如果你需要一片阿斯匹林，我有。

*Imagine a doll that has your face and is your doll! Everyone will want **one***.（one 等於 *a doll with its owner's face*。）
設想有這麼一個布娃娃，它面孔像你、而且是你的，肯定每個人都想有一個這樣的布娃娃。

*The green light went out, **the red one** came on*.
綠燈熄了，紅燈亮了。

*The top front teeth are **the ones which are most at risk from tooth decay***.
上門齒是最容易受到腐蝕的牙齒。

*Who are your favorite tennis players? Who are **the ones that when you watch a championship you're hoping will win**?*
你特別喜歡的是哪幾位網球選手？看錦標賽時，你希望獲勝的選手是哪幾位？

*He is one of those actors who has made a lot of films but **few good ones***.
他是一個拍過多部電影，但沒有幾部成功的演員之一。

**5.8** ▶注意◀ 用在上述情況的 one、ones 主要是起到籠統地替代其他詞的作用，而 it、them 直接指稱 "現實世界" 的事物。

*Merely having enough houses for the number of families that claim to want **one** would not remove the housing problem*.（one 等於 *a house of some kind*，某種住房。）
單單向要求住房的家庭提供足夠房屋解決不了住房問題。

*The house is in the hands of the agents, but until **it**'s sold **it**'s yours to use if you want **it***.（it 等於 *that particular house*，那個特定的住房。）
那住宅房還在房產經紀人手裏，但是只有等到出售時，如果你要這個房子才屬於你，你想用就可以用。

也請注意下面例句中 it 和 one 的區別。

*He felt he had to tear off the label and replace **it** with an identical one*.
他認為他需要把那個標簽撕掉，再用一個相同的標簽去替換原先的那個。

**5.9** 有時幾個不同的代詞全部都返指被提及過的同一事物。

*Small meteorites hit the Earth all the time. Most of **them** incinerate in the atmosphere. The cores of the larger **ones** survived to pulverise craters on the earth; many of **them** have been eroded or obliterated by glaciation, but **some** have survived. **Others** have landed in the deep Antarctic ice: **they** are regularly retrieved and studied because **they** are less likely to be contaminated with earth material. **Some** come from outside the solar system, **a few** are believed to have come from Mars.*

小流星時時都在碰撞地球。他們中的絕大多數在大氣層中燒燬。較大流星的核心部份未被燒燬在地球上砸出隕石坑。多數隕石由於冰蝕作用已被侵蝕或消失得無影無蹤，但其中有部份卻保留下來。有的流星落入南極厚厚的冰層之中：由於他們不大可能被地球物質污染，所以常常被取出來進行研究。有的流星來自太陽系以外的地方，少數據信是來自火星。

上文所有粗體部份的代詞都以一定方式指代落在地球上的流星。然而，隨着行文的擴展，文中代詞起到的具體指代作用有了下面的變化：them 指代 small meteorites；ones 泛指流星；them、some 指個體較大的流星；others 再一次泛指流星；they、they 指埋入南極冰層中的流星；最後 some、a few 又一次地泛指流星。

## 指稱地方和時間
## Referring to place and time

here, there

**5.10** 副詞 **here**、**there** 可作為**替代形式**指代文中提及或暗指的地方。在會話中，根據語境把 here 的意義理解成進行會話的地方；沒有必要用其他指稱把地方表示出來。

*The house stood near a quiet sandy beach facing across the vast distances of the Lake of Oulu; **here** she could wander and imagine herself on the edge of a great sea.*

那座房屋豎立在寂靜的沙灘附近，面對芬蘭歐路湖浩瀚的湖水；她可以在這裏漫步，想像自己在大海之邊。

*His first call had been at his lawyers. **Here** he had learnt that none of the cases had been decided one way or another.*

他首先是走訪了他請的律師。那裏他獲悉所有的案件都未作出某種判決。

*Soon, he was on Adalbertstrasse. Number eighty-four would be less than a five-minute walk. **Here** was the worst bomb damage he had seen.*

不久，他就到了阿達貝斯查斯。離 84 號公路步行不到 5 分鐘。這裏是他所見到過的遭受炸彈破壞最嚴重的地方。

*My father expects to land at Portsmouth within the fortnight. It would mean so much to me to be **there** on the dock, waiting for him.*

我父親希望在兩週內在朴茨茅斯上岸。在那裏的碼頭上等候他對我來説意義重大。

*Dad's at the hospital with Sam. The police are going to take us **there**.*
爸爸同山姆在醫院裏。警察打算把我們送到那裏去。

## now, then

**5.11** 作為時間替代形式的 **now**、**then** 的使用方式與 here、there 類似。 Now 在會話中一般指稱現在時間,但在書面語裏卻不盡如此,可以表示過去,含義是 at that same time (在那同時),指已提及或暗示出來的時間。

*They told her it was the rainy season **now** where Peter was.* (*...the time when the snakes are most active, she recalled.* ……她回憶起那是蛇最活躍的時候。)
他們告訴她彼得所在地方當時是雨季。

*Through the telescope the hunter saw Sementsev move forward. **Now** he was the perfect target.*
獵手通過望遠鏡看見塞門澤夫向前移動。他這時成了獵手的理想目標。

*Sharpe looked behind again and saw his closest pursuers were **now** just fifty yards away.*
夏普又往後看了看,發現離他最近的追捕人當時離他只有 50 碼。

*From 1985-90 I was an instructor at the regional party headquarters. After that I went back to work in a factory. **Then** I had no idea what a casino was.*
從1985年到1990年我是地方黨部的教員。隨後我回到一家工廠工作。當時我不知道賭場是甚麼樣的地方。

*We left just after one-thirty. By **then** the wind had risen almost to gale force.*
我們剛過一點半就離開了。到那個時候風力已經增強到接近 8 級。

# 替代分句
# Substitution for clauses

## this, that, it

**5.12** 有的代詞,尤其是 **this**、**that**、**it** 可以替代語篇中先行的分句或先行的語段。這樣的替代並不是一定要逐詞對應,讀者通過上下文會理解替代詞替代的是甚麼。下列例證的粗體部份表示代詞返指的是甚麼。

*He employed a housekeeper about whom he would sometimes remark, rather unkindly, that **not only was she of indeterminate age**, **but also of indeterminate sex**, unaware that **this** was exactly what others frequently said about him.*
他僱了一個人料理家務,講起此人時他有時會說,而且是很不友善地說,她不僅年齡難定,而且性別也不明,殊不知他的這番話恰恰是別人經常對他的議論。

*They had thought that **they might climb out under the cover of darkness**. It only took a few minutes to discover that **this** was impossible.*
他們本來以為他們可以在夜幕的掩護下爬出去的。不過,只用了幾分鐘就發現那是完全不可能的事。

*Upon its introduction to Europe **coffee was hailed as an aphrodisiac**, which made it very popular. It was perhaps with **this** in mind that Voltaire drank sixty cups a day.*

咖啡剛剛引入歐洲時，被奉為春藥，受到廣泛的歡迎。大概是基於這種信念，伏爾泰一天要喝60杯。

*We lived together, off and on, for two years. **This** was way before **that** was an acceptable thing to do.* (this 等於 our living together，that 等於 any couple living together。)

我們那時住在一起，時斷時續，有兩年的時間。這是早在男女同居得到社會承認之前的生活方式。

*'I wonder if the police have managed to get hold of Matt. **I'll try and find out**,' Brand assured her. '**That** would be a relief,' she said gratefully.*

"我不知道警方是否已經抓住了馬特。我設法去打聽清楚。"布蘭德向她保證。"這將解除我們的擔憂，"她感激地說。

*At first I thought that **this reorganization was simply an attempt on his part to gain more power**. But **that** is not the explanation.*

起初我以為這種重組只不過是他獲取更大權力的企圖，但是我這種想法解釋不通。

*'**I'm so lonely**.' I said it aloud, trying to mean **it**, trying to feel the ache.*

"我感到多麼孤獨。"我大聲說，盡力表達出這種感覺，盡力去體會這種感覺帶來的痛苦。

*They go to motor racing to watch cars crash, but it's a pretty unattractive thought.*

他們要去賽車場看汽車相撞，但是這是一種非常不得體的想法。

**5.13** This（而不是 that）、it 可以預指語篇中後隨的分句和語段。

*I hate to say **this** but I don't think they're kidding.*

我不願這樣說，但我認為他們不是在開玩笑。

*I know him better than any of you, and I can say **this**: nobody's going to make him work any faster.*

我比你們誰都更了解他，我可以說這話：誰也不能使他工作得更快些。

*Well, I'm ashamed to say **it**, but I don't care for my war duties at all.*

唉，我真不好意思說出自己的這種看法，我根本不願履行我的戰爭義務。

## so, not

**5.14** So、not 可返指並替代分句，尤其在轉述動詞及 I'm afraid、it appears、it seems 這類表達式之後。

*They hated children. I heard them say **so**.* (...so.即：...that they hated children.他們討厭孩子。)

他們討厭孩子。我聽到他們這樣說過。

*'Actually, when you see somebody die gradually they go so thin, you know.'* — *'Yeah, I believe **so**.'*

"實際上，當你目睹有人瀕臨死亡時，他們會變得很瘦，你知道。"——"是的，我相信是這樣。"

*'But you'll be taken prisoner, won't you?'* — *'I hope **not**.'*

"不過你會被俘，對嗎？"——"我希望不會這樣。"

*'Were there any survivors?'* — *'No, sir. I'm afraid **not**.'*
"有幸存者嗎？"——"沒有，先生，恐怕是沒有。"

*Is he being honest with the people? So far, it appears **not**.*
他對那些人誠實嗎？到目前為止，他似乎並不誠實。

*'How did the accident occur? I assume it was an accident.'* — *'It seems **so**.'*
"事故是怎樣發生的？我認為那是一次事故。"——"似乎是這樣的。"

If so、if not、even so 等表達式裏的 so、not 也用來替代分句。另見 2.40 和 2.53 節。

*Did Rose have a passport? And if **so**, where was it?*
羅斯有護照嗎？如果有的話，又在哪裏呢？

*Ask her if it is a convenient time. If **not**, can she suggest another possible time?*
問問她那個時間方便不方便。要是不方便，那可不可以提出一個可行的時間呢？

*Iris avoided wine with her meal but even **so** she felt unutterably drowsy afterwards.*
艾麗斯用餐時不喝酒，但即使這樣，她飯後還是感到不可言狀的昏昏欲睡。

**5.15**   So 尤其是 not，也用在 perhaps、probably、maybe、possibly 之後替代分句。

*'I am sure he would tell you were you to ask him.'* — *'Perhaps **so**, but I do not wish to risk a snub.'*
"如果你問他，我肯定他會告訴你的。"——"也許是這樣的，不過我不想遭到他的冷遇。"

*Perhaps this time we will make a better job of it. Or perhaps **not**.*
也許這回我能把工作做得更好。也許不能。

*'Does it matter?'* — *'No, probably **not**,'* said Irena.
"要緊嗎？"——"不，也許不要緊，"艾琳娜説。

*'You're probably better equipped to do it than he would be even if he were here.'* — *'Maybe **so**. But it's hard all the same.'*
"即使他在這裏，你也許比他更有條件做這事。"——"可能是這樣的。不過也一樣難啊。"

*Maybe the police would believe it, maybe **not**.*
警方也許會相信，也許會不相信。

*'I don't know any secrets.'* — *'Possibly **not**. But it's more probable that you do know some but haven't recognized their value.'*
"我不知道甚麼秘密。"——"可能不知道。不過更大的可能性是你知道一些，但卻沒有意識到它們的價值。"

**5.16**   作為替代分句的 so 有時用在分句或句子之首，以示強調。這種情況主要出現在有表示想法和説法的動詞（即轉述動詞）的句子裏。

*It's an example of Victorian architecture, **so** I've been told.*
那是維多利亞時代建築的範例，有人對我這樣説。

*'Everything about him was well documented.'* — *'**So** I believe.'*
"有關他的所有情況都有完備的資料。"——"這我相信。"

有 so 的分句常常含有對先行分句內容的真實性表示懷疑或不相信的成分。

*'He made a genuine mistake.' — 'Yeah, **so** he says.'*
"他犯了個名符其實的錯誤。"——"是的，他是這樣講的。"

*Choosing which type of greenhouse was a simple task; or **so** I thought.*
挑選何種類型的溫室是不難的工作；或者說我是這樣想的。

*Nothing changes, or **so** it seems.*
沒有出現任何變化，或者說似乎是這樣的。

# 用 do 作替代形式
# Substitution using 'do'

**5.17**　**Do so**、**do it**、**do that** 可替代謂語部份（即不把主語包括在內的整個分句）。Do 的時態形式會在替代中變化。

*He tried to remember where he might have seen her before, but could not **do so**.*
（…but could not do so. 等於 …but could not remember. 卻記不起來。）
他盡力回憶可能在甚麼地方見過她，卻記不起來。

*I always read a lot and I **am doing so** more than ever while preparing a new TV programme.*（…and I am doing so more than ever… 等於 …and I am reading more than ever… 我閱讀的東西比平常更多。）
我總是大量閱讀，在準備一個新的電視節目期間，我閱讀的東西比平常更多。

*She nearly died at the age of 95 in June, and finally **did so** in July.*
95 歲時她在 6 月裏差點兒死去，不過最後還是在 7 月裏死去了。

*Faraday made a note in his diary in 1822: 'Convert magnetism into electricity!' It was 1831 before he **did so**, and what a revolution it caused.*（…before he did so… 等於 …before he converted magnetism into electricity… 在他把磁力轉化成電力之前。）
法拉第於 1822 年在日記裏記錄這麼一句話："把磁力轉化成電力。"他是在 1831 年完成這種轉化，這引起了一場了不起的變革。

*We can make a difference in the world in which we live. We can **do it** because we believe in the power and the spirit of our own will.*
我們能對自己生活的世界產生重大的影響。我們能夠做到，因為我們信賴自己意志所具有的物質和精神力量。

*Now we'll go and talk to your mother. Don't you want to **do that**?*
那麼我們去找你母親談。你不想去嗎？

# 用泛義名詞指代
# General nouns used for reference

**5.18**　返指另一個名詞（或名詞詞組）通常是用帶 the、this、such 等限定詞的名詞。有時，用相同的名詞返指，但常常是用原名詞的同義詞（即意義大體上與原名詞相同的名詞），或者用涵蓋面更廣、包括被指稱名詞意義的泛義名詞。譬如，child 包括 daughter，即 child 的意義比 daughter 的涵蓋面更廣。有時，在常識範圍內，用大家都能理解的名詞來指代另一名詞。例如，在下列的第二個例證裏，如果將蛋黃醬和馬鈴薯泥拌混在一起，這兩樣東西就成了一種拌和物。

> *Beside her slept her two-year-old daughter, Belle.* **The child**'s *forehead was damp with perspiration.*
> 她身旁睡的是她兩歲的女兒貝麗。這孩子的額頭汗津津的。

> *Combine the thick garlic mayonnaise with the mashed potatoes and spread* **this mixture** *on rounds of toasted French bread.*
> 把濃的帶蒜蛋黃醬同土豆泥拌和起來，再把這種拌和物塗在整塊的法式烤面包片上。

某些意義非常廣泛的名詞經常用來指稱(返指或預指)文中出現的名詞，不僅指稱名詞，而且指稱句子，譬如說指稱描述動作、事件、想法或陳述的句子。

## thing, case, way

**5.19**　**Thing** 是泛義名詞中最為普通的名詞，可以用來替代表示物體的名詞。

> *He brought out the compass which he'd removed from the lifeboat. 'This* **thing**'s *virtually useless, but at least it does show changes in direction.'*
> 他拿出自己從救生艇取下來的指南針。"這個東西實際上沒有多大用處，不過它至少可以指明方位。"

更重要的是，thing 指稱的可以是想法、動作、事件或狀況等。

> *Trying to avoid or minimize risk, however, is not the same* **thing** *as trying to eliminate it.*
> 然而，努力避免或降低風險與消除風險卻不是一回事。

> *Infection and inflammation are not exactly the same* **thing**.
> 感染和發炎並不完全是一回事。

> *Why is it that feminists always say 'women feel' when what they mean is 'feminists feel'? It is not at all the same* **thing**. (即：這兩種說法並不表示相同的概念。)
> 為甚麼女權主義者在自己的意思是"女權主義的感覺"時，總是說"婦女的感覺"？這兩者是根本不同的概念。

> *I coerced Ray, who wasn't religious at all, to attend the church with me and convert, which was a big mistake, because the next* **thing** *I knew, he'd become a fanatic.*
> 我強迫根本不信教的瑞依跟我一道去做禮拜並皈依宗教，這是一個極大的錯誤，因為我後來才知道，他成了宗教的狂熱分子。

> *The* **thing** *I like about Wallace is that he is not worried about failure.*
> 我喜歡華萊士的地方是他不為失敗犯愁。

**Case** 是另一個意義廣泛的名詞，指稱事件、狀況或環境。

*Some visitors may come by road from Zaire; in that **case**, they will probably enter Zambia through Kaumbalesa or Mokambo.*
部份參觀的人可以從扎伊爾乘車去；在這種情況下，他們或許要通過考姆巴薩或莫康卜進入贊比亞。

*You'll be a lawyer or a policeman, and in either **case**, your studies will stand you in good stead.*
你將成為律師或警察 ，但不管是當律師還是當警察，你的學習將對你很有幫助。

**Way** 可以指稱做事的方式或方法。

*If an unemployed worker refuses training or a job his benefits are stopped. In this **way**, Sweden has virtually abolished long-term unemployment.*
如果失業人員拒絕接受培訓或一項工作，就要中止給他的補助金。用這種辦法，瑞士差不多完全消滅了長期失業。

*We have decided to use the jam you sent us only with our evening cup of tea, and in that **way** it will last us a long time.*
我們決定只在喝夜茶時才用你送的果醬，這樣一來，就可以用上很長時間。

用了另外一些泛義名詞的例證可在以下幾節看到。有關用來表示返指或預指的名詞的詳盡論述，見第 6 章。

# Such 的用法
# Uses of 'such'

**5.20**　起返指作用的 such 既是限定詞又是代詞，主要有兩種用法：

- 第一， such 與其他詞一起構成名詞詞組，用來表示像那樣、是那樣的物、人或行為。

- 第二， such 用在短語 as such 中，含義按先行詞或短語的確切意義來解。

**Such**（帶形容詞或不帶形容詞）用在具數名詞的單數、複數形式前，也用在不具數名詞前。

*There have long been rumours that they have been trying to acquire anti-aircraft missiles, but this is the first time they have claimed the use of **such a weapon**.*
（…such a weapon. 等於 …an anti-aircraft missile.）
長期來都有謠言傳說他們一直在謀求防空導彈，但這是第一次他們宣稱用了這樣的武器。

*He had never seen a woman in his close family openly lose her temper with a male relative, and believed that only bad women did **such a thing**.* （…such a thing. 等於 …lose their temper with a male relative 。）
他從未見過自己近親家庭的一名女性公開地對男性親戚發火，並認為只有壞女人才做這樣的事。

*He is quite ambitious and is prepared to work hard.* **Such people** *should be given a chance to get on.* (Such people... 等於 People who are ambitious and prepared to work hard。)
他雄心勃勃而且有苦幹的準備。這樣的人應該給予出人頭地的機會。

*Ultimately developing countries would like to be able to generate their own technology. In the interim,* **such countries** *must depend primarily on imports.*
所有的發展中國家最終都希望能開發本國的技術。在過渡期間,這類國家必須主要依賴進口。

*He cheerfully travelled economy class, even though his height was beginning to make* **such cramped conditions** *uncomfortable.* (...such cramped conditions... 等於 ...the sort of cramped conditions that are typical of economy class。)
他開開心心地乘坐經濟艙位旅行,雖然他的身高在開始讓這種經濟艙位顯得狹窄。

*Their experimental method gives rise to accusations of bias. But* **such 'bias'** *cannot be wholly explained as the product of personal views of staff members.*
他們的實驗方法引發了對偏見的種種指責。不過,這樣的偏見是不能完全説成是工作人員意見的產物。

*My friends would take the children out and keep them for a night to give me a break. And my doctor continued to listen, to believe, teaching me how to cope. I was very lucky to be surrounded by* **such understanding and love**. (...such understanding and love. 等於 ...the understanding and love shown to me by my friends and my doctor.)
我的朋友們會把孩子們帶出去並留他們過夜,給我一次休息的機會。我的醫生繼續傾聽我的意見、信任我,教我應付辦法。我為自己生活在這種被人理解和關愛的氛圍之中感到十分幸運。

**5.21**　**Such** 之後也可以跟 all、any、many、no、one、some,而且偶爾還會省略這些短語後的名詞。

*All social theories are designed to either advance the science of society or to promote fraudulent ideas concerning society. Thus,* **all such theories** *are developed with some use in mind.*
所有社會科學理論的構想都旨在促進社會科學的發展,或者鼓吹對社會的欺騙性的看法。所以,所有這些理論的形成都是有實用目的的。

*She had threatened to inform London that she could no longer take responsibility for working with me. I warned her against* **any such course**. (course 等於 course of action,行動步驟)
她威脅説要通知倫敦方面她不再對同我一道工作負責。我警告她不要採取這樣步驟。

*Marcia recognized the evening as one which Robert had decided not to enjoy. There were* **many such**. (...many such. 等於 ...many evenings like that.)
馬希亞認識到那個晚間聚會是羅伯特已經決定不愉快度過的一次聚會。這樣的情況有過多次。

*'I'll tell you what I'll do, catch the first plane back to Los Angeles.' Even as she said it she knew she would do* **no such thing**. (...she would do no such thing. 等於 ...she would not catch a plane back to L.A.)
"我告訴你我的打算,即乘第一班飛機飛回洛杉磯。"甚至在她説這話時,她就知道她不會這樣做的。

*'I just want justice.'* — *'There's* **no such thing** *any more and you're not being honest. You want revenge.'*
"我只要正義。"——"不再有正義這樣的東西了。你不誠實,你要報復。"

*Festivals often had huge orchestras. In the Tang dynasty **one such** had 120 harpists alone.* （...one such... 等於 ...one huge orchestra...）
節日常有大型樂隊。在唐代，有一次樂隊單是彈奏豎琴的就有 120 人。

*Anthony, darling, is one of us about to say that this is stronger than us, or **some such nonsense**?* （...some such nonsense... 等於 ...some similar absurd statement...）
安東尼，親愛的，是不是我們中的一個人打算説這比我們更具有實力，或者類似的蠢話嗎？

*He personally hoped that the Nature Conservancy or **some such body** would buy up the island.* （...some such body... 等於 ...some similar organization...）
他個人希望自然資源管理委員會或類似的機構會買下那個島嶼。

## as such

**5.22** **As such** 返指緊靠的先行詞或短語，含義按先行詞語的確切意義來解。
*He had no plan of action **as such**.* （即：He had no actual plan, though perhaps he had various ideas about what to do. 也許他對要做甚麼有各種各樣的想法，但卻沒有確切的計劃。）
他沒有確切意義上的計劃。

*The note was a blatant attempt to evade mail censorship and **as such** was against prison regulations.*
那張條子是明目張膽逃避信件檢查的企圖，從嚴格意義上説是違反監獄法規的。

*Escaping prisoners of war could expect to be treated **as such**. Unidentified strangers masquerading as foreign workmen could expect to be dealt with as spies.*
逃跑的戰俘會得到應有的處理。身份不明、冒充外籍工人的陌生人會當作間諜處理。

**5.23** ▶注意◀ 有時 so 可替代前面提到的形容詞。
*I found the street where Eddie lived. It was narrow, made more **so** by the cars parked on both sides.* （...made more so by... 等於 ...made narrower by...）
我找到了艾迪住的那條街。街道狹窄，停在街邊的汽車使它更顯狹窄。

作補語用的 so（比如作動詞 be 的補語）常常置於句首，後接倒裝的主語和助動詞，以示強調。與 5.16 節比較。

*Gwendolen, you're crazy. I know, and **so** are you.* （...and so are you. 等於 ...and you are crazy too.）
昆多倫，你瘋啦。我知道，而且你也瘋啦。

*Life is great. **So** are you, and the flowers aren't really enough to express it.*
生命力偉大。你也偉大，朵朵花兒實在不足以表現這種偉大。

**Such** 偶爾也置於句首，與 so 的用法類似。

*She was struck by a picture of a woman with a long dress and a plunging neckline and a tall hair-do. **Such** were the fashions in those days.* （例證的第二句等於 That is what the fashions were in those days.）
一幅身着低領口連衣長裙、髮型高聳的仕女畫給她留下深刻的印象。這是那個時代流行的衣着打扮。

# Sort 、 kind 、 type 的用法
# Uses of 'sort', 'kind', and 'type'

this sort/kind/type, that sort/kind/type

**5.24** 敘述某人某物像（或者不像）提及過的另一人或物的辦法之一是用 "this/that+sort/kind/type+of+ 名詞" 或者 "名詞 +of +this/that+sort/kind/type" 構成的短語。因此，that kind of book 和 a book of that kind 的意義差不多，表示那種/類書。

*I have played a lot of glamorous women who have broken men's hearts, so people tend to see me as **that sort of** person.*
我已扮演過許多使男人傷心的、富有魅力的女角色，所以人們往往把我看成是那種人。

*We often blame ourselves for things that happen to other people. **That kind of** belief is not at all unusual.*
我們經常為發生在他人身上的事而自責。那樣的想法並不奇怪。

*So now this has been definitely diagnosed as the Plague. There has been consternation everywhere, because when **this sort of** disease is brought into a country there is no knowing how far it will spread.*
所以，這種病已經被確診為一種瘟疫。到處是一片恐慌，因為當這種疾病傳染到一個國家，就無法知道它會擴散到甚麼地方。

*We ended up teaching mainly foreigners, teachers, journalists and people **of that kind**.*
我們後來教的對象主要是外國人、教師、記者以及類似身份的人。

*Many 'scientific' journals have a disgraceful attitude to parapsychology and completely reject and suppress any publications **of that type**.*
許多 "科學" 雜誌對靈學採取了一種有失體面的態度，並完全拒絕、壓制這類出版物。

**5.25** This type of thing、that kind of thing 這樣的短語用得很廣，其中的 thing 常常表示行為或事件，而不是具體的物。

*They heckled him, and threw things. Quite nasty, but of course if you're a minister these days, with current standards of behaviour, you have to get used to **that sort of thing**.*
他們對他進行詰問，向他扔東西。行為惡劣，不過，當然了，要是你現在當部長，根據現行的行為標準，你必須對這樣的事習慣起來。

*He was not suited to the role of detective: there were professionals who did **this sort of thing**, and did it far more efficiently.*
他不適合當偵探：有做這種工作的專業人員，而且他們幹起來要有效得多。

*Some of them are drinking beer, partying late at night, **that kind of thing**.*
他們中的一些人在喝着啤酒，舉行社交聚會，深夜不散，如此等等。

*People keep asking me to do things. Reviews, articles, **that kind of thing**.*
人們不停地要我做事。寫評論、文章之類的事。

*It is specially important to guard against accidents. All good parents have fire-guards and gates at dangerous places, but I strongly advise you to get **this kind of thing** thoroughly organized some time before it actually seems necessary.*

防止事故於未然尤其重要。細心的家長們都設置有壁爐爐檔，在容易出事的地方裝有安全門，但我強烈地建議你們把這類東西安排得有條有理以備不時之需。

*'What sort of bother?'* — *'Well, running off without paying and **that type of thing**.'*

"有甚麼煩惱的事啊？"——"唉，如拿走東西不付錢之類的事。"

**5.26**　雖然 "these/those+sort/kind/type+of+ 複數名詞" 裏的 sort、kind、type 明明是單數形式，但人們可以聽到、特別在口語裏聽到這樣的短語。但是許多人都認為這種用法不合語法，所以在書面語裏常設法避免。

*I was asking her what it was like, you know, I mean, what's your weather like and all **these sort of boring questions**.*

我問她那裏情況如何，我的意思是你們那裏天氣如何以及諸如此類枯燥無味的問題。

*People like us shouldn't work **these kind of hours**.*

像我們這樣的人不應該在這樣的時辰工作。

*He is very good-looking if you like **those sort of looks**.*

要是你喜歡這種模樣的人，他還是長得挺好看的。

*That way we don't have to provide the showers, the food services, the washers and dryers, **those type of things**.*

那樣安排的話，我們就不必提供淋浴、餐飲服務、洗衣機、烘乾機之類的東西了。

# 比較形式
# Comparative forms

**5.27**　從定義上說，比較的條件至少要有兩個人、兩個物或兩種概念，所以比較時用的替代形式 (其中包括 another 和 other) 在一定意義上總是指稱另外的人或物。有時另外的人和物由語境暗指出來，而不必在先行語句裏明白表達。

*Can I have **another** coffee?*

可以再給我一杯咖啡嗎？

*Where's the **other** sock?*

另一隻襪子在哪裏？

**5.28**　在多數情況下，比較常用預指，也就是說，句子裏先用比較級形式的形容詞、副詞及其描述的人、物或行為，然後再用進行比較的尺度。比較的尺度這時用 **than** 引導 (或者在同級比較時，用 **as** 引導)。另見 2.84 – 2.87 節。

*The latest earthquakes are **smaller than** the one which shook the area on Sunday.*

最近幾次地震比星期日發生在該地區的地震要小些。

*We must move to accept the idea that two parents and one or two children are an **easier** equation **than** one parent and one or two children.*
我們有必要提議接受這樣的看法，即有一、兩個孩子的雙親家庭比有一、兩個孩子的單親家庭更容易協調內部、處理好各種關係。

*Some words tend to occur **more often than** others.*
有些單詞往往比另一些的出現頻率高。

*I hope I look **as good as** you when I'm your age.*
我希望等我到了你的年齡時長得和你一樣好看。

在別的情況下，比較級形式可以返指已經提及或者暗示的人、物或行為。

*This is a junior school. You'll go to a **bigger** one for girls of your age.*
這是一所初級學校。你將去一所學生年齡與你相同、規模更大的女子學校。

*There are probably about a thousand Americans, and a lot of other nationalities, in **smaller** numbers.*
那裏大約有一千個美國人，還有人數較少的其他許多國家的人。

*They should visit the North West where everything is **cheaper**.*
他們應該到物價更便宜的西北去訪問。

*Some broken bones heal quickly and some **more slowly**.*
有的骨折癒合得快，而有的癒合得較慢。

*Make the music hearable, both to the people in the audience and, just **as important**, to the onstage musicians themselves.*
要讓觀眾聽得見演出的音樂，讓前台的樂師們自己聽見也同樣重要。

## the former, the latter

**5.29** 返指兩個不同的人或物，對他們進行一定的比較時，可以用 **the former** 指代第一個被提及的人或物，用 **the latter** 指代第二個被提及的人或物。這兩個替代形式在語體上比較正式，但除用於書面語外，也用於口語，有時可以後接名詞。

*There are rules which govern not only the working lives of our nurses, but also their off-duty lives. While I demand adherence to **the former**, I am, I hope, sufficiently realistic to realize that **the latter** are mostly out-of-date.*
現行的規定不僅管我們護士的工作，還要管她們的下班的生活。雖然我要求遵守前一類規定，但是我希望，我是個足夠現實的人，能意識到後一類規定大多已經過時。

*You know what Democritus said on the subject. 'Do not trust all men, but trust men of worth.' **The former course** is silly, **the latter** a mark of prudence.*
你知道古希臘哲學家德謨克利特對這個問題的看法。"不要信任所有的人，但要信任真正有價值的人。"前一種態度是糊塗，後一種態度是深謀遠慮的標誌。

*I couldn't tell if he was being careless and unstructured, or if he was a clever interrogator. I was beginning to suspect **the latter**.*
我不能肯定他當時是否故意粗心大意、缺乏條理，也不能肯定他是否是個聰明的審訊人。我開始懷疑他屬於後者。

# 是相同還是不同？
# The same or different?

the same, the opposite, the reverse

**5.30** Same、opposite、reverse是無比較級形式的形容詞，但其基本意義是比較。

可用 **the same** 、 **the opposite** ，偶爾也用 **the reverse** 返指事件、想法或一段話語。必要時，可把動詞用在這幾個形容詞之前。也可以把這幾個替代形式擴展成帶有名詞的短語。

*Their questions were clear and concise. **The same** could not be said for the answers.*
(The same... 即：The answers were not clear and concise. 對問題的答覆不清楚不扼要。)
他們的問題簡明扼要。答覆就是另外一回事了。

*I have a friend who went to France as a male au pair without any trouble. I do not see why I cannot **do the same** here.* (...do the same... 即：...be a male au pair... 當換工，學習本地語)
我有一個朋友去了法國，順利地當上換工學習法語。我不明白為甚麼我不能在這裏仿效他的作法。

*'Do you enjoy your job?' — 'I could ask you **the same**.'*
"你喜歡自己的工作嗎？" —— "我也想問你這個問題。"

*His coldness angered her. She had made her impulsive offer in a spirit of straightforward friendliness, and she wanted him to accept it in **the same way**.*
他的冷淡使她生氣。她以直率友好的態度向他提出一個感情衝動的建議，並想他以同樣態度接受她的建議。

*Morris has played well in both matches and I would say **the same thing** for Andrews.*
莫瑞斯在兩場比賽中都表現出色，我對安德魯斯的評價也是一樣的。

*She realized that compared with most women she was remarkably inexperienced in this sort of thing. What worried her more than anything else was that Mike might think exactly **the opposite**.* (...the opposite. 即：...that she was experienced. ......她有經驗。)
她意識到自己與大多數婦女相比，在這種事情上非常缺乏經驗。但最使她擔心的是麥克對她的看法恰恰相反。

*He remained silent, resisting the impulse to encourage Stephen to talk, which he knew might well have **the opposite effect**.*
他仍然沉默不語，克制住鼓動斯蒂芬說話的衝動，他知道這樣可能會起到相反的作用。

*I hope that anything I report will have the effect of being useful to our purpose, not **the reverse**.*
我希望我報告的事會給我們的目標帶來有用的影響，而不是起到相反的作用。

*The interview had not reassured Tweed. Rather **the reverse**.* (...the reverse. 即：It had worried him. 倒是使他感到擔心。)
那次會見沒有消除特威德的疑慮。倒是起到了一定的反作用。

☞ 另見 **at the same time**：2.60 節。

## likewise, otherwise

**5.31**　**Likewise**、**otherwise** 總是返指。第 2、3 章的例證説明它們作連接語的用法，作連接語時，它們多少游離在句子之外。它們也可以用在動詞之後。**Do likewise** 是替代do the same（做同樣的事）、act in the same way（以相同方式行事）的另一種形式。

*The boy and his mother emerged from the next-door house, got into their respective cars, and drove away. As soon as they were out of sight, Bernard **did likewise**.*
（*…did likewise.即：…got into his car.*……上了自己的汽車。）
那個男孩及他的母親從隔壁房子裏走了出來，分別上了各自的車，駕車而去。當他們的車一消失，波爾那德同樣也上了自己的車。

*He put family honour above all else, and taught us to **do likewise**.*
他把家庭的榮譽放在首位，並教育我們也這樣做。

**Otherwise** 只用在動詞do 及某些籠統地表示想法的動詞（如decide、know、pretend、prove、suggest）之後，其含義是differently（不同地）或the opposite（相反）。

*He pleaded guilty in spite of considerable pressure to **do otherwise**.*
儘管有相當的壓力叫他不要這樣，他還是認了罪。

*You should still continue your course of these drugs to prevent the infection recurring, unless your doctor **advises otherwise**.*
如果大夫沒有不同的醫囑，你就應該繼續服用這些藥物，免得重新感染。

*He was hurt and it was no use **pretending otherwise**.*
他受到了傷害，裝作無事的樣子沒有用處。

*'Do you think she really is what she says?' — 'I think she is sure that there is nothing we can do to **prove otherwise**.'*
"你以為她真的是她所説的那樣嗎？"——"我認為她肯定我們無法證明她的話與事實不符。"

## identical, similar, different

**5.32**　這三個形容詞都用於比較兩個或更多的人或物。它們同常用的比較級形式一樣，可以返指或預指。返指時，它們都帶上各自特有的介詞，與比較的尺度相連接。它們相應的副詞形式 identically、similarly、differently 有時也這樣使用，即帶上介詞，再加上表示比較尺度的詞語。

説 something is **identical to /with** something else（一人一事與另一人、一事相同）時，是表示它們完全相同或者很相像。要知道，相像的雙胞胎通常是難以分辨的啊!

*I joined a group of women dressed in turquoise sweatsuits **identical to** mine.*
我加入了一羣婦女們的活動，她們跟我一樣身穿蘋果綠運動服。

*I was very reluctant to accept that robots were **identical with** human beings.*
我很難接受機器人與人類一模一樣。

*It would be easy to produce a balanced composition by echoing a line on the left side of the painting with an **identical** line on the right.*
在畫的右邊畫出一根與左邊相同的線條來完成一幅對稱性好的畫作是一件容易的事。

*Cobuild appears to have been confused with an **identically** named company based in Greater Manchester.*
柯比爾德這個縮寫好像同本部設在大曼徹斯特的一家同名公司混淆起來了。

不完全相同的人或物可以說成是 **similar to** each other（彼此類似的）。作連接語用的 similarly 見 3.11 節。

*The accident was **similar to** one that happened in 1973.*
這個事故與發生在 1973 年的事故類似。

*Place the almond and coconut oils together in a double saucepan or **similar** utensil over a low heat.*
把杏仁油和椰子油一起放在雙層蒸鍋或類似的炊具裏微火加熱。

*These theories of brain function sound less compelling when you learn that in the 19th century a **similar** argument raged about the function of the lobes of the brain.*（注意，argument 在本例證裏是作 theory 的近義詞用的。）
當得知19世紀有關腦葉功能的類似理論鬧得沸沸揚揚時，這些腦功能理論聽上去就不那麼使人非相信不可了。

*Germany's diplomatic service is structured **similarly to** that of Britain.*
德國外交事務在組織結構上與英國類似。

*'I'm so sorry,' I muttered, or something **similarly** inadequate.*
我咕嚕地說了"對不起"或其他類似的不能充分表達歉意的話。

相比之下不同於他人、它物的人或物可說成是 **different from** them（與他們不同的）。

*London was **different from** most European capitals.*
倫敦與大多數歐洲國家的首都不同。

*The figures suggest that the company is surviving the recession better than most, but the second half may tell a **different** story.*
這些數據表明，那家公司比大多數公司更順暢地度過蕭條期，但是另一半數據反映的情況可能就不一樣。

*They still get treated **differently from** almost every other contemporary British band.*
他們受到的待遇幾乎不同於當時任何一個英國樂團。

*What had begun as a command ended up quite **differently**; it came as close as John could get to a threat.*
開始當作命令的話結果完全變了樣，它幾乎成了約翰能發出的威脅。

**Different to**、**different than**（這主要是美國英語的用法）也用來表示不同於他人它物的人或物，不過，有的人認為只有 different from 才是正確的用法。

> *Soya beans are quite **different to** any other bean in flavour and texture.*
> 大豆在味道和質地上不同於其他任何一種豆類。

> *We have a **different** relationship with horses **than** we do with cattle and sheep and pigs.*
> 人類與馬的關係不同於與牛、羊、豬的關係。

▶注意◀ 當後接的是從句時，different than 就很適用。如果說話者在上列的第二個例證裏一定要用from，那麼就不得不採用a different relationship from the kind we have with cattle, sheep, and pigs 這樣的別扭說法。

**5.33** ▶注意◀ Differently 有時的作用簡單得就像動詞賓語，其含義與 the opposite 或 otherwise 差不多。

> *She had started the business and had come to believe it would fail without her. The last few months **had taught** her **differently**. The company was thriving in her absence.*
> 她辦起了公司並認為公司沒有她就辦不好。但是過去幾個月的情況卻使她有了不同的認識。公司在她不在時運轉得紅紅火火。

> *Until now I thought that this sort of accident was the owner's fault but now I **know differently**.*
> 過去我一直認為這類事故是車主的過錯，但現在我有了不同看法。

## equal, additional

**5.34** Equal（包括 **equally**）、**additional** 都能返指。如果說一人、一事與另一人、一事相等，是指他們在大小、價值等方面一樣，具有程度相同的某種特徵。

> *Each Christmas Anthony sent him carefully chosen and expensive presents. He received letters of gratitude composed with **equal care**.*（…with equal care.即：…with as much care as the care taken in choosing the presents. 寫信的精心程度與挑選禮品時的精心程度一樣。）
> 每次聖誕節，安東尼都送給他精心挑選、價格昂貴的禮品。安東尼收到的是同樣精心寫成的感謝信。

> *She was not used to making apologies and she was **equally nervous** about developing relationships.*
> 她不太習慣向人道歉，也同樣害怕與別人發展關係。

> *Nick was already nursing a grudge against her because of what happened this morning. She did not want to give him any **additional cause for grievance**.*（第一個理由是"上午發生的事"。）
> 因為上午發生的事，尼克已經對她懷恨在心。她因此不想再給他增添不滿的理由。

Equally、additionally 作連接語的用法，見 3.12 和 3.4 節。

# 書面語中習慣用語
# Written conventions

**5.35**  本章已經討論過的詞語既能用於口語又能用於書面語。不過有些詞語是專門為寫文章的人在指稱語篇中的另一部份時使用。

## as we have seen, as we saw (earlier), as we shall see

**5.36**  寫文章的人有時為了引起讀者注意，用 **as we have seen** 或 **as we shall see** 這樣的短語說明自己在指稱文章的某個部份。As we have seen 後的 earlier 可用也可不用；as we shall see 後的 later 也是可用可不用。

> ***As we have seen**, the increase in the prison population is due to an increase in long-term sentences.*
> 正如我們已經知道的那樣，監獄裏人數的增加是由於被判長期徒刑的人數增加之故。

> ***As we saw earlier**, the evidence of the past is hard to read, but easy to interpret wrongly.*
> 正如我們早些時候了解的那樣，過去的證據不易讀懂，卻容易被作出錯誤的解釋。

> *For this reason, **as we saw in Part Two**, a fat such as butter is better to cook with than sunflower oil.*
> 正如我們在第二部份讀到過的那樣，由於這個理由，黃油這類油脂比向日葵油更適合於烹飪。

> *The acquisition of this technology places a great burden on the foreign currency resources of the underdeveloped countries, although **as we shall see later on** this may be lessened by various forms of aid.*
> 獲取這種技術給不發達國家外匯資源帶來沉重的負擔，雖然，正如我們稍後會了解的那樣，這種負擔可以通過多種形式的援助得以緩解。

## above, below

**5.37**  **Above** 和 **below** 只用於書面語，通常返指和預指同一章裏出現的語篇。

> *As we saw **above** in the section on product quality and service, the customer will pay more readily if the product and service match expectations.*
> 正如我們在上面討論產品質量和產品服務一節已經了解到的那樣，如果產品質量和產品服務達到預想的要求，顧客就會樂意掏出更多的錢。

> *The numerical symbols in the Index (pages 2-3) are explained **below**.*
> 索引部份（第 2 頁至第 3 頁）用數字表示的符號解釋如下。

## as follows, the following

**5.38**  **As follows**、**the following** 也差不多只用於書面語，在它們後面緊接的是任何列舉的事實或解釋。短語 the following 可以有自己的名詞。

*Prepare a mayonnaise sauce **as follows**: In a bowl place egg yolks, mustard, salt and pepper. Pour the oil in gradually while beating with a whisk.*

製作蛋黃醬的程序如下：把蛋黃、芥末、鹽和胡椒粉放進碗裏。用攪拌器攪拌時緩緩倒進食油。

*The question at issue is **the following**: what does scientific criticism of ideals and value-judgements mean and what is its purpose?*

審議中的問題如下：對理想和價值判斷的科學評論的意思是甚麼以及這種評論的目的是甚麼？

*Please therefore place in the Boston Globe automobile classified advertising section **the following notice**: 'WANTED: Blue Mercedes Benz'.*

因此請在波士頓環球報的汽車分類廣告欄內刊登如下啟事："求購：藍色梅塞德斯奔馳轎車"。

*The orders for a trip to Italy included **the following instructions**: All players will report to the Great Western Railway Hotel, Paddington, London, in time for dinner early on Saturday evening.*

對意大利之行的命令包括如下的指示：全體球員去倫敦帕丁敦的火車西站大飯店報到，及時趕上星期六晚上時間較早的晚餐。

## chapter, section

**5.39**　書的作者希望讀者了解自己是在進行返指或預指時，可以提及被指稱的章、節。

*We saw in a previous chapter that audio tapes playing suitable music can be very useful as preparation for meditation.*

我們在上一章已經了解到，用錄音帶放送合適的音樂可以作為默想的有用的準備。

*As we've already discussed in an earlier chapter, we warm more to people who we assume are similar to ourselves than to those who don't appear to be.*

正如我們在前面一章已經討論過的那樣，對認為是與自己相像的人與看上去不像自己的人相比，我們對前者更容易產生好感。

*We shall see in the next chapter that language plays an exceedingly important part in the process of memory.*

我們將在下一章了解到，語言在記憶過程中起着極其重要的作用。

*As was noted in the previous section, policies of prevention and community care in all the services led to a renewed interest in family welfare.*

正如前一節說過的那樣，預防措施和全方位服務的社區關愛會導致人們重新對家庭福利產生興趣。

*The next section looks at the causes of stress in more detail.*

下一節將更為詳盡地討論緊張關係的起因。

▶注意◀ 請留意上列例證裏與 as we saw、as we have seen、as we shall see 類似的其他不同的形式。

## the last chapter

**5.40**　從理論上說，**the last chapter** 會產生歧義，理由是它可以指 the previous chapter to this（本章前的一章），也可以指 the final chapter of the book（本書

的最後一章）。不過在實際運用中，寫話者指稱自己的語篇時，它總是返指前面出現的一章，這從動詞時態可以看出。

> ***As we have seen in the last chapter***, *competitive, pluralistic politics is likely to mean that a wide variety of points of view and interests is brought to bear on matters of urban development.*
> 同我們在上一章已經了解的那樣，相互競爭的多元政治可能意味着形形色色的觀點和利益都可能影響都市發展的問題。

> ***In the last chapter we looked briefly at*** *the idea that language acquisition is partly genetic and partly the result of experience.*
> 我們在上一章對語言習得部份屬於遺傳、部份出自經驗這一說法進行了簡要的論述。

# 6 指稱：名詞
## Reference: nouns

**6.1** 第 5 章裏的一些例證含有對描述行為、事件、想法、說法等的語段進行返指用的泛義名詞。論述過的名詞包括 thing 、 case 、 way 。從嚴格語法意義上講，這些詞都不是連接語，對它們的使用主要從語義出發，以它們的詞彙意義為依據，不過，當這些詞作泛義名詞使用時，通常要帶 the 、 this 之類的限定詞。所以，它們作為連接標記，有助於把句子黏合成篇，即我們理解的語段，而不是彼此毫不相干的句子隨意堆積。

我們在本章將繼續把這樣的論述擴大到更多的泛義名詞。第一，要注意這些名詞都要帶限定詞，第二，雖然這一章的大多數例證中泛義名詞都返指，但有的例證中泛義名詞卻預指。

本章的安排如下：

- 指稱各種動作、事件、情況的名詞在 6.2 − 6.15 節討論。
- 指稱事實、說法、想法的名詞在 6.16 − 6.33 節討論。
- 指稱作為語篇的語篇成分在 6.34 − 6.37 節討論。

## 行為、事件和情況
## Actions, events and situations

**6.2** 許多指稱動作、事件、情況的名詞大都屬於中性名詞——即不管指稱的是好事、壞事還是不好不壞的事，說話人都持不偏不倚的態度。但有的（如以下例證所示）卻表示出說話者是贊同還是反對的態度。

act, action, activity, course (of action), move, process

**6.3** Act 、 action 都是 "動作、行為、舉動" 的意思，含義相似。說話者用 **act** 時，表示單個的和馬上就能完成的動作，而 **action** 更偏重於動作的目的和過程。

> *He decided to put the car away in the garage. He saw **this act** as something that it was absolutely necessary for him to do at the moment.*
> 他決定把汽車放進車庫。他認為這是他當時務必要採取的行動。

*Finally he cleans all the parts of his bike in the sink so carefully that his granny, who interrupts him in **the act**, thinks he's doing the dishes.*

最後，他把自行車的各個部件在洗滌槽裏進行清洗，洗得那麼仔細以致他的祖母中止了他的行動，還以為他是在洗碗碟。

*The government says environmental taxation will be introduced only when competitor countries take **the same action**.*

政府宣稱，只有當與其競爭的國家採取相同的舉動時才徵收環境稅。

*The diploma will be duly prepared and, after it has been signed by the proper officers, it will come forward to you by registered post. I hope that **this action on our part** will afford you a small part of the pleasure which we have received in performing it.*

畢業證書將按規定製作出來，由有關官員簽字後，用掛號信寄給你。我希望我們方面的行為會讓你分享一部份我們從這項工作中得到的樂趣。

*He looked up at the sky, **the first action of any person who's been locked away against his will**.*

他抬頭望天空，這是任何一個不情願地被關押起來的人表現出的第一個動作。

*US fighters intercepted that plane and forced it to land in Italy. Now, **this action** was taken at great personal risk to those military personnel.*

美國戰鬥機攔截了那架飛機並迫使它在意大利降落。這種舉動是在冒着給軍事人員帶來巨大危險的情況下採取的。

*As for banning a record for being offensive, **such actions** often have the reverse effect. 'Relax' went straight to number one.*

至於對冒犯行為不准記錄在案，這樣的舉動常常會適得其反。"放鬆點兒"才是最好的方法。

用 **activity**（活動）時，強調涉及許多的事情發生，而且是很"繁忙"的動作。

*If you're a bricklayer or an athlete you will need more food to 'fuel' **that activity** than if you are a secretary or a student.*（that activity 即：...the activity involved in being a bricklayer or an athlete. 與砌磚工或運動員有關的活動。）

如果你是砌磚工或運動員，你的工作就比當秘書的或當學生的需要更多的營養來支持你的活動。

*A hospital has many functions to perform, including the prevention and treatment of disease, the education of both health professionals and patients, and the conduct of clinical research. **All these activities** must be conducted with an overriding concern for the patient.*

醫院有多種功能，包括防治疾病、教育醫務人員和病人及進行臨床研究。所有這一切活動的進行都必須把對病人的關心擺在最重要的位置。

通常用 **course of action**（辦事程序）或 **move**（舉動）指稱有計劃的行為。單獨用 course（即不帶 of action）比較少見，語體也比較正式。

*What he would really have liked to do was to dig his garden. However, **this course of action** was out of the question.*

他原來很想做的事就是在園子裏挖地。然而，這個行動是不可能的。

*There is little chance that any bank will introduce charges on credit balances this month, or even this year. **Such a move** would be exploited instantly by its rivals.*

任何一家銀行在本月、甚至今年收取貸方餘款費用的可能性都不大。因為這一舉措會馬上為其競爭者所利。

*Almost all state enterprises should be sold off or closed over the next few months. As with the constitution and decentralisation, **these moves** create both promise and risk.*

幾乎所有的國有企業都應該在今後的幾個月裏賣掉或者關閉。如同憲法和權力分散的情況一樣，這些舉動帶來的既有希望又有風險。

*As was the custom among Suki's people, her father said nothing to his daughter about his plans for her marriage. **Such a course** would never have entered his mind.*（Such a course 即：the idea of telling her about his plans，想把他的計劃安排告訴她）

蘇姬的父親不告訴蘇姬他對她婚事的計劃，這是他們那樣的人的習慣做法。他根本就不會想到把他的計劃告訴她。

**Process**（步驟、過程）表示一系列的動作或連續的動作。

*These huge trees, in fact, are feeding on themselves, for the moment their leaves fall they decay and become the 'food' on which the trees feed. So rapid is **this process** that only a thin topsoil is able to form.*

這些巨樹是在給自身提供食物，因為這種樹的葉子一落地就腐變成樹木的食物。這個過程進行得那麼迅速，結果只有一層薄薄的表土形成。

*He leapt on me and took away the knife, wounding me in the **process**.*

他向我撲來奪走了那把刀，接着把我刺傷。

## circumstance(s), context, position, situation, state of affairs, state

**6.4**　有時人們需要提及伴隨某事的事件或者指出某事發生時的情況。這些作為"背景"的事件或情況可用上列泛義名詞加以指稱。用複數形式 circumstances 遠比用其單數形式普通。另見 **case**：5.19 節。

*This extra production, combined with a seasonal slump in demand, has caused sharp falls in the prices of some crude oils in recent weeks. Under **these circumstances**, present market weakness is hardly surprising.*

這種額外的石油生產，加上季節性的需求下降，在最近幾週裏已經引起了原油價格的大幅度下降。在這樣的情況下，目前的市場疲軟一點兒也不令人吃驚。

*The Nuremberg trials took place in the aftermath of a great war and total surrender. **Such circumstances** are rare and do not exist in the Bosnian case.*

紐倫堡的審訊在大戰和無條件投降之後進行。這樣的情況罕見而且在波斯尼亞案件中並不存在。

*The nurses were all very nice and helpful and assumed that I knew nothing about what would be done. I'm glad they did. In **this circumstance** I am a patient, not a doctor.*

護士們都和氣、樂於助人，而且認定我對要做的事一無所知。我很高興他們有這種看法。在這種情況下，我是病人，不是醫生。

*Now at this point two odd circumstances met together. The landlords were, in fact, a religious society of the strictest Protestant principles. That was **one circumstance**. **The other** was this: the firm wrote their letter begging for a slight delay on 'Unknown World' letter paper.*

在這時，兩個奇特的情況同時發生了。那些房東們事實上屬於遵循最嚴格的清教徒教規的宗教團體。這是一個情況。另一個情況是：那家公司寫信請求暫緩製作印有未知世界的信紙。

*Not only did stress literally save our lives, but we almost became addicted to the stress reaction, liking to fight even when not necessary. In **this context**, modern man's behaviour begins to make sense.*

壓力不僅挽救我們的生命，而且我們幾乎對壓力習慣地作出反應，在沒有必要的時候也會抗爭。在這樣的情況下，現代人的行為開始有了意義。

*'I'm living on massive bank overdrafts.' — 'I understand,' Jefferson murmured, 'I'll help you.' — 'No, no,' Mahoney said, 'I'm just explaining **my position**.'*

"我是靠大量的銀行透支過日子。"──"我明白，"傑弗遜低聲說，"我會幫助你的。"──"不，不，"馬洪尼說，"我不過是在說明我的境況罷了。"

*Not much is usually said about these students who feel ashamed, embarrassed and failures. Hence it is important to know what can be done for those who find themselves in **this position**.*

人們通常不大談論那些感到羞愧、窘迫以及認為自己是失敗者的學生。因此了解到底能為那些發覺自己處於這種狀況的學生做些甚麼是重要的。

*The headlines were mostly about the current unrest and the government's inability to get on top of **the situation**.*

新聞標題的內容主要涉及目前的動亂以及政府在控制這種局面方面表現出的無能。

*I realized one morning that, in the near future, there would only be the two of us at breakfast. The two of us: **that state of affairs** which I secretly hoped for.*

一天早晨我意識到，在不久的將來，吃早飯時只有我們兩人。就我們兩人：這是我悄悄期待的情況。

*The rest of the children were illegitimate, **a very terrible state of affairs** in those days.*

其餘的孩子都是私生子，這在當時是一件很糟的事情。

*The only thing that irritated me was that I could not shave. I could feel the stubble on my face, **a state of affairs** I have always found intolerable.*

唯一使我煩燥的是我無法刮臉。我能感到自己臉上長出的短髭，這樣的情況是我一直不能忍受的。

**State** 通常指稱某人在精神、軀體或情感方面的狀況。

*Being in an hypnotic trance is rather like being on the borderland between sleep and waking. You feel warm and comfortable and drowsy. While in **this state** your logical mind fades into the background.*

處於催眠後的恍惚狀況很像入睡和甦醒之間的臨界狀態。你感到暖和、舒適和昏昏欲睡。在這種情況下，你的邏輯思維能力逐漸退到次要的地位。

*He'd obviously been drinking and he looked flushed and angry. I've never seen him in **such a state** before or since.*

他顯然剛喝過了酒，臉孔紅紅的、一付生氣的樣子。我在過去和此後都從來沒有看見他處在那樣的狀態。

## plight, predicament

**6.5**　名詞 **plight** 指處於艱難的、有時是危險的境況。

*When her husband died of tuberculosis, she had been turned out of her cottage with her nine-year-old daughter. Walking by chance in a lane close to Oldbury, she met my father and told him of **her plight**.*

她丈夫死於肺結核時，她和自己 9 歲的女兒被趕出了自家的小屋。在她漫無目地走在一條靠近歐爾貝瑞的小巷時，碰見我的父親並向他講述了自己的苦境。

*Schrader was horrified when he saw the conditions the slum children had to live in. He donates hundreds of thousands of dollars every year to ease **their plight**.*

席拉達看到貧民區兒童生活條件時感到震驚。他每年捐出大量的金錢來緩解他們的困境。

名詞 **predicament** 與 plight 的意義相似，但可以指一個人面臨麻煩必須作出選擇或決定的境況。

*This remarkably sensitive thinker stood at the crossroads of the 'modern' and the 'post-modern', but felt nothing but despair in **this predicament**.*

這位特別敏感的思想家處在 "現代" 派和 "後現代" 派的十字路口，在這種窘局下他只能感到絕望。

*He realized that the barge had stopped. He knew by the hum of the engine that it was out of gear. He began to worry about **his predicament** and studied the river bank, hoping to find a place to climb out. There was none.*

他意識到駁船已經停了下來。從發動機的嗡嗡聲他判斷傳動裝置出了問題。他開始為自己的困境擔心，仔細看着河岸，希望能找到一個地方爬上去。但那裏卻沒有。

## result, development, effect, outcome

**6.6**　以上列出的是這類名詞的一部份，可用來表示被看成是由別的事件或動作引起的各種事件或狀態。

*By 1985 the share of manufactures in the exports of these countries was approaching that of industrialized countries. **This result** should dispel the notion that developing countries are dependent on exports of agricultural products.*

1985年之前，這些國家製造業在出口方面佔的份額已經接近工業化國家的水平。這樣的業績理應消除認為發展中國家的出口依賴農產品的看法。

*During another experiment, though, she saw two images. **This result** was unexpected but turned out to be extremely important.*

然而，在另一次試驗中，她看到了兩個映像。這個結果出乎意料，但卻證明是極為重要的。

*Through sheer grit and determination he managed to climb back from 26th to sixth at the finish. 'I could be very pleased with **this result** later,' he said.*

全靠毅力和決心，他成功地從第 26 樓爬回到終點的 6 樓。 "我以後也能對這樣的成績而感到高興，" 他說。

*Politically, a Russian military commitment would be a great fillip. But Moscow's leaders seem effectively to have ruled out **such a development**.*

在政治上，俄國的軍事承諾或許會帶來很大的促進。不過，莫斯科領導人似乎在實際上已經排除了這一進展。

*Chemistry was continually advancing knowledge of both the organic and inorganic world. Moreover, many of **these developments** were directly useful in industry.*

化學在不斷推進人們對有機界和無機界的認識。此外，許多認識方面的新進展在工業上有直接的用途。

*Vegetarians have significantly thinner blood and lower blood pressure than meat eaters. **This effect** is caused partly by a reduction in the number of red blood cells.*

素食者比肉食者的血紅濃度更為稀薄、血壓更低。這樣的情況部份是由血紅細胞數量減少所致。

*The court decided that the time she had already served in prison was sufficient punishment for the manslaughter charge. **This outcome** could just as easily have occurred with a male defendant.*

法庭判決，她在牢房服刑的時間已經是對她過失殺人罪的足夠懲罰。這樣的判決無疑也可以發生在男性被告身上。

## episode, event, experience

**6.7** 已發生的重要的或非同尋常的事可以説成是 **episode**（重要情節、插曲）、**event**（要事、大事）或 **experience**（體驗、經歷）。

*If you should remember anything else about that visit of yours to the garage, anything at all, give me a ring. The more you go over **the episode** in your mind, the more real it will become.*

如果你回憶起你去車庫所經歷的別的情況，甚麼情況都行，請給我打電話。你越是反覆回憶事情的主要情節，整個情況就會變得更加真實。

*I had to walk a mile and a half before I found a petrol station that had a tow truck. One of the mechanics drove me back to the car, took off the damaged tyre, and took it back to the station to be patched. After it was repaired, he brought it back to the car and put it on. **The entire episode** took over two-and-half hours.*

我不得不步行一英里半路才找到一個有拖曳車的加油站。那裏的一個機械師駕車把我送到我汽車的出事地，取下壞掉的輪胎並把它帶回加油站修補。輪胎修好後，他又把它帶回去安裝好。整個事件用了兩個半小時。

*The husband subsequently pleaded guilty to the assault and was convicted. At the time of **the event** the victim was 38 and had four children.*

後來，那個丈夫對施行強暴認罪並被定罪。事件發生的時候，受害人 38 歲並有四個孩子。

*Of course if you are going to a party, or performing an important public role, that's different. Just make sure your make-up all comes off after **the event**.*

當然，你去作客或者充當一個重要公眾人物，那就不同了。不過在事後一定要卸去你的化妝。

名詞 **experience** 強調從事件參與人的立場來看待事件。

*To his surprise, he was met by sullen apathy.* **The experience** *disturbed him, he was used to an enthusiastic welcome.*

使他吃驚的是，他受到冷淡的待遇。這種經歷讓他感到不安，他習慣受到熱情歡迎。

*And now came perhaps* **the worst experience of all** — *fire. Not fire aboard the ship* — *that would have been easy to escape* — *but fire on the surface of the sea.*

後來有了也許算是最糟糕的經歷 ——火災。不是在船上的火災 ——這樣的火災容易脫逃 ——而是發生在海面上的火災。

偶爾把物體而不是把人說成有過某種經歷。這是比喻性的用法，為了達到幽默的效果。

*Most of the furniture had spent the last six months in storage and some of it, she thought, looked a little worse for* **the experience**.

絕大多數傢俱近半年之久都在貯存之中，在她看來，其中的部份因為有了這段經歷，看起來就比過去稍差了一些。

☞ 比較 **incident**；見 6.15 節。

## manner, method, means, practice, system

**6.8**　有的名詞指稱做事的方式方法。**Method** 表示的是有目的而慎重的方法；**practice**、**system** 表示的是有規律的或者重複的做法。

*My children lay down upon the earth, and in* **this manner** *we passed the entire night.*

我的孩子們躺在泥地上，我們就這樣度過了整個夜晚。

*Before killing them, they fire shots in the air in order to attract the attention of people living nearby. In* **this manner**, *the soldiers ensure that the executions are witnessed by friends and families of the victims.*

在處死他們之前，士兵們對空鳴槍以引起附近居民的注意。士兵們以這樣的方式確保死者的朋友和家人成為他們行刑的見證人。

*Leave the beans to stand for 6-8 hours in a cool place, then drain. The harder the bean, the more it will benefit from longer soaking so* **this method** *is advisable for soya beans, chick peas and butter beans especially.*

把豆子在陰涼處放置 6 — 8 個小時，然後把水滴乾。豆子愈是乾硬，就愈能得益於較長時間的浸泡，所以用這種方法處理大豆、雞豆、尤其是腎形豆等是可取的。

*In 1823 acupuncture was mentioned in a leading medical journal and in 1824 Dr Elliotson, a physician at St Thomas's Hospital, London, began to use* **this method of treatment**.

1823年，一份第一流醫學雜誌提到了針刺療法。1824年，艾略森醫生，倫敦聖·托馬斯醫院的一名內科大夫，開始使用這種治療方法。

*The elite troops should be sent in to attack at whatever point the enemy appeared to be weakened. By* **this means** *the decisive attack would come as a surprise.*

應該派遣精銳部隊對敵方的看來正在削弱的地方進攻。這種方式就會使起決定作用的進攻成為突襲。

*Where agriculture gave poor returns, people had to search for **other means** to supplement their diet.*
在農作物收穫差的地區，人們不得不想其他辦法補充主食的不足。

*Claude may have done some painting outdoors and certainly Constable did, but **the practice** was not widespread at this time.*
克羅德大概在室外作過一些畫，而康斯特布爾肯定在室外作過，不過這種做法當時並不盛行。

*We found that the management was passing discounts in cash to individuals who gave them business. When I found out I gave the management three months to stop **the practice**.*
我們發現經理部把打折部份用現金付給同他們做生意的個人。當我了解這種情況時我給了他們三個月時間停止這種作法。

*You may set up a trust fund in which you place cash in trust for whomever you wish. **This system** avoids the highest levels of taxation and often carries out your instructions well.*
你可以設立信託基金把你要給任何他人的錢託管起來。用這種辦法可以避免最高稅收，並且常常能保證執行好你的指示。

*A further act of Parliament took the regulation of admissions and detention of mental patients out of legal hands and gave it over to doctors. Most psychiatrists felt that **this system** worked well.*
後來的國會法案把接收和阻留精神病患者的權利從司法部門轉交給醫務人員。大多數精神病醫生認為這種作法很有作用。

## phenomenon, possibility

**6.9  Phenomenon** 表示相當奇怪又為人們目睹發生的事。這是一個較為正式的詞。

*Steve opened his mouth as if to speak, but stopped talking even before he had started. Rose knew **that phenomenon**. She still saw it daily, as if Steve had words ready to pour out to her and bit them back.*
史蒂夫張開口彷彿要說話，但是還沒有說出口又停住了。羅斯熟悉這個現象。她每天都看見這個現象，彷彿史蒂夫已經想好了話要向她吐露卻又縮回去了。

*The pilot recalled some difficulty in reading the thermometers, not realizing that he was suffering from an inadequate supply of oxygen. **This insidious phenomenon** leaves its victim in a state of euphoria, unaware that his physical and mental processes have been seriously affected.*
飛行員記得自己讀溫度表度數時感到很費勁，而沒有意識到自己當時已受供氧不足之苦。這種暗中為害的現象使他處於過度欣快的狀態，殊不知自己的心理和生理過程已經受到嚴重的影響。

**Possibility** 表示可能發生的事。

*'The police may have the car followed and may even have it stopped on some pretext', Rebet persisted. 'I have foreseen **that possibility**; that is why a second car will follow the first one'.*

"警察可以對那輛車進行跟蹤並且找借口要車停下",瑞別特堅持說:"我已經預見到這種可能性;那就是為甚麼會有一輛車跟着前一輛的原因。"

*The thyroid gland can either over- or under-function. Either of **these possibilities** causes a change in the person's psychological functioning as well as in their physical well-being.*

甲狀腺的功能可能亢進也可能減退。兩種可能性中的任何一種除改變人的生理健康外,還改變人的心理活動。

## achievement, exploit, feat

**6.10** 這三個名詞都用來指稱需要努力才能完成的動作。用**achievement**不一定指要用體力的動作,而可能是通過考試或力勸他人做事之類的動作。**Exploits**、**feats** 指一般都要用體力完成的動作,而 feat 常常指相當困難的動作。在通常情況下, achievement 、 feat 都表示稱讚:把某個動作説成 exploit ,是因為説話者認為該動作勇敢和有趣,但也可能是説話者並不贊成。

*Many famous and successful people have mastered the outward skills of confident behaviour and their very success in a credit to **this achievement**.*

許多有名望和成功的人都學會了外表上表現出自信的技巧,他們的成功就是對這種成就的褒獎。

*She has now learned to walk about with the help of crutches and stand while resting against chairs or tables. But the numerous scars on her frail, underdeveloped legs bear testimony to the suffering involved in **these achievements**.*

她現在已經能借助拐杖走來走去並能扶着椅子或桌子站立起來。但是她那虛弱、發育不全的雙腿上的無數傷疤證明她取得這樣成功的過程中所經受的折磨。

*Louis Bleriot flew his light aircraft across the Channel to Dover on 25 July 1909. **This achievement** ranks alongside that of Lindbergh.*

路易斯·布萊里奧於1909年7月25日駕駛輕型飛機越過英吉利海峽抵達多佛。他的這個成就可與林德伯格的成就相媲美。

*After graduating from high school, having learned nothing except how to put the school paper to press, he joined a friend in canoeing 2,200 miles from Minneapolis to Canada's Hudson Bay. **The exploit** helped land him a job as a copy boy on the Minneapolis Journal.*

中學畢業後,除了送校報去付印外,他甚麼技術都未學會,後來他與一個朋友一道駕獨木舟從美國的明尼阿波利斯到加拿大的哈德遜灣行程 2 千 2 百英里。這一壯舉使他在明尼阿波利斯日報謀到一份工作,當上了送遞稿件的勤務工。

*Rebels have been operating with a captured fishing boat, and also with coastguard vessels taken from the government. Among **their other exploits** they managed to hijack a cargo ship laden with rice and divert it to their headquarters.*

叛亂分子一直在用一艘掠奪的漁船及從政府手裏搶來的海岸警衛船隻進行活動。他們的其他活動還包括把劫掠來的一艘運大米的貨船改裝成自己的指揮部。

*He paid an architect to design a house for him, and had it built far enough under the estimate (**not too difficult a feat** in those years of falling prices) to be able to afford a swimming pool.*

他出錢聘請一名建築師為他設計了一幢房子並把房子以遠遠低於預算價格造好（在那價格不斷下降的歲月裏這不算難以辦到的舉動），因而能造一個游泳池。

*He jumped as high in the air as he could and jumped backwards over the fence. She could see the gleeful expression on his face as he dared her to attempt **the same feat**.*

他高高地躍起往後一跳翻過圍欄。她看得出他向她挑戰要她作同樣的動作時所表現出興高采烈的樣子。

## affair, business

**6.11    Affair** 是一個常見的具有幾種意義的詞，其中一個意義表示為人們不贊成的一個事件或一系列事件，理由是事件裏含有不誠實或犯罪的成分。

*They argued that the letter bombs and equipment in Mr Byrne's flat had been planted. Certainly, **the affair** seemed to have been conducted in an extremely amateurish way.*

他們認為波爾恩的公寓的書信炸彈及其設備是事先安放的。可以肯定，這事看來是由很外行的人所為。

*The theft of $10,000 was serious enough, or so the police thought. They found his assertion that he had also tried to assassinate the Vice-President scarcely credible. The full truth of **the affair** was hushed up until 1993.*

警方認為偷竊一萬元已算夠嚴重的了。而對他試圖暗殺副總統的證供，警方更感到難以置信。這件事被遮掩起來，直到 1993 年才真相大白。

*Why would he take the dog along with him at the risk of being bitten? Odder still, why had the dog followed this stranger? Leonora sighed. None of the questions could be answered. Everything about **this affair** offended her innate sense of order.*

為甚麼他冒着被咬傷的險也要帶着那隻狗呢？更奇怪的是，為甚麼那隻狗會跟着這個陌生人？利奧諾拉嘆了口氣。以上的問題沒有一個能得到解答。關於這件事的一切都不合她內在的思考條理。

**Business** 也能表示某種事件。它有時指一件複雜的或困難的活動、令人迷惑的事件或難以處理的問題。

*A full medical history and examination will be carried out of both of you. The **whole business** may be rather depressing, and you could well be letting yourself in for a whole series of tests and investigations spanning several years.*

將對你們兩人的健康史和身體情況作徹底的了解和檢查。整個了解和檢查可能使人感到相當壓抑，你們可能陷入拖延數年的一系列測試和調查之中。

*Finishing his drink, he went to bed, **a business** easily accomplished by him these days as he simply took off some clothes and crawled under the sheets.*

喝完酒後，他就去睡覺，這事對他來說很容易，因為在這些日子裏他只要把衣服一脫往被單下一鑽就行了。

## crisis, difficulty, problem, dilemma

**6.12**　不幸的情況或無論如何都需要作出的困難決定可以看作是 **crisis**（危機）、**difficulty**（難事）、**problem**（難以處理的事）或 **dilemma**（進退維谷的困境）。

*Nearly all the factories in the nation have closed, and food and money are scarce. News of **this crisis** is only beginning to spread beyond its borders.*
那個國家幾乎所有的工廠都關閉了，食物和貨幣短缺。關於這一危機的消息已經開始擴散到外國。

*Though the small body was cold and senseless, the doctor could detect a faint pulse and he was able to massage him back to consciousness. The child survived **this crisis** to make a complete recovery.*
雖然幼小的軀體冷而無知覺，醫生仍能感到微弱的脈動，能用按摩使他恢復知覺。孩子度過了這場危機並完全康復過來。

*The industry is remarkably secretive one and both sellers and buyers are reluctant to reveal the cost of transactions. To **these difficulties** should be added those of fluctuating sterling/dollar rates and significant and rapid changes in production costs.*
工業界的運作是出奇地守口如瓶，買賣雙方都不肯披露交易的費用。除了上述困難外，還有英鎊/美元匯率波動以及生產費用巨大而迅速的變化所造成的困難。

*Increased flexibility in the eyeball may cause vision to deteriorate as the day wears on. **Another difficulty** is that in about one in four patients, the effect of the operation is progressive, causing them to end up long-sighted.*
眼球的活動隨着一天時間的推移而增加，這可能引起視力減退。另一難題是每 4 個病人中約有 1 人，由於手術效果是累進的，最後可能成為遠視眼。

*Texts in exotic and unfamiliar foreign languages are far, far harder for singers to memorize than texts in their native languages. That has been **a recurring problem** with such operas.*
對演唱者來說，用奇異的、不常見的外語寫成的歌詞比用他們自己的母語寫成的歌詞記憶起來難上加難。這是排演這類歌劇時一直遇到的困難。

用 **dilemma** 強調難以確定的抉擇，這時不管用哪種解決辦法都不是完全令人滿意的。

*I used to wonder what responsible choice we could make: using paper destroys trees while plastic pollutes the planet. Lately I've been avoiding **this dilemma** by bringing my own canvas bags when I go to the store.*
我曾常常尋思，怎麼才算負責任的選擇：用紙袋會造成伐木毀林，而用塑料袋又要污染地球。最近我去商店時帶帆布袋避開了這個進退兩難的問題。

*The two aims might come into conflict: you will need to consider how you might steer your way through **such a dilemma**.*
這兩種目的可能相互衝突：你需要考慮如何才能把握好方向，度過兩難的困境。

## solution

**6.13**　問題(problems)，不管是否被看作問題，都需要解決辦法(**solutions**)。

> 'Rehabilitation is often thought of as restoring an area of land to its original conditions,' says the bank's report. 'However, **this solution** is rarely feasible. Often', it says, 'rehabilitation will mean simply restoring a cover of vegetation to eroding soils.'
>
> "復原通常被理解為恢復一片土地的原有狀況，"銀行的報告說。"然而，這個解決辦法的可行性不大。通常，"該報告接着說，"復原的含義僅限於為受浸蝕的土壤恢復植被。"

## accident, disaster, tragedy

**6.14**　不幸的事件可以說成 **accident**（事故），事故有大小之分。

> Three people died yesterday when a light aircraft crashed into trees and burst into flames soon after takeoff. **The accident** occurred at about 3 pm near Denton aerodrome.
>
> 昨天，一架輕型飛機起飛不久就猛撞在樹上墜毀，燃燒起來，有三個人死亡。事故發生在下午三時左右，在丹頓機場附近。

> You wouldn't be able to argue that your pregnancy was **a little accident** you couldn't prevent.
>
> 你不可能爭辯你的懷孕是一次自己無法阻止的小事故。

嚴重的事件或情況可以說成是 **disaster**（災難、禍患）或者 **tragedy**（悲慘事件、悲劇）。

> Thousands of persons were made homeless by the storm. The persons displaced by **this disaster** were advised to report to centers set up by the Red Cross and the Salvation Army.
>
> 暴風雨使成千上萬的人無家可歸。因為這次災難被迫撤離家園的人被告知向紅十字會和基督教救世軍設立的中心報到。

> Three months later Ian was dead. Luckily she had not been with him on the night he lost control of his car and careered into the woods. It was after **that tragedy** that Sharon decided to emigrate.
>
> 三個月後依安就去世了。所幸的是在他汽車失控衝進樹林的那天晚上，她沒有同他在一起。正是在這次悲劇之後謝爾潤才決定移居外國的。

> Although not a word about **the tragedy** appeared in the newspapers, the famine that raged in the 1930s throughout southern Russia was a matter of common knowledge.
>
> 雖然報紙上對這場饑荒悲劇隻字未提，但30年代在俄羅斯南部肆虐的饑荒是盡人皆知的事。

> On 30 July 1898 **the most appalling tragedy** struck. Thomas and his father were out in a boat when a sporting gun that was lying across Thomas's knees accidentally went off, killing his father.
>
> 1898年7月30日，駭人聽聞的慘劇突然發生了。托馬斯和他的父親在外面的一條船上，這時橫放在托馬斯膝部的獵槍意外走火，將他父親射死。

## incident

**6.15**　麻煩的或令人不快的事件，或者不平常的事件，可以説成是 **incident**（事變）。

*Ward started shouting and gesticulating and the broadcast was brought to an abrupt end. **The incident** made front page headlines.*
沃德開始大喊大叫、指手劃腳，電視播放立即就停止下來。這事件成了頭版新聞。

*If you have been the subject of a crime, try to find witnesses, and report **the incident** to the police.*
如果你成了犯罪的受害人，就要設法找到證人並向警方報告。

*In the second round of the 110 metres hurdles, Browne survived a fall, but dismissed **the incident** with a reassuring word.*
在110米跨欄賽的第二輪，布朗差點摔倒，但他對這一事故未予理會，還説了句恢復自己信心的話。

*There was just one outburst of firing during the night — **a minor incident**, compared to the pitched gun battle which took place yesterday.*
夜裏只有一次短暫的槍擊 —— 與昨天發生的對陣槍戰相比，只算是一件小事。

# 事實、陳述和想法
# Facts, statements and ideas

**6.16**　返指語篇（或有時預指語篇）可以通過把語篇描述的動作或情況加以歸類，即劃分出肯定的事實或需要討論的事（如 fact、topic）或者對某事件或情況所作的解釋（如 purpose）。前面的語篇描述的是"口頭行為"時，不管是直接還是間接引語，都可用 answer、excuse、suggestion 這樣的名詞來指稱。要是前面的語篇描述的是"心理行為"，可用 belief、idea、theory 這樣的名詞來指稱。6.16 － 6.33 節將對這類名詞進行詳細的論述。

## fact, factor

**6.17**　如果將某個事件或某個情況説成 **fact**（事實），就是毫不懷疑地承認其真實性。

*When they are told that they are suffering from some strange illness, they may not accept this straightaway. But gradually they will come to accept **the fact**.*
當告知他們患着某種怪病時，他們也許不會馬上接受。不過他們會慢慢地接受這一事實的。

*Something was convincing her that she was trapped, that escape was impossible. As **this fact** sank in, all her initial revulsion returned.*
有某種東西使她隱約地感到自己陷入了圈套，要逃出去是不可能的。當她最終充分意識到這個事實時，她最初的厭惡感又湧上心頭。

*We all had one thing in common, we had been selected to fight unwinnable parliamentary constituencies. Despite **this fact** we all learnt a great deal from our experiences.*

我們大家都有一個共同點，即我們都曾被推選出來在我們無法獲勝的議員選區裏競選。事實雖然如此，我們大家都從自己的經歷中學到了許多東西。

**Factor**（要素、因素）表示能對事態產生影響的一個事物或環境。

*Cameras can't make the kind of adjustments the brain does and **this factor** means that a drawing of a place and a photograph taken of the same spot look very different.*

照相機無法像人腦那樣作出調整，這一因素意味着表現一個地方的畫作與在同一地方拍攝的照片看起來有很大差別。

*It was a case of bad leadership, inefficient organization, lack of equipment, and **various other factors**.*

這是由於領導不力、組織鬆懈、設備缺乏及其他一些因素造成的一種情況。

## issue, matter, subject, topic

**6.18** **Issue**（爭端、重要的議題）、**matter**（思考內容、主題）、**subject**（主題、對象）、**topic**（論題、題目）用來指稱被考慮、討論或辯論的對象。Issue 常常指有爭議的事。

*Cider makers say they will be put out of business by Eurocrats who want to classify the drink as a wine because it is made from fruit. Duty on a pint could go up 500 per cent after the EC debates **the issue** this week.*

蘋果酒製造商說他們將被歐洲經濟共同體官員弄得歇業，這些官員因為蘋果酒是用水果製造的，要把這種飲料劃入果酒類。歐共體在本週對這個問題進行辯論後，對這種飲料每品脫的徵稅可能上升百分之五百。

*Andrew asked her again what she thought she had seen. She had been considering **the matter**. 'I did see him. I'm sure I did.'*

安德魯再次問她，她到底認為自己看見過甚麼。她一直在想這個問題。"我確實看見過他。我肯定看見過他。"

*He was tough on drug abuse. Sure, he'd been addicted himself but he had picked himself up and persevered with the cure. His unyielding attitude on **this subject** was that since he had done it, so could everyone.*

他對濫用麻醉藥品態度強硬。不錯，他自己曾經對麻醉藥品上癮，但卻能自拔並鍥而不捨地治癒了毛病。他在這個問題上不動搖的態度是既然他能擺脫惡習，其他人也能做到。

*I read extensively about the cholesterol issue and met most of the scientists conducting research on **the topic**.*

我大量閱讀過有關膽固醇問題的文獻，並會見了從事這個課題研究的大多數科學家。

*The chapter refers only briefly to the suitability of different parrot species to conditions in captivity. A thorough discussion of **this important topic** is, to my mind, the most significant omission from this book.*

該章只簡略地提及不同鸚鵡物種對關養條件的適應程度。在我看來，本書的最大疏漏就是缺乏對這一論題的詳盡論述。

*She believes that cannabis is less harmful than alcohol and tobacco, both of which are legal, The women intend to raise **the issue** at their national conference. 'We have studied **this subject** very closely,' she says.*

她認為大麻的害處不如酒精和煙草，而後兩樣是合法的。這些婦女打算在全國婦女大會上提出這個問題。她說，"我們對這個問題已經進行了仔細研究。"

## aspect, respect

**6.19** **Aspect**（方面）表示計劃、問題、情況或活動等某一特定特徵。

*In some ways I think avoiding the way back to smoking is more difficult than the stopping. Here are some helpful tips on **this aspect** of the problem.*

我認為防止戒煙後再抽在一定程度上比戒煙更難。這裏有幾項告誡，有助於克服這方面的困難。

*'But who might want Mrs Brown dead? That's the next question for you to tackle.' — 'We've already started on **that aspect**, sir.'*

"不過，是誰希望布朗太太死呢？這是要你解決的下一個問題。"——"先生，我們已經着手在解決這方面的問題。"

**Respect**（方面、着眼點）同 aspect 的意義相似。作為返指的名詞，常常用在 in this respect（在這方面）、in that respect（在那方面）這樣的短語裏。

*He was determinedly cheerful, and seemed dedicated only to enjoying himself. **In that respect** he was like his mother. But Tony knew that behind his half-closed eyes Richard hid a much more complex nature.*

他打定主意過得快快活活，似乎只熱衷於享受。在這方面，他像他母親。不過托尼明白在理查德半睜半閉的眼睛後面隱藏着他那更為複雜的本性。

*Our superiors were every bit as tied to their jobs as we were. It was long hours for everybody. We may have been their inferiors in the job hierarchy, but at least **in this respect** we were their equals.*

我們的上級同我們一樣完全忙於自己的工作。大家的工作時間都很長。在工作等級上可以說我們是他們的下級，不過，在忙的這方面，我們是平等的。

## purpose, end, reason

**6.20** 說話者提到 **purpose**（目的、意圖）、**end**（目的、目標）、**reason**（理由、道理）這幾個名詞時，就是在試圖解釋某種事實，或者比如說，解釋某事發生的理由。For this purpose（為此目的、為此）、to this end（為這個目標、為此）都返指某個計劃或打算，然後再說明為實現目的而進行的努力。For this reason（因為這個理由）指稱即將說明的、已發生的或將發生的事的理由。

*One poor soldier, whose leg they were about to amputate, having been laid upon a table **for this purpose**, had the other leg taken off by another cannon ball in the very middle of the operation.*

一名可憐的士兵的一條腿即將被截去，為此目的他已被放在手術台上等着。在手術中間，他的另一條腿又被一顆炮彈炸斷。

*When I go there it may be necessary for me to purchase the goodwill of certain influential men. **For this purpose** I have a fair amount of gold.*

到那裏後，我也許免不了要去收羅某些有權勢的人的友善。為此目的，我帶了相當數量的黃金。

*With archive film of the period now available, my first plan was to make an hour-long television documentary, and **to this end** I telephoned the BBC in London.*

由於能夠獲得那個時期的檔案膠片，我的第一個計劃就是製作一部一小時長的紀錄片，而且我還為此給倫敦的英國廣播公司打了電話。

*The world can, he believes, be designed so that behaviour likely to be punished seldom or never occurs: **to this end**, control of the population as a whole must be delegated to specialists, to police, priests, teachers, therapists and so on.*

他認為，還可以把世界進行一定的設計，以使可能受罰的行為很少發生或不再發生。為此目的，世界人口的控制問題必須委託給專家、警察、牧師、教師、治療專家等。

*I'm interested to find out what's universally alike in human behaviour and **for this reason** I want to see cultures which have not yet had any contact with the outside world.*

我很有興趣去發現人類行為的普遍相似之處。因為這個理由，我想去了解與外部世界迄今尚無任何接觸的文化。

*The job sometimes entailed physically searching for the victim, often under fire. It was **for this reason** that the people who flew the rescue helicopters were treated with considerable respect.*

這個工作有時需要實地查找受害人，常常是冒着炮火。正是因為這個理由，駕直升機救援的人備受尊敬。

## announcement, comment, declaration, message, remark, statement

**6.21**　表示"口頭行為"的名詞常常用來直接指稱在口頭或書面上表述過的原話。

*His eyes gleaming, the man went on, 'The original tables have hidden drawers in them. It's said that one of them holds a great secret.' **This announcement** startled the three girls.*

那人眼睛閃着光亮，繼續説道："那些新穎的桌子都有暗抽屜。據説其中一個藏有重大的秘密。"這一宣佈使三個姑娘大吃一驚。

*But I said briskly, 'Oh, I don't know. I should think most women would act like that in her position.' She looked slightly taken aback. I wondered if she resented **my comment**.*

但是我爽快地説："啊，我不知道。我倒是認為絕大多數處在她的地位的婦女都會這樣行事的。"她看上去有點吃驚。我不知道她是否對我的話有反感。

*The Minister denied that he would resign. He made **his declaration** as he arrived for lunch at the headquarters of the Arts Council in London.*
部長否認自己要辭職。他的這一聲明是在到達倫敦的美術協會總部用午餐時宣佈的。

*Attached was a small card and on it a single line in Arabic. Belle's knowledge of written Arabic was scant, and although she examined the card she had not understood **the message**.*
附在一起的有一張小卡片，上面有一行阿拉伯文字。貝爾的阿拉伯書面語知識有限，雖然她仔細看過卡片，仍然不明白那一行字的意思。

*He read the telephone number, and **the message**. It was from Ben Gibson. He had tried to ring Arnold; would Arnold be kind enough to ring him back?* （注意，此例 message 預指前部份。）
他看過電話號碼和留言。那是本‧吉布遜給他的。他試圖給阿諾德打過電話；阿諾德願意給他回電嗎？

*'I know she must be sad that Gran died, but money's always a great consolation.' — 'Now, now, Roger, I'm sure you didn't mean it, but **that remark** was in very poor taste.'*
"我知道她一定為格蘭的去世感到悲哀，不過，金錢總是一個大的安慰。" ——"好了，好了，羅傑。我肯定這話不是你的本意，不過，你的那句話不得體。"

*'There was a team of policemen here all evening after dinner,' he said. To his surprise Milton accepted **the statement** without question.*
"晚飯後整個晚上都有一隊警察留在這裏，"他說。米爾頓對他這一宣佈並不表示異議，這使他感到吃驚。

## account, description, information, reference

**6.22** 另外一些指稱書面或口頭上某種敍述的泛義名詞有 **account**（敍述、報道）、**description**（描述、說明）、**information**（信息、情報）、**reference**（指稱、參照）。

*The book tells us that the Archbishop of London, in union with the bishops and nobles of the land, made Arthur, then a youth of fifteen years of age, King of Britain in the year 516. Although no mention is here made of his coronation in London, it seems to be implied in **this account**.*
這本書告訴我們，倫敦的大主教，聯合了國內的主教和貴族，在公元 516 年立阿瑟這個當時只有 15 歲的青年為英國國王。雖然書中不曾提及在倫敦舉行加冕典禮，但是書中的敍述似乎已經使這事不言而喻。

*'Well, Robert. So you're going to be one of our avenging angels.' Robert did not particularly relish the description.*
"好啊，羅伯特。瞧你將成為我們復仇天使中的一員。"羅伯特並不特別喜歡對他進行這樣的描述。

*'I think I was home by about quarter past four. I know I had afternoon tea as soon as I got in.' — 'I see,' I said. My mind was chewing over **this information**.*
"我想我大約在四點一刻前就到了家裏。我記得一到家就吃下午茶點。"——"我明白了，"我說。我心裏琢磨他提供的這一信息。

*Somebody described Barnett and his staff as a black hole surrounded by a vacuum. Quite good, yes. Although Williams laughed at **this reference** to the current chairman, his mind was elsewhere.*

有人把巴那特和他的員工形容成真空包圍起來的黑洞。對，説得好。雖然威廉斯為這樣説及現任主席而感到好笑，但心裏卻想着別的事。

## belief, conclusion, idea, plan, theory, view, viewpoint

**6.23**　有些名詞用來專門指稱心理過程，不過這類過程當然可以在後來的口頭或書面敍述中加以表達。

如果説一個人有某種 **belief**（信念），則表示此人確信某事的真實性。

*In fact I thought she must be dead by now, though I had no reason for **this belief** since she was younger than I am.*

實際上我認為此時他肯定已經死了，雖然我的這種信念缺乏道理，因為她比我年輕。

*Any form of racism is distressing to witness, but Suki found it even more disturbing to encounter **such beliefs** amongst her own community.*

目睹任何形式的種族歧視都是令人苦惱的，但是蘇克發現自己所在社區存在這類信念時，她更感不安。

用 **conclusion**（結論）表示經過仔細考慮後得出的結果。

*He must have dropped his shoes when he sank in the canal. Just as he came to **that conclusion** the light from the windows disappeared.*

他肯定是在運河裏下沉時把鞋弄丟了。就在他得出這個結論時，燈光從那些窗戶裏熄滅了。

*'You mean somebody tried to kill us?' Bess asked. Nancy frowned. 'I don't think we can draw **that conclusion** from the evidence,' she said slowly.*

"你是説有人試圖殺害我們嗎？"貝斯問道。南希皺了皺眉。"我想我們無法從那個證據得出這種結論，"她慢慢地説。

**Idea**（主意、意見、想法）的意義有時與 belief（信念）、opinion（意見、看法）、theory（意見、揣測）相似；有時它的意義又與 suggestion（建議、提議）或 advice（忠告、建議）接近。

*He doesn't know I'm here because **the idea** hasn't occurred to him.*

他不知道我在這裏，因為他腦子裏從來不會出現這種想法。

*What better place to start the TV series than the island of Corfu where I had lived as a child. I was pleased with **this idea** since I had not visited the island for many years.*

拍這部電視連續劇沒有任何地方比我兒時生活過的科孚島更好。我為有這種主意感到高興，因為我已經多年不去那裏了。

*We were a player short and the priority was to determine whether Geoff Cook would be joining us. Frankly, I believed he would, as he had earlier seemed quite keen on **the idea**.*

我們少一名球員，首先要考慮的事就是確定吉弗‧庫克是否願意加盟。坦率地說，我認為他會願意的，因為他早些時候表示出對這一意向的興趣。

**Plan**（計劃、方案）表示預先確定某事如何進行。

*The French President and the German Chancellor have proposed a joint army corps that could be a basis for a European defence force. **This plan** was outlined in a letter to the leadership of the European Union.*

法國總統和德國總理建議成立作為歐洲防務力量基礎的聯合軍團。在給歐洲聯盟領導層的一封信裏對這個計劃作了概述。

*She denied reports that the United States was to build a military training base in northern Peru. She said there were **no such plans** at present.*

她否認有關美國打算在秘魯北部建立軍事訓練基地的報道。她說眼下還沒有這樣的計劃。

**Theory**（意見、揣測）表示雖無法證明但卻認為是真實的事。

*I'll bet you this is where it happened, because these are the sort of scratches a woman's heels would make on the floor. To test **my theory**, I walked a few steps away and scraped my own high heel against the tile.*

我肯定這是事件的發生地，因為這些是女性的鞋跟在地面上磨出的痕跡。為了證明我的推測，我走開了幾步，邊走邊用高鞋跟刮擦地上鋪設的地磚。

*They were all overjoyed, and secretly, although I have no evidence to support **the theory**, I believe Her Royal Highness was equally pleased.*

他們非常高興，而且我還私下認為，公主殿下也同樣高興，不過我還無法證實自己的推測。

**View**（想法、看法、見解）、**viewpoint**（觀點、見解）與 opinion 大體上同義。

*I really believe that one is a doctor in order to save life, anywhere and at any time. For forty years I have never departed from **this view**.*

我真的認為當醫生是為了救死扶傷，何時何地都是這樣。40 年來我從未背離過這種觀點。

*As far as Galton was concerned, a person's intelligence was a relatively fixed quantity. **This viewpoint** of Galton's found a ready audience among American psychologists.*

在戈爾頓看來，人的智力是一個相對穩定的量。他的這個觀點立即在美國心理學家中得到共鳴。

## suggestion

**6.24** **Suggestion**（想法、建議）主要指（在口頭或書面上）提供給他人的意見和計劃。因此，有時它的意義與起解釋作用的 idea（想法）或 theory（揣測）差不多。

*People in the town started saying we were burning bodies. But it is not true. Until then, no one had even made **such a suggestion**.*

城裏人開始說我們是在燒死人屍體。但那不是事實，在此之前，誰也沒有提出過這樣的想法。

*A rumour went round the capital that he had heart disease. Officials would not comment on **this suggestion**, even to deny it.*

說他患了心臟病的謠言在首都不脛而走。官員們對這種揣測不加評論，甚至也不予否定。

但有時 suggestion 指稱可以加以實施的建議。

*Trade union leaders appealed for the government to suspend the price rise until Monday. But **this suggestion** was rejected by the finance minister.*

工會領導人呼籲政府把物價上調推遲到星期一。但是，這一建議被財政部長拒絕了。

*'I shall speak to him myself,' Nina said firmly. 'If you wish, dear,' Tom sighed. He knew from experience that if he opposed **the suggestion** too violently Nina would become more obstinate.*

"我要親自找他談談，"尼娜堅定地說道。"那就隨你吧，親愛的，"湯姆嘆息道。他從經驗中知道，對她的意見過於反對，她反倒會更加固執己見。

## promise, question, request, answer, reply, response

**6.25**　有幾個名詞常常用來指稱屬於不同類型的口頭敍述（不過，它們也能指稱書面敍述）。這些名詞包括 **promise**（承諾、答應）、**question**（質疑、問題）、**request**（請求、懇求）、**answer**（回答、應答）、**reply**（答覆）。

*'Paloma,' she whispered, 'Paloma, I'm here. I've come to take you home.' She made **the promise** for both of them.*

"帕樓瑪，"她低聲說，"帕樓瑪，是我。我來把你們領回去，"她向他們倆作出這樣的承諾。

*He kept Paul talking, asking **questions** about the hotel. 'Did the Kemptons own it? Or merely manage it? Was it they who had extended it?' And among **such questions** he slipped in more personal ones.*

他使保爾不停地說話，一再問他有關飯店的問題。"飯店是肯普頓家的嗎？還是由他們家經營？是他們家擴大了飯店的規模嗎？"他問着問着就插進了更帶私人色彩的問題。

*'Now, please leave me alone.' He ignored **her request**, 'So I have done something to upset you? What?'*

"行了，請不要打擾我。"他沒有理會她的請求，"是我做了讓你不開心的事嗎？是甚麼事呢？"

*'There must have been dozens of people who'd seen him.' Connors had **a ready answer**. 'He was obviously wearing a wig. Nobody would connect the man in your photo with him.'*

"肯定有許多人見過他。"康納斯對這個問題有現成的回答，"顯然他戴着假髮。誰也不會把照片上的人同他聯繫起來。"

*'I presume you kissed her, did you?' — 'Yes.' **The reply** was almost a whisper.*

"我認為你吻過她，是嗎？"——"是的。"他的回答低得像耳語。

有時，**response** 與 answer、reply 的意義大體相似，但由於它表示某種感情或心理反應，所以在詞義上與 answer，reply 相比，中性意義的成分更少（Response 的意義還包含不用詞語表示的反應）。

*The report brought **this response** from one local inhabitant: 'Your broadcast today has left me a bit confused'.*
報告上有一位本地居民的反應：“你們今天的播放有點把我弄糊塗了。”

*Laura then relayed to her husband the psychoanalyst's shattering pronouncement.*
***His response** was delivered in a sharp tone of voice. 'How much did it cost you?!'*
勞拉後來向她丈夫傳達了精神分析學家那令人震驚的看法。他以刺耳的聲音作出反應：“花了你多少錢？”

## argument, assertion, claim, criticism, objection, opinion, point

**6.26**　人們的態度，通常是不可動搖的並且是堅定地表達出來的，可以用不同的方式指稱。 **Assertion**（斷言、聲明）、**claim**（主張、斷言）都表示堅定的陳述、聲明。

*'You take what you can get in this world, Johnny.' Pilarski held up his hand. 'No. You take what you deserve. No more, no less.' Charlie turned to me. 'We have **this argument** all the time.'*
“約翰尼，一個人應該獲取他在世上能夠得到的東西。”皮拉斯基舉起了一隻手。“不，一個人應該獲取他該得到的東西。不多，也不少。”查理轉向我說。“我們一直都有這樣的爭論。”

*More political leaders tend to be assassinated in times, if not of peace, then at least when their countries are not fighting for survival in a formal state of war. Some evidence for **that assertion** will be discovered in the assassination index which forms part of this study.*
更多的政治領袖可能遭到暗殺，即使不是發生在和平時期，但至少也不是他們國家為求生存而處於戰爭狀態的時期。這一斷言的某些證據可以在構成這份研究報告一個部份的暗殺指數中發現。

*I asked a woman in the factory how they coped with the terrible smell on bad days. 'Ach, we don't really notice it,' she said, with a wry smile that cancelled out **the claim**.*
我問過那家工廠的一名女性，她們在壞日子裏如何應付那種難以忍受的氣味。“艾奇，我們真的沒留意到這種氣味，”她苦笑着說，抵消了我的斷言。

*The claim is that such trees are alien and basically unattractive. **This criticism** needs, however, to be set against the fact that they account for less than a third of all woodland.*
有這樣的斷言，說這種樹木格格不入而且實際上就難看。然而，這樣的批評需要與所有林地上這種樹木佔不足三分之一這一事實一起考慮。

*The result is a pattern of land use which represents only the preference of bureaucrats responding to the demands of pressure groups or vested interests. **A further criticism** of planning made by Hayek stresses the connection between economic and political freedom.* （後來的批評表明前面的話也是一種批評。）
結果是有了土地使用格局，它只代表對壓力集團或既得利益集團的要求作出響應的官僚們的偏愛，後來由海葉克對該規劃提出的批評強調經濟自由和政治自由之間的聯繫。

*The drinks trolley came along the aisle. Jeanne said it was too early for alcohol. But Ryle overrode **her objection**.*
裝飲料的手推車順着通道行進。珍妮說時間還早，不到上酒的時候。但是賴爾對她的反對意見不予理會。

*'I tell you, man, the whole thing is crazy!'* — *'Is that **the opinion** of the Press?'*
*'Is it something very valuable, then?'* Alistair asked. *'Oh, no, it isn't valuable,'* Henry
answered, *as if **the point** were not of much interest.* (...the point... 即：...the point of
whether it was valuable or not... 是值錢還是不值錢的問題。)

"老兄，聽我説，整個事件真荒唐！" ——"那是新聞界的意見嗎？"
"那麼，那是不是一件非常值錢的東西呢？"阿里斯塔爾問道。"啊，不，不值錢，"享利答道，彷
彿對值不值錢的問題並無多少興趣。

## accusation, allegation, threat

**6.27** 這幾個名詞可以指稱相當敵對的或不友好的看法、評論（當然這種評論也可
以用書面語表達）。

*He claimed I was jealous of Elliott. Which was **a manifestly baseless accusation**.*
他斷定説我嫉妒艾略特。這顯然是毫無根據的指責。

*I am to be accused of treason and conspiracy. I not only admit the factual truth of
**the accusation**. I regard that treason and that conspiracy as evidence of my patriotism.*
我將被控犯了叛國罪和陰謀罪。我不僅承認這種指控屬實。我還認為這樣的叛國和陰謀是我愛國主
義的證據。

*It has often been alleged that Diana Winters practises witchcraft, and now she
regretfully admits that **the allegation** can no longer be denied.*
經常有人説戴安娜·溫特斯耍弄巫術，她現在懊悔地承認這種指控再也無法否認。

*He accused the team of not working hard enough, and attacked the manager too,
who was astonished by **the allegation**.*
他指責運動隊不夠努力，並且還攻擊了經理，後者對這樣的指責大為吃驚。

*'I see your arm has not recovered yet. How would you like the other one broken?'
Although **the threat** was suavely spoken, Kemp felt a spasm of fear.*
"我看你的手臂還未康復。難道還想把另一隻也弄斷嗎？"雖然這種恐嚇他的話説得溫和，但肯普還
是感到一陣恐懼。

## advice, warning

**6.28** 有的名詞是用來指稱奉勸他人該做甚麼或不該做甚麼的。**Warning**用來通
知他人可能有不愉快的事會發生（尤其是在這個人不肯根據他人建議採取行動
時）。

*Arthritis patients, it is claimed, should not eat meat in any form. Many people who
have followed **this advice** and eaten fresh vegetables and fruit have found a marked
improvement in their health.*
據説，關節炎病人不應該吃任何種類的肉食。許多採納這個忠告並食用新鮮蔬菜和水果的人發現自
己的健康有了明顯的改善。

*If you want **my advice** — which you've never taken in the past — keep out of the
whole thing.*
如果你想要我給你提出勸告 —— 你過去從來就沒聽取過 —— 那麼，你對那件事就不要沾邊。

*Gough and his staff had many times in the weeks prior to the attack alerted GHQ about the danger on the 5th Army front, but **these warnings** were ignored.*

戈夫和他的參謀人員在受到進攻之前的數週裏已經多次提醒統帥部第5軍團前線存在這種危險性，但是這些警告都被置之不理。

*'There is the possibility not only of open murder but also of poison secretly administered: a most reliable source tells me that you should take very great care.' — 'Thanks for **the warning**.'*

"不但有公開兇殺的可能性，也有暗地下毒的可能性：一個非常可靠的消息來源通知我，要你格外當心。" —— "謝謝你的提醒。"

## apology, admission, confession, excuse, explanation, denial, refusal

**6.29  Apology** （道歉、認錯）指一個人對自己做的事表示歉意、遺憾。如果是一次對他人的嚴重冒犯或重大的失誤，就得加以認錯（**admission**）或坦白（**confession**）。

*'He'd certainly have reported anything irregular. I'm so sorry you've been inconvenienced.' Grudgingly the American accepted **the apology**.*

"他肯定報告過任何異常情況。我對給你帶來的不便表示歉意。"那個美國人勉強地接受了這個道歉。

*'Yes, I'm sorry. It's my fault.' Latimer made **the admission** at once.*

"是的，我很抱歉。那是我的過失。"拉迪摩爾立即認錯。

*'Frankly I'd be ashamed if Yoller or my parents knew that we were friends.' **This confession** depressed Hunter even more.*

"說真的，如果約勒爾或我的父母知道你我是朋友，我會感到慚愧的。"他的這番自白使亨特更加難受。

人們又可以用不是那麼抱歉的口吻對自己做過的事或說過的話找個藉口（**excuse**）或者作出解釋（**explanation**）。

*'You said your dog didn't bite.' — 'I'm sorry, but we thought you wouldn't come if we said how bad he was,' Mrs Williams replied. **This excuse** sounded familiar.*

"你說過你的狗不咬人。" —— "真對不起，但是我們認為，如果跟你說了這條狗多麼厲害，你就不會來了，"威廉斯夫人回答說。 她的這一藉口聽起來好熟悉。

*'My car had a flat tyre…' Mather seemed wholly uninterested in **the explanation**.*

"我汽車的輪胎癟了……"梅達對這樣的解釋似乎毫無興趣。

*The girl's mother had three kids from an earlier marriage, and so did her father. Then they had two more together. So the total is eight children, but the father and mother each had five. Even after **this explanation**, it took the rest of us a few minutes to get the point.*

那姑娘的母親與前夫生過三個孩子，她的父親也與前妻生過三個孩子。後來他們結婚後又生了兩個，所以加起來一共有八個孩子，不過父親、母親各自有五個孩子。甚至在她作出這一解釋之後，我們想了好幾鐘才明白了這話的意思。

說話者可能以比較生氣或憤慨的口吻否認自己說過的話或做過的事（**denial**），或者拒絕去做某事（**refusal**）。

> *'Why were you in my room?' — 'I wasn't in your room.'* **His denial** *was flat. I didn't know whether to believe him.*
> "你為甚麼進我的房間裏？"——"我沒進過你的房間裏。"他斷然否認。我不知道該不該相信他的話。

> *The baron picked up his revolver and turned to Federico. 'Go up to your room. Now,' he ordered him. 'No,' Federico replied.* **This refusal** *made the baron wince.*
> 男爵抓起左輪手槍對着弗德瑞科。"走，到你房間去，快點。"他發出命令。"不，"弗德瑞科答道。他的拒絕倒使男爵退縮了。

## attitude, doubt, fear, guess, hope, objection, wish

**6.30**　有些指稱篇章的名詞描寫個人看法。

> *Leo's view is that if a thing is worth doing, it's worth doing as well as it can possibly be done, so he will work just as hard at his hobby as at his career. One of the advantages of* **this attitude** *is that at any time a hobby can be turned into a career.*
> 利奧持有這樣的觀點，值得一做的事就應該全力以赴去做好，因此他從事業餘愛好同他從事職業一樣努力。這種態度的優點之一就是業餘愛好在任何時候可以變為一個人的職業。

> *Could it really be argued, they asked, that governments were instituted to secure man's right to the pursuit of happiness? Was it as axiomatic as Jefferson proposed that all men were created equal? Despite* **these doubts and objections** *on the evening of 4 July 1776 the text of the American Declaration of Independence was formally signed.*
> 他們問道，是不是真的可以這樣爭辯說，政府的成立是為了確保人們追求幸福的權利？人生來就平等是否像傑弗遜提出的那樣是不言而喻的？儘管有這種種的疑慮和異議，美國獨立宣言的正文還是於1776年7月4日正式被簽署。

> *She was afraid the children would compare her unfavourably with their mother and dislike her. I sympathised with* **this fear**, *which did indeed represent an unpalatable reality.*
> 她擔心那些孩子會把她與他們的母親作不利於她的比較後而不喜歡她。我同情她的擔心，因為這種擔心確實代表了一種使人不快的現實。

> *Around 1500 BC, the Hindu priesthood decided that creation had occurred 2 billion years ago. The accuracy of* **this guess** *was unsurpassed until the 20th century.*
> 約在公元前1500年左右，印度的僧侶界就斷定創世發生在20億年前。這一猜想的準確度直到20世紀才被超越。

> *Men and women through the ages have testified that inner peace can be found through God despite excruciating pain. Euthanasia is the despair which rejects* **this hope**.
> 長期以來，天下的男男女女已經證明，儘管有極度的痛苦，卻能通過上帝找到內心的平靜。安樂死是拒絕這種希望的絕望。

*I kept hoping that if I didn't look at them they would quietly go away. When I had finished, I opened my eyes and discovered that, unfortunately, **my wish** had been granted. There was only one person left in the audience.*

我心裏一直希望，如果我不看着他們，他們就會靜悄悄離去。等我結束時，我睜開雙眼，很不幸，發現我的這一願望已經實現了。聽眾只剩下一個人。

## Compliment

**6.31  Compliment**（稱讚、恭維）表示說話者讚許或欽佩他人時說的好話。

*'She's pretty,' says Erica, 'You resemble her a lot.' I smile appreciatively, though I cannot take **the compliment** seriously.*

"她長得漂亮，"艾瑞卡説，"你長得很像她。"我感激地笑笑，不過我不能把這種稱讚當真。

*'I love watching you,' he said. 'The way you move.' She smiled at **this compliment** the way she always did.*

"我喜歡看你，"他説，"喜歡看你的動作。"對這樣的恭維她像平常一樣報之一笑。

## rumour

**6.32  Rumour**（流言、謠傳）表示人們相互之間傳來傳去的話。可以是令人愉快的但常常是令人不愉快的；可以是真實的也可以是虛假的。

*He drank too much, so **the rumour** went.*

他飲酒過多，人們這樣謠傳。

*I was told that flu was about but I didn't take **the rumour** seriously until one or two of my visitors began to disappear.*

有人告訴我説流感盛行，但直到有一、兩位客人不見人影了，我才對這傳聞予以重視。

## stuff

**6.33**  有時用 **stuff**（廢話、荒唐話）指稱說話者很不贊同的評論或意見。

*She wondered, for the hundredth or thousandth time, how Paul could say and write the things he did. Did he really believe **that stuff**?*

她多次自問，怎麼保爾會説出那樣的話、寫出那樣的東西？難道他真的相信那種荒唐事嗎？

*What an extraordinary story. Do you actually propose to print **stuff like that**?*

真是離奇的故事。難道你真的打算把那種亂七八糟的東西付印嗎？

*Ghosts and demons? Don't tell me you still believe in **all that stuff**!*

牛鬼蛇神？你是説你仍然相信那樣的荒唐話嗎？

## 指稱作為語篇的語篇成份
## Text as text

### word, phrase, sentence, paragraph

**6.34**　有的名詞可以指稱作為語篇的口頭或書面語段。

*'And now if you'd just like to give me an account of your own whereabouts after you left the party.' — 'Of course! You want my alibi.' Conder rolled* **the word** *round his tongue in a way that made the questioner feel faintly ridiculous.* (the word 指 alibi，當時不在犯罪現場的證明)
"現在可不可以説説你離開聚會後的去處。"——"行！你是要我提供當時不在犯罪現場的證明。" 孔德把最後一個詞發得十分誇張，讓發問人自覺有點可笑。

*Polly hurried into the house, muttering to herself. 'Doctor. Ambulance. Blanket to keep him warm. Police.'* **The last word** *had come unbidden to her mind and hastily she rejected it. His fall had been an accident.*
帕麗匆忙走進房子，低聲地自言自語説出了"醫生。救護車。給他保暖用的毯子。警察。"這最後 一詞不由自主地出現在她的腦際裏但她又很快地打消了這個念頭。他跌跤是一件偶然的事。

*'He would certainly have told you to do what I ask.'* **These words** *deprived me of all power of resistance. 'Very well, I'll do it,' I said.*
"他肯定告訴過你我要你做的事。"他這話使我再也無力反對。我説，"好的，我照你説的辦。"

*What is all this about 'a far seashore'? Why have I got* **this phrase** *in my head? My thoughts are getting all mixed up.*
這"遠方的海濱"到底是怎麼回事？我腦子裏為何出現這個詞組？我的腦子全糊塗了。

*'Do you mean it's a badge or a trademark or something?' — 'I don't know.' — 'Well, don't be too late if you can help it.' There had been an urgency in* **that last sentence** *which would not have been there if she had expected everything to go smoothly.*
"你的意思是説那是一種徽標，還是商標，還是別的甚麼東西？"——"我也説不清。"——"好 吧，你可得快點兒弄清楚。"她的最後一句話説得很緊迫，彷彿她指望着一切都進行得順利。

*Now, he thought, I must think very carefully what to do.* **This sentence** *occupied his mind for some time to the exclusion of all else.*
這時他想：我必須仔細考慮要做的事。在較長的時間裏，他腦子就裝着這個問題，別的甚麼都考慮 不進去。

*The report was scathingly satirical and closed with* **this paragraph**: *'The young ladies at the Tallis School deserve better from our police department than they are getting. If Mr Lane is indeed the mystery intruder, as the police claim he is, he should have been more carefully watched.'*
整個報告是滿紙刻薄的挖苦諷刺，並以這樣一段話結尾："塔裏斯學校的年輕女士們理應從警方得 到比現在更好的照管。如果萊因先生是警方所稱的神秘的騷擾者，那就應該更加警惕地對他進行監 視。"

## quotation

**6.35** **Quotation**（引言、引語）指從書本、劇本或別的語篇中引用的一個短語或句子。

*' "The past is a foreign country", isn't that what you once quoted to me?' — 'There's another half to the **quotation**: "They do things differently there." '*
'"過去是人們不熟悉的世界"，這不是你曾經引用給我聽的那句話嗎？'——'這句引語還有另一半沒說，即"那裏的人們做事不一樣。"'

## passage

**6.36** 書本、演講或其他語篇的**passage**（段落、一段話）指說話者特別關注的段落。段落可長可短，可以包括幾個句子，不過，在多數情況下，其長度比一段更長，或用 passage 加以替代。

*He had not tried to disguise in his diaries what he knew would happen to the soldiers. They were being sent back, he said, 'to torture, slavery and death'. Why had he not cut out **this passage**?*（this passage 指代與士兵命運有關的那一節。）
他在日記裏並未試圖把自己知道的會發生在士兵身上的事掩蓋起來不說。他說，士兵被遣返回去"受刑、受奴役並被處死"。他為何沒有把這段話刪掉呢？

*In one of Wodehouse's stories, Bertie extols the genius of his butler, Jeeves, finishing with **this passage**: 'There are no limits to Jeeves' brain-power. He virtually lives on fish.'*
在沃德豪斯出版的一篇短篇小說裏，伯特讚揚了他的男管家吉夫斯的聰明才智，小說以這樣的一段話結尾："吉夫斯聰明絕頂。他幾乎全靠魚來維持日子。"

*Consider **this passage**: 'You need to train yourself to prepare impromptu speeches, speak with enthusiasm, and use eye contact. The more you speak, the more you'll be able to use parts of an old speech in a new one.'*
請考慮以下這段話："你需要培養自己即席演講的能力，演講要有熱情，要接觸聽眾的目光。演講得愈多，你就愈能在以後演講裏用過去演講中用過的部份。

## dialogue

**6.37** **Dialogue**（對話）表示兩個人之間的交談。

*During dinner, the mother kept calling attention to the fact that her daughter needed to lose weight. Now it should be obvious that the public setting was not an appropriate place for **such a dialogue**.*
用餐時，母親不斷地提醒說她的女兒應該減輕體重。很明顯，在公眾場合是不宜進行這樣的交談的。

*Soon a voice announced that we were to have the opportunity of tasting the Ethiopian national dish, wot. A military-looking Englishman in the seat in front of me summoned the stewardess. 'What is this food?' he demanded. 'Yes, wot is that food,' said the stewardess. 'What?' said the man. 'Wot,' nodded the stewardess. 'It's what?' said the man. 'Yes, it's wot,' said the stewardess. 'What?' said the man. 'Wot,' agreed the stewardess. 'What?' 'Wot.'* **The dialogue** *was unstoppable.* (注：what 和 wot 的發音完全一樣，把那個英國人給弄湖塗了。)

不久就有人宣佈說，我們將有機會品嚐埃塞俄比亞的國菜 —— 沃特（wot）。坐在我前面的一位軍人模樣的英國人把女服務員叫了過來。"這是甚麼樣的食物？"他問道。"是的，就是沃特，"女服務員答道。"是甚麼？"他說。"是的，就是沃特，"她點頭說。"是甚麼（what）？"男的又問。"沃特！"她贊同說。"甚麼？""沃特。"這場對話沒完沒了，一直進行着。

# 會話中的連接手段
## Links in conversation

**7.1**　所有用於書面敍述的連接詞、連接語及其他具有連接作用的詞語都可用於口語，儘管它們中的一部份只能用於非常正式的口頭敍述。在第 1 章和第 2 章中，我們已經提到了一些在書面和口語中都較常用的詞語。

此外，還有一些在口語起着特殊作用，或者幾乎只用於口語的單詞和短語。

某些在會話中用的"**話語標記**"，把一個説話人的若干句子連接起來（雖然實際上説話用的句子沒有像書面敍述時那麼界限清晰）。但有時，這些標示語又為另一個繼續對話的參與者所使用。

## 表示猶豫的語氣詞
## Hesitation noises

**7.2**　有時在説話時，説話者會發出一個音，僅用來表示自己還沒有結束自己的話，不過正在想接下去講些甚麼。這些語氣詞（幾乎都不能算作單詞）在書面中通常用 **er**（哦）、**erm**（呃）、**uh**（嗯）等表示。此外，還有很多能起到這種作用的詞。

**7.3**　表示一個人正在傾聽他人的話，可以使用如 **mm**（嗯）、**yes**（對）、**yeah**（哎）、**right**（對）及 **oh right**（哦，對）等。這些詞可用來表示聽話人同意説話者的話，也可僅用來表示一個人已經聽到了對方的話。有時，還可用yeah（耶）表明聽話人想提出自己的不同看法。

> *A: And **erm** it's just unfortunate for people who want to watch something else, isn't it?*
> A：呃，對那些想看看其他東西的人來説，這是不幸的，不是嗎？
>
> *B: **Mm** well **yeah** but **erm** the people who can't manage to see the match obviously want to see it on TV.*
> B：嗯，對，哎……，不過，呃，對那些不能到現場觀看比賽的人來説，他們顯然想在電視上看到現場直播。
>
> *A: How do governments and councils find out about what is happening to the populations?*
> A：地方政府和議會是如何了解人們中間發生的事呢？
>
> *B: **Yeah** but...*

B：哎，不過……

*A: And how do they plan for what people are doing?*

A：他們對人們所做的事又作何打算呢？

*B: **Yeah** but you…they've already got this information on computer or in a file.*

B：哎，不過你……他們早就從電腦上或文件上得知這個消息了。

*A: No one dares do anything to me; besides I wear glasses.*

A：沒有誰敢對我怎麼樣；而且我還帶着眼鏡呢。

*B: **Oh right**.*

B：哦，不錯。

*A: It's the national language.*

A：這是國語。

*B: **Yes** indeed. **Yeah** I wasn't quite sure what you were saying there for a minute, **yeah**.*

B：對，確實。哎，我對你剛才說的那些話不是很清楚。

*A: **Oh right**.*

A：哦，是這樣。

*B: **Yeah**.*

B：哎。

*A: **Erm** I mean **er** it is a very difficult issue.*

A：呃，我的意思是說這是個很難的問題。

*A: I didn't go this Thursday.*

A：本週四我沒去。

*B: **Oh right**.*

B：哦，是啊。

*A: …which is rather a nuisance*

A：……這真是個麻煩。

# 使話語保持流暢的補白語
# Fluency fillers

**7.4** 我們有時把表示猶豫的語氣詞和起到這種作用的詞稱為**補白語**，因為它們使說話者的話聽起來更流利。如果沒有它們，說話中就會有無聲停頓。從這個角度來說，它們在對話中具有功能性作用——表示說話者還沒說完，還不到他人的說話的時機輪；同時又表示受話者正在傾聽，而且聽懂了說話者的話。

用作補白語的單詞和短語肯定具有意義，其作用就是連接對話的內容。

但在話語的開頭，補白語對保持口頭敍述繼續進行所起的作用也許與它們本身的意義同等重要。

很多動詞表達式可用於口頭敍述中，它們有時起強調作用，但同時又起補白語的作用。7.5－7.8節將討論這些動詞表達式。

## I mean, you know, you see

**7.5** 可以用 **I mean**、**you know** 和 **you see** 強調所説的話，並常常隨後作進一步的解釋。説話者可以用 I mean 或 what I mean is... 來解釋或糾正自己剛説的話。如果用 you know 或 you see，則表示説話者認為他人理解自己的話，或者在説服他人同意自己的話。

*'It's true,' Nancy said, beginning to feel better. '**I mean**, I do complain when Ned's in training.'*
"沒錯，"南希説，開始感覺好受了些。"我的意思是，當奈德在訓練時，我確實有意見。"

*They've had proportional representation in other countries and, **you know**, you sort of don't get anywhere. **I mean** the political system in this country is good basically.*
在其他國家他們實行議會選舉的比例代表制，你知道，在你們那裏這樣的辦法就不大行得通。我的意思是説，在這個國家裏，政治體制從根本上説還是不錯的。

*And when I say the war was over, I don't mean May '45, **I mean** autumn '44, when the Resistance had stopped blowing trains up.*
當我説戰爭結束時，我並不是指 1945 年 5 月而是指 1944 年 8 月，因為當時抵抗組織已經停止炸毀火車。

*Because of the money I was persuaded by certain people in the forces to volunteer for four years and get extra money which I did. **I mean** at that age you're quite vulnerable, you listen to older people.*
為了錢，我被軍隊中的某些人説服自願服了四年兵役，並為此多掙了些錢，我的意思是説，在那樣的年紀，人容易受別人影響，往往聽從年紀比自己大的一些人的話。

***What I mean** is that we spend most of our time not living in the moment. We're either regretting the past or worrying about the future.*
我的意思是大部份時間我們都沒有把握住此刻。我們往往不是為過去惋惜，就是為將來擔心。

*He was short of money but **you know** he was mean as well.*
他是缺錢，不過你知道，他就是有錢也不大方。

*Well, there's a lot of argument about that, **you see**.*
唉，你看，關於那件事大家爭論不休。

***You see**, you're making a sweeping generalisation.*
你看，你的結論下得過分籠統了。

*I don't know that it's an election issue. **I mean** I'm not sure. **You see** I have very mixed feelings over this.*
我不知道那事與競選有關。我的意思是我不確定。你瞧，我對這件事有一種相互矛盾的交集感情。

**7.6** 不過，這些動詞表達式有時只起補白語的作用。

*But **I mean** this man was **you know**, he was sort of picking on the afflicted more than anything.*
但我的意思是説這個人，你知道，他總是專找那些備受折磨的人的茬。

*I said I'll, **you know**, feed the animals and then just go up the road.*
我説你知道，我會餵完這些動物後再上路。

*And, er, **you know**, **I mean** I'd like to defend all accents really. I think, er, we all grow up with our culture.*

哦，你知道，我的意思是我真的願為不同口音辯護。我認為，哦，我們都是在一定的文化中長大的。

*Well now the dealer, erm, **you see** he's in Stoke-on-Trent.*

那麼現在那個商人，哦，你瞧，他在英國的特倫特河畔斯托克市。

***You see** but and then, I think I ought to write back and enclose these.*

你瞧，但這樣一來，我想我應該回信並附上這些。

*Well I don't think …**I mean you see** the Welsh and the Scots are very…are fiercely proud of their nationalities.*

我不認為……我的意思是你知道威爾士人和蘇格蘭人非常……十分以他們的民族自豪。

***I mean** it raises sort of ethical problems really doesn't it **you know**.*

我的意思是這真的引起了某些道德問題，你知道，難道不是嗎。

***I mean** I'd like to because **I mean** I suppose **you know** it must be fun to see but I mean I wouldn't do it.*

我的意思是，我心裏挺願去看，因為，我的意思是，我猜想，你知道，那看起來一定很有趣，但我的意思是，我不會去。

## you mean, do you know what I mean, if you see what I mean

**7.7** 人們有時把 you mean 當成一個問句來問，以檢查自己是否已經理解了他人的話。

*A: And anyway what made you think I'd change my mind just because he asked me?*

A：不管怎麼說，你怎麼會認為我改變主意僅僅是因為他要求我這麼做？

*B: **You mean** your father?*

B：你是說你父親？

說話者要檢驗別人是否理解了自己的話，可以用 **do you know what I mean?**，**do you see what I mean?**，**if you see what I mean** 等表達式，不過，這些表達式有時似乎僅僅是起到補白語的作用而已。

*A: Yes, where's your scar?*

A：對了，你的疤痕在哪裏？

*B: Well, it's between my shoulder blades. And it's on the right side but nearest the spine. **Do you know what I mean**? Right next to my spine.*

B：就在我的肩胛骨間。在身體右側靠近脊椎的地方。你懂我的意思嗎？就在我的脊椎旁邊。

*A: I don't see anything wrong with her.*

A：我不覺得她有甚麼不對勁。

*B: Oh it's sort of messy.*

B：哦，多少有點混亂。

*A: Well yeah.*
A：是這樣。

*B: Rather than …ha, ha…anything normal.*
B：不是，……啊，哈……不是，那麼正常。

*A: Yeah.*
A：耶。

*B: **Know what I mean**?*
B：懂我的意思嗎？

*Now that may be not good enough for you or me but it may be good enough for him. He may be doing the best job as he sees it. **Do you see what I mean**?*
那對你我來說也許不夠好，但對他而言，已經夠不錯的了。照他看來也許是他的工作已經做得再好也沒有了。你懂我的意思嗎？

*Will you ask her? But, you know, only if she really doesn't mind **if you see what I mean**.*
你會問她嗎？但是，你知道，只有她真的不介意你才能問，不知你是否懂我的意思。

*A seminar is no better or worse than a conversation but we want both **if you see what I mean**.*
研討會與隨意的交談很難說有甚麼好壞之分，但我們這兩種形式都要。不知你是否懂我的意思。

## I know, I see

**7.8** 如果一個人說**I know**，那就表示此人對所表述的觀點表示贊同，或者接受他人所說的話是真實的。

*A: I mean they're not slums. They're nice houses, George.*
A：我的意思是那些房屋並非貧民窟，是一些很不錯的房屋，喬治。

*B: **I know**, **I know**, I've seen them all being built.*
B：我知道，我知道，我看到它們正在興建。

**I see** 並不一定表示贊同，它僅表示"我懂你的話"。

*A: You line the cake tin and then sort of build the paper up round the outside.*
A：你給蛋糕烤模襯上一層紙，再在外面圍上一圈紙。

*B: Oh **I see**, yeah, I'm with you, yeah.*
B：哦，懂了，耶，我同意。

# 引起注意，改變話題
# Attracting attention, changing the topic

**7.9** 人們用不同的單詞和詞組改變話題來引起他人的注意（以便開始對話）或改變話題。

## right, all right, okay

**7.10**　　**Right**、**all right** 和 **okay**（也寫作 **OK**）常被用來改變話題。在一定程度上，它們意味著"對，我已經聽到了，並懂了你的話"，但這些短語常暗示說話者只對已經說過的話表示贊同。也許說話者認為關於某個話題已經沒甚麼再要講的了，於是希望改變話題——或者進行另一活動。

**Right**, that's it. I'm going to bed now.
對，就這樣，現在我要去睡覺了。

'We have already suggested that on previous occasions.' — '**All right**, well we'll come back to that.'
"我們以前已經提議過這事了。"——"好的，那麼，讓我們再舊話重提。"

**Okay**, so are we agreed on going north?
好的，那麼我們對去北方已達成一致意見了？

**All right**. So stand up on your left leg and get your right leg swinging round in a circular motion clockwise. All right that's what you've got to do. And then while you're doing that I want you to shake your head. **Okay** so you're standing on your left leg swinging your right leg clockwise. Difficult isn't it?
好的。那麼你就用左腿單立，右腿以順時針方向打圈。對，就那麼幹，現在，在你做這些動作的同時，我要你再晃晃腦袋。好，現在你左腿單立，右腿順時針方向打圈，怎麼樣，難吧？

**7.11**　　如果說話者處於權威地位，那麼他說的 **All right** 或 **right** 就可以帶有命令的份量了。

The cop then rammed Kelly against the Land Rover, still on his knees. '**All right**, hands behind you.'
警察把凱利往蘭德牌越野車上猛撞，他仍然跪着。"好，現在把手放到背後。"

**7.12**　　如果以問句的方式說這些短語，就可檢驗聽話人到目前為止是否同意或理解說話者的話。

There's a little village a few miles north of Portsmouth, off the old London Road. Denmead. Ask for Stanmore Hall there. Or follow the signs, **all right**?
在舊倫敦大街那邊，朴次茅斯以北幾英里有一個小村莊，叫鄧米德。你到了那兒再打聽斯坦莫爾會堂的位置。或者按照路牌自己去找，好嗎？

Anyway, don't tell me, let me guess. You're gonna show me a picture. A girl probably, **right**?
不管怎樣，先別告訴我，讓我猜猜看。你將給我看一張照片，也許是張女孩子的照片，對嗎？

We had to cut a third of our staff. Terrible thing, letting people go, but that's business, **right**?
我們必須裁掉三分之一的職工。讓人家失業，真糟糕，但做生意就是如此，不是嗎？

*So you'll put down the number that you'll calculated in percentage form. **Right**? You'll write three percent or minus two percent or minus twelve percent. **Okay**? On the top line.*

那麼你將在百分比表格中寫上計算出來的數字，是嗎？你可以寫上3%或-2%或-12%。對嗎？寫在第一行。

*Try to be more careful next time, **okay**?*

下次更小心點，好嗎？

**7.13** 如果把這類短語用作回答，則可以表示説話者贊同他人的説法，但也可以僅用來表示説話者聽懂了他人的話。在這種情況下，也可用oh right （另見7.3節）。

*A: I'll come with you, Doreen.*
A：我和你一起去，多琳。
*B: **All right** then.*
B：那好吧。

*A: It hasn't got a name yet.*
A：它還沒名字呢。
*B: **Oh right**.*
B：行。

以下的例證取自電台的熱線節目。在每個例證裏，都是由電台主持人先説話。

*A: We're getting towards the end of the programme and I want to squeeze another caller in, **all right**?*
A：我們的節目就要結束了，讓我抓緊時間，再接一個電話，好不好？
*B: **Right okay** fine.*
B：對，好，好的。

*A: Dave, nice to talk to you.*
A：大衛，和你交談很愉快。
*B: **All right**.*
B：好的。
*A: Cheers mate, bye bye.*
A：再見，朋友，再見。

## now, well, so

**7.14** 像 right、all right 和 okay 一樣，**now, well** 和 **so** 這三個詞也可以表示説話者想改變話題或提供新的信息。7.15 － 7.18 節將着重探討這三個詞在起相同作用時的不同用法。

**7.15** **Now**（有時也作 **now then**）可用來引起他人的注意或開始對話。

*'Now ,' he said. 'We had better have another meeting, so that I can tell everyone.'*
"現在，"他説，"我們最好再開個會，以便我把這事告訴每一個人。"

A: ***Now then*** *I want to ask you. Does angora involve cruelty to rabbits?*
A：那麼現在我想問問你，使用安哥拉毛紗是否需要對安哥拉兔子施虐？
B: *No, it's from an angora goat. It's nothing to do with rabbits.*
B：不，這種毛是從安哥拉羊身上剪下來的，與安哥拉兔無關。

**7.16**　如果改變話題前使用 **well**，就表示説話者在每個人都理解自己剛才的話後，從原來的話題轉向一個新的話題。不過，有時 well 只起到一個補白語的作用。

*He and I were special friends. He had taught me a few words of his language and I was able to make myself understood now and then. I taught him some of my words too. **Well**, Wamgum and I went out. The sun was high in the sky…*
他和我是特殊的朋友。他教了我一些他們語言裏用的詞，於是我不時能讓他聽懂我的話。我也教了他一些我的語言裏的詞。好了，就這些。瓦姆古姆和我那天出門。時逢豔陽高照……

A: *I'm waiting for one of them to knock on my door.*
A：我正等着他們中的一個人來敲我的門。
B: *Good man.*
B：好樣的。
A: *Because they're not going to get away very easily.*
A：因為他們是輕易出不去的。
B: *No. **Well** let us know what they say.*
B：沒錯。好了，告訴我們他們説了些甚麼。

A: *Go on then, carry on then. What do you want to talk about?*
A：別停，往下講。你想講甚麼？
B: ***Well**, I was just phoning up about er British Telecom really.*
B：好了，我只是在打電話給，呃，給不列顛電信公司。

A: *Can I have them delivered late afternoon?*
A：下午晚些時候能將東西送出嗎？
B: *Yeah.*
B：行。
A: *No later than six, if that's possible.*
A：可能的話，不要遲於6點。
B: *No later than six. **Well**, we wouldn't do it later than six anyway.*
B：不遲於6點。好的，我們在6點之前就送出。

A: *By then it'll be too late.*
A：到那時就太遲了。
B: ***Well**, anyhow, we'll work that one out when the time comes.*
B：行了，不管怎麼説，到時我們一定會把那事了結。

'Happy birthday, Leigh,' he said, leaning down to kiss me. I turned my cheek, but he kissed me quickly on the lips. '**Well now**,' he said standing. 'I have some things to do in the office.'

"生日快樂，利，"他説着，並彎下身吻我。我把臉轉過去，但他卻飛快地吻了一下我的嘴脣。"好了，現在，"他直起身子説，"我辦公室還有事要辦。"

**7.17** **So** 也表示説話者的話已為他人理解，接下去説話或者提問。

I somehow got the impression you were telling me something. **So** what was it? **So** who was it?

我多少感到你剛才是有話要對我講。那麼，是講甚麼事呢？又是講誰呢？

*A:* We used to have an assistant editor who could help us with it — on Wednesdays. What's happened to her by the way?

A： 我們過去有一個助理編輯幫我們幹這事，時間是在每週的星期三。順便問一下，現在她人呢？

*B:* I don't know.

B： 我不清楚。

*A:* **So** who's doing her job?

A： 那麼，現在誰在幹她那份工作？

**7.18** 通常把 **well** 用來有禮貌地將批評或糾正的話的語氣緩和下來。

'I ought to go out and get something else.' — '**Well**, what's the matter with these gees?' Sam put an arm round her. 'You had certain other things on your mind too.'

"我該出去再買點別的東西。"——"那麼，這些雞蛋怎麼辦？"山姆用一隻手臂摟住了她，"你腦子裏一定在想其他甚麼事情。"

'He never mentioned that he was resigning.' — '**Well**, I don't think he would have done under the circumstances.'

"他從沒提到過他要辭職。"——"行了，在這種情況下，我也不認為他會提。"

説話者也可以用 well 表示將糾正自己的話。

Tell him we'll be there in three days time. **Well**, three and a half.

告訴他我們三天後到那兒。對了，是三天半之後。

'Weren't you engaged to her?' — 'No, **well**, no, not exactly.'

"當時你不是同她訂了婚嗎？"——"沒有，嗯，沒有，並不完全是這樣。"

**7.19** **Well, well**！表示驚訝，或者假裝的驚訝。

To his delight a familiar, tall, languid figure lowered itself down the steps. '**Well, well**! I'm glad you're alive.'

令他高興的是，一個熟悉的、無精打采的高個子緩慢地往樓梯走下來。"啊，啊！我真高興你還活着。"

'**Well, well, well**,' I crowed. 'Fancy that! What have we here!'

"喲，喲，喲，"我歡呼道。"太神奇了！看看我們這兒有甚麼啊！"

## so what?

**7.20 So what?**（意思是"那又怎麼樣？"）用來表示某事並不重要，或不會產生任何影響。這個短語有時聽起來較為粗魯。

> *A: Toby, we're not students any more, you know.*
> A：托比，你知道，我們再也不是學生了。
> *B: **So what**? Why are you so conventional, all of a sudden?*
> B：那又怎麼樣呢？你怎麼會一下子就變得這麼傳統了？

> *They are no better than me. They are just people who have got money. **So what**?*
> 他們和我一樣糟。他們只是有錢而已。那又怎麼樣？

## oh well, well then

**7.21** **Oh well** 和 **well then** 有時表示"在那種情況下"或"既然那樣"。

> *A: I've got to go and get some stamps.*
> A：我得去買些郵票。
> *B: Oh have you? **Oh well**, you can pick me up some airmail envelopes while you're there.*
> B：是嗎？既然這樣，你在那兒就可幫我買幾個航空信封。

> *A: The publishers want the text in by the second of March.*
> A：出版商想在 3 月 2 日前收到文本。
> *B: **Well then** we can do it.*
> B：既是這樣，我們能辦到。

## then again, there again

**7.22** 可以用 **then again** 或 **there again** 預示說話者在剛擺出的觀點或事實之後，將補充某個與原來不一樣的新的觀點或事實。因此，這兩個表達式可用來引出相反的觀點。這兩個表達式都可用於書面語中，不過在口語中更常見，其意思與 on the other hand（另一方面）基本相同。

> *The frog pauses, stock still. Possibly it is thinking what to do next, but **then again** possibly it has no recollection of what it did last.*
> 青蛙停頓了一下，一動不動。也許它在考慮下一步該怎麼做，但另一方面也可能它已記不起來剛剛做了甚麼。

> *I suppose I should be ashamed, she thought. But **then again**, why?*
> 她想，她自己應該感到羞愧。但再想想，又為甚麼要羞愧呢？

> *You might get them to take action, but **then again** you might not.*
> 也許你能讓他們採取行動，然而，也許你不能。

*I do believe that in a decade from now there will be a significant and growing number of employee-controlled companies in the UK. But **there again**, I have always been an optimist.*

我確實相信十年以後，在大不列顛聯合王國將不斷湧現大量由僱員控制的公司。不過，從另一方面講，我這人一直是個樂觀主義者。

*A: It's very easy to get a child to sit in front of a television, it's far easier than getting it to read a book.*

A：讓孩子坐在電視機前看電視並不難，這比叫孩子看書要容易得多。

*B: But I mean, **there again**, but television is also very educational.*

B：但我認為，從另一個角度講，電視也很有教育意義。

## oh, oh dear

**7.23**　**Oh** 是一個感嘆詞。可用來引起注意或表達某種情緒（如：驚訝、煩惱或愉悅），或者有時候只起到補白語的作用。

***Oh** Ned, Nancy cried to herself, why did you have to leave me?*

哦，內德，南希還哭着對自己說，你為甚麼一定得離開我呢？

*A: He didn't send me a Valentine card.*

A：他連一張情人卡也沒寄給我。

*B: **Oh**. **Oh** how disappointing.*

B：哦，哦，多麼令人失望。

*A: Okay, what made you move to Old Windsor?*

A：好了，你們為甚麼要搬到溫莎古堡呢？

*B: Well we thought it was a better place.*

B：嗯，我們覺得那兒更好。

*A: **Oh** I see yes.*

A：哦，我知道了，是的。

**Oh dear** 也可用來表示煩惱、同情或失望之類的情緒。

*A: And Michael's out and I'm lonely.*

A：邁克出去了，我很寂寞。

*B: **Oh dear**.*

B：哦，親愛的。

*A: I feel like I want to cry.*

A：我覺得我想哭。

*B: **Oh dear oh dear**.*

B：哦，親愛的，親愛的。

*A: Poor me.*

A：我真不幸。

*B: Poor you.*

B：可憐的！

## by the way, incidentally

**7.24**　如果想改變主題，可以用 **by the way** 或 **incidentally**。也可以用這兩個短語提示説話者將提供並不太重要的附加信息。

> *He didn't tell me, **by the way**; I found out by accident.*
> 順便提一下，他沒告訴過我；是我自己湊巧發現的。

> *'She doesn't like being told about that kind of thing.' He paused and then said rather awkwardly. '**By the way**, I suppose you cannot tell me when we shall be back in Bucharest?'*
> "她不喜歡人家告訴她那種事情。"他停頓了一下，而後尷尬地説，"順便提一句，我想你也不知道我們得何時回布加勒斯特吧？"

> *Let me remind you **by the way**, on Tuesday of next week, don't forget, the show is coming live from the Assembly Rooms in Derby.*
> 讓我順便提醒你一句，下週二，別忘了，表演將在德比市的會議大廳以現場直播的方式播出。

> *You're listening to John Taynton on BBC Midlands Radio. The lines are going mad here. **By the way** if you want to try and get through, please be patient; the team are answering calls as quickly as they can.*
> 您正在收聽BBC英格蘭中部電台約翰・泰英頓的節目。這裏的電話忙極了。順便提一句，如果您想打通電話，請務必耐心，受話小組正以最快的速度應接電話。

> *It's really good of you and I'm immensely grateful, but I think I ought to stay here. **Incidentally**, how are you yourself?*
> 您太好了，我非常感激。不過我想我該待在這兒。順便問一聲，您自己身體怎麼樣？

## speaking of... , talking of...

**7.25**　可以用這類短語來改變主題，但新話題必須與他人或説話者自己剛剛所説的話有某些文字上的聯繫。

> *'I keep remembering what you said. Forget about the past. Think of the future.' — 'That's right. **Speaking of** the future, I'm going to be in London tomorrow. I would like to take you to dinner.'*
> "我一直記着你説過的話。忘掉過去，考慮將來。"——"那是對的。説到將來，我明天要去倫敦。我希望到時能請你吃飯。"

> *'September's my favourite month. Still warm and sunny enough to sit outside during the day, but cool in the evening, and when everyone's safely home you can draw the curtains and be cosy.' — '**Talking of** being safely home,' Guy said, 'shouldn't Angie be back by now?'*
> "九月是我特別喜歡的一個月。白天還很溫暖，陽光燦爛，可以坐在室外。而晚上則較涼快，當大家都安全地到了家了，就可以放下窗簾，溫暖舒服一下。"——"談到安全回家，"蓋伊説道，"現在安吉該回家了？"

## look, listen

**7.26** 説話者可以用 **look** 或 **listen** 這兩個詞來引起他人對自己接下來要講的話的重視，因為説話者認為接下來的話很重要。

> **Look**, I'm sorry. I didn't mean it.
> 瞧，我很抱歉。我是無心的。

> **Look**, girl, you and me gotta talk!
> 瞧，姑娘，你我要談話了！

> **Listen**, I'm acting under the orders of the District Attorney.
> 聽着，我是照着地方檢查官的指示辦事的。

> **Listen**, how about some coffee?
> 嘿，喝點咖啡怎麼樣？

如果説 **look here** ，就表示説話者可能生氣了。

> Now **look here**, you're wrong.
> 現在聽着，你錯了。

> By six o'clock I was exhausted and at 9 o'clock I told the producer, '**Look here** I'm going to leave at 10.'
> 到6點的時候，我已經筋疲力竭了；到9點鐘時，我對製片人説，"聽着，我10點鐘一定得走。"

## guess what!, as it happens

**7.27** 提到某個令人吃驚的事情前，可以用 **guess what!** 引起他人的注意。

> **Guess what**! I've been promoted to manager!
> 猜猜出了甚麼事！我被提升為經理了！

> We checked the dead guy's fingerprints, like we always do. **Guess what**. He wasn't one of our men at all.
> 我們像往常一樣，檢查了死者的指紋。猜猜出了甚麼事。他根本不是我們的人。

**As it happens** 有時可用來強調某件很令人驚訝的事，但也可用來表示某件並不重要的事。

> 'When did he last see a baseball match?' — '**As it happens**, last Sunday.'
> "他甚麼時候最後一次觀看壘球賽？"——"碰巧是上週日。"

> Genetics didn't have a damn thing to do with it, although, **as it happens**, my father was also a cop in New York.
> 遺傳學跟這事完全不相關，不過，我爸爸湊巧也是紐約市的一名警察。

> The minister would not comment on the case yesterday when, **as it happened**, he was visiting a forensic science laboratory.
> 部長對昨天他在碰巧參觀法庭科學實驗室時聽到的案子不發表任何意見。

## anyway, anyhow

**7.28** 這兩個詞在口語中很常用，用法很像 well（見 7.16 節），表示可以回到先前曾提到的某件事上來改變話題。

> ***Anyway**, let's have some food.*
> 不管怎樣，讓我們先吃點東西吧。
>
> ***Anyway**, to answer your question properly, no, I don't hate Jeffries himself.*
> 不管怎樣，讓我對你的問題作出恰當的回答，不，我不恨傑弗里斯本人。
>
> ***Anyhow**, so we became friends and everything, and we call each other on the phone all the time.*
> 不管怎樣，我們成了好朋友，並一直通電話。

也可以用兩個詞中的任何一個引出一段話中的重點。

> *And I was thinking well if they've put him through that what are they going to put me through. And I thought well why postpone things. Why not just walk out now. So **anyway** I walked out and I came back here.*
> 我在想如果他們那樣處置他，不知又將如何處置我呢。於是我想到那麼為甚麼還耽擱呢，為甚麼不現在就出走。於是，不管怎樣，我出走了，並回到了這兒。

☞ 比較 2.54 和 3.5 節。

# 強調某一點
# Emphasizing a point

## believe me

**7.29** 可以用 **believe me** 強調説話者在説的話是真實的或重要的。

> *Look, I know you're in a hurry, but **believe me**, in this kind of situation hurry gets you nowhere. Take it easy, play it cool.*
> 瞧，我知道你很急，但相信我，在這種情況下，着急無濟於事。別緊張，冷靜點。
>
> *You're doing fine, **believe me**. Fine.*
> 你做得很好，相信我，真的很好。
>
> *I've tried it and it does work, **believe me**.*
> 我試過了，真的有效，相信我。

## the fact is… , the thing is…

**7.30** 如果想強調所説的話屬實，可以使用 **the fact is…** 或 **the fact of the matter is…** 。

*I didn't have a chance to defend myself. I was sent home. And **the fact is**, a lot of other young people who were there are going to draw their own conclusions from that.*

我根本沒機會為自己辯解，就被送回了家。不過事實是，很多在那兒的其他年輕人將從這事中得出他們自己的結論。

*Well, people often complain that CDs are cheaper in the States but **the fact is** that, of course, everything in America.*

是啊，人們經常抱怨在美國激光唱片比其他地方便宜，但事實是，在美國無論甚麼東西都比在其他地方便宜。

**The fact of the matter is** *you have to decide.*

事實是你必須作出決定。

如果想提出解釋或找個借口，也可以用 **the fact is...** 或 **the thing is...**。

*Well, look love I'm sorry, **the fact is** I'm going to Greece tomorrow.*

得了，瞧，親愛的，我很抱歉，事實是，我明天得去希臘。

*I suppose **the thing is**, people wear things more now to please themselves and for comfort than maybe they used to.*

我認為事實是，人們現在穿衣服可能比以前更注重給自己帶來愉快和舒適。

*I mean, **the thing is**, of course, we have a different relationship with horses than we do with cattle and sheep and pigs, don't we?*

我的意思是，事實上，我們與馬的關係，跟我們與牛、羊、豬的關係當然是不同的，不是嗎？

**The thing is** *now, English is not my mother tongue, but I really loathe it when people can't speak correct grammar.*

事實是，儘管英語不是我的母語，但我對人們說話時不能運用正確的語法，真的感到很厭惡。

也可以用 **the thing is...** 強調某個急待答覆或解決的問題。

**The thing is**, *what do we do next?*

事實是，我們下一步怎麼辦？

*But **the thing is**, how am I going to know what standard I'm at?*

但是事實是，我將如何得知自己處於哪個水平？

# the point is...

**7.31**　如果想強調論證中最重要的部份，可以用短語 **the point is...**。

*And you see **the point is**, if you've got less staff, you've got more money to spend on books.*

關鍵是，如果你少僱些人手，就可以省下錢來買進更多的書。

*I think there are differences, but **the point is** they were all looking for unskilled work 'cos they couldn't get skilled work.*

我想這有所區別，但關鍵是，他們都在找那些無需技能的工作，因為他們找不到需要技能的。

*So many people today say 'Well that part of the Bible does not apply today'. But* **the point is**, *every part of the Bible applies today as regards principles.*
今天很多人都在説："得了，聖經中的這部份如今不再適用。"但關鍵是，就其原則而言，聖經中的每一部份在當今還是適用的。

## as I say, as I said, as you say

**7.32** 人們有時通過重複來強調某一點，而説話者也可以用 **as I say** 或 **as I said** 來表示這個意思。

也許會令人多少有點吃驚，這些短語有時也確實出現在實際的書面語中（並不僅僅局限於口語的書面記錄）。不過，此類文章的語體是相當非正式的。

*'So how would you rate him then? Mildly amusing or what?' — 'Amusing I suppose, but* **as I say** *he's not my type of comedian at all.'*
"那麼你怎麼評價他？是有些滑稽，還是甚麼？"——"是有些滑稽，不過正如我所説的，他算不上我心目中的那種喜劇演員。"

*Yeah, they were really lovely, the people in the group, but* **as I say** *it was a bit frustrating so I started hating it.*
是的，人羣中的人確實很可愛。但正如我説的，這事太令人灰心了，以至我開始憎恨起整件事來。

**As I said** *most of the national rugby stadiums are all covered now, and all seater, and a lot of the top rugby clubs have got tremendous facilities now.*
正如我所説的，大多數的國家橄欖球館現在都有拱頂了，全有座位。很多甲級橄欖球俱樂部都有了大量的設施。

**As I said** *at the beginning of this chapter, women have a lot of good business skills, although we tend to underrate ourselves.*
正如我在本章開頭所説的，女子擁有很多高超的經商技能，儘管我們傾向於低估自己。

也可以使用 **as you say** 來重複或提及某人先前所説的話，以表示説話者贊同此人的意見。

*It is a very simple device,* **as you say**, *very much like a ballpoint pen.*
這是個很簡單的裝置，正如你所説的，簡直就像一支圓珠筆。

*'I understand your point of view completely,' he said. '***As you say**, *it could have happened to anyone.'*
"我完全理解你的看法，"他説道，"正如你所説的，這事可能在任何人身上發生。"

在非正式語體中，也可用 like 來替代 as，但是大多數人認為這樣説是錯的。

**Like I say**, *I don't necessarily agree with everything he's done.*
正如我所説的，我不必對他所做的每件事都表示贊同。

*I think,* **like you say**, *the meetings are a good idea.*
我認為，正如你所説的，開會是個好主意。

## as far as

**7.33**　如果説話者想説話時留些餘地，即想説自己對所説的事實並不十分有把握，但又認為自己所説屬實，則可使用 **as far as I know**。

*I was given no training whatever; nor was Peter, **as far as I know**.*
我沒有得到過任何培訓，而且據我所知，彼得也沒有。

*Stan has always been a bachelor **as far as I know**, so my remarks about women were of no relevance to him.*
據我所知，斯坦一直是個單身漢，因此，我關于女人的評論與他無關。

***As far as we know**, no one has ever been killed by computer hacking.*
據我們所知，還從未有人被電腦黑客行為所殺。

**7.34**　**As far as I can see** 和 **as far as I'm concerned** 表示説話者就個人而言或發表自己的觀點。

*Lots has been lost and nothing **as far as I can see** has been gained.*
損失了不少，依我看，卻一無所獲。

*It's a particular pleasure **as far as I'm concerned** because it's the first time we've had anybody from the literature department coming to talk to us.*
依我看，這是莫大的榮幸，因為這是我們首次請到來自文學系的人士給我們作報告。

# 結束談話
# Ending conversation

**7.35**　説話者可以用多種方式暗示談話的結束。兩個較常用的單詞是 well 和 anyway。

***Well** I must dash. Wish me luck.*
好，我得走，祝我好運吧。

***Well** I must get back. I left the potatoes on.*
好，我得回去了。我出門時，土豆還在爐火上呢。

***Well** I must be off.*
好，我得走了。

*A: As you say, everything seems to change so quickly, doesn't it? **Anyway**, nice to have met you.*
A：正如你所説的，事事都變得真快，不是嗎？不過，還是很高興遇到你。

*B: Okay, thank you, bye bye.*
B：好的，謝謝，再見。

# 8 句子附加狀語
## Sentence adjuncts

**8.1** 在第2、第3章中討論的連接語主要指單個的副詞或其他的狀語。它們顯示了説話者或寫話者如何看待他們所敍述的兩件事情之間的聯繫。例如：一件事情是另一件事情的結果呢，還是那另一件事情的一個例證，或者連接語本身只是標誌着用不同的詞來重複原來的話？在各種不同的用途中，連接語與連接詞（第2章)有些相似之處，但是，連接語對於句子結構更具獨立性，並且還可能在事實上起着句子與句子之間的連接作用。

另一類狀語，對於句子結構也有相當的獨立性，稱為**句子附加狀語**(有時也稱為**評註性狀語**）。與連接語不同的是，它們並不起聯繫句子(或分句)的作用，而且從語法上來説，也不是連接詞。但是，它們在體現寫話者或説話者對話語的態度上起了重大作用。通過使寫話者或説話者的態度明朗，它們在使句子的意義更加明瞭方面起着重要的作用，從而把寫話者或讀者聯繫起來。因此，本書把這些狀語也包括進來。

**8.2** 注意指稱這類狀語用的術語繁多。**句子副詞**這一術語，有時也被其他寫話者使用，在這本書中，卻沒有使用。因為該術語既可指句子的附加狀語(本章討論的主題)，又可指連接語，即任何獨立於句子其他部份的狀語。在有些語法書中，**句子附加狀語**被稱為**評註性狀語** ，而**連接語**則被稱為**連接性狀語**。

句子的附加狀語分成多種：

- 用來解釋説話方式的狀語。如："老實説"（frankly），"坦白講"(to be honest) 和 "總的來説"（generally speaking）。這些都可歸在同一個主題 "説話者説話的方式"(8.4－8.16節)之下。這類詞和詞組有時被稱為**語體評註性狀語** 。它們一般用於非正式語體，特別是用於口語、轉述口語及小説的對話中。

- 用來解釋説話者對自己所述事情(8.17－8.43節)的可能性和真實性所持的態度的狀語。例如："當然"（certainly）、"毫無疑問"(no doubt)、"當然"(of course ) 及 "也許"（perhaps）。

- 用來表示敍述人對自己所敍述或所描寫的事情所持的態度的狀語。這些狀語常用於表現説話者對所述事情是好還是壞的看法和評判。例如："令人煩惱地"

（annoyingly）、"幸運地"（luckily）和"可理解地"（understandably）。

- 用來表示或強調説話者對自己敍述的動作的實施者所持的態度的狀語（8.71－8.87 節）。説話者用這些狀語把自己對這種人的行為的看法表示出來。如："勇敢地"（bravely）、"正確地"（correctly）和"愚蠢地"（foolishly）。

以上提及的後三類狀語中的詞和詞組有時也被稱為**內容評註性狀語**，因為，它們表示説話者對自己所述內容的看法。

**8.3** 儘管附加狀語可以出現在句中很多不同的位置，但是最具特徵性的位置一般是句子的開頭，或者，在從句中，緊跟在連接詞之後。

*Frankly, Thomas, this question of your loan is beginning to worry me.*
老實説，托馬斯，我開始為你的貸款擔心了。

*Lynda can't spend more time at home because, frankly, the family need the second income.*
琳達不能再留在家裏不工作了，因為，老實説，家裏需要第二份工資。

*No doubt many will regard these as harsh words, but regrettably they are true.*
無疑很多人會認為這些話很刺耳，但是，令人遺憾的是，這些全是實話。

*Fortunately, the weather that winter was reasonably mild.*
幸運的是，那年冬天的天氣相當溫和。

*Correctly, he had trusted her integrity.*
他相信了她的誠實，他這樣做是對的。

附加狀語的另一常見的位置是在主語和動詞之間。

*Many people, to my mind, spoil it for themselves.*
在我看來，很多人自己把這項活動搞糟了。

*The situation, frankly, struck me as all but hopeless.*
老實説，局勢依我看幾乎毫無希望。

*He went for X-rays which fortunately showed his leg was not fractured.*
他去拍了 X 光，幸運的是，拍片顯示他的腿骨沒有斷裂。

*The officials reportedly became annoyed.*
據報導説，官員們都發火了。

*We actually think we need more policemen.*
實際上，我們認為我們需要更多的警察。

當句中不止一個動詞時，附加狀語常用在第一個助動詞之後。

*The contract for this will no doubt be widely advertised.*
毫無疑問，為此所簽定的合同將被廣而告之。

*He had obviously been hiding.*
很明顯，他一直在躲藏着。

*Classes had evidently ended.*
顯然，課已經結束了。

*Her husband was **mysteriously** killed.*
她的丈夫被神秘地殺害了。

*It is now **definitely** accepted.*
如今這已經肯定為人們所接受了。

但是，當句中的動詞只是 be 的某一形式時，附加狀語常常用在該動詞之後。

*I was **frankly** astonished at the degree to which different singers can affect the interpretation of a song.*
老實説，歌手對一首歌曲影響差別之大令我震驚。

*The balance of power in Europe is **fortunately** stable and likely to be permanent.*
幸運的是，在歐洲的勢力均衡格局很穩定，並有可能永遠保持下去。

附加狀語也有可能位於包括句末的其他位置。在句末時，附加狀語對於句子本身的獨立性常由逗號表示，儘管有時逗號並不需要。

*We're getting a little tired of it, **frankly**.*
我們有點厭倦它了，老實説。

*See you at the next meeting, **no doubt**.*
不用説，下次開會再見。

*Anyway, that hadn't got far, **fortunately**.*
不過，那事還沒太離譜，真幸運。

*That's a mistake **perhaps**.*
也許那是個錯誤。

*The company said yesterday, **no doubt correctly**, that it had increased its share of the beer market.*
公司昨天宣佈，無疑是正確的，公司在啤酒市場的份額增加了。

跟在不及物動詞或及物動詞及其直接賓語後面的一般是方式副詞，因此那些可以充當方式副詞的句子附加狀語應盡量避免用在這個位置。要格外注意某些以 -ly 結尾的副詞，免得把方式狀語和句子附加狀語混淆起來。以下的三個例證中都有方式副詞，即用來強調動詞動作的方式的副詞。

*You can talk **frankly** to me.*
你可以對我直言相告。

*Please speak **clearly**.*
請説得明白些。

*Did I pronounce your name **correctly**?*
你的名字，我叫對了嗎？

但是不可能產生歧義時，這類副詞可以跟在不及物動詞或及物動詞及其直接賓語之後，即使用作句子附加狀語也可以如此。

*That's a mistake, **clearly**.* （...clearly. 等於 ...obviously. ……很明顯。）
那是個錯誤，顯而易見。

*He's made a terrible muddle, **frankly**.* （...frankly. 等於 ...to be frank with you. 對你實説了吧。）
他搞得糟透了，老實説。

當然，對那些不作方式副詞的附加狀語來説，跟在不及物動詞或及物動詞及其直接賓語之後是不會產生任何問題的。

*That's a mistake **perhaps**.*
也許那是個錯誤。

*It's only a theory, **admittedly**.*
必須承認，這只是一種揣測。

*He's lost his job **unfortunately**.*
不幸的是，他丟了工作。

☞ 有關以 -ly 結尾的副詞的位置，詳見 8.71 節。

# 說話者說話的方式
# How you are speaking

### personally

**8.4**　如果説話者説 **personally**（從個人角度）來看待某事，那麼在某種意義上就暗示也許別人並不持有這種觀點。但同時，像其他許多這類作語體附加狀語的詞語一樣，personally 起着一定的強調作用。

*I had read the book with interest, but **personally** I thought it was greatly inferior to Lawrence's other work.*
我懷有興趣地讀這本書，但依我看，這部作品遠遠比不上勞倫斯其他的作品。

*But that's your choice. **Personally**, I think you and Chris would be better off, far better off, here in the States.*
那是你的選擇，但依我看，我認為你和克里斯在美國境況會更好，會好得多。

*I **personally** think that your custom of burning dead bodies is much more hygienic than burying them, as we do.*
我個人認為，你們把屍體火化比像我們實行土葬要衛生得多。

***Personally** I blame it on television.*
我個人認為那應歸咎於電視。

***Personally** I think a jolly good smack occasionally never did a child any harm.*
我個人認為偶爾給孩子一個愉快而適度的響吻不會給孩子帶來任何危害。

## in my opinion, in my view, to my mind,
## from my point of view

**8.5**　也可以用一些其他不那麼常見的詞組來強調説話者所説的話是自己的個人意見。

*'Surely you have other sources of information.'* — *'I do. And I want to count you among them. You are eminently qualified **in my opinion**.'*

"當然你有其他的消息來源。" —— "是的，我有。並且我想把你也算作其中之一。依我看，你完全夠資格。"

*There are several books on the market at the moment, which give listed remedies for various women's ailments. **In my opinion** these are too confusing and worse than useless to the uninitiated.*

當前在市面上有好幾種書，它們為各種婦科疾病羅列了一些藥方。但照我看，這些書太令人無所適從，對外行來說，比沒用還糟糕。

*Most of the negotiations between unions and management break down because of a lack of trust, so the Church, **in my view**, has a role to play in the real world.*

大多數勞資雙方的談判都因為缺乏信任而破裂，因此依我看，在現實世界中教會可以發揮一定的作用。

***In my view** the cost of living is not the most important thing for the working man to consider.*

在我看來，有工作的人要考慮的頭等大事並非是生活費用。

*I have never discovered anything better than sailing to cut yourself off from the world and all its worries. But many people, **to my mind**, spoil it for themselves by racing.*

我不能找到比航海更好的方式來使人遠離塵世及所有世間煩惱。但很多人，依我看，卻以航海競賽的方式，自己破壞了這項活動。

*Unfortunately you know a lot of bad music, **from my point of view**, gets into the charts.*

不幸的是，你知道，很多依我看挺差勁的歌曲擠進了每週流行唱片選目。

*The girl who's just been appointed there was, **from my point of view**, utterly hopeless, useless.*

剛被委派到那兒的那個女子，據我看，無可救藥，不起作用。

## honestly, frankly

**8.6**　有時說話者想陳述一種觀點或某一事實，但同時也認為這種觀點或事實有可能使人感到失望或不快。這時，通過使用 **honestly** 或 **frankly** 這樣的詞，就可以以一種相當禮貌的方式強調話語的真實性或肯定性，同時又承認了該話語可能引起他人的不快。注意與這兩個副詞相關的變體詞語。

*I've got lovely ideas for the front of the house, but **quite honestly** I don't know if it's worth it.*

我對房子的正面有一個不錯的構想，但老實說，我不知道該設想是否值得。

*My mum belongs to the local choral society and **quite honestly** I ignored her singing meetings and things.*

我母親參加了本地的詩班合唱團，老實說我對她的唱歌聚會及有關的事都置之不理。

*There's been gossip here. **Honestly**, Joan, I'd rather not go into detail.*

這兒有些傳言。但老實說，瓊，我寧願不將其細節一一說出。

*I don't **honestly** know.*
我確實不知道。

***In all honesty**, aren't there already far too many pages of scientific research published every week, every month, every year for us to read and absorb?*
老實説，每週、每月、每年出版的供我們閱讀和吸收的關於科學研究的資料，難道不已經太多了嗎？

*I'm desperately trying to remember whether it worked. I can't **in all honesty** remember whether it did or not.*
我竭盡全力回憶它是否奏效，但老實説，我實在記不起來。

*Mr Cameron, my husband hasn't been well. It's…**Frankly**, it's not something I can explain over the phone.*
卡梅潤先生，我丈夫身體不好。是……老實講，這事我在電話裏講不清。

*The situation, **frankly**, struck me as all but hopeless.*
老實講，形勢給我的印象是幾乎毫無希望。

*This woman came up to me at a party and started paying me clumsy compliments. **Frankly**, I thought she must be drunk.*
這個女人在晚會中走到我跟前，開始對我進行不得體的恭維。老實講，我想她一定是醉了。

*After I lost some hair I felt I looked **frankly** distasteful.* （注意本句的詞序。）
脫落了些頭髮之後，老實説，我覺得自己看起來令人厭惡。

***To be frank**, I found her fascinating.*
老實講，我覺得她很迷人。

*I'm here on business of a kind which requires me to carry large sums of money. **To be frank**, I would be happier if I had a pistol.*
在這兒，我所從事的工作要求我攜帶巨款。因此，老實講，如果我有支手槍，我會更自在些。

當講話人不得不承認某些自己不太願意承認的事情的時候，可用 **to be honest**。

***To be honest**, I faint at the sight of blood.*
坦白説，我一見血就發暈。

*I don't know if we could ever get to a normal life there, **to be honest**.*
坦白説，我不清楚我們能否在那兒過上正常人的生活。

☞ 比較 **really**、**truly**：見 8.26 節。

## briefly, realistically, seriously, quite simply

**8.7**　還有一些帶 -ly 的副詞可用來交代説話者説話的方式。以下是一些例證。

***Briefly**, we found out which soldiers wanted to desert; then we informed them that we would organize it when opportunity offered.*
簡而言之，我們發現了哪些士兵想逃跑；於是我們就通知他們一旦有機會，我們將組織逃跑。

*I can save you the trouble of reading it. **Briefly**, no less than nine of our agents have passed information to the enemy.*
我可以省去你看材料的麻煩。簡而言之，我們機構中至少有九個特工向敵方提供過情報。

*So what's new about tuberculosis that has renewed interest in the disease?* ***Briefly****, HIV.*

那麼，是結核病的甚麼新情況又引起了人們對這種疾病的關注呢？簡而言之，是人體免疫缺損病毒。

***Realistically****, with many patients, there is no way to help the underlying problem without first tackling the addition.*

現實地説，對於很多病人，如果不首先解決他們藥物成癮的問題，就無法幫他們解決其他潛在的問題。

*Hypnotists tell us that they cannot make us do anything that we would not normally want to do.* ***Realistically****, however, we all have only limited power with which to resist suggestions from those in authority.*

催眠術師告訴我們他們無法讓我們做任何我們通常不想做的事情。但現實地説，我們對於抵制來自權威人士的建議的能力都相當有限。

*'Keeping old age at bay is one reason for playing again,' he said. '****More seriously****, I thoroughly enjoy the game and was pleased the club asked me to help in whatever capacity I could.'*

"防止衰老是我重新參加比賽的一個原因。"他説道。"説得認真些，則是由於我極其喜歡這項運動，並且對俱樂部邀我隨便以甚麼身份盡力感到高興。"

*'Anyway, thank you for making me get the dresses.* ***Seriously****, do look OK?'* — *'You look terrific, Anastasia.'* （Seriously 用在問句裏，所以它的意義等於 tell me truthfully。）

"不管怎麼説，謝謝你讓我得到了這衣裙。老實講，我看來還可以嗎？"——"你看起來漂亮極了，阿娜絲塔夏。"

*Most of them,* ***quite simply****, drank.*

很簡單，他們中的大多數人都喝酒。

*Do not expect any personal revelations from me.* ***Quite simply****, the woman was an enigma.*

別指望從我這裏了解到甚麼有關個人的意想不到的情況。很簡單，女人是個謎。

***Quite simply****, these are the finest novels on magic ever written.*

很簡單，這些是有史以來有關魔術的最好的小説。

# literally

**8.8**  **Literally** 是一個相當奇怪的副詞，可以用來強調所述事情的真實性，以及説明説話者在使用有關詞的準確和基本的意義。

*We have planted* ***literally*** *thousands of trees.*

確切地説，我們已經種了幾千棵樹。

*With a wave of her hand she was off,* ***literally*** *running up the path before Sven realized what had happened.*

她揮了揮手就跑了，在斯溫還沒搞清發生了甚麼事之前，就已經跑到了小徑盡頭。

但該詞常常只用於強調，而句子中其他詞的字面意思不一定完全真實。

*Dead fish **literally** carpeted the banks of the river downstream.* （即：*The banks of the river were covered in dead fish.死魚鋪滿了河流下游的堤岸。*）
死魚簡直像地毯一樣密密麻麻地鋪在下流的河岸上。

*You're a brilliant barrister, everybody says so. But you're an incurable romantic, darling, your head **literally** in the clouds.* （即：*Your mind is far away on other things.你的腦子遠離現實在想其他事情。*）
你是個才華橫溢的律師，每個人都這麼說。但是親愛的，你還是個無可救藥的浪漫主義者，你的腦子真的像是在雲霧之中。

*And it seemed to Bunbury that his companion in crime was almost **literally** driving by the seat of his pants and arguing off the top of his head.* （*By the seat of one's pants 的含義是 "本性"；off the top of one's head 的含義是 "未加考慮"；這兩個短語都屬比喻性用法。*）
邦伯瑞似乎覺得他自己參與犯罪是本性驅使及不經思考的結果。

## to be fair, in all fairness

**8.9**　除了表明自己誠實或坦率之外，說話者還可以說自己是公正的。這類詞組常用於說話者在自己表明或暗示指責後提出一種相反的觀點。**In all fairness** 是to be fair 的變體，意義是 "公正地說"。

*Until I or some other MPs get the opportunity to raise this matter in parliament, we will not know the government's position, though, **to be fair**, I believe ministers can't really do much about it anyway.*
在我或其他的議員找到機會在議會中提出這件事之前，我們無從知道政府的立場，不過，公正地說，我認為部長們對此事也無能為力。

*'I'm disappointed in the BBC for giving it so much coverage.' — 'I don't think it's just the BBC **to be fair**. I mean I think we're being bludgeoned by it in the newspapers.'*
"我對英國廣播公司很失望，因為它對這事報道得太多了。"——"公平地說，我認為這並非只是英國廣播公司，我的意思是我認為所有的報紙都對這事大加報道，為此我們感到震驚。"

*He just picked up the notebook and marched silently from the room, several pairs of eyes following him in astonishment. **To be fair to Geoff**, this was an isolated instance; he does not usually behave like that.*
他只是撿起筆記本，然後一聲不吭地從房間裏走了出去，房間裏的人都驚訝地瞪着他。但公正地說，傑夫這種表現是偶然事件，他平時不會有這樣的舉止。

*Some road-building schemes may be good, some are clearly bad and some dubious for various reasons. There is much more to be said, **in all fairness**, on both sides of the issue.*
有些公路建築方案交待得很清楚，有些很糟，還有些出於各種原因，難以評判其質量。公平地說，這一問題的兩個方面都還有很多東西值得探討。

▶注意◀ 副詞 fairly 不用作句子附加狀語。

## to put it… , to say the least

**8.10**　另一種表示説話方式的辦法是使用含 put 的詞組，表示説話者以某種特定的方式表達自己的意見。最常見的表達式有：**to put it mildly…** ，**to put it bluntly…** 和 **to put it crudely…** ，不過還有其他許多相似的短語都可用，例證如下：

*In the circumstances he was being pretty brave, **to put it mildly**.* （即：He was being *extremely brave.* 他表現極為勇敢。）
説得婉轉些，他在那種環境下表現得很勇敢。

*Regrettably, alongside the real figures, a small number of women whose historical standing is, **to put it mildly**, more than a little doubtful have been taken to the hearts of feminists.* （即：Some fairly unimportant historical women have been presented by feminists *as important.* 女權主義者把一些歷史上不那麼重要的婦女尊為要人）。
令人遺憾地是，與那些真正重要的歷史人物相提並論的還有幾位婦女，她們的歷史地位，保守地説，很令人懷疑，但卻也很受女權主義者們的重視。

*They are family orientated holidays and **to put it bluntly** they don't want old people there. It's not a nice thing to say, but families don't want them.*
這是專為家庭安排的度假，直截了當地説，他們不希望有老人在場。儘管這麼説不太好，但家庭成員們確實不要老人。

*We cannot, **to put it crudely**, open a baby's head and look inside.*
我們不能，粗魯地説，把嬰兒的腦袋打開，然後往裏看。

*'You still love her, I think.' — 'Oh yes,' Villiers said. 'Loving is easy. It's the living together that's so damned hard.' — 'So what was the problem?' — '**To put it simply**, my work.'*
"你依然愛她，我認為。"———"是的，"維利爾斯説，"愛是簡單的，但要生活在一起就極為困難。" ——"那麼問題在哪兒呢？"——"簡單地説，我的工作。"

*Some management games, in which young stockbrokers hunted one another around country estates armed with toy guns, were, **to put it charitably**, eccentric.*
在一些管理人員的聚會遊戲中，年輕的股票經紀人們手執玩具槍在鄉村莊園中互相追逐，他們看起來，説得寬厚些，有些古怪。

**To say the least** 的意思與 to put it mildly（保守地説）大致相同，即説話者原可以更強硬地表達自己的態度，但出於禮貌，沒有那麼做。

*The evidence for all these charges seems, **to say the least**, unlikely to prove convincing in court.*
所有這些指控的證據，説得婉轉些，在法庭上似乎不大可能令人信服。

*Conversation in the room during the meal was, **to say the least**, difficult.*
要在吃飯的時候進行交談，説得輕點，是很困難的。

**8.11**　▶注意◀ **To put it in another way** 的意思大致與 in other words（換句話説）相同。因此，這是一個表示換一種説法的表達式，見 3.15 節。

*Why should you believe a word they say? Or, **to put it another way**, how can you decide which words to believe?*

你為甚麼要相信他們説的話？或者，換句話説，你怎麼能決定哪些話該信？

## generally / broadly / roughly speaking, in general

**8.12** 有時，説話者用含有 **speaking** 的短語表示自己在怎樣説話（或者在怎樣進行書面敍述）。

**Generally speaking**、**broadly speaking** 和 **roughly speaking** 都可用來指所説的話是大致或通常如此的情況。

***Generally speaking**, even very young children are quite good at making the most of their pocket-money.*

一般説來，就連很小的孩子都善於充分使用他們的零花錢。

*The refugees who were to be involved in the resettlement programmes fell, **broadly speaking**, into two categories.*

重新安頓計劃內的難民，大致説來，分為兩類。

*So we've established a norm that, **roughly speaking** pay goes up by three percent a year, okay?*

那麼我們就確定了條規矩，大體上説，工資每年漲 3%，行嗎？

**In general** 也具有相似的意義。

*Human freedom **in general** means the free exercise of human ingenuity in the satisfaction of an ever-widening range of desires.*

人類自由，一般來講，意味着人類自由發揮自己的聰明才智來滿足不斷擴大的要求。

***In general** they like quick results so anything requiring long periods of study or work is not likely to appeal.*

一般來説，他們急功近利，因此任何需要消耗很長時間的學習或工作的事對他們來説都毫無吸引力。

***In general**, short-acting drugs are better for this condition than those with a prolonged action.*

一般來説，對這種病症，見效快的藥物比見效遲緩的藥物更好。

# 含有 speaking 的其他表達方式
# 'Speaking' in other ways

**8.13** **Strictly speaking** 意味着説話者認為自己在進行準確、精確的敍述。

*Somebody pointed out that, **strictly speaking**, electricity was a discovery, not an invention.*

有人指出，嚴格地説，電是一種發現，而非一種發明。

'Can I leave money to my cat?' — '**Strictly speaking**, an animal can't inherit, although an animal charity can.'
"我可以把自己的錢遺留給我的貓嗎？"——"嚴格地説，動物是無權繼承的，不過動物慈善機構可以。"

It does help to remember that they're referring to a single point. They're not referring to the whole structure **strictly speaking**.
記住他們提到的一個要點是有所幫助的。嚴格地説，他們所指的並非整個結構。

**8.14** 也可以用如 **technically speaking** 、 **medically speaking** 這樣的短語，其意思是指説話者從技術上或醫學上的觀點來進行敘述。不過，technically speaking 與 strictly speaking 常具有相同的意思。

Savings are, **technically speaking**, that part of income which is set aside, to be translated later into spending or investment.
儲蓄金，用專門術語來説，是工資中保存起來以備將來使用或投資的一部份。

Sometimes the monasteries made too many demands on the peasants who worked on their lands, although **technically speaking**, each monk was supposed to go and beg for his food.
有時修道院對在其領地上工作的農民要求太多，儘管，嚴格地説，每位修士應以化緣的方式獲得食物。

The crews are fit and, **medically speaking**, we have ensured that this fleet is one of the best equipped for trans-ocean racing.
船員們身體健康，而且從醫學角度上説，我們已經確保船隊是一支適於越海比賽的最佳組合。

Women, **statistically speaking**, receive 75 per cent of the average wage for men.
女性，按統計來説，獲得的工資是男性平均工資的75%。

## as it were, so to speak, in a manner of speaking

**8.15** 短語 **as it were** 或 **so to speak** 常用來表示説話者認為自己所使用的並非最確切的字眼。這也許是因為説話者一時找不到最合適的詞語，雖然他説的話有一定的真實性；或是因為説話者想指出他在打比方或使用成語。但不管怎麼説，這兩個短語在口頭敘述中相當常見。**In a manner of speaking**，相對而言，則是個較少見的變體。

Suddenly, overnight **as it were**, South Africa was part of not just the Olympics but the big wide world.
忽然，似乎是一夜之間，南非不再僅僅是奧林匹克運動會的一部份，而且成為了這個大世界的一部份。

We don't start and invent, **as it were**, on a piece of paper, these new chemicals.
我們並非只靠一張紙就着手發明了這些化學新藥，儘管看起來似乎如此。

Health-care workers, police and others accept the saving of lives as an everyday occurrence–another day at the office, **as it were**.
從事保健、警察等職業的人把救人看成每日發生的事，—— 好像在辦公室又工作了一天。

*Another of Alistair's brilliant ideas was to have me start the programme and set the scene while standing, **as it were**, hand in hand with a white rhino.*
阿里斯塔另一個聰明的主意是讓我站在一頭白犀牛旁，似乎正和它手拉手，作為節目的片頭和場景。

*You can't even trust yourself **so to speak**, cos the habit, the addiction is stronger than you are.*
可以說，有時你甚至連自己也不信任，因為習慣、嗜好比個人的力量更大。

*I ought not to tell you but I will, since you're in the family, **so to speak**.*
我本不應告訴你，但我還是要說，因為可以說，你是家庭中的一員。

*Were she not his best friend's niece, he would deal more sharply with her whining. Tell her where to get off, **so to speak**.* （ tell someone where to get off 意思是對他人的某種行為表示不滿，並要他停止這種行為。）
如果她不是他最好的朋友的侄女，那麼他面對她的哀訴會嚴厲得多。可以說，會喝令她停止。

*Oh you know how it is when you work with people but don't mix with them socially. You know them and you don't, **in a manner of speaking**.*
如果你不在社交上與同事打成一片，也就是說，你認識他們，但不這樣做，其結果將會怎樣你是知道的。

## in retrospect, with hindsight, on reflection

**8.16**　有時，說話者也許想說，由於自己對往事的回顧，發現自己對某事的看法已經改變了。用來表示 when I / you think about it （當我 / 你想起此事時）的表達式有好幾種。

***In retrospect** our responsibility looks daunting, but at the time it did not worry us in the least.*
回想起來，我們當時的任務實在是令人膽怯，但在那時我們一點也不發愁。

*It might be thought that my work would have suffered from my obsession, but **in retrospect** I can see that during that period I reached the zenith of my career.*
也許人們會以為我那時的着迷會影響我的工作，其實回想起來，恰恰是在那個階段，我的事業達到了頂峰。

*As ever stubborn, I could not bring myself to agree with the board judgement, but **with hindsight** they were right.* （即：I now realize they were right，我現在意識到他們是對的。）
我一向固執，因此一直不同意董事會的評價，但事後想起來，覺得他們是對的。

*The decision I then took was a faulty one. **With hindsight**, and a clear head, it would have been better to have surrendered.*
我當時所做的決定是錯的，事後冷靜下來思考，發現當時如果投降，情況可能會好一些。

*Only my family and my self-belief got me through. **On reflection**, the year made me stronger. I sorted out my values.*
正是我的家庭和我的自信伴我度過那段艱難時期。現在回想起來，那一年使我變得更堅強，我理出了自己的價值。

*He has just issued a statement saying that **on reflection**, he regretted the remarks and withdrew them.*
他剛剛發表了一份聲明，說他經過事後考慮，為自己先前所說的話感到抱歉，並收回那些話。

## 說話者對可能性的看法
## Your opinion as to likelihood

**8.17**　在 8.18 – 8.43 節中所討論的句子附加狀語表示說話者就事件或情況發生的可能性有多大發表自己的意見。

### of course

**8.18**　如果說話者認為某事確實無疑，而且自己的聽話者 (或讀者) 不可能持有不同意見 (或者不給聽話者任何機會表示異議！) 那麼，可用 **of course** 來強調自己的話的真實性。

*She's Paul's sister **but of course**, you know that.*
她是保爾的姐姐，當然這你是知道的。

*Scotland Yard is **of course** called into these cases as a matter of routine.*
作為一種常規，倫敦警察廳刑事偵緝部理所當然地被請來參加這些案子的調查。

**Of course** 也可用於口語中，作為表示贊同的簡短回答。有時，這類回答是相當禮貌的；可有些時候，這類回答則令人感到說話者相當不耐煩 (如：That's so obvious, why say it? 這是顯而易見的嘛，還有甚麼好說的？)。

*'Do you know Davina Norris?' — '**Of course** I do. Everybody knows Davina Norris.'*
"你知道大衛娜‧諾里斯嗎？"──"當然，我知道，哪個不知道大衛娜‧諾里斯呀。"

*'But you wouldn't refuse?' — '**Of course** not.'*
"但您不會拒絕吧？"──"當然不會。"

*'Do you still need me?' — 'But **of course**, my dear chap.'*
"你還需要我嗎？"──"當然囉，我親愛的小傢伙。"

*'You never told me that.' — '**Of course** I didn't.'*
"你從沒告訴過我。"──"當然沒有。"

### obviously, clearly, plainly, manifestly

**8.19**　這四個副詞有時可以替代 of course。但它們更具有 "客觀" 的意思，即聽話者 (或讀者) 必須贊同說話者的觀點，因為客觀情況或環境證明該觀點是正確的，也就是說，說話者所說的話可以從一些客觀的事實中推導出來。**Obviously** 最為常用，特別常見於口語中。而 **manifestly** 則用得較少。

*'But who's responsible, David?'* — *'**Obviously** somebody who wants the truth published as much as we want to publish it.'*

"但這該是誰的責任呢，大衛？"——"當然是那個和我們一樣想把真情公佈於世的人了。"

*A candidate must have capacity for technical understanding at a very advanced level and the ability to express himself clearly both orally and in writing. Enthusiasm and aptitude for the job is **obviously** essential.*

一名候選人必須有很高的專業技術能力，並具備清晰的口頭和書面表達能力。當然，對工作的熱情和才能也是必要的。

*I turned to my left to see a small boy with dark, inquisitive eyes staring up at me from the corner of the couch. He had **obviously** been hiding behind it.*

我向左轉身，看到一個小男孩在沙發的角落裏睜着一雙烏黑、好奇的眼睛瞪着我看。很明顯他正躲在那裏。

*You have suffered losses at some past date and **obviously** don't wish to do so again.*

你過去遭到過損失，顯然不希望再發生那樣的事。

***Obviously**, at an eighty per cent tax rate there's going to be a lot more tax evasion.*

很明顯，當稅率高達 80% 時，將會有更多的逃稅現象。

*One of the police officers took off his helmet. **Clearly**, he considered this was a method of defusing a dangerous situation.*

警察中有一名摘下了頭盔。很明顯，他認為這麼做是一種緩解危急狀況的方法。

*She clutched something against her chest. It was a grey manilla envelope, and whatever it contained was **clearly** the cause of all this anxiety and tension.*

她把一件東西貼着胸口緊緊地捏着。那是一個灰色的牛皮紙信封，很明顯，一切的焦灼和緊張都是由於這封信裏的東西引起的。

*Some of his good humour had now returned to him, but he was still **plainly** baffled and worried for his business.*

現在，他又有些恢復平日的幽默了，但很明顯，他依然還在為自己的生意困惑和擔心。

*The content of BBC news bulletins is **manifestly** dependent on the uncontrolled succession of events.*

英國廣播公司新聞快報的內容很明顯來自於不斷發生變化的各類事件。

## unmistakably

**8.20**　如果說某事是 **unmistakably** 真實，就是指其真實性顯而易見，不可能有其他的解釋。

*Each was wearing a long white coat and one had a stethoscope round his neck. They were **unmistakably** doctors.*

每個人穿着白大褂，其中一個的頭上還戴着聽診器。錯不了，他們準是醫生。

*He kissed her warily. Instantly, **unmistakably**, he felt her recoil.*

他小心翼翼地吻了她一下，沒錯，他立即感到她退縮了。

## probably, perhaps, maybe, possibly

**8.21**　**Probably** 的含義是very likely（可能性很大）; **possibly** 的含義是not very likely（可能性不很大）。**Perhaps** 和 **maybe** 含義介於這兩者之間。

*By the time he came to retire at least two of the young managers would **probably** be ready to take over.*
到他退休的時候，至少有兩名年輕的經理可能已經準備好了接他的班。

*Now she was ten, **perhaps** they would stop calling her 'little Bessie'.*
現在她已十歲了，也許他們不會再叫她"小貝茜"了。

*The Americans had already helped him. **Perhaps** they might help him again.*
美國人已經幫過他一次了。也許他們還會再幫他一次。

*Some soldiers have died, others have been wounded. Still others are missing and **perhaps** have drowned.*
有些士兵死亡了，有些受傷了。還有一些失蹤了，也許已經淹死了。

*All sorts of stories seem to go around. **Maybe** people make them up because nothing is actually known.*
各式各樣的傳聞四處流傳。也許是因為人們都不知道到底是怎麼回事，因此編造了不少故事。

*They'll get him. **Maybe** not today, but sooner or later.*
他們終將抓住他，也許不是在今天，但那是遲早的事。

*Artie went where he pleased, and saw whom he pleased. **Possibly** he liked the excitement of the risk.*
阿提隨心所欲，想去哪裏就去哪裏，想見誰就見誰。也許，他喜歡冒險的刺激。

## likely

**8.22**　**Likely** 在標準英語中是一個形容詞，但如果加上了一些諸如most、very 或 quite之類的修飾語後，有時就用作副詞 —— 儘管有些人認為這是不正確的用法。其意思與 probably（可能地）相似。

*I'll have to tell the police all about it and **most likely** they'll want to know why I came here.*
我將必須向警察講明事情的全部情況，而且極有可能，他們會想知道我為甚麼來到這兒。

*The decisive event would **most likely** come in 1917.*
決定性的事件極可能發生在 1917 年。

*During the day a sense had been growing in her that there was no point in going on expecting him because **very likely** he would never reappear.*
在那一天中，她逐漸產生了一種想法，即繼續盼他是沒意義的，因為他很可能不會再出現。

*These troops, he warned, would **very likely** encounter enemy cavalry.*
這些軍隊，他警告說，很可能碰上敵人的騎兵。

*No, **quite likely**, he would not have told me.*
不，很可能，他本不會告訴我。

*Quite likely*, however, the refugees may resist making contact with charitable organizations.
不過，很有可能這些難民大概會拒絕與慈善機構聯繫。

## potentially

**8.23**　説某事 **potentially**（潛在地）是真實的，説話者的意思是指那事目前並非如此，但有可能會變成如此，因為相關的情況會朝着那個方向發展。當感到某事將變得危險或有害時，常常會用該詞。但該詞也可以用來指正面的情況。

*It would be impractical and **potentially** dangerous for anyone other than a local person, with total knowledge of the language and culture, to attempt to communicate with the kidnappers.*
除了完全掌握方言和熟悉該地文化背景的當地人外，任何人試着和綁匪交談都是不可行的，並且具有潛在的危險性。

*Here, **potentially**, is a machine that can learn from 'experience'.*
這兒的一台機器，從其潛能來看，能從 "經驗" 中學習。

*Here is, **potentially**, a machine with something approaching a real brain.*
就潛能而言，這兒的一台機器很可能在將來具有與人腦相近的功能。

*Planners find themselves in a similar position, expected to offer decisions that will satisfy a number of people who are **potentially** or actually disputing the use of land.*
規劃者們發現他們正面臨相同的處境，要作出決定以滿足那些在將來潛在地會為或現在正為土地使用而爭執的人們。

## actually, in(actual) fact, in point of fact

**8.24**　**Actually** 尤其常見於口語，用於強調説話者相信某事的真實性，或強調某事發生過——特別是當説話者認為這麼説會令聽話人詫異。因此 actually 可用來表示説話者不同意他人已表示的看法。

*Well we **actually** ended up sitting in seats where the backs had been broken off.*
得了，我們最後實際上坐在那些椅背斷了的座位上。

*We've asked for five but we **actually** think we need more. We think we need seven tape recorders.*
我們已經要了五台，而實際上我們認為自己還需要更多台。我們認為自己需要七台磁帶錄音機。

*He had a little dog called Ella which he brought with him and this dog **actually** used to go into battle with him and she was **actually** killed in a battle.*
他曾有一隻叫葉拉的小狗，他把她帶着，她過去確實常跟他上戰場，並且確實在一次戰役中喪生。

**In fact**（以及下面 in fact 的變體）也用來強調説話者的敘述也許會令人驚訝。因此，它也可以用來表示與先前説的話相反或對照。

*He waited what seemed an age, but was **in fact** one minute, for the whisky.*

他似乎覺得那杯威士忌他已經等待很久很久，但實際上卻只有一分鐘。

*May I point out that 'grass snake' is a misnomer? A grass snake is **in fact** a large, legless lizard.*

我可以指出"草蛇"的叫法是用詞不當嗎？草蛇實際上是一種體大、無腿的蜥蜴。

*It hadn't damned well even snowed! **In fact**, rain was splattering the windows, which wasn't the same thing at all.*

老天連一場雪也沒下過！實際上，只有雨水劈裏啪啦地打在窗子上，這跟下雪完全是兩碼事。

*Well I mean what is happening to you is insanitary, isn't it? It's a health hazard **in actual fact**.*

那麼，我的意思是正發生在你身上的事對你的健康是有害的，難道不是嗎？實際上那對健康是危險的。

*Seafarers like me swear all the time, don't they? It's common language. **In actual fact** I've managed to conduct myself in here, I think, without using one swearword.*

像我這樣的海員們成天詛咒發誓，難道不是嗎？那是這兒的通用語言。但實際上，我想我在這兒尚能表現良好，從沒有用過詛咒語。

***In actual fact** you've only got fifteen days' water and it takes forty days to get rescued.*

實際上，你只有可供 15 天的用水，而獲得援救卻要 40 天。

*She met and eventually married a man considerably younger than herself who claimed to be a pilot with Air France. **In point of fact** he was a chauffeur working for a car-hire firm.*

她遇上了一名年齡比她小得多，並自稱是法國航空公司飛行員的年青人，並最終與之成婚。實際上，他只是個租車公司的司機。

## as a matter of fact

**8.25   As a matter of fact** 與上述詞語的意思相似，可用於強調其後的信息。

*It's not just an old wives' tale, you know, that full moons and madness have an affinity. **As a matter of fact**, as recently as last year at the University of Pennsylvania, an extremely interesting study was done along those lines.*

你知道，滿月與精神病有密切的聯繫這一說法並非只是愚蠢之談。實際上，就在去年，在賓夕法尼亞大學就開展了一項與此類似的極其有趣的研究。

*Now some people have such confidence in the unborn child's hearing ability that they sing and talk to him and he actually responds! **As a matter of fact**, the unborn child has a completely developed auditory structure about half-way through pregnancy.*

現在，有些人對自己尚未出世的嬰兒的聽力如此自信，以至於他們常為他唱歌並與之交談，而嬰兒確實有反應！實際上，未出世的嬰兒在母體懷孕中期，其聽力系統就已完全發育。

有時，**as a matter of fact** 也可用在作出解釋、辯解或承認某事之前。

*As a matter of fact*, there's a complication in the present situation which has made us rather careful of what we say to her.

實際上，目前的情況很複雜，以至我們跟她說話時都非常小心。

## really, truly

**8.26**　作為句子附加狀語，**really** 和 **truly** 均起強調作用，不過有時在口語中，只是為了讓話語流暢而插入。Really 在口語中特別常見。

*Well I think that it's such an infringement of the sovereignty that we've fought for long and hard in this country over a great many hundreds of years really*.

我認為這是對我們主權的侵犯，而為了主權我們在這個國度中真的艱苦卓絕地戰鬥了千百年。

*And really I ought to write to him and tell him that I'm sending someone to see him.*

我真的應該給他寫信告訴他我正派人去見他。

*I don't really know what to say to you about this.*

我真的不知道關於這事我該對你說些甚麼。

*I'm really looking forward to Thursday and seeing you all again.*

我真心期望能在星期四再次見到你們大家。

*She did not truly know him; theirs had been a brief afternoon encounter more than twelve years before.*

她並非真的了解他；他們倆只在 12 年前一個下午短暫地意外會見而已。

也可用 **truly** 強調正在敍述的是真實的。

*Darling I respect your opinions, truly I do.*

親愛的，我尊重你的意見，真的尊重。

*I am sorry, Stella. I truly forgot.*

我很抱歉，斯特拉，我真的忘了。

*Truly, love is blind.*

真的，愛是盲目的。

▶注意◀　Really 和 truly 的含義常與 very 相同，用以強調形容詞或副詞。因此在以下 3 例中，它們不再是句子附加狀語。

*I'm going to be very honest with you, Joey, because this is really important to me.*

我將對你直言不諱，鳩益，因為這對我很重要。

*You need to take this really seriously.*

你要很認真地對待這事。

*Their efforts were truly remarkable.*

他們的努力是非常卓越的。

**8.27**　**Really** 的第二個用法是強調真實情況與表面情況不相符合。

*Try to find out why they're **really** here and what it is they **really** want.*

設法搞清楚他們到底為甚麼來這兒以及他們到底想要甚麼。

*What some of these students **really** want is a parent to take them in hand and tell them what to do.*

這幫學生中的一些人實在需要的是由家長牽着他們的手，告訴他們該做甚麼。

## in reality

**8.28　In reality** 與在 8.27 節中討論的 really 的第二種含義相同。說話者在講解事實，這些事實與人們想像的可能不一樣。

*Many of them wrongly assume that the surviving partner will inherit whereas, **in reality**, he or she may receive nothing.*

他們中的很多人都錯誤地認為，幸存的配偶將繼承財產，然而實際上，他或她可能甚麼也得不到。

*In the distance a fox began to cry, **in reality** calling for a mate, but sounding as if in agonized torment.*

遠處一隻狐狸開始嚎叫，實際上它在召喚配偶，但聽起來卻像是身受痛苦折磨而發出的聲音。

## surely

**8.29**　如果說話者認為某事是顯而易見的，或肯定是正確的，並企圖勸說他人也相信自己所說的話，就可使用 **surely**。該詞的意思是 I can't believe you don't agree with me（我不認為你反對我）或 You agree, don't you（你同意，對嗎？）。

*We had been sentenced in our absence, without an opportunity to plead our defence, which under the laws of natural justice is **surely** wrong.*

我們在未出庭的情況下就被宣判了，根本就沒有機會為自己辯護，這麼做據自然判決法肯定是錯的。

*The police have **surely** questioned him thoroughly.*（即：I cannot believe they have not questioned him thoroughly. 我不相信他們還沒仔細審問過他。）

警方肯定已經仔細地審問過他了。

*Well what about the ironing, John. I mean that's only about an hour isn't it? There's not a lot of work in that **surely** for a young strapping fellow like you.*

把衣服燙一下怎麼樣，約翰。我想大約只要花一個小時就行了，是不是？對你這麼個棒小夥子來說，這肯定不是甚麼重活。

***Surely** you don't think I went off in my swimming costume, murdered my husband and pushed him into the water, and then returned to change?*

你肯定不會認為我穿着泳裝走開，殺了我丈夫並把他推到水裏，然後再回來換上衣服吧？

**8.30**　當說話者確信某事已經發生或正在發生或將要發生時，也可使用 **surely**。

*Name a famous conductor, and almost **surely** he has encountered difficulties.*

隨便說出一個著名指揮，幾乎可以肯定，他都遇到過困難。

*Food and drink culture in Britain is **surely** changing, has **surely** changed over the last two decades.*

在英國，飲食文化肯定正在不斷地發生着改變，並且在過去二十年中肯定已發生過不少變化。

*Long before nuclear ores are exhausted, better energy sources will **surely** be developed.*

在核能源用盡之前，更好的能源肯定會被開發出來。

**Slowly but surely** 則是為了強調儘管某種活動發生的速度不快，但它的發生是必然的或肯定的。

*The number of women alcoholics is **slowly but surely** catching up on their male counterparts.*

女性酗酒者的數量必定會遲早趕上她們的男性同道。

**8.31** 也可用 **surely** 表示 Yes, definitely（是，必定）、 Yes, of course（是，當然）的意思，以回應他人的話。

*'Would you all join me tonight?' '**Surely**,' said Mather, 'That would be very kind.'*

"你們今晚都到我這兒來嗎？""當然，"馬瑟說，"你們太好了。"

## definitely, certainly

**8.32** **Definitely** 與 **certainly** 在口語中極其常見。可用來強調說話者的話不容置疑，等於 I am certain that...（我確定……），It is certain that...（這是肯定的……）。Definitely 的語意更強，不過不能用於句子開頭（除非在短句中，如："Definitely not!" "當然不！"）。

*This procedure requires a doctor who is a skilled expert. It **definitely** should not be done by yourself or by a beauty specialist.*

這個程序需要一名技術精湛的醫學專家來完成。絕對不能由你本人或一名美容師來完成。

*Zinc is now **definitely** accepted as being essential for the combatting of infections.*

現在，鋅已經確定無疑地被看作是一種抗傳染病的必要元素。

*You must be prepared to cope with unusual situations, local inadequacies and unpredictable events as and when they occur. Our kind of travel is **definitely** not suitable for people who expect to be cosseted or pampered.*

你必須準備好應付各種不同尋常的狀況，當地設施欠缺，會發生意想不到的事件。我們這種旅行絕對不適合那些嬌生慣養和受到溺愛的人參加。

*Contrary to what some people believe, massage is not difficult to learn, although it is **certainly** true that someone will get better at it through practice.*

不像一些人想像的那樣，其實學習按摩並不很困難，儘管有的人通過實踐肯定能掌握得更好些。

*What can be wrong with clean air? Nothing. Everybody wants it. I **certainly** support it.*

空氣清潔有甚麼錯？沒有。每個人都要清新的空氣。我當然也支持這種觀點。

*I **certainly** don't agree with the drugs scene.*
我不同意有關吸毒的一場。

**8.33　Certainly** 當放在句子開頭時，有時會有一點讓步的意義，相當於 It is admittedly true that... (誠然⋯⋯)。

*He didn't look as if he'd had a day's illness in his life. **Certainly** his operation hadn't made him lose weight.*
他看起來這一輩子好像都沒得過一天病。當然，他的那次手術並沒使他消瘦。

*It was rumoured that the town's traffic system had already cost the sanity of ten motorists. **Certainly**, one had been found slumped over the wheel of his car, sobbing in a highly emotional manner.*
有傳聞說該鎮的交通體制已經讓10名駕車手失去了理智。確實，其中有一個被發現倒在車輪旁，情緒激動地抽泣着。

**8.34** 作為一種簡單回答，**certainly** (當然) 與 of course 的含義相同。

*'Well, sir, perhaps we could begin by your telling me just what you were doing Sunday night and Monday morning.' — '**Certainly**,' said Chantrey.*
"那麼，先生，也許我們可以開始了，先由你告訴我你週日晚上和週一上午在做甚麼，怎麼樣。"
——"當然可以，"錢特里答道。

## undoubtedly, without(any) doubt, doubtless, no doubt

**8.35** 這四種表達式，儘管看起來形似，意思卻並不相同。

**Undoubtedly** 和 **without (any) doubt** 語意最強。表示完全的肯定：There is no doubt at all that... (毫無疑問⋯⋯)；It is quite certain that... (這是肯定的⋯⋯)。

*People who gave comfort or help to the enemy in this war are liable to be tried for treason. Some will **undoubtedly** be hanged.*
那些在戰爭中向敵軍提供支持和幫助的人將會以判國罪受到審判。有的無疑將被處以絞刑。

*'Teaching from a blackboard is boring and **undoubtedly** turns people off,' he claimed.*
"單靠板書教學是令人厭倦的，而且毫無疑問會令人討厭，"他說道。

*Conflict there **undoubtedly** was, but it was very one-sided.*
毫無疑問會有衝突存在，但那只是單方面的。

*Although hostile, Ron thought, Sammy was **undoubtedly** lonely.*
儘管依然抱有敵意，羅恩認為，薩米毫無疑問很孤單。

*Those who sink to drug abuse are **without doubt** the weakest and least desirable of the population.*
那些沉溺於嗜用麻醉毒品的人無疑是人類中最脆弱和最不可取的人。

*Stress is **without doubt** the single most significant factor in raising blood pressure.*
緊張無疑是引起血壓升高的唯一最重要的因素。

***Without any doubt** there is need for further change in Europe.*
毫無疑問，歐洲有必要作進一步改革。

**Doubtless** 與 **no doubt** 則語意相對較弱，意思大致與 probably（可能地）或 presumably（大概地）等同。

*I've more to tell you than you **doubtless** read in the paper.*
你可能從報上讀到了一些，不過，我要告訴你更多。

*The turtles were removed from our bat (**doubtless** to the relief of the maids who serviced our room) and placed in a suitable container.*
海龜已從我們的浴缸中取走（這可能會讓替我們打掃房間的女傭鬆一口氣），放到了一個合適的容器內。

*People who are told that they are unattractive, will **no doubt** eventually see themselves as being unattractive.*
那些從小被告知自己容貌平常的人，最終很可能就會把自己視為其貌不揚之輩。

***No doubt** love for their fellow man played its part, but there were sound economic reasons too.*
很可能他們對同胞的愛也起了一定作用，也有堅實的經濟因素。

▶ **注意** ◀ 作為句子附加狀語的 no doubt 要嚴格與放在 that-從句或以 about 引導的介詞短語前的 no doubt 區分開來，儘管它們看起來很相似。用在從句或介詞短語前的 no doubt 表示的是絕對肯定的意義。

*There was **no doubt** Greenfield was infatuated.*
格林菲爾德肯定是癡情的。

*He had **no doubt** that the enemy must be ruthlessly crushed.*
他堅信對敵人一定要無情地加以摧毀。

*He will go back to London; there is **no doubt** about that.*
他會回到倫敦來的，這一點毫無疑問。

## unquestionably, undeniably

**8.36** 這兩個句子附加狀語在書面語比在口語中用得更多，表示肯定的意思。不過它們強調的是敍述內容明白無誤，以至於根本不可能提出質疑或異議。

*The squabblings of the art historians cease to matter. These paintings are **unquestionably** some of Italy's finest.*
藝術歷史學家們的爭執變得無關緊要了。這些繪畫毋庸置疑是意大利繪畫中的精品。

***Undeniably**, political stability and human progress in the country depend on greater economic success.*
不可否認，國家政治的穩定和人的進步都依賴於更大的經濟繁榮。

## apparently, presumably, evidently, seemingly

**8.37** 四個詞中的任何一個均可用來限定所説的話的真實性。表示説話者所説的看起來是如此,但他本人並不保證它是如此。

如果使用 **apparently**,説話者的意思是説自己被告知過某事是真實的,或者此事看起來是如此。**Seemingly** 的意思與 apparently 差不多,但使用得較少。

*Apparently your father was warned, but never said a word.*
很明顯,已經有人警告過你父親了,不過他從未吐露過。

*He talked to some of the children, apparently.*
很明顯,他跟一些孩子談過了。

*He had been found by a friend, apparently dead of a heart attack.*
他的一個朋友發現了他,很明顯,他死於心臟病發作。

*Her parents had seemingly borne their troubles well.*
她父母表面上看起來似乎能承受他們的煩惱。

**Evidently** 的意思與 apparently(明顯地)相似,不過強調敍述是有據可查的,此類證據常是説話者本人或他人看到的直接見證。

*Voters are evidently angry now that he broke that promise.*
由於他不恪守諾言,顯然選民們都生氣了。

*Classes had evidently ended for the day because the campus was virtually deserted.*
那天的課顯然已經結束了,因為校園裏已經沒有人了。

*He bet a lot of money. Evidently, he lost a lot.*
他押上了一大筆賭注。顯然,他輸了不少錢。

使用 **presumably** 表示説話者所説的是自己推測的情況,即根據他自己所知的事實和環境作出的一個較為合理的推測。

*He stayed here a short while. Presumably he booked in like every other visitor.*
他在這兒待了一會兒。也許他也像其他參觀者一樣已辦理登記手續。

*The new edition came out last month. So presumably the library will have that.*
新版本上個月就問世了。因此圖書館可能有這本書。

## allegedly, supposedly, reportedly

**8.38** 這三個詞在書面語比在口頭語中用得更多,與上一節的四個詞相比,這三個詞進一步限定了説話者對自己所説的話的真實性的承諾。其中 **allegedly** 和 **supposedly** 使説話者置身於事外,即他所説的是他人的想法,而對這種想法,他本人卻深表懷疑。

*Faith healers have allegedly produced miracles just through the laying on of hands.*
據稱,從事信仰治療的大師們只要行按手禮,就能創造奇跡。

*He regards socialization as now largely the preserve of the state. It is **allegedly** accomplished by means of education, welfare agencies and the subsidized arts.*
他把社會化看成在很大程度上是國家的專有範圍。據稱，這一進程是通過教育、福利機構以及為人文學科提供補助的方式來完成的。

*A woman could rub this material into her face and it would **supposedly** eradicate the lines on her face.*
婦女們可以把這種材料搽到臉上，據稱可以消除皺紋。

*From time to time during the slow journey, announcements were made over the loudspeaker system, **supposedly** to tell passengers the name of the next stop, but the voice was distorted and the information given in what appeared to be an unknown language.*
在漫漫旅程中，擴音器中不時傳來通知，據稱是向旅客報告下一站的站名，但糟糕的是，擴音器裏的聲音變了調，使通知聽起來像是用一種大家都聽不懂的語言來廣播的。

**Reportedly** 則是較為中立的説法，相等於 It is reported that…（據報道……），説話者也可能相信這種報道。

*Her childhood was **reportedly** stressful.*
據報道，她的童年生活很艱難。

*The officials **reportedly** became annoyed when they learnt that the article in the New England Journal of Medicine did not mention their plan.*
據報道，當官員們得知新英格蘭醫學雜誌中的文章沒有提及他們的計劃時，都惱怒了。

## theoretically, in theory, in practice

**8.39** **In theory** 及其變體 **theoretically**，表示某些行為或狀況據説將發生或存在，或者應該發生或存在。説話者通過使用這些詞語，暗示了現實，即**實際上**（**in practice**）發生的情況並非如此。

*Although **theoretically** the land was owned by the State, the nobles and the monasteries held large estates, and peasants also owned land.*
儘管理論上土地屬於國家，但實際上，貴族和修道院都佔有大量地產，農民也佔有一部份土地。

***In theory** at least, musical skills seem to presuppose intelligence of the conventional kind. Yet it is possible to find musically gifted individuals who score very low indeed on standard intelligence tests.*
至少在理論上，音樂技能要求常人的智力水平。當然，有些音樂上極具潛質的個人可能在標準智力測試中得分極低。

*Though **in theory** he knew that he risked being killed or kidnapped, **in practice** he took for granted the immunity of the foreigner.*
儘管在理論上他知道自己冒被殺害或被綁架的危險，但實際上，他認為作為外國人當然有豁免權。

*Yes I do consider that the present arrangements are inadequate. Not **in theory**, maybe, but definitely **in practice**.*
是的，我認為目前的安排不太妥當。也許理論上沒錯，但在實際上確實欠妥。

## officially, ideally, superficially, nominally, hypothetically

**8.40** 這五個副詞 —— 有點像 theoretically —— 指出所說的話和真實情況形成對照。**Officially** 表示 "根據官方提供情況" (according to some official source) ，但說話者卻對此表示懷疑。

> The meeting would be handled by his assistant. He, **officially**, would be somewhere else.
> 會議將由他的助手掌握。而他本人，據官方說，正在外地。

> I can recall a time when **officially** your position didn't exist.
> 我還可以回想起那段你的職位根據官方說法還不存在的時光。

> And so to this day we **officially** maintain that your department is only a figment of the popular imagination.
> 因此直至今天，根據官方說法，我們依然堅持你們部門只是公眾想像出來的，純屬子虛烏有。

**Ideally** 表示，在理想的世界裏，說話者的話會成立。

> **Ideally** two sketch books are necessary: a small one ,which will go in a large pocket, and a bigger one which will enable quite a large drawing to be made.
> 理想的是需要兩本素描本；小的那本可以放進隨身大口袋裏，大的那本可以用來作較大的畫。

> **Ideally**, the school should have spacious, open buildings and be in open grounds.
> 理想的是學校應該有寬敞的、開放式的建築和開闊的場地。

> **Ideally**, all wine should declare any additives used during the winemaking process and should also list any pesticides or other chemicals introduced to the vineyard.
> 理想的是各種葡萄酒都應該說明釀製過程中用過的添加劑，還應該列出葡萄園中使用的殺蟲劑和其他化學製劑。

**Superficially** 的含義是 on the surface (表面上看) 或 at first glance (第一眼看上去) 。

> Many of these killers are frequently glib and **superficially** charming, helpful, sweet and kind.
> 這些殺手中有許多人通常油嘴滑舌，並且表面上看上去富有魅力、樂於助人、和藹可親且心地善良。

> Although **superficially** these industries seemed to be under public regulation, they were thus in fact mostly privately regulated.
> 雖然表面上看，這些工業似乎被置於公共管理之下，但實際上他們大多為私人管理。

**Nominally** 表示某事的名稱或正式描述使人誤解或不十分精確。

> It was **nominally** a non-political trip, but this did not unduly inhibit the president's campaigning style.
> 雖然這名義上是一次非政治性的旅行，但是這對於總統的競選風格並沒有太多的約束。

> Although they are both **nominally**, and I believe genuinely, volunteers, they are both constantly asking for money.
> 雖然他們倆在名義上，而且我也深信，都是自願者，但是他們一直在要錢。

**Hypothetically** 表示某事理論上是可能的，但可能性不大。

*There is no evidence that he knew, though it remains **hypothetically** possible.*
雖然理論上仍然是可能的，但實際上他並不知道任何證據。

*Within every EU state there are thousands of employers which could **hypothetically** offer employment to a British graduate. However, such employers will very probably have well established recruitment practices in their home countries.*
理論上講，歐盟的每個國家都有成千上萬名僱主可以向一名英國大學畢業名提供職業。但是，這些僱主也許很可能已經在他們本國確立了他們的招聘辦法。

## admittedly, arguably, conceivably

**8.41**　這三個副詞主要用於書面語。**Admittedly** 有一種讓步的意思——寫話者承認，了解情況，因而在某些方面削弱了自己敍述。

*It is only a theory, **admittedly**, but the pieces fit together, and in my opinion it's worth pursuing.*
確實這只是一個推測，但是它的各部份有機聯繫，並且我認為值得對它探討下去。

*To have survived acute thirst, a near drowning, and almost freezing to death is a tribute to his courage. **Admittedly** he had little choice in the matter.*
熬過極度的乾渴，做到溺水不死或挨凍而不死都顯示了他高度的勇氣。不過在這件事上，他確實沒有甚麼選擇。

**Arguably** 表示有可能對某特定觀點進行論證 (one could argue that...)。寫話者可能非常相信該論證，但實際上沒有説出來。所以arguably可以視作對敍述的削弱。但是在某種意義上講，有時它可以加強敍述，即暗示這是推理論證的結果，而不只是個人的意見。

*Though Yeats was **arguably** the greatest modern English language poet, Eliot was undoubtedly the most important and influential.*
雖然稱耶茨是最偉大的現代英語詩人值得商榷，但是艾略特卻毫無爭議的是最重要且最具有影響的現代英語詩人。

*This satellite had saved thousands of lives and was **arguably** the most useful and efficient result of America's space program.*
這個人造衞星救了許多人的性命，毫無爭議它是美國太空計劃中最實用及最有效率的成果。

**Conceivably** 只表示有可能構想出或獲得某種意見，但寫話者並未表態。

*When we first got the letter I wondered if Mollie could **conceivably** have written it to herself.* （即：*Was it possible to imagine that she had written it to herself?* 是否有可能設想她把這封信寫給自己呢？）
當我們剛收到這封信時，我懷疑莫麗是否有可能把這封信寫給她自己。

## basically, essentially, fundamentally

**8.42** 這三個詞強調說話者在提到的是情境的最重要（最基本的、最本質的）方面。可能會增加更複雜的細節，但說話者的敘述通常都是真實的。這三個詞都可用於口語和書面語，其中 **basically** 最常用，並且最常用於口語。

*Basically that argument was simply that the country could not afford to go on expanding non-productive sectors such as social services.*
基本上講，理由就是這個國家無力繼續擴大像社會服務這樣的非生產性部門。

*Basically, a stroke is the result of damage to part of the brain caused by an interruption to its blood supply.*
基本上講，中風是部份大腦損傷的結果，這種損傷是由對大腦的血液供應中斷引起的。

*The diet consists basically of fresh meat, fish, fruit and vegetables, with water to drink.*
該飲食基本上由鮮肉、魚、水果和蔬菜組成，還有飲用水。

*In other words all societies are essentially capitalist, and all people are businessmen.*
換種說法，所有的社會在本質上都是資本主義的，並且所有的人都是商人。

*Essentially, given the potential of modern technology and large-scale producing organizations, there is no technological reason for hunger or inadequate shelter, medical care and the like.*
本質上講，在有了現代科技和大規模生產機構的潛力，飢餓、住房不足、醫療等的缺乏從技術上來說就沒有任何存在的理由。

*Fundamentally, they were both thinking like bureaucrats. People who spent their lives in bureaucracies were typically afraid of breaking rules.*
從根本上講，他們倆都像官僚一樣思考問題，那些一輩子都在官僚政治中度過的人害怕打破陳規。

## hopefully

**8.43** 說話者可以用 **hopefully** 取代 I hope（我希望）或 we hope（我們希望），表示自己希望某事發生。有些人認為這種用法不正確，但已被廣泛使用。

*Angel and I were off to another life, another world, which was hopefully a much happier one than the one we had known at the orphanage.*
安琪爾和我出發走向另一種生活、另一個世界，我們希望它比我們在孤兒院時所知道的世界更快樂。

*Data for the scientific discoveries that made nuclear power possible has been collected by Nick Kollerstrom and will hopefully be published.*
有關使原子能成為可能的科學發現的資料已被尼克·科勒斯特勞姆收集，希望將會發表。

*Hopefully some basic investigations will have already been carried out by the family doctor.*
希望這位家庭醫生到時已經做過了一些基本的檢查。

# 説話者對事件的意見或判斷
# Your opinion or judgement of events

**8.44** 有時候在報道某件事時，説話者並非只對它進行客觀報道，而且還要表明自己對其的態度，即對該事件的好、壞、是否合理、是否令人吃驚等作出評價。有許多句子附加狀語可以用來表示自己的態度—有時候也可表示被報道事件中所涉及的人的態度。它們中有許多相當於一個起引導作用的分句，例如：surprisingly 等於 It is surprising that... 。

表示某件事令人驚奇(或者表示某事在意料之中因此不令人驚奇)的句子附加狀語將在8.45 - 8.57節討論。表示對運氣好壞的看法的句子附加狀語在8.58 - 8.62節論述。接下去在8.63 - 8.71節則涉及表示其他各種判斷的句子附加狀語，其中表示認為某件事是重要的這種看法的句子附加狀語在8.63節討論。

## 某事令人驚奇
## Something is surprising

surprisingly, remarkably, amazingly, astonishingly

**8.45** 有幾個詞可以表明説話者對已發生事物的驚奇，其中以 surprisingly 最為常見。

*The management has discovered unexpected benefits from employing over-50s.*
***Surprisingly**, they take fewer days off sick.*
管理層已經發現僱傭50歲以上的人所帶來的意外好處。因為令人驚奇的是，他們更少請病假。

*Her eyes met Nick's and she caught his happiness. Suddenly, **surprisingly**, she felt like a young girl again.*
她的目光與尼克的目光相遇，並且她捕捉到了他的快樂。令人驚奇的是，突然她感到自己又成了一個年輕姑娘了。

*On this occasion however, Rawlinson persevered, and Herbert **surprisingly** relented.*
儘管這一次洛林森仍然堅持，但令人驚奇的是，赫伯特卻變得態度緩和。

*The factory had, **remarkably**, escaped Allied bombing.*
這家工廠令人驚異地躲過了同盟國的轟炸。

***Remarkably**, the book contains not a single photograph.*
不同尋常的是，這本書沒有一張照片。

*I repeated the command once more and **amazingly** he obeyed me.*
我再一次重複了命令，令人驚異的是，他居然對我服從了。

*We thought the house had been empty for ten years. **Amazingly**, there was a telephone standing on the floor by the big windows.*
我們認為這棟房子已經空置了10年了。令人驚異的是，那些大窗戶邊的地板上居然放着一台電話機。

*In 1952, she had been the success story of the Hollywood year, the London–Broadway actress who had caught the critics' attention, and **amazingly**, the public's also.*

1952年，這位倫敦一百老匯女演員成了好萊塢當年的成功故事，她不僅贏得了評論界的注意，而且令人驚異地贏得了公眾的注意。

***Astonishingly**, seven out of ten people in Britain have not made a will.*

令人驚異的是，在英國每10個人中就有7個沒有立過遺囑。

## curiously, strangely, oddly, interestingly, funnily

**8.46**　有時候說話者可能想要強調某件事不僅令人驚奇，而且相當怪異。**Interestingly** 強調說話者認為自己的信息是令人感興趣的，那是因為有時該信息與人們的想法相反。

*He had a short beard which, **curiously**, served to make him look younger than his years.*

他有一臉短短的鬍子，令人難以理解的是，這居然使他看起來比他的歲數更年輕。

***Strangely**, the idea that she might have left Berlin did not occur to me until I got to the station.*

奇怪的是，在我到達車站之前，我從沒想到她可能已經離開柏林了。

*Around his neck, **oddly**, was a small green scarf.*

真古怪，他脖子上圍着一條小綠色圍巾。

***Interestingly**, it appears that those who are good at analytical, rational thinking, do not do so well when confronted with new circumstances.*

令人感興趣的是，看來那些擅長分析與理性思考的人在遇到新情況時並不很擅長這樣做。

**Funnily** 必須後跟副詞 **enough**。這種表達式主要用於口語。本節討論的其他詞也經常後跟 enough。

*The main ingredient is sugar, **funnily enough**.*

主要成分是糖，真好笑。

*I smiled and kissed him. **Funnily enough**, I was suddenly very hungry.*

我笑了並吻了他。好笑的是，我突然感到餓了。

*One of my guides in the desert with me got forty-three stings and was very ill. **Curiously enough**, I alone was not stung.*

在沙漠裏，跟隨我的向導中有一位被蜇了43次，而且症狀嚴重。非常令人難以理解的是，只有我沒被蜇過。

***Strangely enough**, the Hollywood gossip columnists and paparazzi showed similar respect and left the movie star couple pretty much alone.*

非常古怪的是，那些好萊塢饒舌的專欄作家和名人攝影師居然表示出相似的尊重，沒怎麼去打擾那對電影明星夫婦。

*The talk, **oddly enough**, was drifting towards politics.*

非常奇怪，這次談話的話題漸漸地轉向了政治。

*Oddly enough*, he performed well at school.
非常令人奇怪的是，他在學校裏表現得很好。

*Interestingly enough*, I found that there were more women working in Hollywood prior to 1920 than at any other time since.
非常令人感興趣的是，我發現 1920 年前在好萊塢工作的婦女比那以後任何時候都多。

## mysteriously, inexplicably

**8.47**　如果說話者說某件事神秘地（**mysteriously**）發生了，那麼是在強調這件事不只是古怪，而且令人困惑，可能仍是一個未解的謎。

*A few months after the divorce, her husband was **mysteriously** killed by a hit-and-run driver. But he, the husband that is, hadn't changed his will yet, so she got all the money.*
離婚幾個月以後，她的丈夫被一名肇事後開車逃跑的駕駛員神秘地害死了。他，即她的先夫，還沒有修改遺囑，因此她得到了他所有的錢。

*Two psychiatrists from the famed Massachusetts General Hospital recently reported on a group of children who were **mysteriously** taken ill.*
最近，來自著名的馬省總醫院的兩名精神病醫生就一羣神秘得病的孩子提出了報告。

**Inexplicably**（難以解釋地）的含義是對已發生的事在過去或現在都無法說明。

*Suddenly and **inexplicably** I began to sob. I hadn't cried for years and why now?*
突然，莫名其妙地我開始抽泣起來。我已經多年沒有哭過，為甚麼現在要哭呢？

*The car pulled cautiously onto the grass and for a few moments it just sat there, **inexplicably** with its engine running and its lights on.*
汽車小心翼翼地駛到草地上，它就在那裏停了一會兒，難以理解的是，它的發動機在轉動，車燈也開着。

## incredibly, unbelievably

**8.48**　如果說話者使用 **incredibly** 或 **unbelievably**，那是在說所敍述的事情是那麼令人驚奇，以至儘管事情屬實，但卻令人難以相信。

*Incredibly, our army was not attacking, fearful that a hostile advance might mean death for the hostages.*
令人難以置信的是，由於擔心一次敵對的推進可能意味着人質的死亡，我們的部隊居然沒有攻擊。

*Incredibly, it seems that he was unaware that he had shaken off his pursuers.*
令人難以置信的是，他看來還沒有意識到他已經擺脫了追捕他的人。

*Unbelievably, the fourth game was also drawn.*
令人難以相信的是，第 4 場比賽還是平局。

*As we always tell prospective patients: if you want me to help you, you must be prepared to help yourself. **Unbelievably** this quickly eliminates about 40 percent of those who contact us.*

正如我們總是告訴那些可能成為病人的人那樣，如果你們想要我幫助你們，那麼你們必須要準備好幫助你們自己。與我們聯繫過的人中有 40% 居然令人難以置信地沒來看病了。

## unexpectedly

**8.49**　如果某件事出人意料地（**unexpectedly**）發生了，那麼這當然令人驚奇，但是說話者強調的是，當時有關的人之所以感到驚奇是因為他們沒有指望事情會發生。

*They had driven **unexpectedly** down a one-way street and got away with it.*
他們出人意料地在單行道上逆行，並且居然未被人發覺。

***Unexpectedly**, I've been offered a wonderful job.*
出人意料的是，我得到了這麼好的一份工作。

## coincidentally

**8.50**　如果兩件事情令人驚奇地同時發生或在某個方面令人驚奇地相關，但純屬偶然（而非由於任何計劃），那麼這就是巧合（**coincidentally**）發生的事。

*Nora spent most of her considerable leisure hours with her two adopted sisters, Magda and Suki, who were both **coincidentally** also residing in Canton.*
諾拉將她可觀的空閒時間的大部份用於和她的兩位收養的姐妹瑪格達和蘇琪呆在一起，她們兩位湊巧也住在堪頓。

*The new housing minister was a former aristocrat, to whom one of the now crumbling palaces, **coincidentally**, once belonged.*
這位新任住房部長原是位貴族，那些已破舊不堪的宮殿中有一座碰巧一度曾屬於他。

# 意料之中或恰如其分的事
# Something is expected or appropriate

**8.51**　有時說話者想要說明所發生的事並不令人驚奇，而是相反，即預料中要發生或可能會發生的事。

## not surprisingly, unsurprisingly

**8.52**　評論某事並不令人驚奇的方式是使用 **not surprisingly**。在8.45節中別的表示 surprise（吃驚）的副詞不能這樣加以否定。**Unsurprisingly** 則是一種較少使用的變體。

*Not surprisingly*, *the bodyguards opposing them were sometimes brutal also, and being male, expressed masculine brutality.*
反對他們的保鏢們有時顯得野蠻，而且作為男性，顯示出男性所具有的野蠻，這並不令人感到意外。

*The bad news was that the van, **not surprisingly**, was in an appalling condition and needed another thirty-six hours in the garage.*
壞消息是，當然這也不令人感到奇怪，這運輸車情況糟得可怕，還需要在修理間再呆上36個小時。

*It's an alphabetically ordered file, starting with A and finishing **unsurprisingly** perhaps with Z or something.*
這是份按字母順序排列的文件，從 A 開始，也許以 Z 或別的甚麼字母結尾也不會令人感到奇怪。

***Unsurprisingly**, there is little enthusiasm in the City, or in Whitehall, for such wholesale reform.*
倫敦的金融商業區或白廳，對這麼一場大規模的改革並未表現出甚麼熱情，這並不令人感到奇怪。

## inevitably, predictably

**8.53** 如果説話者認為某件事過去或現在注定要發生或注定是如此，就可以用 **inevitably**，其字面上的意思是指某件事過去或現在無法避免。

*Rose was mostly liked and respected as an employer, but **inevitably** she had her critics.*
作為僱主，羅斯通常受到人們的愛戴或尊敬，但不可避免的是，她也有她的批評者。

*A more elderly population combined with rising home ownership rates will **inevitably** result in more elderly owners.*
老齡人口的增加和擁有自己住房家庭的比例上升不可避免地產生越來越多的年長房主。

較不常用的 **predictably** 的含義是指任何人都能預先猜測到某事會發生或某事會如此。

*First reports from the various hospitals and emergency services indicated that excessive use of force by the police had been responsible for the protestors' deaths. **Predictably**, pubic reaction was mixed.*
來自不同醫院和急救服務機構的最初報告顯示警察使用過分的暴力造成了抗議者的死亡。不出所料，公眾對此的反應顯得有褒有貶。

***Predictably**, the new rule prohibiting goalkeepers from handling passes kicked deliberately towards them has caused initial confusion among even the most experienced.*
不出所料，即使是最有經驗的守門員起初也對這條禁止守門員用手處理有意傳給他們的球的新規則感到困惑不解。

*There was silence round the table. **Predictably** it was broken by Janet.*
整張桌子的人顯得一片沉默。不出所料，這種沉默被簡妮特打破了。

## necessarily, not necessarily

**8.54** 如果説話者説某事物勢必（**necessarily**）如此，那就是説從邏輯上講此事應該如此。所以它的意義類似於 inevitably（儘管 inevitably 還帶有不可避免的結果的意思）。

*The acquisition of valuable and extensive property thus **necessarily** requires the establishment of civil government.*
因此，貴重而大片地產的取得勢必有賴於文職政府的建立。

*There will **necessarily** have to be some further instructions.*
勢必需要有進一步的指令。

*Lynch firmly believed that the repository of all important knowledge in a small town was, **necessarily**, the chief barman of the local pub.*
林奇堅信，在這座小鎮裏所有重要知識的貯存庫勢必是當地那間酒吧裏的那位領班招待。

Necessarily 的反義詞是 **not necessarily**，暗示某種結果或結局並非不可避免，不過，當然，它總還可能發生。

*Of course if they didn't see him it does**n't necessarily** mean he wasn't there.*
當然，即使他們沒有看見他，也並非一定意味着他不在那裏。

*A small child does **not necessarily** love his brothers and sisters: often he obviously does not.*
一個小孩並非一定要愛他的兄弟姐妹：顯然，他通常就不愛。

*Conscious envy is **not necessarily** destructive.*
有意識的忌妒並不一定具有破壞性。

**8.55** ▶注意◀ **Unnecessarily** 的意義則大不相同。它指說話者對認為是浪費時間（事實上是沒必要）的行為的評論。

*Elsie's mother came over with the coffee, **unnecessarily** carrying the cup on a tray.*
艾爾西的母親帶着咖啡走過來，毫無必要地把咖啡杯子放在一個托盤上端過來。

*'His throat's been cut,' I said **unnecessarily**, just to say something.*
"他的喉嚨被切開了，"我毫無必要地這樣說，只是為了沒話找話說而已。

## typically, characteristically

**8.56** 如果說話者認為某事物通常以自己描述的方式發生，或某人以自己預想的方式行事，那麼就可以使用 **typically** 或 **characteristically**。Typically 比較常見並常用在口語中。

*He had pleaded to be allowed to go there but **typically** at once began to have doubts once permission had been given.*
他曾請求允許到那裏，但一旦被允許，他又是一貫的樣子，馬上產生疑慮。

*Such calculations are **typically** made by bureaucratic decision.*
如此的估算典型地出自官僚主義決定。

*I begged him to see another doctor. **Characteristically** he was unwilling.*
我請求他去看另一位醫生。他不願意，這是他的本性。

*I discovered I had, **characteristically**, lost the notebook.*（即：*I am always losing things.* 我總是丟東西。）

我發現我把筆記本丟了，我總是這樣。

## naturally, not unnaturally, understandably

**8.57**　如果說話者說某事自然如此（**naturally**），那是指在當時的境況下那是可以預料的事（因此 naturally 有時大致相當於 of course）。

*Everybody thinks you ought to take a holiday in any case. Will you come? All expenses paid, **naturally**.*

每個人都認為你無論如何應該休假。你來嗎？自然，所有的費用我們付。

*She ran screaming into the street, blood running down her face, and the neighbours **naturally** rang the police.*

她尖叫着衝上大街，鮮血沿着她的臉直往下淌，鄰居們很自然地給警察打了電話。

*Do you like bodies? Dead bodies? **Naturally**, you do not.*

您喜歡屍體嗎？我是說屍體？你自然不喜歡。

*Some sort of platform, **naturally**, was necessary for Irene Byrd to stand on when she made her speech.*

當艾琳·伯德作演講時，當然她需要站在某種講台上。

**Not unnaturally** 的使用範圍更小，其含義是並不令人驚奇。

*Different muscles in the body have, **not unnaturally**, different roles to play.*

人體中的不同肌肉起着不同的作用，這並不令人驚奇。

*Barker still had his arm in plaster so, **not unnaturally**, press photographers appeared from nowhere and took photographs of the Prince about to be flown by a one-armed pilot.*

巴克的手臂仍敷着石膏，因此許多雜誌攝影師不知從何處冒了出來，給將由一名獨臂駕駛員駕駛的王子號拍照，這一切並不令人驚奇。

***Not unnaturally**, the primary concern of the French army was the expulsion of the invader from French soil.*

並不令人驚奇，法國軍隊主要關心的是將入侵者從法國本土趕出去。

如果說話者使用 **understandably**，是表示自己打算原諒某種行為或舉止，因為該行為或舉止在當時環境下是一件自然而然的事。

*Many touchingly spoke to me of their painful experiences, but **understandably** declined to be filmed or directly quoted.*

許多人曾令人感動地與我談過他們痛苦的經歷，但可以理解的是，他們不願意將這些經歷拍成電影或直接加以引用。

*The syllabuses of military academies were **understandably** dominated by the study of conventional war.*

可以理解的是，軍事學院的課程大綱把學習常規戰爭擺在主導的地位。

## 屬於幸運或不幸的事
# Something is fortunate or unfortunate

**8.58**　有時候説話者評論説某事的發生是好事或壞事。

## happily, fortunately, luckily

**8.59**　可以使用這三個副詞中的任何一個來表達對所發生之事的喜悦或贊許。**Happily** 暗示説話者對該事件感到高興，**fortunately** 有時暗示了一種幸運的成分，前兩個詞要比 **luckily** 常見。如果説話者希望提及究竟誰是幸運的，可以增加一個用 for 引出的介詞短語。

*Even if they found a house that was within Mark's limit he could not obtain a mortgage without a regular income. **Happily** his mother-in-law came to the rescue and lent them the money.*
即使他們找到了馬克能買得起的房子，由於沒有穩定的收入，他沒法取得抵押貸款。使人高興的是，他的岳母過來救了他們，把錢借給了他們。

*Such discord is, **happily**, absent in my present parish.*
令人高興的是，這樣的不和諧在我目前所在的教區還沒有。

*Brian passed me a rope and I managed to pull myself up onto a wet, sloping ledge. **Fortunately**, the rock was rough and my deck shoes held.*
布萊恩遞給我一根繩子，然後我設法把我自己拉向一個濕漉漉的斜面岩礁。幸運的是，這是一塊粗糙石頭，我的登山鞋能踩得住而不打滑。

*Eventually the plane hit a house, but **fortunately** there was no fire.*
這架飛機最後撞上了一棟房子，但幸運的是，沒有造成火災。

*Eight out of ten of us suffer this miserable condition at some time in our lives. **Fortunately** for most of us, it's an isolated event.*
在我們的生活中的某個時候，10 個人有 8 個經受過這種可悲的情況。對我們中的大多數人來説，很幸運，這只是個孤立的事件。

*Once when she slipped, her bicycle headlamp fell out of her pocket and skidded away down the track; **luckily** it wasn't broken.*
當她一滑倒，她的自行車頭燈就從她的口袋裏掉了出去，在跑道上向下滑去；幸運的是，燈沒被打破。

*He simply called the police and **luckily** there was a squad car nearby, so they were caught.*
他只是給警察局打了電話，幸運的是，附近有一輛巡邏車，所以那些人被逮住了。

## unfortunately, sadly, unhappily, unluckily

**8.60**　可能大多數人都是悲觀論者。無論如何，通常在英語口語中，**unfortunately** 看來要比 fortunately 常用！這裏還有其他三個選擇：**sadly**，**unhappily** 和 **unluckily**。

*In the course of time his wife had **unfortunately** become an invalid.*
歲月流逝，他的妻子不幸成了傷殘。

***Unfortunately**, my car broke down and I was stuck here while it was being repaired.*
不幸的是，我的車壞了，在修車的時候，我就被困在那裏了。

***Sadly**, what should have been a very minor incident ended in disaster.*
不幸的是，本是件很小的事故最後卻成了一場災難。

*They do have an endless stream of traffic hurtling by which, **sadly**, drowns the beautiful music.*
他們確實聽到不斷的車流飛馳而過，令人沮喪的是，它淹沒了美妙的音樂。

***Sadly for company morale**, and perhaps for its future ability to recruit the best graduates, shocked employees read about the sackings in the newspapers.*
對公司士氣以及也許對公司將來能招聘到最好的畢業生的能力來說都是件不幸的事，驚呆了的職員在報紙上看到被解僱人員名單。

*This was not, **unhappily**, the view of everyone in the game.*
令人不快的是，這不是這場比賽中每個人的看法。

***Unhappily**, although the traitor had been seized, the chief enemy agent had escaped.*
令人不快的是，儘管叛徒抓住了，但主要的敵方間諜卻逃走了。

***Unhappily for you**, things didn't work out as you'd planned.*
令你不快的是，事情不按照你所計劃的那樣進行。

*Some people **unluckily** achieve suicide when they only meant to attempt it.*
不幸的是，一些人本來只是為了嘗試一下自殺，卻真的自殺成功了。

***Unluckily for him** the fraud officers were watching this flight too.*
對他來說，不幸的是，那些欺詐的官員也在觀看這次飛行。

## thankfully, mercifully, miraculously

**8.61** 如果因為某事發生，或者可能因為某件極不令人愉快的事已經結束，而感到寬慰時，說話者可以用 **thankfully** 或 **mercifully**。如果認為某事既幸運又使人驚奇，則可以使用 **miraculously**。特別是使用miracifully 和miraculously時，有可能暗示是上帝或命運造成了這件幸運之事的發生。

***Thankfully**, the land has so far escaped being developed.*
謝天謝地，至今這塊土地尚未開發過。

*There are, **thankfully**, exceptions to this approach.*
值得感謝的是，除了這種方法之外還有別的方法。

*That morning the Atlantic, **mercifully**, was calm and almost windless.*
值得慶幸的是，那天早上大西洋平靜而無風。

***Mercifully** there is no snow on the ground. Walking should not be hard.*
慶幸的是，地上沒雪。走路應該不難。

*Violent incidents were **mercifully** uncommon .*
謝主慈悲，暴力事件並不常見。

*Miraculously*, ten survivors had crawled out of the terrible wreckage, hysterical, astonished to be alive.
不可思議的是，10名幸存者從可怕的斷垣殘壁中爬了出來，並且為自己居然還活着而感到歇斯底里和驚懼。

*He used his skill as a negotiator to set up a conciliation force that since July has **miraculously** managed to keep the peace.*
作為一名談判代表，他運用自己的能力建立了一支和解隊伍，竟從7月起不可思議地成功地維持了和平。

## alas, tragically, regrettably, disappointingly

**8.62** 此外，還有用來評述某事件或情境如何令人感到傷心、悲慘、後悔或失望，以上列出的四個詞就屬於這類句子附加狀語。

*No, I married, but **alas** it has been a failure.*
是，我結過婚，但是，唉，這是一次失敗的婚姻。

***Alas**, there are no longer any battles worth fighting.*
唉，再也沒有值得打的仗了。

***Tragically** and unexpectedly he died six months later.*
6個月後他就死了，這真是悲劇性的而且出乎意料。

*The army has always claimed that the rebels fired first, and it seems probable that the two sides **tragically** misunderstood each other's intentions.*
軍方總是宣稱是反叛者首先開的火，看來雙方都可能誤解了對方的意圖，這真可悲。

*Business success is **regrettably** not about fairness but about making a profit.*
不幸的是，商業成功不講公道只講賺錢。

*Human beings **regrettably** are not omnipotent.*
不幸的是，人類並非萬能。

***Regrettably**, these authors supply no systematic evidence to document their views.*
不幸的是，這些作者沒能提供系統的證據來佐證他們的觀點。

*Hughie, rather **disappointingly**, chose an obscure restaurant.*
令人相當失望的是，休吉選了一家沒有名氣的餐館。

# 某事是重要的
# Something is important

## significantly, importantly

**8.63** 如果想強調某事件或情況對某事有重要影響，可以使用 **significantly** 和 **importantly** 作為句子附加狀語，importantly 經常出現在 **more importantly** 或 **most importantly** 這類短語裏。

*His death was more than just his own end. More **significantly**, it marked the end of Indian resistance throughout the Midwest and South.*
他的死並非僅是他自己一生的結束。更重要的是，它標誌着印第安人在整個中西部及南部反抗的結束。

*He ended, **significantly**, not with recommendations, but 'intentions'.*
重要的是，他結尾時用的是"打算"而不是建議。

*He'd made his point. **More importantly**, he'd distracted them from making enquiries about his affairs.*
他已經把他的論點說清楚了。更重要的是，他轉移了他們的注意力，使他們不再詢問他的情況。

*Don't hide your ambitions. **Most importantly**, you should ask what your area of responsibility, if any, will be.*
不必隱藏你的抱負。最重要的是，你應該問一問，如果有你的職責範圍的話，那會是甚麼。

*It will depend on the drug you have been on, how long you have taken it, and **very importantly**, how long it takes your body to get back to normal.*
這取決於你一直在服用的藥，你服用了多久，另外，非常重要的是，這種藥要用多長時間才能使你的身體恢復正常。

# 說話者作出的其他反應
# Other reactions

**8.64**　可以使用其他各式各樣的句子附加狀語來表示說話者對自己說及的事所作的反應。

## ironically, paradoxically

**8.65**　**Ironically** 通常強調某事件或情況是有關的人未想到的，並且還可能是他們不希望發生的。

*And **ironically**, the evidence suggests that, by feeding animals and ourselves with antibiotics the bacteria and viruses develop resistance, so new drugs have to be invented.*
並且具有諷刺意味的是，有證據表明，通過給動物和我們自己吃抗生素，細菌和病毒逐漸產生了抗藥性，因此，又不得不發明的新的藥。

***Ironically**, those who report feeling safest are statistically at highest risk — men.*
具有嘲諷意味的是，那些宣稱自己感覺最安全的人，根據統計卻是處在最危險之中的人——那就是男人。

**Paradoxically** 強調某件事不僅與預期的相反，而且有可能非同尋常或不可理喻。

***Paradoxically**, what we take to be objective, the real world outside us, they conceived as a spiritual phenomenon, a psychic event.*
矛盾的是，我們認為我們外部的真實世界是客觀的，但他們卻認為是一種精神現象、是一種心靈的事件。

*Intelligence often means being self-critical while, **paradoxically**, having confidence in what you are doing.*

智慧經常意味着自我批評，但自相矛盾的是，同時又意味着對你所做之事有信心。

## appropriately, conveniently

**8.66** 正如這兩個詞的字面意思所提示的那樣，把 **appropriately** 和 **conveniently** 用來表示某事無論是一般來說還是從某特定人物的觀點來看都是合適的或方便的。

***Appropriately** perhaps, since the main character is a moderately famous film actress, the other characters have only supporting roles.*

也許是恰如其分吧，由於主要角色是一位小有名氣的女演員，別的角色只能做陪襯了。

*Both children, unable to articulate the rage that might more **appropriately** be directed towards the parent, now begin to direct it towards each other.*

兩個孩子無法清楚地表達出本來更應是針對父親或母親的怨氣，現在開始向對方發怒。

*The machines are **conveniently** located at Post Offices, leading retail outlets and Banks and Building Societies.*

這些機器被放在各郵局、重要的零售直銷店、銀行以及建房互助會裏，很是方便。

說話者還可使用 **conveniently** 來表示某事對有關的人是方便的，但說話者自己卻不贊同。

***Conveniently**, he had developed amnesia about that part of his life.*

於己方便的是，他對自己的那段生活得了健忘症。

*'She's insane,' he thought, **conveniently** absolving himself from blame.*

"她瘋了，"他想，倒也方便，這樣自己便能免於責難。

## amusingly, annoyingly, suspiciously

**8.67** 這些詞表示說話者對所發生之事感到好笑或氣惱，或者感覺到某人的行為令人懷疑。

***Amusingly**, she tells her story from the point of view of a middle-aged woman doctor.*

令人好笑地是，她以一個中年女醫生的觀點來講述自己的故事。

***Annoyingly**, the suitcase was just too big to fit into the cheap wardrobe in the bedroom.*

令人感到氣惱的是，這隻手提箱太大了一點，無法放進臥室裏那隻廉價的衣櫃裏。

***Suspiciously**, the 'sickness' rate jumps sharply on Fridays and Mondays.*

令人起疑的是，一到週五和週一得病率就突然大幅上升。

## absurdly, ridiculously

**8.68**　當說話者希望評述所發生的事荒謬可笑時，可以使用這些詞。

*'You're wearing Robyn's perfume!' **Absurdly**, he made it an accusation.*
"你在用若拜因的香水！"令人感到荒謬的是，他居然以此來責備我。

*The death of someone you had, **absurdly** of course, always assumed would be there for you can be devastating.*
你一直認為某人為了你還堅持活着，這當然荒謬。他的死會令你一蹶不振。

*The anxious expression on the doctor's face made her, **ridiculously**, feel sorrier for him than for herself.*
荒謬可笑的是，醫生臉上急切的表情使她覺得為醫生比為她自己更難過。

## preferably

**8.69**　說話者用 **preferably** 來陳述自己寧可某事而不是另一事發生，或者說明某事比另一件事好。

*She can't spend the night in that cottage. **Preferably**, leave her with friends.*
晚上她不能呆在那間小屋裏。寧願讓她和朋友們在一起。

*Grab a friend, **preferably** a fellow job-seeker, and run through several mock interviews. Keep switching roles. Practise, practise, practise.*
抓住一位朋友，最好也是一位求職夥伴，然後連着進行幾次模擬招聘面試，不斷地交換角色。演練，演練，再演練。

## famously, notoriously

**8.70**　如果說話者認為自己在敍述的事件或行為是廣為人知的，可以用 **famously**。但如果是壞事，就用 **notoriously**。當然所涉及的人或事通常會由此而成名（或變得臭名昭著）。

*As Descartes **famously** concludes:' I think, therefore I am.'*
正如笛卡爾的著名結論所說："我思考，所以我存在。"

*As the late great manager of Liverpool, Bill Shankly, **famously** remarked:' Football is not a matter of life and death; it's more important than that.'*
利物浦足球隊偉大的已故經理比爾·顯克利說過一句名言："足球並不是生死攸關的事，它比生死更為重要。"

*There he fought cases that ended racial discrimination in housing contracts. Most **famously**, in 1954 he persuaded the Supreme Court that segregation in the public schools was unconstitutional.*
在那裏，他進行了一些旨在結束住房合同上的種族歧視的法律訴訟。其中最著名的是，1954 年他說服最高法院認定公立學校的種族隔離是違反憲法的。

*He's no detective. Also, he's **notoriously** been no friend of the police.*
他根本不是偵探。另外，他從來就不是警方的朋友，這是眾所周知的。

*I do not wish to set up as ideal the mindless, unending competition that **notoriously** drives men into early graves.*
我不希望把這種臭名昭著地促使人們過早進入墳墓的輕率的、無休止的競爭樹為一種理想。

# 說話者對有關的人的看法
# Your opinion of the people involved

**8.71**　有時候，在敍述一個動作或另外某個行為時，說話者對所發生的事表達的意見也適用於與此事有關的人。有這種用法的多數副詞源於相應的、可說明主語的形容詞。因此，說話者說 The employee has unreasonably refused... 時，又可以用 The employee was unreasonable to refuse...（那個僱員已經無理地拒絕了……）來表達：

當用在動詞之後，即只描述動作進行的方式時，作為這類句子附加狀語的許多副詞是普通的方式副詞。但是當它們位於動詞之前和位置接近句首時，則會產生兩種效果：

* 該副詞指整個句子或分句。

* 該副詞強調說話者對他人動作的評判。

讓我們對下面兩個例句進行比較：

> *I was eating **sensibly**.*
> 我合理地吃着。

> *And you very **sensibly** declined to listen to this rubbish.*
> 你很有理智地拒絕聽取這種胡説八道。

當然在兩個例句中，句子的主語，存在於現實世界之中，是可以感知的。但在第一句中，強調的是人吃東西的方式——以一種合理的方式吃着，挑選合理的食物。但這並不意味着I was sensible to eat。相比之下，第二句的含意是You were sensible to decline to listen to this improper and insulting stuff（你拒絕聽取那種不妥的、侮辱性的話，説明你有理智）。

另外，讓我們再比較一對句子：

> *The enemy fought **bravely** and well.*
> 敵人勇敢而高明地進行戰鬥。

> *Mr. Kim **bravely** stood up to authority.*
> 基姆先生真勇敢，挺身反對權威。

第一句句子告訴我們敵人是如何戰鬥的——既驍勇又善戰。對敵軍下決心開戰則根本沒有提及，因此不能改寫成 The enemy were brave(to decide) to fight（也許他們根本不想打仗，但一開戰，則很英勇）。相比之下，第二個句子強調基姆先生在整個行動中表現出來的勇敢——他敢於對抗權威，他的行動本身是勇敢的。

▶ 注意 ◀ 8.72 － 8.87 節中討論這些用於表示對人的看法的句子附加狀語與 8.44 － 8.70 節中的那些主要用於評判事件的句子附加狀語之間的差別。例如，一般來説我們不能用表示對事件看法的句子附加狀語的形容詞形式來改寫原來的句子，也不能用這樣的形容詞説明句子主語。

✘ *She was surprising to feel like a young girl again.*

✘ *I was inexplicable to begin to sob.*

✘ *Human beings are regrettable to be omnipotent.*

## reasonably, unreasonably

**8.72** 如果説話者認為某人以某種方式行事時，表現得合乎情理或不合乎情理，可用這兩個詞。

*The earlier results were in line with expectations, so we can **reasonably** assume that the machine was not malfunctioning during the previous experiments.*
早些時候得出的結果與預期的相同，所以我們可以合乎情理地假定，這台機器在以前的試驗中沒有發生故障。

*The trouble is that the conventional training and development of marketing executives, quite **reasonably**, has focused on the external environment of customers.*
麻煩是，高級營銷管理人員的傳統培訓和提高相當合乎情理地把重點放在客戶的外部環境。

*The employee has **unreasonably** refused an offer of reinstatement from the employer.*
這位僱員不合常理地拒絕了僱主提供給他的復職機會。

*A waiter threw a plate of curry at one of the customers, who **not unreasonably** aggrieved.*
一位侍員把一碟咖喱扔給一名顧客，這位顧客並非毫無道理地覺得受到冒犯。

## rightly, wrongly, correctly, incorrectly, justly, unjustly

**8.73** 有時候説話者認為某人以某種方式行事時做得對（或做得不對），或者認為做的事是對的或正當的(或者不對或不正當的)，那麼可以使用這些詞來把自己的意見表示出來。

*The Pope's visit to this country has been **rightly** seen as an important exercise in Christian unity.* （即： *People were right to see it this way.*人們這樣看待這件事是正確的。）
教皇對這個國家的訪問已被正確地視為是體現基督教團結的一次重要活動。

*Breast milk is quite **rightly** said to be the most perfect food for babies.*
說乳汁是嬰兒最完美的食物，這一點相當正確。

*It is very wrong if parents encourage young children to go out, demand what they want and threaten violence if their demands are not met. If adults behaved like this they would be arrested, and **rightly** so.*
如果父母鼓勵年幼的孩子走出去，去索要他們想要的東西，如果要求得不到滿足就以武力相威脅，這是非常錯誤的。如果成年人如此行事，那麼他們將被逮捕，並且該被捕。

*Who got the money? The million pounds Captain Blake was **wrongly** accused of stealing?*
誰得到了這筆錢？即布萊克船長曾因此而被錯誤指控盜竊的那一百萬英鎊？

*The reason for the sheer boredom, as you **correctly** say, is unemployment.*
你說得很對，全然的無聊是失業引起的。

*As Haig **correctly** perceived, the resignation would not be seen as a 'purely personal matter' but as an acceptance of blame.*
赫格的看法很對，不能把辭職視為純粹個人的事情，而是要視為對指責的接受。

*A man who, for instance, is a taxi-driver can **correctly** be described as 'self-employed'.* （即：People are correct to describe a taxi-driver as self-employed. 人們把一名出租車司機描述為自我僱傭是正確的。）
例如，一名出租車駕駛員就可被正確地說成是自我僱傭的人。

*Many lady golfers **incorrectly** straighten the right knee in the backswing.*
許多玩高爾夫球的婦女在向後揮杆時不正確地將右膝挺直了。

*In our obituary of Arnold Jameson yesterday we **incorrectly** gave his Christian name as Andrew in the headline and in the first two paragraphs.*
在昨天我們為阿諾德‧傑姆森所寫的訃告中，在標題和前兩段中我們錯誤地將他的基督教名寫成了安德魯。

*No government can **justly** claim authority unless it is based on the will of the people.*
沒有一個政府可以理所當然地要求承認其權威性，除非它是基於人民意志之上的。

*Scotland is **justly** proud of its magnificent scenery and famous heritage.*
蘇格蘭可以理所當然地為它的壯麗風景和著名文化傳統而感到驕傲。

*The Report of the Study Group condemned the action and implied, quite **unjustly**, that Waite alone had been responsible.*
研究小組的報告指責了該項活動，並且相當不公正地暗示只有魏特一個人負有責任。

但是，如果說話者想強調對某事的是非沒有看法，而只想說明某事發生，可以使用 **rightly or wrongly**。

*The retreat also taught him, **rightly or wrongly**, how unreliable were his allies.*
無論是對還是錯，撤退給他的教訓是他的聯盟是多麼不可靠。

***Rightly or wrongly**, they believe they have been persecuted.*
且不論是非，他們認為他們已經受到迫害。

*Whether **rightly or wrongly**, they criticize me.*
無論是對還是錯，他們都批評我。

# consistently

**8.74** 如果某人行事 **consistently**，是指此人總是以同樣的方式行事或保持同樣的意見或態度。

*The truth is I've **consistently** exploited you.*
事實是我一向是在剝削你。

*Both animal and human studies have **consistently** demonstrated the significant effect oat bran has on cholesterol levels.*
對動物和人的研究一直表明燕麥麩對膽固醇水平有顯著影響。

*The choice could be restricted to people who have **consistently** followed some vocation or profession.*
選擇範圍可以限於那些一貫從事某種行業或職業的人。

# kindly, sincerely, politely, generously

**8.75** 可以使用這些詞來讚揚他人好心、真誠、禮貌或慷慨。

*He had **kindly** brought them back after their visit to the animal sanctuary.*
在他們參觀動物保護區之後，他好心地把他們帶了回來。

*He had **kindly** invited us to what he called a light lunch.*
他已經好心地邀請我們參加他稱作輕便午餐的餐會。

*Anyone who **sincerely** doesn't want to be biographized can cover his tracks while he's still alive.*
任何一位真誠地不願讓別人為他寫傳記的人，在世時都可以隱匿他的行蹤。

*I drove home, through the fires, and in Edgware Road, a policeman stopped me, and **politely** explained that there was no through route from here to Victoria.*
我開車回家，經過大火現場，在艾奇維爾路上被一名警察攔住，他禮貌地解釋說，從這裏沒有通向維多利亞的路。

***Politely**, Martin addressed remarks to her, but she would not reply.*
儘管馬丁曾禮貌地對她說話，但她卻沒有回應。

***Generously**, he gave part of the money to his spokesman and the rest to his bodyguards.*
他慷慨地把那筆錢的一部份給了他的發言人，其餘的就給了他的貼身護衛。

*Members should **generously** share work materials.*
成員們應該慷慨地分享工作材料。

*The owner of the company **generously** promised to invest £100,000 over a period of three years.*
公司的所有者慷慨地許諾在 3 年內投資 10 萬英鎊。

*They had **generously** voted an exceptionally large sum for his inauguration.*
他們已經慷慨地投票批准為他的就職撥一筆極大的款項。

**8.76** ▶注意◀ 對比此處 kindly 的用法與它在表示要求和命令時的用法。在要求和命令中，它通常具有諷刺意味，這時說話者要麼是在惱怒地要求甚麼，要麼是有權力下命令。

*Will you **kindly** authorize your officer to remove his security bodyguard in the passage outside the door.*
你可否授權你的官員撤走門外通道上他的保鑣。

*Would you **kindly** describe to us your activities on Thursday afternoon and evening.*
你可否向我們說說你在週四下午和晚上的活動。

*You will **kindly** not instruct me in elementary physics.*
請你行行好，別對我講授初等物理。

***Kindly** cable your reply to these questions soonest possible.*
請盡快把你對這些問題的答覆用電報傳過來。

提要求時，用 please 比較穩妥，而且可以緩和要求的口氣，不過這裏的第三例即使用 please，聽起來仍然很不耐煩。

## bitterly, angrily, fiercely, crossly, resentfully

**8.77**　如果某人對某事物感到怨憤，通常是因為他認為某事不公平或因受到不公正待遇而感到極為惱怒和失望。**Bitterly** 是語氣很強的詞；**resentfully** 意思與之相近，但用得較少。

*She took his cold hand and held it, **bitterly** thinking that she was completely useless.*
她拿起他那隻冷冰冰的手，緊緊地握住它，心裏痛苦地想着她自己真是沒用。

*Most scientists **bitterly** oppose the move to patent these fragments because their function in the body is not yet known.*
大多數科學家強烈反對將這些零星的成果拿去申請專利的動議，因為它們在人體中的功能尚不清楚。

*It never occurred to me to try for university myself, something I **bitterly** regret not doing.*
我從未想過自己努力去進大學，我對未進大學極其後悔。

*For the second day running Ryle returned to the hotel during siesta and disturbed the dozing concierge, who **resentfully** produced his room key.*
為了第二天的賽跑，萊爾在午休時間回到旅館，打擾了正打瞌睡的看門人，此人顯然不滿地拿出了他的房間鑰匙。

如果說話者認為某人在做某事時感到憤怒的話，可以用 **angrily** 或 **fiercely** 來描寫此人的行為。但 fiercely 並不總是暗示憤怒或挑釁（如 a fierce animal 一頭兇猛的動物）；它通常的意思是強烈地（intensely）或非常活躍地（very actively）。

***Angrily**, Joe socked Starkey on the jaw to knock him out.*
喬憤怒地猛擊斯塔基的下巴，欲將他擊昏。

*He put a hand over hers, but she **angrily** shook it off.*
他將一隻手放在她的手上，但她卻憤怒地甩脱了他的手。

*He **fiercely** denied reports that he has made a secret deal.*
他憤怒地否認有關他做了一筆秘密交易的報道。

***Fiercely**, she assured me that she hated small men.*
她極力使我相信她討厭個子矮小的男人。

***Fiercely**, he brushed away the tears from his eyes; he must force himself to do something.*
他急速地擦去眼中的淚水；他必須強迫自己做些事情。

説話者説某人發火地（**crossly**）説話或行事，多半是批評他生氣了。

*'Oh, stop it!' she said with a sigh of irritation and **crossly** tugged her skirt down over her leg.*
"喔，別這樣，別這樣！" 她帶着惱怒的嘆息説道，並發火地把她的裙子往她的腿下拽了一把。

*'Never mind all that,' Mum said, **crossly** lugging her shopping bags. 'We've got to get home.'*
"甚麼都別管了，" 媽媽説着，生氣地拎起她的購物袋。"我們該回家了。"

## reluctantly, willingly, unwillingly

**8.78**　如果某人勉強（**reluctantly** 或 **unwillingly**）做某事，則表示他們實際上不想去做。

***Reluctantly** the night porter decided that he would have to disturb the sleeping guests.*
雖不情願，那位夜間服務員後來還是決定他必須打擾一下那些睡覺的客人。

***Reluctantly**, but with no real choice, John Kempton made up his mind.*
由於實際上沒有甚麼選擇，約翰·肯普頓勉強下了決心。

*He had **reluctantly** come to admit that life outside the great cities had its advantages.*
他已經勉強承認大城市外的生活有它自身的優勢。

*She hesitated, then **unwillingly** related the episode of the breadknife.*
她猶豫了一下，然後不情願地敍述了有關切麵包刀的那一情節。

**Willingly** 當然是 reluctantly、unwillingly 的反義詞。

*He had **willingly** joined the conspiracy.*
他自覺自願地參與這個陰謀。

*They **willingly** assume responsibility for the success or failure of a venture and are answerable for all aspects of it.*
他們自願承擔一次商業冒險成敗的責任，並且對其所有方面負責。

## calmly, casually, patiently, impatiently

**8.79**　如果説話者認為某人在困境中表現了相當程度的自我控制，可以説此人辦事鎮靜（**calmly**）。

> The oddest thing was that Norman Davies **calmly** refused to admit the existence of the problem.
> 最奇怪的事是，諾曼·戴維斯鎮靜地拒絕承認這個問題的存在。

> **Calmly**, looking into the policeman's eyes, he repeated his account of his ill-timed walk.
> 他顯得很鎮靜，盯着警察的眼睛，重述他那不合時宜的散步。

説話者説他人行事隨隨便便（**casually**），是指此人沒把事放在心上，或者至少是假裝不把事情放在心上。

> Bellamy **casually** reached for the oysters.
> 倍拉米漫不經心地把手伸向那些牡蠣。

> The Friar **casually** kicked a dog out of his way.
> 這位修道士隨意地把一條擋住他去路的狗踢開。

> **Casually**, Fred said to one of the colleagues in his room, 'Has anybody seen the Chief of Staff since he returned?'
> 弗雷德對他房間裏的一名同僚隨意地説道："參謀長回來後，有人見過他嗎？"

> 'What would you give for it, madam?' **Casually** she muttered a price.
> "您願意出甚麼價，夫人？"她隨隨便便地咕嚕出了一個價錢。

説話者使用 **patiently**（耐心地）時，是暗示某人準備等候或不着急。

> A splodge of fake 'blood' began to trickle down his cheek. The make-up girl **patiently** mopped it up.
> 一塊假血的斑點開始沿他的臉往下滴，那個化妝的女士耐心地把它抹掉。

> **Patiently**, the interrogating officers piece together the puzzle.
> 負責審問的官員們耐心地把有關疑團的點點滴滴拼湊起來。

**Impatiently** 當然用來表示相反的意義。

> He put the phone down and was turning away, his brain already clicking into gear, when it rang again. **Impatiently** he turned and picked it up.
> 他放下電話，轉身走開，當電話再次響起時，他的腦子已正常工作。他不耐煩地轉過身，拿起了電話。

## thoughtfully, intelligently, shrewdly

**8.80**　説話者用這些副詞來評論某人的行為所表現出的明智、聰明或慎思。

*The Prime Minister has **thoughtfully** kept the industry job and several minor jobs unfilled, ready to reward loyalists.*
首相已經深思熟慮地讓工業部門的職務以及幾個次要的職務空缺着，用於獎賞他的忠實支持者。

*He put the list away, and then took it out and studied it again. **Thoughtfully**, he added another item.*
他收好那份清單，然後又將它取出來並且仔細地研究，最後又在認真推敲中增加了一個項目。

*She, **intelligently**, left at about 11.45. I stayed talking.*
她在 11 時 45 分明智地離開了，我卻繼續説着。

*The England captain **intelligently** played the ball wide to Steve MacManaman, magnificent again on the wing.*
這位英格蘭隊的隊長明智地將球再次橫傳給遠處的斯蒂夫·麥克馬拉曼，使邊鋒又處於有利的位置。

***Shrewdly**, he offered to provide financial backing on condition he became an equal partner.*
他精明地主動提供財政支持，條件是他成為對等的合作夥伴。

*Kate **shrewdly** recognised the usefulness of the work grapevine and managed it to her advantage.*
凱蒂精明地認識到這條獲取秘密信息的渠道的用處，並且設法為她所用。

## bravely, courageously

**8.81**　説他人做事勇敢（**bravely**），或者甚至使用語氣更強的 **courageously** 時，説話者顯然為他人表現出的勇氣感到欽佩。

*Once, long before, a snake had got loose in our living room, and my father had **bravely** trapped it in a shopping bag.*
很久以前，曾經有條蛇在我們客廳裏逃脱，我父親勇敢地設法將它誘進了一隻購物袋中。

*Even more **bravely**, she is preparing to have her thick plait of red hair shorn and dyed white.*
更為大膽的是，她準備把她的紅頭髮辮子剪掉，並把頭髮染成白色。

*In spite of spinal injuries he **courageously** returned to the burning wreck to rescue the ship's logbook.*
雖然脊椎受了傷，他仍勇敢地回到燃燒着的船的殘骸上，搶救出這艘船的航行日誌。

## desperately

**8.82**　説話者在談論某人的行為時用 **desperately**（不顧一切地鋌而走險），暗示此人正處於一種極端條件下，並且幾乎願意冒任何風險去改變它，儘管也許成功的希望不大。

***Desperately**, he tried to think clearly.*
他絕望地試圖理清思路。

*Mahoney **desperately** climbed and climbed towards that tiny square of light way up at the top of the well.*
馬亨尼絕望地向井口一小方塊透光處不斷地爬去。

## proudly

**8.83** 在說及他人的行為時用 **proudly**，說話者也許會、也許不會因這種行為欽佩此人，這部份地取決於他認為此人的驕傲是否有道理。

*We **proudly** brought our new car home.*
我們驕傲地把新汽車帶回了家。

*She **proudly** declined all his attempts to help her with money.*
她驕傲地拒絕了他用金錢幫助她的所有試圖。

***Proudly**, he shows off the array of weaving and knitting machines.*
他驕傲地炫耀那一排編織和針織的機器。

*He **proudly** told Sharpe that he had stolen the food.*
他驕傲地告訴夏普，他偷了那食物。

## wisely, sensibly, cleverly, prudently

**8.84** 說話者可能會認為某人在行事方式上的表現是明智的、有道理的或聰明的。這裏列出的幾個副詞就能表示說話者的這些看法。**Prudently** 表示此人小心翼翼，躲避風險。

*The pilot **wisely** decided to return to base as quickly as possible before the aircraft began to blaze.*
飛行員明智地決定在飛機着火之前盡快返回基地。

***Wisely** preparing for any outcome, the good nuns were not taking sides in the conflict.*
這些好心的修女在明智地準備應付任何結局的同時，不打算在這次衝突中支持任何一方。

*His aircraft hurtled towards the crowd, which **wisely** scattered as he hit the fence.*
他的飛機衝向人羣，而人羣在飛機撞上圍欄時明智地散開了。

***Sensibly**, successive councils had tried to retain the atmosphere of the town and there had been very little development.*
連續幾屆地方議會都明智地試圖保持住小鎮的氣氛，因而幾乎沒有甚麼發展。

*The townspeople **sensibly** stayed indoors and closed their shutters.*
鎮上的人明智地呆在家裏並且關上了他們的百葉窗。

*Rather **cleverly**, he had now parked his car near the bar, so we had a good view of it.*
他相當聰明地把他的車停在酒吧附近，這樣我們能清楚地看到它。

*After the funeral I questioned her about her age and she **cleverly** replied 'that was a printing error.'*
葬禮後，我問過她的年齡，但她聰明地回答道，那是個印刷錯誤。

*In the face of growing hostility, the Imperial envoy **prudently** decided to withdraw his official support.*
面對不斷增長的敵意，帝國公使審慎地決定收回他的官方支持。

*The majority of the population was against the Communists but **prudently** avoided making a public stand.*
大部份人反對共產主義，但卻審慎地避免作出公開表態。

## innocently

**8.85**　如果某人舉止幼稚(**innocently**)，那是説此人可能不明白自己在做的事的重要性，或者可能知道但卻想表現出不知道的樣子。

*One was always, you know, **innocently** committing some awful offence.*
你知道，一個人總會無知地犯法。

***Innocently**, I said I'd take a look round.*
我幼稚地説，我將四處看一看。

## unwisely, foolishly, stupidly, rashly

**8.86**　如果説話者認為某人行為不明智或缺乏理智，可用這裏列出的副詞來表示這種評判。這類副詞在書面語中用得比口語中多。

*Many members of the public **unwisely** assume that scientists must be better informed than themselves.*
公眾中有許多人不明智地認為，科學家一定比他們自己更見多識廣。

***Unwisely**, the Tibetans subsided within the sheltering shield of their mountains and tried to keep the rest of the world at bay.*
西藏人不明智地退隱於他們四面環山的天然屏障裏，試圖與外界隔絕。

*The girl who took his call **foolishly** lost her note of the conversation.*
為他接電話的那個女孩愚蠢地把電話記錄給弄丟了。

*Adam remembered how the Persian-speaking boys at school had laughed when, **foolishly**, he had confided his pet name.*
亞當記得，當他愚蠢地把自己的小名透露出去時，學校裏那些講波斯語的男孩是如何笑話他的。

*The blackmailer had **stupidly** left his name and address on the magazine, and I tracked him down.*
那個勒索者愚蠢地將他的名字和地址留在這本雜誌上，於是我據此追查到他。

*Yesterday **stupidly** I tried to get from one side of London to the other side, right.*
昨天我愚蠢地試圖從倫敦的這一邊一直走到另一邊。

***Rashly** he had criticised Mao's policies in a letter to the Soviet Communist party.*
在一封給蘇聯共產黨的信中，他魯莽地批評了毛的政策。

*I spent nearly forty years writing books and made quite a lot of money, but I **rashly** gave most of it away.*
我花了將近40年寫書，並掙了不少錢，但我將其中大部份輕率地送了人。

## carelessly, lazily, cunningly, wilfully, arrogantly, dishonestly, childishly

**8.87**　有些副詞用來表達非常具體的批評，這裏列出的是其中的幾個。

*Clements **carelessly** let the car wind itself up above the 110 kilo-metres-an-hour speed limit.*
克萊門茨毫無顧忌地讓車以超過110公里／小時的速度限制疾駛。

*Soon after his birth, however, the queen's serving-woman **carelessly** falls asleep and the child vanishes.*
但是這小孩剛出生不久，女王的僕女就粗心地睡着了，小孩也不見了。

*One of the cricketers — who caught practically nothing from the bat all the week— snatched a bird out of the air after it had **carelessly** flown into the school building.*
其中一名板球運動員——他整整一星期幾乎連一個擊打球都沒有接住——卻從空中抓住一隻大意飛進校舍的鳥。

***Lazily**, she thought that she should be changing for dinner, and dismissed the thought at once.*
她懶散地想到她應該換好衣服去用正餐，但是馬上又打消了這個念頭。

*Sharpe had an impulse to move back into the shelter of the trees, but **lazily** stayed where he was.*
夏普有一種退回到可供隱蔽的樹林中去的衝動，但卻懶散地呆在原地不動。

*The staff **cunningly** got round this by serving drinks by the fire at 7.45pm and not showing us to the table until 8.*
職員們傍晚7點45分在爐火旁給我們喝飲料，直到8點才把我們領到桌邊就座，這就狡猾地迴避了這件事。

*He has **wilfully** disregarded the instructions we gave him.*
他對我們給他的指令固執得不加理會。

*They **arrogantly** maintained that they had a mandate to govern.*
他們傲慢地宣稱他們已被授權管轄。

*Berkowitz had **dishonestly** handled stolen property.*
伯科維茨不誠實地處理贓物。

*In those days it was **childishly** believed that if government went round every industry to ensure that its exports exceeded its imports then, hey presto, balance of payments problems would disappear.* （即：People were childish to believe this. 人們幼稚地相信這種想法。）
那些日子，人們幼稚地相信，如果政府巡視每個工業部門，以保證它的出口超過其進口，那麼說變就變，像變戲法一樣，支付平衡的問題就會消失。

# 練習

**練習 1**（第 1 章）

用括號內的連接詞將下列各組句子連接成複句，並在句子裏作出相應的改動。第一組句子已經替你連成複句。

0) The house was built of good stone. And it was kept in good order. The garden also was kept in good order. (both…and)

   <u>The house was built of good stone. And both it and the garden were kept in good order.</u>

1) The beer and sandwich made him feel better because he had been hungry. It also made him feel better because for a while he could pretend that this was just a normal day. (both…and)

   ...........................................................................................................

   ...........................................................................................................

2) There was, she realized now, more than one way of looking at a key. It opened a door. It kept it locked. (both…and)

   ...........................................................................................................

   ...........................................................................................................

3) He doesn't look like his uncle. He doesn't look like his aunt. (either…or)

   ...........................................................................................................

4) No one would know what became of them. No one would care what became of them. (either…or)

   ...........................................................................................................

5) Sometimes you got the order. Sometimes you didn't get the order. (either…or)

   ...........................................................................................................

6) Her nails weren't long . They weren't painted either. (neither…nor)

   ...........................................................................................................

7) She didn't weep. She didn't despair. But she planned. (neither…nor)

   ...........................................................................................................

8) Anthony was not a skilled mechanic. Fred wasn't skilled mechanic either. (neither...nor)

   ......................................................................................

9) Now when he moved his head he felt the pain of the bruise. He also heard the crinkle of the papers concealed in his pillow-case. (not only...but also)

   ......................................................................................

10) She paid him a top salary. And the job kept him moving and happy. (not only...but)

   ......................................................................................

11) He would be made familiar from maps with the layout of Geneva. He would be made familiar from a large-scale model too. (not only...but also)

   ......................................................................................

12) Presumably the river carried the body down. It follows that this is where the body entered the water. (if...then)

   ......................................................................................

13) Maybe land was nearby. If so, they might be able to obtain fuel and take off again before the plane was swallowed up by the sea. (if...then)

   ......................................................................................
   ......................................................................................

14) Maybe this view is right, but that would mean that perhaps we have been applying the wrong tests to the animal kingdom. (if...then)

   ......................................................................................
   ......................................................................................

**練習 2** (第 2 章)

用括號內的詞語將下列各組句子改寫成新的句子，盡量保持原句意義。在新句裏作出必要的改動。第一組句子已經替你改好。

0) While I was reaching for the glove compartment she was getting out of the car. (meanwhile)

   I was reaching for the glove compartment.

   Meanwhile, she was getting out of the car.

1) It was unfortunate that he was tone deaf. Otherwise he might have made a fortune as a singer. (if )

   .......................................................................................................

2) Though Tibetan was to be taught during the three years of primary school, all secondary education was in Chinese by Chinese teachers. (however)

   .......................................................................................................

3) You won't get any fruit off these trees unless you prune them.(otherwise)

   .......................................................................................................

4) Elsie poured out tea and after they'd all drunk a cup, Aunt Mamie announced that she was going up to rest. (soon afterwards)

   .......................................................................................................

5) They were living at the house with another young couple with their babies and a shared nanny, Meanwhile the war drew closer and bombs began to fall on Glasgow. (while)

   .......................................................................................................

   .......................................................................................................

6) I wanted to be seen from the outer office but not overheard, so I moved the chair back from the doorway. (so that)

   .......................................................................................................

7) I was prescribed this medicinal cream for my face. I used it for about two to three years, generously applying it every morning. As a result my skin is now quite thin on my face. (so that)

   .......................................................................................................

   .......................................................................................................

8) 'And you'll go to Tasmania for your trout fishing?' — 'I suppose I shall, unless the police want me to stay here.' (provided that)

   .......................................................................................................

9) Whereas Ireland worked as a team with clever passing among the forwards, England relied on individual efforts. (by contrast)

   .......................................................................................................

10) Whereas unemployment seems to have contributed to increasing crime rates, this has not generally resulted in more people being sent to prison for longer periods of time. (however)

........................................................................................................

........................................................................................................

11) Much as he had enjoyed the lively company of his friends in Edinburgh, his work, he felt, demanded solitude. (all the same)

........................................................................................................

12) While some UN sources expressed hope that a deal would be struck, the Americans were less optimistic. (on the other hand)

........................................................................................................

13) Although they knew it was wrong to steal a car, most of those interviewed, all under 17, did not consider themselves criminals. (despite)

........................................................................................................

........................................................................................................

14) 'I can't do anything for several days.' he said. 'There's an important murder trial going on and I'm the main police witness. It won't matter a lot, though.' (still)

........................................................................................................

........................................................................................................

15) Then she made some sandwiches and coffee and put them on a tray to take into the sitting-room for their supper. While she was doing it Patrick and Margaret talked quietly. (meanwhile)

........................................................................................................

........................................................................................................

16) We had our money stolen on the last day. Otherwise we had a wonderful time there. (except that)

........................................................................................................

........................................................................................................

**練習 3** (第 2 章)

有的詞語在外表上相似，但在意義和用法上卻不一樣。從每條題目前的兩個詞語中，挑選最合適的一個詞語填入空白處，使句子意義完整。

1) by contrast　on the contrary

   a) Tobacconists, booksellers, and stationers also reported falling activity. ............................. chemists, grocers, shoe shops and leather stores all said business was better last month than in January.

   b) There was no anxiety on the flight deck, no shouts of warning: ......................, the pilots commented to each other on the awesome beauty, the majesty and tranquillity of what they were seeing.

   c) There had been no elections, no campaigning, no consulting the people. ............................., helpless civilians had been shot, the radio station closed down and a puppet government installed.

2) though　although

   a) It seemed that the new government was the only topic the King would allow to be spoken of, .............................. at the same time he would say almost nothing about it himself.

   b) The tour continues through some beautiful wine towns whose vineyards can be visited and wines tasted. In truth, ..............................., the opportunities for tasting are fairly infrequent in this part of the tour.

   c) It was such a pleasant town, barely a city, even .............................. it was the capital.

3) for that matter　no matter

   a) We haven't been a real world power since the end of the war, .............................. what we've pretended.

   b) For some unexplained reason, ................................. how hot it would get, Eric never seemed to perspire.

   c) The cabin was unlocked . It didn't even have a lock ..............................

4) in case　in any case

   a) She went on with her search, knocking on each door before entering the room .............................. the occupant was lying down, or perhaps asleep.

   b) But perhaps you have a private number just ..............................

something interesting which I could pass on emerges in any conversation or discussion I might have.

c) The pale furnishing colours they had enjoyed in their last house were not going to be practical here. ............................... they wanted something different.

5) given (that)    granted (that)

a) She has health problems. ............................... that's not her fault, but all the rest is.

b) ............................... theory consists of a set of ideas, those ideas must come from somewhere.

c) I don't see what I can do for you, ............................... you have, I repeat, no evidence.

6) all the same    at the same time

a) 'I don't suppose you've any facts to support that?' 'No hard evidence,' Brand admitted. 'I thought not. ............................... I'd like to hear your story for myself.'

b) The only person I could think of asking was my husband, and yet ............................... he was the one I was supposed to be running away from.

c) 'There's nothing to be done for him. He's dead. This is one time the kiss of life won't help,' she said. '..............................., you were splendid trying to save him like that.'

7) above all    after all

a) Each sentence ought to be balanced, so that it sounds right if it is read aloud; it should end before a reader runs out of breath. ............................... it should say exactly what it means, in the simplest way.

b) He earned a reputation for sound, logical and ............................... honest performances in the House of Commons.

c) He was beginning to feel foolish about criticizing the police. .............................., what did he know about questioning murder suspects?

8) in the meantime    meanwhile

a) The BBC are trying to get independent confirmation of this story;

..............................., please do not use this version.

b) One of his ventures was an overseas bank. His son Nigel directed it. ............................... another of his sons, Ernest, was sent to prison in Hong Kong for corruption.

c) We need a new system which takes into account the real educational needs of London's children. ..............................., the government should stick to the present arrangements.

**練習 4** (第 2 章)

有的連接詞的意義不止一個。從下列詞語裏找出相應的詞語來替代原句的劃線部份。第一對句子劃線部份的替代詞語已經替你找出。

| | | |
|---|---|---|
| all the time when | although | although…greatly |
| because | earlier than | from the time when |
| in order that | in the way that | more or less the same as |
| provided that | rather than | the whole time that |
| whereas | with the result that | |

0) <u>As</u> he drew closer, picking his way through the rocks, he could see that his son was excited.

00) He felt ashamed that he had not offered to serve in the French army <u>as</u> many other settlers had done.

Meaning: 0) *all the time when*    00) *in the way that*

1) I haven't been back <u>since</u> I left before the war as a girl.

2) Water containing high levels of nitrates or nitrites should not be given to babies, <u>since</u> these minerals increase the risk of blood disorders.

Meaning: 1) .......................................    2) .......................................

3) In the centre of the lawn a figure stood motionless. It must have stood there <u>as long as</u> she had.

4) He didn't care what the flowers were, <u>as long as</u> they were yellow.

Meaning: 3) .......................................    4) .......................................

5) She held the telephone firmly against her ear <u>so that</u> no telltale sound could leak out.

6) The effects of time and blackcurrant juice have healed her throat, <u>so that</u> she can speak normally again now.

Meaning: 5) .......................................... 6) ..........................................

7) He looked young and earnest, <u>much as</u> he'd always done.

8) You will always be welcome when you get back but <u>much as</u> I should like to see you, I believe it is best for you to stay where you are.

Meaning: 7) .......................................... 8) ..........................................

9) They'll kill you <u>sooner than</u> let an outsider cause trouble.

10) The Bank is likely to lower interest rates <u>sooner than</u> expected.

Meaning: 9) .......................................... 10) ..........................................

11) <u>While</u> chemical control of pests is not the only option, its use far outstrips other techniques.

12) Meat and bread prices will go up three times, <u>while</u> tea, butter, and cigarettes will cost double.

Meaning: 11) .......................................... 12) ..........................................

## 練習 5 （第 2 章）

用下列連接詞完成句子，每個連接詞只能用一次。

| | | | |
|---|---|---|---|
| as though | even though | for | in case |
| lest | on condition that | so | until |
| wherever | yet | | |

1) We had no worries about where to get off .......................................... we were to be met by our uncle.

2) She wore black of course, and she looked enchanting. He guessed, correctly that Veronica never looked anything but enchanting, .......................................... black suited her best of all.

3) I got here too early. I left home in plenty of time .............................. I had trouble finding the place.

4) They were allowed to play anywhere in the park .............................. it had a special playground.

5) A six o'clock start got him to the airport with half an hour to spare .......................................... he bought two newspapers.

6) He would have to avoid saying anything to Ginny ..........................................

he bring the same fate on her.

7) He slashed the air with his sword ........................................ it was a whip.

8) Nancy followed them, keeping a safe distance, sticking close to the trees ........................................ there were any.

9) I will decide what programme of work will be carried out. You will not take any action ........................................ you have precise instructions from me. Is that clear?

10) I will live with you ........................................ you never look inside my handbag without my permission.

**練習 6**（第 2、3 章）

從下列各組句子裏挑選出劃線部份中最合適的連接語。

1) She was a good judge of character and felt he spoke the truth. <u>Besides</u> / <u>Instead</u> / <u>Nevertheless</u> she didn't care for him.

2) The traffic was so heavy that the driver went slowly and was often forced to stop. Soon, <u>furthermore</u> / <u>however</u> / <u>moreover</u> we were on a faster road, and we picked up speed.

3) She had thought she would be grateful for their company on the drive back to Algiers, but <u>for one thing</u> / <u>instead</u> / <u>likewise</u> they were making her nervous.

4) You can now telephone our credit card hotline on 0121 414 6203. <u>Accordingly</u> / <u>Alternatively</u> / <u>Equally</u> complete the order from and return it to the address printed.

5) Tom's mother had been determined that he should not become a coal miner like his father and brothers. <u>Accordingly</u> / <u>All in all</u> / <u>At the same time</u>, she had sent him away to live with her sister, who was married to a shopkeeper in Hereford.

6) I believe my career has been well spent. <u>At last</u> / <u>At least</u> / <u>At the same time</u> that is my view.

7) As one grows older, so all the body processes slow down and food is less well utilized than it once was. Extra vitamins are <u>in addition</u> / <u>instead</u> / <u>therefore</u> need to compensate for this.

8) The recent recession has destroyed a high proportion of vacation jobs. <u>Hence</u> / <u>However</u> / <u>Nonetheless</u>, we would expect student debt to be on a sharp rise at present.

9) I take my two dogs with me everywhere I go. <u>Even so</u> / <u>For that matter</u> / <u>So</u> my friends are pretty used to them by now.

10) That's why I've come here today, to tell your mother that her brother needs more money. Well, that's my excuse, <u>also</u> / <u>anyway</u> / <u>indeed</u>.

11) This was not a well-travelled road. <u>Even so</u> / <u>For example</u> / <u>Moreover</u>, it was an extremely dusty one.

12) Disappointingly, though, the symptoms continued; <u>indeed</u> / <u>otherwise</u> / <u>similarly</u> it is only in the last few weeks or so that I have been free of them.

13) It is appropriate at the end of this important period to reflect upon a major development of benefit to all aircraft, <u>namely</u> / <u>likewise</u> / <u>or rather</u>, navigational and automatic piloting equipment.

14) He pulled a small enamel box out of the pocket of his jacket and placed it on the table in front of him. <u>Next</u> / <u>Then again</u> / <u>Thus</u> he tore a blank page from his notebook and folded it in two.

15) We will ensure that anything you ask for is delivered directly to your hotel room. <u>Likewise</u> / <u>Otherwise</u> / <u>Thereby</u>, if you wish to visit the ballet or opera, this too will be arranged.

**練習 7** (第 4 章)

用虛線前寫出的詞改寫下列各組句子，並在經過改寫的句子裏的 that-從句或wh-詞從句下劃出橫線。第一組已經替你改寫完畢並劃出了橫線。

0) He saw something. He didn't like it.

He <u>*didn't like what he saw.*</u>

1) I'll do something or other, and it will be well thought out.

Whatever ................................................................................

2) It must be Pete's brother! This suddenly dawned on me.

It ................................................................................

3) What are we looking for? We don't know.

We ........................................................................................................................

4) This man is your brother. We are certain of it.

   We ........................................................................................................................

5) Something or other was going on in the investigation; he felt he was closer to it than he had been before.

   He ........................................................................................................................

6) Improved breathing would bring better co-ordination. This was the vital factor.

   The ........................................................................................................................

7) Why should they wish to look like that appalling man? It's beyond me.

   It's ........................................................................................................................

8) We have 28 professionals. You can't run away from that fact.

   You ........................................................................................................................

9) The document has been wrongly dated and ought to read 1932 instead of 1931. This is clear from the contents.

   From ........................................................................................................................

10) Someone said history repeats itself first as tragedy, then as farce. They were right.

    Who ever ........................................................................................................................

11) I am going to say something. Please listen carefully.

    Please ........................................................................................................................

12) Who does it belong to? That's something they are still arguing over.

    They ........................................................................................................................

13) Whose money is it? That doesn't matter!

    It ........................................................................................................................

14) How should we handle this? Let's talk about it.

    Let's ........................................................................................................................

## 練習 8 (第 4 章)

用非限定小句或無動詞小句替換原來句子裏的劃線部份。第一個句子已經替你改寫完畢；第 11、15、17 句還有提示。

0) <u>When he looked at his watch</u>, he saw that it was half past five.
   *Looking at his watch, he saw that it was half past five.*

1) <u>After he left the hotel early in the morning</u>, he headed for the public library, <u>and took up his usual position on the steps</u>.

   ..............................................................................................................

2) He grew impatient <u>if he was told</u> that something could not be done because it had not been done before.

   ..............................................................................................................

3) He stared vacantly at the people <u>who were milling around</u> <u>as if they were unaware</u> of the commotion.

   ..............................................................................................................

4) They said they were so busy they would need a week <u>before they took action</u>.

   ..............................................................................................................

5) <u>Even when she was asked a direct question</u> she scarcely bothered to answer.

   ..............................................................................................................

6) These schemes should be fairer to taxpayers, but they would still be expensive, <u>especially if they were available</u> to all.

   ..............................................................................................................

7) He poured himself another drink; <u>he was unwilling to lose</u> the moment and the memory.

   ..............................................................................................................

8) I've heard that Joe Wilson, <u>though he is unwilling to part with any money during his life</u>, will leave everything to her after his death.

   ..............................................................................................................

9) Do you think that <u>while he was still in motion</u> his cycle was kicked from behind?

..............................................................

10) How do we choose? <u>When we have chosen,</u> how do we know that this is the best choice?

..............................................................

11) <u>She didn't realize it, but</u> she was moving along the road, <u>and she was unaware of its crystal-hard covering of ice.</u>

Without

..............................................................

12) <u>Because she realized</u> that she was blocking his path, she stepped cautiously to one side.

..............................................................

13) <u>Although they were unhappy with the opinion polls,</u> Republicans argued yesterday that they would receive a boost from their convention in August.

..............................................................

14) He finished the tea and laid the cup aside, <u>because he wasn't expecting her to answer.</u>

..............................................................

15) Mother had had a fainting fit <u>when she heard the news.</u>

on

..............................................................

16) The doctors have been marvellous <u>in the way they have explained everything.</u>

..............................................................

17) Joanna startled Enid: <u>she gave her an utterly inappropriate hug.</u>

by

..............................................................

18) <u>His eyes were fixed on the lake:</u> he made the sort of meaningless remarks that the occasion required.

..............................................................

**練習 9**（第 5 章）

指出下列各組句子裏劃線部份所替代或指稱的部份。第一句已經替你做好。

0) 'How do you know no one else saw her?' — 'Someone might have, sir, but <u>if so,</u> they haven't come forward yet.'

*if someone else saw her*

.................................................................................................

1) He wanted to extend a hand, touch the body lying there, but he could not nerve himself to <u>do so</u>.

   .................................................................................................

2) Send them along, and if they arrive before I leave, well and good. <u>If not</u>, the responsibility will be mine and you'll have done your duty.

   .................................................................................................

3) Few drivers left the highway here, although there was a grassy area which made <u>this</u> possible.

   .................................................................................................

4) They're nightmares. Terrible, hideous, frightening nightmares. I don't feel joy. I feel pain. But the first <u>ones</u> weren't <u>like that</u>.

   a) ones ...................................................................................

   b) like that ............................................................................

5) He was trying to decide whether to advise Robin to go to a London hospital or to a local hospital in Sussex. Finally he thought he would advise <u>the latter</u>. When I asked his reason for <u>this</u> he replied that he thought the Sussex hospital a good <u>one</u> and that <u>it</u> would be much more pleasant for me, visiting Robin, to be in the country and not too far from home.

   a) the latter ............................................................................

   b) this ....................................................................................

   c) one .....................................................................................

   d) it ........................................................................................

6) 'Have you any valuables anywhere else in the house that need checking?' — 'I don't think <u>so</u>. My wife and I gave our son a great many things when he married. It seemed to us that <u>that</u> was the sensible thing to do.'

   a) so .......................................................................................

   b) that .....................................................................................

7) He would sit at his desk staring at the telephone, aware every moment that nothing was happening and that people wanted to know <u>why not</u>.

   .................................................................................................

8) People who talk soppy to their dogs almost always <u>do it</u> in public as well as in private. As a vet's wife I'd noticed <u>that</u>. But Martin <u>did it</u> in private, and adopted a brisk, no-nonsense approach in public. <u>It</u> just didn't make sense.

a) do it ..................................................................................................

b) that ...................................................................................................

c) did it .................................................................................................

d) It ......................................................................................................

9) You're the one who asked me to help. I can't <u>do that</u> if you lie to me.

..................................................................................................

10) If you do decide to buy, you should not <u>do so</u> through one person but through several, your agent, your banker, and a couple of stockbrokers.

..................................................................................................

11) The poorer patients paid cash when money was available, and <u>if not</u>, asked that the fee be charged to their account. More often than not <u>this</u> resulted in the fee never being paid at all.

a) if not ..................................................................................................

b) this ....................................................................................................

以下句子裏 do so 的用法不精確，試改寫此句使它在語法上更準確。

12) Andrew did not feel that they were expecting to be offered a drink, so he did not <u>do so</u>.

..................................................................................................

## 練習 10 （第 5 章）

說明下列句子的劃線指稱的對象是甚麼。第一句劃線部份指稱的對象已經替你寫出。

0) The old greed for power? <u>It</u> is one, if not the most important, source of wars, conflicts, and family quarrels, more than <u>any other</u>, come to think of it.

a) it *=the old greed for power* ..................................................

b) any other *=any other source of wars, conflicts, and family quarrels* ...............

1) 'Is there anything the matter with my sisters? Is that why you're phoning?' The voice sounded anxious, less aggressive. 'To the best of my belief there's nothing the matter with <u>either of them</u>,' Andrew replied.

.................................................................................................................................

2) There was a great deal of talk about the restoration needed after the storm. The damage had not been so very great but, as in <u>all such cases</u>, more work was going to be required than I had at first thought.

.................................................................................................................................

3) Truth was truth. When in doubt tell <u>it</u>. His confession looked terrible on paper. He screwed up his first three efforts after only a line or <u>two</u>, decided that <u>the fourth</u> was as bad as <u>the others</u>, but that <u>it</u> had to stand. He had to give them the full story. Explain to them how <u>it</u> happened.

a) (tell) it ...................................................................................................

b) two ........................................................................................................

c) the fourth .............................................................................................

d) the others .............................................................................................

e) it (had to stand) ...................................................................................

f) it (happened) ........................................................................................

4) If one member of staff can do so much damage any visitor, nurse, doctor or consultant, could <u>do likewise</u>.

.................................................................................................................................

5) Another point to remember when planning a diet is that it is not always necessary to cut a type of food out completely, but simply to replace it with <u>something similar</u> but more suitable, carob powder instead of chocolate for example.

.................................................................................................................................

6) This interest in preventive medicine has taken many years to develop, but at last government money is becoming available for further research, <u>The same</u> cannot be said to be true for research into the effects of chemical residues in food.

.................................................................................................................................

222

7) After 'The Shetland Bus' I wrote two novels. One was a thriller. <u>Both</u> are forgotten now, and deserve <u>it</u>. But <u>they</u> taught me I was not about to make my fortune as a novelist.

    a) Both ..................................................................................................

    b) it ......................................................................................................

    c) they ..................................................................................................

8) But, he claimed, 'the public increasingly question the utility of institutions like the House of Lords, the judiciary, and the honours system. These institutions depend powerfully on deference, and obfuscation. <u>Neither</u> is compatible with a fully functioning democracy.'

    ..................................................................................................

9) Anthony loved the place and, in his will, John had made over to <u>him</u> most of the land, but <u>he</u> doubted if <u>his son</u> would ever live in the house. He certainly would not <u>do so</u> alone. This house needed children, women, voices, confusion. Still <u>it</u> might happen. Anthony might yet settle down.

    a) him ..................................................................................................

    b) he ...................................................................................................

    c) his son .............................................................................................

    d) do so ...............................................................................................

    e) it .....................................................................................................

## 練習 11 (第 6 章)

說明下列句子劃線部份的名詞指稱的對象是甚麼。

1) The line of people waiting to be questioned pressed forward, as if by <u>this action</u> they could hasten <u>the process</u>.

    a) this action ........................................................................................

    b) the process .......................................................................................

2) People who organize their own disappearance may believe themselves to be acting rationally. Often <u>the operation</u> has been thoroughly planned and deep psychological problems that prompt <u>such actions</u> are well hidden.

    a) the operation ....................................................................................

    b) such actions .....................................................................................

3) As you release your breath, let your left leg hang further so as to stretch your stomach muscles. The same procedure should be repeated on the other leg three or four times. This action will help to strengthen the muscles.

a) the same procedure ...................................................................................

b) this action ...............................................................................................

4) It is very likely indeed that the child will pretend that his homework doesn't have to be handed in for ages, and that he needn't do it until next week. The chances are that he will be saying this because he wants to watch a favourite TV programme, so look out for the situation.

...........................................................................................................................

5) 'Ingrid appears in public, maybe has her meals in the hotel dining-room. That way we make them think her sister is still here in Stockholm. But she is not.' He cleared his throat and I guessed he was about to raise an awkward subject. 'But are we sure we can trust Ingrid?'

a) That way .................................................................................................

b) an awkward subject .................................................................................

6) Environmental opposition delayed procedures for acquiring land, which forced the railway authority to put large stretches of new line into tunnels. This in turn caused another problem. Entering a tunnel at high speed creates pressure pulses that cause unpleasant sensations in passenger's ears.

a) another problem .....................................................................................

b) And what was the first problem? ...........................................................

7) At the time the realization that his best friend had murdered three people didn't seem to bother Wolfe, but since then I had come to see that the whole business had really shaken him.

...........................................................................................................................

8) What we have here is a very neatly organized basic textbook for first-year mathematics students. If our students knew all of this stuff when they arrived, or even when they left, to be honest, I would be more than happy.

...........................................................................................................................

9) Mrs Williams was reading a magazine. Diana was busy talking to Stephen about something. The children were playing quietly in a corner. 'A

dreadful thing has happened,' said Sophie as soon as she was sure they could not be heard. 'Your brother, my brother, I mean dear Philip, of course, has run away from school and declares he will go to sea with you.'

......................................................................................................

10) Another theory could be that the wounds had been inflicted after death. There wouldn't have been much bleeding in that case. I wondered how carefully the doctor had examined the body.

......................................................................................................

## 練習 12 （第 6 章）

選出下列各組句子裏劃線部份的最合適的詞，並説明其指稱的對象。

1) Even today, when it has been widely filmed and photographed, Tibetan-style debating remains an astonishing spectacle, with its stamping, posturing and hand-clapping. No outsider since Desideri had regularly taken part in this act / action / activity.

......................................................................................................

2) If something won't go right in a painting, the solution is to return to the original subject and try to see with greater clarity what you are aiming to recreate in paint. Sometimes in these circumstances / this context / this position / this experience it can be helpful to put down your brushes and make a separate drawing of the subject.

......................................................................................................

3) Inform air-traffic control that your aircraft has been taken over by terrorists and that you are changing course and proceeding to Cyprus. When you have done that, tell the passengers of this development / effect / result and warn them not to make any stupid moves.

......................................................................................................

4) Of course he'd been talking in his sleep and of course he'd not known what he was saying. But the fact that he'd said that name meant it must be in mind. Sometimes, when she reached this point, she was able to dismiss the whole episode / event / happening as nonsense.

......................................................................................................

5) Hyperventilation, or overbreathing, is breathing in a rapid, shallow way using the upper chest instead of the abdomen. Breathing in this <u>manner</u> / <u>method</u> / <u>means</u> produces more oxygen than the body needs.

..............................................................................................................................

6) Pressure to get tough on international fossil thieves has grown steadily, along with the prices collectors pay for top-grade specimens. The <u>fact</u> / <u>issue</u> / <u>topic</u> has come to a head over a piece of moon rock now in the hands of a private collector in the US.

..............................................................................................................................

7) 'Here's what to do. If the police ask you, just say you can't remember who bought you the drink. Say the place was full of rich tourists and it must have been one of them.' This <u>plan</u> / <u>theory</u> / <u>view</u> seemed to please the boy, who grinned and said 'Right. No problem.'

..............................................................................................................................

8) Suppose you do have one hundred people who do like and approve of you. Are you happy? No, because you are worried that the one hundred and first person might not like you. This <u>argument</u> / <u>belief</u> / <u>criticism</u> condemns you to never being able to enjoy the positive feelings of those who do like you fully.

..............................................................................................................................

9) I am sure that there is some way in which a couple who have been turned down for adoption can be given an adult explanation for the <u>denial</u> / <u>excuse</u> / <u>refusal</u>.

..............................................................................................................................

10) I am going to help your parents get you better. We won't let you get any more ill, nor let you die, and nor will we let you get overweight, which I know is another <u>doubt</u> / <u>fear</u> / <u>objection</u> you have.

..............................................................................................................................

**練習 13** (第 8 章)

用句子附加狀語改寫下列各組句子裏的劃線部份。有的句子需要作少許更改。注意第 4 句、第 10 句要求用一個完全不同的詞語。第一句已替你改寫好。

0) I am being serious when I say that we'd be enormously grateful if you'd stay till we get back.

   <u>Seriously we'd be enormously grateful if you'd stay till we get back.</u>

1) And she knew that, <u>if she was realistic about it</u>, no edition of the paper could be put together, printed, and distributed the same day if the news came later than 3.45.

   .............................................................................

2) <u>We are lucky that</u> there are some clear fingerprints on the knife.

   .............................................................................

3) <u>It is obvious that</u> politics is becoming an increasingly dangerous game.

   .............................................................................

4) They may be mad, but – <u>you must agree, don't you?</u>–they don't want to starve.

   .............................................................................

5) <u>It appears</u> he's been prescribed some kind of pills, and we're supposed to make sure he doesn't drink.

   .............................................................................

6) Truman's performance during what <u>you could argue</u> was the most crucial week of his presidency was of a very high quality.

   .............................................................................

7) If he sued and won he would – <u>there's no doubt about it</u>–be awarded a very large sum of money indeed.

   .............................................................................

8) <u>It is interesting to note that</u> the things some of us find frightening, other people experience as exciting.

   .............................................................................

9) <u>It was very sensible of you</u> to decline to listen to this improper and insulting stuff.

   .............................................................................

10) You've got to remember that a microphone was put under my nose immediately I got off the horse. Of course <u>when I think about it now</u>, I would rather have not spoken on television.

......................................................................................................

## 較長語篇中用的連接詞語

本書到目前為止都是展示兩個或三個句子之間是怎樣用連接詞語或其他指稱手段進行銜接的。但事實上，這些詞語和手段也對段落與段落之間的銜接發生作用，使較長的語篇黏合成完整的話語。本書練習 14、練習 15 和練習 16 的設計旨在讓讀者能在使用和解釋語篇中使用的連接詞語方面得到訓練。練習 14 和練習 15 用的是書面語語篇，而練習 16 用的是電台熱線電話的對話，其目的是為了展示第 7 章中討論過的許多在英語口語才用的詞語。

為了有助於讀者做練習，將把一個作為例證的較長書面語語篇，以及對該語篇使用的連接詞語和指稱手段的說明安排在練習 14、練習 15 之前。練習 16 包括對熱線電話的對話中用到的、只在口語中才使用的連接詞語的說明，然後才是該練習的正文部份。

下面列出的是摘自《每日電訊報》(1995.8.20) 的一篇新聞報道。這篇文章報道的是其他星球上存在外星人的可能性和有人報告說看見過的神秘不明飛行物體 (UFOs 飛碟)。文章使用的不同的連接詞語和指稱手段的下面都劃有橫線。為了閱讀方便，又給文章的段落編了號。

## CLOSE ENCOUNTERS AND CONSPIRACY OF SILENCE

**1** Many scientists are perfectly happy with the idea that aliens exist in our galaxy. But ask <u>them</u> if <u>those same aliens</u> have visited the Earth, and <u>the question</u> will be met with howls of derision.

**2** The cartoon image of the Unidentified Flying Object debate has led to the emergence of <u>a 'politically correct' stance</u> on <u>the issue</u>, adopted by virtually all scientists: UFOs are definitely not alien spaceships.

**3** <u>Few</u> will risk their scientific reputations by publicly discussing the thousands of reports that flood in every year from apparently sane members of the public.

**4** <u>However</u>, <u>many</u> <u>privately</u> admit that the standard of the UFO debate is little better than a bar-room slanging match, with 'scientific' arguments against UFOs as fatuous as claims for <u>them</u>.

**5** Standard put-downs include claiming that aliens would have better uses for the huge amounts of energy needed to cross interstellar space, and that — even travelling at the speed of light — <u>it</u> would take thousands of years to cross the galaxy. <u>Both arguments</u> presume to know the motivations and the technical and physical abilities of any supposed aliens.

**6** <u>Other sceptics</u> insist that aliens would have no reason to visit the Earth, <u>an argument</u> which ignores the somewhat disturbing fact that for the last 70 years radio transmissions announcing our existence have been streaming out from our planet into space — and have passed through hundreds of star systems on the way.

**7** <u>So</u> what is the knock-out scientific argument that proves aliens have not visited us? 'There isn't <u>one</u>. The fact is, we just don't know,' says Professor Freeman Dyson, the distinguished British theoretical physicist at the Institute of Advanced Study at Princeton, New Jersey — and one of the few scientists happy to speak openly.

**8** <u>His</u> reason for not investigating UFO reports is far more down to Earth. 'It's a terrible waste of time — <u>a subject</u> full of interesting stories that one can never check.'

## 説明

Paragraph 1: 'them' = many scientists; 'those same aliens' = aliens who exist in our galaxy; 'the question' refers back to a whole clause — the reported question 'if those same aliens have visited the Earth.'

Paragraph 2: 'a politically correct stance' refers forwards — the scientists' agreed position is that UFOs are not alien spaceships; 'the issue' = the Unidentified Flying Object debate, i.e. the debate as to whether UFOs exist, and if so what they are.

Paragraph 3: 'few' = few scientists.

Paragraph 4: 'however' is used here because there is a contrast with the statement made in Paragraph 3; 'many' = many scientists, contrasting with 'few' in Paragraph 3; 'privately' contrasts with 'publicly' in Paragraph 3; 'them' = UFOs.

Paragraph 5: 'it' is a dummy 'it' referring forwards to the infinitive structure 'to cross the galaxy'; 'both arguments' refers back to the two 'put-downs' (i.e. critical remarks) mentioned, namely, that aliens would have better uses for their energy than visiting the Earth, and that it would take them thousands of years to reach us.

Paragraph 6: 'other sceptics' = other people who doubt whether UFOs are alien spaceships — the word 'sceptic' has not been used before, but 'other' is a referring word, and it takes us back to the people behind the 'standard put-downs' of Paragraph 5; 'an argument' = that aliens would have no reason to visit the Earth.

Paragraph 7: 'so' here indicates a sort of summing up, some result from what has been said so far; in this case it introduces a final question — what is the knockout argument, the argument that would completely destroy the case for UFOs? — to which the answer is 'There isn't one' ('one' = a knock-out argument).

Paragraph 8: 'his' refers to the Professor in Paragraph 7; 'it' = investigating UFO reports; 'a subject' refers somewhat vaguely to UFOs and whether they exist.

## 練習 14

將適當的詞填入練習裏的有編號的空白處。

（白內障（cataracts）指人眼上形成的模糊的雲狀塊，對視力有嚴重影響。）

In addition to cataracts, Tommy Sopwith was suffering from (1) .............................
eye complications, and he went into hospital full of hope (2) ...............................
following an operation his sight would at (3) ......................... be partially restored.
But, (4) ........................., the operation was unsuccessful, and
(5) ......................... was probably the greatest regret of his life. According to his
son: 'The only time I ever (6) ......................... saw him knocked sideways was in
hospital (7) ......................... At the age of 96, Sir Thomas's sight was confined to
shapes and devoid of all detail, then in the following year, (8) ...............................
got steadily worse, until he was unable even to tell (9) ......................... a
photographer had used his flashgun. Sir Thomas never (10) ......................... came
to terms with his blindness.

Even in his late nineties, people still wanted to interview Sir Thomas. By
(11) ......................... his sight had gone and he was rather deaf,
(12) ......................... that was less of a problem thanks to some
particularly good hearing aids. To those (13) ......................... did not know
him,(14) ......................... interviews could be a little disconcerting,
(15) ......................... a question could be followed by a long silence,
(16) .........................the interviewer wondered (17) .........................
Sir Thomas had heard (18) ......................... was being asked. In (19)
......................... he usually had heard, but was determined to be factual
and a suitable answer was being prepared in his mind. It was all part of the Sopwith
character to think (20) ......................... he spoke.

## 練習 15

本練習根據《每日電訊報》的一篇新聞改編。文章的段落次序已經打亂。你能用各
種不同的銜接手段把文章的段落恢復到原來的順序嗎？段落已經編了各種號碼。為
了有助於你做練習，文章的最後一段仍保持原來的位置。

### WAR CRIMES NOVELIST HAS FANTASY LIFE

**1**   The novel provoked public vilification and death threats because it was suspected of following the extremist line of the far right.

**2**   What is embarrassing to the Miles Franklin Award judges is that her book was hailed for its interpretation of 'oral history'.

**3**   Jill Kitson, one of the judges, said: 'The author's background is not what the judging of a literary prize is all about.'

**4**   She claimed that the book was a fictional account of her father's experiences in the camp. In interviews she has said most of his family was killed by Communist Party officials.

**5**   The writer won this year's prestigious Miles Franklin Award for her first novel 'The Hand that Signed the Paper', which tells of a Ukrainian's role in war crimes at Treblinka concentration camp.

**6**   But Thomas Keneally, author of 'Schindler's Ark', said the hoax left her open to charges of making fascist propaganda.

**7**   But Miss Darville's reason for the hoax is a mystery.

**8**   Australia's literary world is in turmoil over disclosures that Helen Demidenko, a 24-

year-old novelist, is herself a work of fiction.

**9** But she is in fact the daughter of Harry and Grace Darville, who migrated from the north of England to Brisbane before she was born.

**10** Her mother said: 'It's fiction, for heaven's sake. She wrote under a pseudonym. Lots of authors do that.'

### 練習 16（第 7 章）

下面是電台熱線電話節目中的一篇對話的一部份。對話中的兩個人分別用字母 H 和 C 表示。H 代表該節目的主持人，C 代表打電話的人，普通公眾的一員。他們在熱線電話上討論的是飲酒開車問題。對話裏兩人相互寒暄和介紹部份已經進行完畢，現在是對話的正文部份，由打電話的人先說。

先通讀對話，再看對話後的說明部份。對話的劃線部份作為在說明部份需要說明的對象或作為練習的材料。為了參閱方便給對話的每一行都編了號。

**1**　C: Erm, there's a lot of mention day after day and er, quite
**2**　　　reasonably of course, it's about drink and drive.
**3**　H: Mhm.
**4**　C: Now this drink and drive thing, er it concerns a lot of
**5**　　　people and it certainly does me because I like to have a
**6**　　　little drink, but I never know whether I'm over the limit
**7**　　　or under. Now some people will say 'Well you can always
**8**　　　solve that by not drinking at all'…
**9**　H: Yeah.
**10**　C: …but I like a drink. Now why hasn't something been
**11**　　　invented er which is a reasonable cost, that people could
**12**　　　buy so they could judge for themselves just as a test
**13**　　　before they go out. If you're over the limit you leave the
**14**　　　car in the garage, right?
**15**　H: Well those … er those things have been invented, to be
**16**　　　honest, and they have been on the market and the
**17**　　　police and I are very much against them because they
**18**　　　actually encourage people to drink don't they?
**19**　C: Erm well, there's two ways of looking at that. It doesn't
**20**　　　encourage people to drink. Oh well, I don't think it
**21**　　　encourages people to drink.
**22**　H: Yes it does, it encourages people to drink up to the
**23**　　　limit. They have a drink and look at the thing and say
**24**　　　'Oh I'm all right I can have another one,' and I
**25**　　　think that's a … that's a dangerous precedent, to be
**26**　　　honest. I think you're much better having, I mean, you
**27**　　　know what you're supposed to have, you know, just a

**28** couple of halves or something like that <u>erm</u> and ...

**29** C: No I'm not ... I'm not quite sure that I've seen these

**30** things. Now <u>I like</u> ...

**31** H: <u>I mean the</u> ...

**32** C: <u>I like</u> a drink of sherry.

**33** H: Yeah.

**34** C: Now I'm not sure. I ... I drink the cheapest sherry <u>you</u>

**35** <u>know</u>, er I've got a litre for about two pounds fifty at

**36** the moment on ...

**37** H: <u>Yeah</u>.

**38** C: ... on special offer. <u>Now</u> I can have some of that and

**39** I feel quite all right but ...

**40** H: You might feel all right.

**41** C: ... but er I should have gone out to a meeting tonight.

**42** H: Yeah.

**43** C: But I didn't go because I felt ... <u>well</u> I'd had some drinks,

**44** I don't know how I'm fixed ...

**45** H: <u>Mhm</u>.

**46** C: ... and I can't afford to lose my licence. Now it'd be

**47** very reassuring to me if I knew er just what effect this

**48** or drink of any sort has on me.

**49** H: <u>Well, I mean, I still think</u> that the people who say if

**50** you're worried about that don't drink at all are the right

**51** ones.

**52** C: But personally I like the idea of these gadgets.

**53** H: Well, they are available, they are on the market.

**54** C: Are they?

**55** H: Yes, they've been around for a year or two now but <u>as</u>

**56** <u>I say</u> the police don't like them at all, and I ... and I

**57** think I support the police fully on this.

**58** C: But it could mean you could er have a drink now and then

**59** and not worry about losing your licence.

**60** H: Well, I mean, <u>the thing is</u> you know, if you want to drink

**61** don't drive, <u>er</u> that's your choice isn't it really.

**説明**

對話每行左側的數字是行數編號。

1, 4, 28, 61, etc: 'Erm' and 'er' are simply hesitation noises. Notice that they are made not only by the caller but also by the radio host, who is a professional broadcaster, who might be expected to speak more fluently.

1-2: C's first remark is very loosely constructed: tidied up it might read 'There's a lot of talk day after day — quite reasonably — about drinking and driving.'

3: H's first intervention is a mere 'mhm', perhaps showing that he accepts drinking and driving as a suitable topic for discussion on the programme.

9:'Yeah' suggests that H agrees with C's previous remark (7-8) — that the solution is not to drink. H also probably feels it is necessary to say something — even though C has not finished speaking.

10:'Now' indicates a new (though related) topic.

14: By saying 'right', C is seeking H's agreement.

15: 'Well' indicates that H is going to give some new information. He then repeats himself ('those … er those things') while thinking what to say. This may partly be because long silences are unacceptable on a radio programme, where the listeners cannot see the speakers.

19-20: C uses 'erm well' to introduce his disagreement politely; he does not think that this alcohol–testing gadget would encourage drinking. But 'oh well' softens his disagreement–He's saying that he is expressing a personal opinion.

24-26: H twice says 'I think'. This phrase can stress that it is only a personal opinion, but it may be a strongly held opinion.

26-27: 'I mean' adds emphasis here to what follows — 'you know what you're supposed to have', i.e. everyone knows the amount of alcohol that is supposed to be safe. (This first 'you know' is not a fluency filler.)

27: The second 'you know' is a fluency filler, though not meaningless. It implies that C must also know that the recommended amount of drink is 'a couple of halves', i.e. no more than two half pints of beer.

31: H is trying to make point here ('I mean the') but he has interrupted C, causing C to repeat 'I like' (30,32) before continuing his remark.

再把整篇對話通讀一次，然後看下列的題目。從每題的三個選項中挑選出最合適的一項。題目中的數字是行數編號。

1) C says 'I drink the cheapest sherry <u>you know</u>' (34 – 35) because

    a) he has already told H this

    b) he expects H to know about cheap sherry

    c) he is checking that H is listening

2) When H says 'yeah' (37), he

    a) agrees that cheap sherry costs two pounds fifty

    b) interrupts because he knows what C is going to say

    c) wants to show he is still in the conversation

3) In '<u>Now</u> I can have some of that …' (38), 'now' implies

    a) C is introducing new information

b) in the past, C could not drink sherry and still feel all right

c) he can only drink sherry because it is cheap

4) C says 'well' (43) because

a) he is starting his remark again

b) he means 'as well', another way of saying 'also'

c) he is showing surprise

5) When H says 'mhm' (45) he means that he

a) doubts what C says

b) is thinking what to say next

c) is listening

6) 'Well, I mean, I still think' (49): The radio host

a) wants to change the topic

b) is gently re-stating his disagreement with what C is saying

c) is sympathizing with C's wish to drink'

7) 'As I say' (55 – 56): The radio host

a) is changing the subject

b) is emphasizing what he has already said

c) is using a fluency filler to give himself time to think

8) 'The thing is' (60): The host

a) is stating his opinion firmly, in the hope of bringing the conversation to a close

b) is changing his opinion on drink-driving

c) is suggesting C is free to choose to drink and drive

# 練習答案

1) The sandwich made him feel better, both because he had been hungry and because for a while he could pretend that this was just a normal day.

2) …It both opened a door and kept it locked.

3) He doesn't look like either his uncle or his aunt.

4) No one would either know or care what became of them.

5) You either got the order or you didn't.

6) Her nails were neither long nor painted.

7) She neither wept nor despaired.

8) Neither Anthony nor Fred was a skilled mechanic.

9) …his head, he not only felt the pain of the bruise but also heard the crinkle…

10) Not only did she pay him a top salary, but the job kept him moving and happy.

11) He would be made familiar with the layout of Geneva, not only from maps but also from a large-scale model.

12) If the river carried the body down, then (it follows that) this is where the body entered the water.

13) If land was nearby, then they might be able to obtain fuel…

14) If this view is right, then (that would mean) perhaps we have been applying the wrong tests…

## 練習 2

1) If he had not unfortunately been tone deaf, he might have made a fortune as a singer.

2) Tibetan was to be taught during the three years of primary school. However, all secondary education…

3) (You must) prune these trees. Otherwise, you won't get any fruit off them.

4) Elsie poured out tea and they all drank a cup. Soon afterwards Aunt Mamie announced…

5) While they were living at the house with … a shared nanny, the war grew closer and bombs began to fall…

6) I moved the chair back from the doorway so that I could be seen from the outer office but not overheard.

7) …I used it for about two to three years, generously applying it every morning, so that my skin is now quite thin on my face.

8) … 'I suppose I shall, provided that the police don't want me to stay here.'

9) Ireland worked as a team with clever passing among the forwards. By contrast, England relied on individual efforts.

10) Unemployment seems to have contributed to increasing crime rates. However, this has not generally resulted in more people being sent to prison…

11) He had enjoyed the lively company of his friends in Edinburgh. All the same, his work, he felt, demanded solitude.

12) Some UN sources expressed hope that a deal would be struck. The Americans, on the other hand, were less optimistic.

13) Despite the fact that they knew OR Despite knowing it was wrong …, most of those interviewed… did not consider themselves criminals.

14) … 'There's an important murder trial going on and I'm the main police witness. Still, it won't matter a lot'.

15) … Meanwhile Patrick and Margaret talked quietly.

16) We had a wonderful time there, except that we had our money stolen on the last day.

## 練習 3

1) a) By contrast
   b) on the contrary
   c) on the contrary
2) a) though OR although
   b) though
   c) though
3) a) no matter
   b) no matter
   c) for that matter
4) a) in case
   b) in case
   c) In any case
5) a) Granted
   b) Given that
   c) given (that)
6) a) All the same
   b) at the same time
   c) all the same
7) a) above all
   b) above all
   c) After all
8) a) in the meantime (OR meanwhile)
   b) Meanwhile
   c) in the meantime (OR meanwhile)

## 練習 4

1) from the time when
2) because
3) the whole time that
4) provided that
5) in order that
6) with the result that
7) more or less the same as
8) although … greatly
9) rather than
10) earlier than
11) although
12) whereas

## 練習 5

1) or
2) yet
3) in case
4) even though
5) so
6) lest
7) as though
8) wherever
9) until
10) on condition that

## 練習 6

1) Nevertheless
2) however
3) instead
4) Alternatively
5) Accordingly
6) At least
7) therefore
8) Hence
9) So
10) anyway
11) Moreover
12) indeed
13) namely
14) Next
15) Likewise

## 練習 7

1) Whatever I do will be well thought out.
2) It suddenly dawned on me (that) it must be Pete's brother.
3) We don't know what we are looking for.
4) We are certain (that) this man is your brother.
5) He felt he was closer than he had been before to whatever was going on in the investigation.
6) The vital factor was that improved breathing would bring better co-ordination.
7) It's beyond me why they should wish to look like that appalling man.
8) You can't run away from the fact that we have 28 professionals.
9) From the contents it is clear that the document has been wrongly dated and ought to read 1932 instead of 1931.
10) Whoever said history repeats itself first as tragedy, then as farce, was right.
11) Please listen carefully to what I say OR what I am going to say.
12) They are still arguing over who it belongs to.
13) It doesn't matter whose money it is.
14) Let's talk about how we should handle this.

## 練習 8

1) After leaving the hotel early in the morning, he headed for the public library, taking up his usual position…
2) He grew impatient if told that something could not be done…
3) He stared vacantly at the people milling around as if unaware of the commotion.
4) …they would need a week before taking action.
5) Even when asked a direct question, she scarcely bothered to answer.
6) …they would still be expensive, especially if available to all.
7) He poured himself another drink, unwilling to lose the moment and

the memory.

8) I've heard that Joe Wilson, though unwilling to part with any money during his life, would leave everything to her after his death.

9) Do you think that while still in motion his cycle was kicked from behind?

10) How do we choose? Having chosen, how do we know that this is the best choice?

11) Without realizing it, she was moving along the road, unaware of its crystal-hard covering of ice.

12) Realizing that she was blocking his path, she stepped cautiously to one side.

13) Although unhappy with the opinion polls, Republicans argued yesterday that they would receive a boost...

14) He finished the tea and laid the cup aside, not expecting her to answer.

15) Mother had had a fainting fit on hearing the news.

16) The doctors have been marvellous in explaining everything.

17) Joanna startled Enid by giving her an utterly inappropriate hug.

18) (With) his eyes fixed on the lake, he made the sort of meaningless remarks that the occasion required.

## 練習 9

1) (to extend a hand,) to touch the body lying there

2) if they don't arrive before I leave

3) for drivers to leave the highway here

4) a) nightmares
   b) terrible, hideous, frightening

5) a) (go to) a local hospital in Sussex
   b) advising a local hospital in Sussex
   c) hospital
   d) to be in the country and not too far from home

6) a) that we have any valuables anywhere else in the house that need checking
   b) giving our son a great many things when he married

7) why nothing was happening

8) a) talk soppy to their dogs
   b) that people who talk soppy to their dogs almost always do it in public as well as in private
   c) talked soppy to his dog
   d) the fact that Martin talked soppy to his dog in private, and adopted a brisk, no-nonsense approach in public

9) help

10) buy

11) a) if money was not available
    b) (the poorer patients) asking that the fee be charged to their account

12) Do so 是一個替代項目，原來想表達的意義是 offer them a drink，但這短語並沒有在句子裏出現。寫話者該這樣寫：Andrew did not feel that they were expecting him to offer them a drink.

## 練習 10

1) either of your sisters

2) all cases of restoration needed after a storm

3) a) the truth
   b) two lines
   c) the fourth effort
   d) the other efforts
   e) the fourth effort
   f) the incident or episode he is confessing

4) do a similar amount of damage too

5) some food similar to the food you are cutting out

6) that government money is becoming available

7) a) the two novels I wrote after 'The Shetland Bus'
   b) to be forgotten
   c) the two novels I wrote after 'The Shetland Bus'

8) neither deference nor obfuscation

9) a) Anthony
   b) John
   c) John's son, Anthony
   d) live in the house

e) Anthony might settle down and live in the house (perhaps with a wife, children, etc)

## 練習 11

1) a) pressing forward
   b) the process of being questioned

2) a) the action of organizing one's own disappearance
   b) acts of organizing one's own disappearance

3) a) letting your leg hang further so as to stretch your stomach muscles
   b) letting your leg hang further and repeating the procedure

4) the situation in which a child pretends that his homework is not urgent because he wants to watch television

5) a) because Ingrid is seen to appear in public, maybe having her meals in the hotel dining-room
   b) the question of whether or not we can trust Ingrid

6) a) pressure pulses that cause unpleasant sensations in passengers' ears, when trains enter a tunnel at high speed.
   b) the requirement to put large stretches of new line into tunnels, made necessary by

environmental opposition

7) the fact that his best friend had murdered three people

8) the information in the basic mathematics textbook

9) the fact that Philip has run away from school and says he wants to go to sea with his brother

10) if the wounds had been inflicted after death

## 練習 12

1) activity = Tibetan-style debating

2) these circumstances = when something won't go right in a painting

3) development = that the plane has been taken over by terrorists and is changing course to fly to Cyprus

4) episode = the man talking in his sleep and saying that particular name

5) manner = a rapid shallow way, using the upper chest instead of the abdomen

6) issue = the problem of what to do about international fossil theft

7) plan = the suggestion that the boy should say he couldn't remember who bought him the drink, probably a rich tourist

8) belief = that the one hundred and first person might not like you

9) refusal = the authorities refusing to allow a couple to adopt a child

10) fear = that you will get overweight

## 練習 13

1) And she knew that, realistically, no edition of the paper could be put together...

2) Luckily (for us), there are some clear finger-prints...

3) Obviously, politics is becoming an increasingly dangerous game.

4) They may be mad, but surely they don't want to starve.

5) Apparently he's been prescribed some kind of pills...

6) ...during what was arguably the most crucial week ... (OR ...during what arguably was the most crucial week ...)

7) ...he would undoubtedly be awarded a very large sum... OR ...he would without (any) doubt be awarded a very large sum ...

8) Interestingly, the things some of us find frightening...

9) You very sensibly declined to listen to this improper and insulting stuff.

10) ...Of course, on reflection (OR with hindsight), I would rather have not spoken on television.

## 練習 14

在原文中出現的詞語放在括號前面，括號裏的是其他合適的詞語。

1) other
2) that
3) least
4) unfortunately (sadly, alas)
5) this
6) really
7) afterwards
8) it
9) when (if, whether)
10) really
11) then
12) although (but)
13) who (that)
14) such (these)
15) because (as, since)
16) while
17) if (whether)
18) what
19) fact
20) before

## 練習 15

段落的原次序是 *8,5,9,2,3,6,1, 7,10*。

## 練習 16

1) b
2) c
3) a
4) a
5) c
6) b
7) b
8) a

# 索引

索引部份列出的單詞、短語後帶有句點的阿拉伯數字指該單詞、短語所在章節而不指頁數。本書正文討論的詞項(即單詞和短語)用**粗體**字母排印。在語法術語表裏列出的術語用***粗斜體***字母排印,其他詞語及語法術語用普通字母排印。

251